Evaria:
A Raven's Flight

By: Angèle Mort

The Flight's Beginning

Selene balanced her bare feet upon the faded tiles that formed the edge of the Elders' Square. A light breeze, cooled by nearby ocean waves, caressed what skin was left bare by ill-fitting funeral robes. The wind carried with it the comforting scent of seaweed and burning wood, but also the hushed voices of those left living. The few condolences offered to Selene's mother by friends and neighbors were cast into shadow by gossip whispered when they fancied themselves out of hearing range.

"May the Spirits protect and guide you."

"If you have need of anything…"

"Nearly a week and still no sign of the boy."

Selene lifted a foot, moving it carefully across a chipped tile.

"…lost her father, and…"

"It was for the best, I say."

"You'll not believe what I…"

"…Marked."

Her foot slipped, causing the edge of the tile to bite into her sole. She landed hard on the damp sand just outside the last line of tiles. Blood mixed lazily with a small puddle of water left by a late rainstorm.

Marked. Her mother had spoken the word countless times, yet refused to reveal its meaning. There was much one could glean from eavesdropping, however. *Their souls are unbalanced. They are a curse to themselves as well as those around them.* No one knew more than that, or at least they were not willing to speak of it. A Marked One was too evil to mention even in fireside stories.

Keep Islyr's secret as well as you have kept your own. Her mother had warned her.

Sand burrowed its way into Selene's wound as she moved. Shivers born of wet clothes and cold stone engulfed her as she sat upon the edge of the Square. She pulled her foot close, squinting to see through the gathering darkness. The cut stretched half the length of her sole. Luckily, it was not deep.

Selene drew a shallow breath and blew lightly upon the wound. Flesh crept quickly over the open space, leaving nothing but a few drops of blood in its wake. She wiped at it until no trace was left.

Something warm pulled her hand back. Her gaze followed. Pyresong robes of flowing silk, the gray of a storm-swept sky, concealed her mother's natural shape.

"Selene, no!" she warned in hushed tones. Her eyes shifted nervously as if to be sure no one was watching.

Tears left dark marks where they touched billowing robes. Selene had never before seen her mother cry. Her hand freed itself from her mother's grasp and moved to touch the mark upon her back.

"I know that this is difficult for you," Maye said, "but you must learn some control."

"Our deepest condolences," Elder Aldyn's approach had been as silent as an owl's flight. Selene had not noticed her until the first word passed her lips. The pallor of Maye's skin as she stared into the Elder's face made even the thickest foam of ocean waves seem a dingy gray.

"Elder Aldyn, forgive me. I did not see you." Maye said with a swift bow.

"So I gather." Elder Aldyn answered. The woman's frown carried more warning than discontent. "This day has been long for us all. You are needed for the Sending Hymn and I wish to speak with the child." The light of a nearby torch turned numerous wrinkles into deep valleys of flesh.

Selene's mother reluctantly turned to the pyre.

Shadows swallowed the Elder's face as she turned from the firelight. It seemed no longer human, this old, dry thing that spoke. "Do not worry for your mother. The pain of your father's death will surely ease with time. Indeed, we all feel lost without his presence. He was a good man and a valued member of the community,"

Selene's chest ached at the thought of her father dead upon the pyre.

The Elder's tongue slid slowly over her parched lips. The harmonized notes of the Sending Hymn caressed Selene as they guided her father's soul to rest before the journey to a new life. Its melody was not enough to put her at ease. Selene's face heated with the threat of tears. She wished desperately to be old enough to join her mother beside the pyre.

"Islyr." A soft hiss escaped with the word, as if a saltsnake was trapped in the Elder's gullet. "It is truly a curse to have a Marked One born into your family. It turns to a crime when you keep that One hidden."

A cold burn washed over Selene's mark. She fought to keep her hand from moving towards it. *Concentrate.* Selene's lungs constricted beneath the ancient woman's gaze.

"We were unable to find your brother's body." Hatred slithered out to rest within the Elder's eyes as she continued. "Be truthful with me now."

Selene wished desperately for Maye to return, though she knew it was impossible. Her mother would remain by the pyre until the final notes of the Sending Hymn had flown away.

"H-he was not marked, Elder." The words came out in a whisper though she had not willed them to do so. No amount of fear would force her to betray Islyr, neither in life nor after. "I swear it."

The Elder leaned closer. "I see." Her jaw twisted.

The sending hymn was nearly finished. The tones of many voices combined to form a solid note.

Elder Aldyn glanced towards the funeral pyre. "If Islyr returns, if his body is found to be marked…"

Selene wished her heart would quiet.

"I protect this village. I ensure that the law of the King is followed. Do you know what happens when someone is convicted of harboring a Marked One?"

It was not truly a question. Everyone knew that hanging was the punishment for Marked Ones as well as those harboring them. "Yes Elder."

The sounds of the Sending Hymn ceased.

"I leave you to mourn, then. May the Spirits protect and guide you on this day and thereafter." Her steps were as silent as they had been at her approach.

Selene drew the chill of night deep into her lungs in a futile attempt to rid herself of the fear that had made its home within her chest. Maye would return any moment.

A soft sound, like that of the wind through river reeds, attracted Selene's attention to the woods beyond the square. There stood a line of palmfruit trees with twisted limbs. A dark shape of feathers and claws flew down from within their branches. A raven. She could have stroked it with little less than an outstretched arm. Never before had one dared to come this close to her, and certainly never at night. The Elders offered a copper piece for each raven's corpse brought to them. *Cursed animals*, or so they said. She had found that she simply did not have the heart to kill one.

The creature folded its wings and stepped towards her. It stood mutely upon the flowing fabric of her robes. Silk and feathers momentarily merged into one. A dark eye turned to scrutinize her. The dying flames of the pyre flashed against its mirrored surface.

"Selene?"

Strange. It was certainly her mother's voice, yet she was nowhere to be seen.

"Selene. Get up. I won't be in again."

Selene struggled to open her eyes. A vision of Maye's face, framed by the light of a single candle, wavered into view.

"What hour is it?" Sleep slurred Selene's words though she tried her best to speak clearly.

"See for yourself. I've breakfast to finish."

Selene glanced through the bubbled glass of the tiny window that graced the room's far wall. It was still dark, though the featherlarks had already begun their song in anticipation of morning. It was still early enough to be on time.

She stumbled to the aged wardrobe she shared with Maye, shivering in the cold of morning. The fire had gone dead some time ago, and heat seeped through old wood like water through a fishing net. Selene pulled her hair into a Rider's knot, secured it with a steel pin, and headed for breakfast. The dream scraped at her concentration. This was not the first time she had relived father's funeral, nor was it the first time that a raven had appeared in her dreams. It had been nearly twelve years since her father's death. The dreams came most often before she went on errand for the Elders.

The smell of burning wood greeted Selene as she entered the main room of the house. Light flowed gently through curtains embroidered with flowers of ochre. Maye had already begun to eat, and did not so much as glance up at Selene as she entered.

Selene's chair tilted dangerously to one side as she attempted to sit. She grumbled at her own clumsiness.

The purpose of each errand was not announced until the time it began for fear of rogue Riders taking it up without a Praecyr's guidance. The notice for this particular errand had only appeared on the board one morning past. The pay was to be better than most, which enhanced Selene's curiosity tenfold. Even knowing that it would drive her mother to anger had not kept her from adding her name to the list.

A poached egg and an end of bread loitered stubbornly on her plate. She was not hungry in the least. Gentle prodding with the point of her knife caused a river of yolk to spill dangerously close to the tabletop. The wide grin she flashed in her mother's direction did not receive anywhere near the response she had hoped for. She had dared to presume that an evening of thought would quell Maye's anger. It seemed only to have made things worse.

Maye's eyes were a peaceful green most often, but when her thoughts turned to anger they became the gray of thick, storm bearing clouds. It was indeed that turbulent gray that glared back at Selene.

"At least have the courtesy to eat something. If I'd known you were only going to play with breakfast I wouldn't have bothered with your half."

"I ride these errands for us. We have been promised ten silver pieces upon the completion of this one. Would you allow such an opportunity to pass us by?" Selene straightened herself as she spoke in an attempt to seem more mature.

Maye did not seem to notice.

"There has not been an errand available in several months," Selene continued. "I must ride this one. It may be longer before the next and the pay will certainly be less." That should sway her a little.

"True," her mother said slowly.

At last, progress. Selene's guilt faded, as did her mother's frown, but the relief was only temporary.

"But do we really need it? I think not. We have money enough to survive the winter."

Guilt grabbed hold of Selene once again and hung there, this time with great tenacity.

"Is your well-being, perhaps your life, worth ten silver?" Maye lowered her voice. "That aside, I know that wealth is not the only thing you seek on these errands."

How irritating it was that Maye always knew her true intentions. Selene took a full bite of bread and pretended to concentrate on chewing. "I'd better go," she said as she crossed the room and looped the belt that held her sword and scabbard in place. The wad of bread in her mouth only impaired her speech slightly. "We're to meet at the Elders' Square. Got to get Cyprus ready."

She took one last bite of bread and stuffed the remaining piece into the leather pouch that hung at her hip.

"Please," Maye began.

"I'll be very careful." Selene cupped her mother's head in her hands and kissed her forehead lightly. She plucked her bedroll and a small sack of dried meat from the floor near the stove. Guilt moved to her stomach and formed a hard lump there. Selene made up her mind to leave before it could overcome her. She grabbed her woolen cloak from its hook by the door and headed out towards the barn.

The pale light of the newly risen sun pulled shadows from the fence posts across the pasture. Selene wrapped her cloak around her. *A few days hence and none of this will be of any consequence.* The thought comforted her. She and Maye would be ten silver pieces richer. That would buy several more chickens and a few yards of cloth for clothing, some pitch to repair the roof, perhaps even that milking goat she had been eyeing at market two days prior. The thought of goat's milk and cheese made her mouth water, although excitement had stolen any real desire for food she may have had.

Frost cooled her hand as she grasped the weathered wood of the pasture gate. A finely built black and white horse trotted out from behind the barn to greet her.

"Good morning Cyprus."

He nuzzled her gently, searching for any snacks that might be hidden beneath her cloak. She took a moment to smooth the soft hair on his neck before heading to the barn for his saddle and blanket. Cyprus eagerly followed her. He was always anxious to be out of the pasture.

In moments they were headed down the packed dirt path that led to the center of town. She would make it with time to spare. The Tides of luck must be with her on this day.

Cyprus' hooves made pleasant clicking sounds as they crossed the intricate pattern of cracked tiles that composed the Elders' Square. A group of three men, all on horseback, stood in the center of the area where years of Elders' council meetings and Tides Festivals had worn the color from the tiles completely. The tallest of the three rode up to meet Selene as she approached. Two massive dogs, each of which stood nearly as high as Cyprus' stomach, shadowed him as he moved. Selene had not seen any of their type before today, though dogs were often used on errands for tracking. The muzzles of these were wide and their heads broad. Their short coats were patched in brown and black, and their tails had been cut short as was most commonly done with smaller dogs for use in hunting rodents. The two looked very much out of place here, as did their master. She guessed by the man's confident stance that he must be the Praecyr for this errand. He wore a pair of leather riding gloves, the fine quality of which placed them very much at odds with the rest of his gear. The deep brown leather armor that covered his chest looked as if it had been quite impressive in its youth. Lengthy gashes ran across its battered surface, some in areas that made Selene wonder at the fact that the man had survived long enough to repair them. A long, battle-worn sword hung casually from his belt. He rested his palm lightly upon it, releasing the weapon only at the last moment to offer his hand in greeting.

"Ranur" he said through a short black beard much like the scrub bushes that grew by the riverside. "You are Selene, I assume."

It was not surprising that he knew her. One could count the number of female Riders within a hundred mile span on a single hand. Anyone who had run errands between Eiboren and the Mortal Sea had heard tell of her, as likely as not. She edged Cyprus closer to him to shake his hand. "Pleasure to meet you."

Cyprus was several hands shorter than Ranur's thick legged, tawny stallion. Although Selene straightened her back and set her feet down in the stirrups she was forced to tilt her head up to meet his gaze. The gloves he wore had been recently oiled and were soft to the touch. She tried to make her handshake firm, as her father had taught her long ago. A strong hand mirrored a strong soul, or so he had been fond of saying. In the end she fell just short of matching the strength in Ranur's grip with her own.

"Wait with the others," Ranur said, turning his horse down the path that led to the Elder's cottage. The skin of his nose and brow creased momentarily, as if something foul was upon the breeze. "I must speak with the Elders briefly. We leave the moment I return."

Selene tapped Cyprus lightly, guiding him to where the other Riders waited. During her first days as a Rider it had seemed odd to trust her life to people she had not laid eyes on before that day. Years of travel with strangers had forced her to accept it, though not to the point of liking.

She turned her attention to the men who would be her companions for the next few days. The closest was a squat, half bald man. What oily hair he had left hung loosely over his disheveled clothes. There would not have been enough to make a riders' knot of it even if he had decided to attempt it. A well-used bow and a quiver of arrows hung at his shoulder. The man did not acknowledge Selene's presence, though the mare he sat upon certainly noticed Cyprus, and was not pleased that he was so close. The horse stepped aside with a snort of displeasure, which was when Selene then received a full view of the group's final member. *Terran.* She sighed heavily. She would have given half her promised pay to be able to ride this errand without him.

Terran noticed her at once and turned his well-muscled gelding in her direction. The shine of its smoke-gray coat mirrored that of the new metal breastplate the man wore. "Selene," he said, flashing her what she was sure he considered to be his most alluring smile. "The Tides bring us together once more."

"Honestly, Terran?" She moved Cyprus as far from him as she could manage while still remaining in the center of the Square. He frequently said the most ridiculous things. The fact that he was here had absolutely nothing to do with the Tides of Fate. She would have wagered her life and the second half of her pay on that.

Relief washed over Selene as Ranur trotted back into view. She would be safe from Terran's obnoxious banter for a short time at least.

The Praecyr wasted no time in giving his commands. "The man we are to track," he said as he pulled his horse around to face them, "was last seen headed northwest into the woods that stretch between Eiboren and this place. The Elders have informed me that he will be a formidable opponent though he is still young." The hand that had previously rested just above his sword lowered, taking a firm grip on its hilt. His gaze settled upon Selene and his brow creased once more. "You three are considered the finest Riders between Maresbane and Vale. Be that as it may, we will need the Tides on our side to return from this errand without incident. The man is to be captured alive and unharmed, with extra silver to be given for his timely return."

The grubby, balding man beside Selene pulled back his lips in a dry smile at the mention of extra silver. Several half rotted teeth jutted from his nearly barren gums. She hoped that his archery was better than his hygiene.

Ranur turned to the man. "Ormun, you're with me."

Ormun's grin faded as he moved his horse to the front of the group. Ranur's stallion towered over the shaggy mare, causing Selene to feel a bit better about Cyprus' stature.

"Tarr. Dai." The dogs' ears perked up as Ranur mentioned their names. They promptly lifted themselves from the ground and loped over to stand by their master, their coats mottled beneath slivers of morning sun. Ranur lowered a strip of blue cloth down to them, allowing them to take in its scent before tucking it into the pouch that hung at his waist.

"You two take up the rear." Ranur nodded towards Terran and Selene. "Any sign of the man we seek should be made known to me immediately." He started towards the woods with Ormun close behind. "Insubordination of any kind will be reported to the Elders upon our return, and a cut in pay will be arranged," he warned. "Just follow my lead and all will be well."

They left the square and started down the one remaining path to Eiboren. There had once been several that led in that direction, but the forest had taken them from the grasp of man and made them hers once more, thus rendering them impassable to those on horseback.

Selene glanced at Terran, who was somewhere between clearing his throat quite a bit more noisily than was necessary and preparing to spit something onto the roadside. It was just one of a great number of irritating habits that he possessed. "Praecyr," he asked when he was finished, "just what is our quarry guilty of?"

"They did not mention his crime." Ranur's voice held a savage bite. "And I did not ask, as there is no need for me to know. That also means that there is no need for any of you to know." His eyes rested solely on Terran, whose face shaded with embarrassment.

It was pleasing to have someone put him in his place.

Ranur turned once again to face the road ahead. "Understood?" he added without looking back.

"Yes Praecyr."

By the Tides Terran had the intelligence to end it there. Selene would also have liked to know the man's crime, though she would never have asked. There were some things Riders simply were not meant to know. Most of them, she had found, a person was better off not knowing.

Days passed with the speed of an early summer storm. There was little wind to speak of and no rain, thus the scent remained clear and strong. The trail was not like any Selene had followed in her years as a Rider. The dogs rarely left the path, though they often wavered from one side of it to the other with the scent. It was almost as if the man did not realize he was being tracked, or else did not care.

Without warning the afternoon of the third day was upon her. The weather was just chill enough to be comfortable, and Selene was quite happily dwelling in thoughts of silver coins until Terran moved his gelding to Cyprus' side. Cyprus snorted irritably. He did not seem to care for Terran's gelding any more than Selene cared for its master.

Terran remained next to her, saying nothing. The words Ranur had spoken to the man upon their departure had kept him silent for the most part. She had very much enjoyed the peace, and as time had passed she had become quite used to him not speaking to her save for pleasantries. Perhaps he simply wished to ride on ahead. What little hope she had vanished suddenly as he turned to face her.

"You are not wearing the pre-caerim pendant I gave you," he said, glancing at her bare neck.

Selene glared at the path ahead. Terran was either quite dense, or completely arrogant. Perhaps it was a bit of both. The pendant was finely crafted. It was easily worth more than she could make in a year on a Rider's earnings. Still, neither its beauty nor his insistence would force her to wear it. Selene had attempted to return the gift on numerous occasions. He had refused to take it. She had entertained thoughts of selling it at times when money had been short. Unfortunately, as it was a gift, she had realized that she simply had too much common courtesy to do so. In the end it had found a permanent home on the top shelf of the wardrobe she shared with Maye. It had gathered dust there since the last Festival of Low Tides, nearly a year ago. In only a few short weeks the next Festival would be upon them.

"I am not wearing it because I do not intend to take vows with you." An irritated tone crept into Selene's voice although she tried her best to keep it at bay. It was not that Terran would have made a horrible husband. He and his father owned what was easily the largest number of fishing boats in Maresbane. He was not prone to violence, and when it came to looks he was treading squarely on middle ground. She may have accepted his offer in another life, for the sake of providing for her mother. Giving in was simply impossible, however. Her mark made it so. After all, one could hardly expect to spend their entire married life fully clothed. Besides that, Terran always managed to burn her patience away like fire upon flashgrass. He surely thought the world should bend to his whim. That must be why her unwillingness bothered him so. She suppressed a sigh and urged Cyprus faster. Terran's gelding took only seconds to match speed.

"I find your attitude to be completely unreasonable." Terran said, seemingly oblivious to her disgruntled expression. "Whoever he is, he most obviously cannot care for you and your mother the way I can. Otherwise you would have taken up with him long ago."

Selene gave no reply. She used her free hand to pull at a stubborn tangle in Cyprus' mane. Perhaps the man would finally choose to go on ahead if she ignored his idiocy.

"Or perchance it is a female with whom you take your pleasure? Let me assure you that I have attended more than the common share of Tides' Festivities and thus I am quite understanding concerning such things. An arrangement can still be made. It is a common enough occurrence in these times. None will think ill of it."

"There is no other, Terran," Selene said with as much of an even tone as she could manage. "You are the only one who pesters me so, thank the Spirits."

Terran made his reply, but his words were buried by the deep barking of Ranur's dogs.

"Stop where you stand, or forfeit your life." Ranur had come to a halt only a few yards ahead. His sword was drawn. Ormun lingered close behind him, his bow ready; holding for the movement of his prey.

A blonde haired man stood in the center of the path. He wore dark breeches and a shirt of midnight blue. The latter struck Selene as odd. That particular tone of blue was reserved most often for those in favor with the king, or so she thought. But certainly no companion of the king would be hunted by Riders. He had stolen it, perhaps. It was the most reasonable explanation.

It was immediately obvious that Ranur's words of warning had not been well received. The blonde haired man started running in less than a Spirit's breath. Ormun loosed an arrow. He and Ranur sped forward. Selene pushed Cyprus to a gallop, leaving Terran gaping behind her on the trail.

"To the north."

Selene could barely hear Ranur's voice over the thundering sound of Cyprus' hooves hitting the packed dirt of the path. She could sense Terran gaining on her, though she had neither the time nor the desire to look back. The path ahead split into two. Ranur slowed in the slightest upon reaching it.

"Terran, Ormun, take the left. Selene, with me," he shouted back at them. It was strange that he would split the party. Something was wrong, though she could not figure out what. Aside from that, no man could outrun a horse at full gallop. Even Ranur's massive dogs were unable to keep up with the horses' gait. *Strange.* She was given no time to think on it, for Ranur's stallion veered suddenly from the path into the woods. He seemed to have no trouble navigating the scattered trees and thick underbrush. Cyprus managed to keep up for a short time, but the forest began to tear at him. Sharp branches and blackberry thorns bit through skin and hide alike.

Selene lost sight of Ranur suddenly. She urged Cyprus to pick up speed. The forest thinned, allowing him to hasten his steps. She breathed a deep sigh of relief as Ranur's tawny stallion came back into view, and another as the pair slowed. They came to a halt a few yards away. She slowed Cyprus and dismounted.

Selene drew her sword as she approached the clearing. The blond haired man lay face down on the leaf-covered soil. An arrow protruded from the rear of his left leg. Tarr and Dai issued rumbling growls of displeasure as they circled him. They had been well trained, for they merely watched the man rather than seizing him. Their master was another matter. Selene watched in horror as Ranur thrust the point of his sword through the man's neck. Blood welled up from the wound. It flowed onto the man's tattered cotton shirt and the soil beneath him, staining it in deep crimson hues.

Selene closed the distance between them at a run. The dream of silver pieces and goat's milk was quickly fading, as was her confidence. The man had done nothing to deserve death. "For what reason did you slay him?" she demanded. Normally she would not have spoken to her Praecyr in such a way, but the rashness of Ranur's actions had stolen all reason from her.

Swift and severe was the punishment for displeasing an Elder. Terran had several lashing scars as a result of disobedience, most of them from years long past. At least one, however, was recent. She had witnessed its placement with two other Riders at her side. There was no fear or pain on Terran's face as Elder Aldyn struck him, only the embarrassment of having failed her. Selene had been lucky enough to escape such punishment thus far. Her marked body, when found, would seal her fate so that even the Tides could not turn it.

"He was to be returned to them alive." The words barely escaped Selene's lips. For a moment she was not certain Ranur had heard her. A soft breeze rustled the leaves overhead, pushing at the silence that enveloped the woods.

"They certainly would have received him as such," Ranur said with a scowl, "was he found to be human."

Selene edged closer to inspect the boy. Save for his blond hair he could have been any man of Maresbane. His strong build reminded her of Terran's younger brother.

Ranur placed one foot on the man's back and used it as leverage to remove his sword. He used what remained of the man's shirt to wipe the blood from its blade before returning his weapon to its scabbard.

"It is here," he said, forming an expression of distaste. He placed a gloved finger on the corner of the man's shirt near the right shoulder and pulled it back to reveal the skin beneath. What had at first seemed to be a dark spot covered by worn fabric was now revealed in its true form. An area of interlocking lines curled like smoke from an extinguished candle across the man's flesh. Selene could feel the blood drain from her face as she gazed upon it.

"Hideous, is it not?" Ranur had clearly mistaken the look of shock upon her face for one of repulsion. "This mark," he said thoughtfully as he traced the tattoo-like symbol with his finger, "is the sign of a soul lingering somewhere between man and beast. The Marked Ones may look as we do, but you cannot let that fool you. They are evil, cursed things. They are a danger to themselves as well as those around them."

A slow burn crept across Selene's mark as Ranur spoke, just as it had during Elder Aldyn's questioning long ago. She had more control over it now, age and practice had seen to that, yet days of travel had made her weary. How many Marked Ones had Ranur killed? Had Islyr been one of them? Curiosity held Selene's feet firmly in place.

"They can change from man to animal at will. By the shape of the mark you will know which beast they are linked to." His expression grew dark as he spoke. "I have seen this pattern before. Not five months ago. Mark of wolf." Ranur backed up a few paces and pulled a square of white cloth from his belt pouch. He wiped his gloved hands with it, as if to rid them of some unseen filth. "Last one escaped me. Not this one though."

Selene's concentration began to slip. Ranur continued speaking, yet his words were lost to her. The world slid away. She reached down to touch the dying man's blood spattered back as if compelled by the Spirits. As she placed her fingers upon him the burn in her mark intensified. One dozen knives, just off the metalsmith's fire, forced themselves through her skin. It was unbearable. Selene's hand slid toward her mark. The burning faded as her fingers left the man's back. She looked up from where she now knelt. Ranur was next to her. His smile had disappeared.

Her error had been as bold as the sun at midday. She withdrew her hand and placed it upon the hilt of her sword, though she made no move to draw it. Ranur watched her calmly. It did not look as though he had noticed anything odd. Selene looked to the east, as if checking upon Cyprus' whereabouts. He was not known to stray, but she was in dire need of some reason to take her eyes from the dying man.

Ranur's pondering expression vanished as he turned from her and mounted. "You are the lightest among us," he said. "Take this *thing* and tie him to your horse. I trust you've enough strength for that."

"Yes, Praecyr." The words came out normally, by luck of the Tides.

"Be ready to ride when I return." He started off at a trot.

Selene willed her breathing to slow. She whistled for Cyprus, who trotted obediently to her side. It would not do to have Ranur return and find her staring numbly at the body.

Selene pulled her spare blanket from Cyprus' saddlebags and unrolled it next to the man. After removing the arrow from his leg and tossing it aside she knelt down beside him and grasped his arm. It was still slightly warm.

Perhaps he was not too far gone. It was an absurd thought, but something within her would not let it go. She had sworn to Maye that she would not use her healing ability where others might see it. But what if he could be saved? She would simply be quick about it. If the man did not rise then nothing would be lost. Selene rolled him over onto the open blanket, trying desperately to ignore the burning that returned to her mark as she touched his skin. It was not as strong now as it had been. She was thankful for that.

It was strange to look upon his unmoving face. He was indeed young, much younger than she had expected. He was no more than a boy. She leaned in close. No breath escaped him.

He did not stir as Selene tore the cloth of his shirt and placed her hands upon the wound that pierced his neck. Every drop of concentration she could muster was channeled into the healing. Her hands grew warm. Her head began to ache. His flesh refused to close in upon itself. She sat back with a sigh. He was most certainly dead. She had been a fool to think that even a Marked once could survive such an injury.

Two bright blue eyes probed her soul from behind golden locks of hair matted with drying blood. She pulled them gently closed, mostly out of respect, but partly to quiet their accusing gaze. "May the Spirits protect and guide your soul on this day and thereafter."

Selene was halfway to her feet when something caught her eye. A leather cord hung around the boy's neck, miraculously untouched by the blade of Ranur's sword. She pulled it gently, taking care not to touch any bare skin. A clear, rounded crystal hung at the cord's end. A setting of silver metal, molded into dragon's talons, held the stone top to bottom leaving the center unobstructed. It seemed such a costly a thing for a young boy to have. It must have been stolen along with the clothing.

Selene moved her fingers across the stone's face to clear the blood that rested there. As she did so a thin line of black smoke swirled through its center. Before she had time to think on it another appeared, this one as white as the other had been dark. They danced swiftly within the orb, nearly touching each other at times yet never mixing. She removed her hand from the stone. The smoke vanished. The pain in Selene's head faded to nothing.

The pendant was an item of magic, that much was certain. She pulled the cord carefully over the boy's head and moved to place it into one of the bags that hung from Cyprus' saddle, but suddenly thought better of it. Riders were entitled to keep any items found while on errand, providing that neither the Praecyr nor the person funding the errand had asked for them. Neither Ranur nor the Elders had mentioned a pendant within her hearing. Furthermore, she simply did not wish to let it go. She pulled the leather strap over her head instead, tucking the crystal beneath her shirt to be sure no one would see it. If it was asked for then she would return it.

In mere moments the body was wrapped and the blanket surrounding it secured with a length of rope. The process of loading the boy onto Cyprus, however, did not go as smoothly as Selene would have liked. His body was heavier than she had anticipated, and freshly dead people were not at all balanced for carrying. To make matters worse, Cyprus did not seem to want anything to do with her as long as she held the dead boy. He snorted and stomped his feet, showing the whites of his eyes as she drew near him. It took quite a few soothing words and a rope from his bridle to the nearest tree to calm him long enough for her to perform the needed tasks. Once she had loaded the body she tied it quickly, before Cyprus had a chance to change his mind. The task was done none too soon, for Ranur rode swiftly into the clearing with Terran and Ormun trailing close behind.

None of the men spoke as they headed back towards the trail. Ormun's silence did not bother Selene, for it most likely came from the vastly diminished probability of receiving extra silver. Ranur's demeanor, however, filled her with uncertainty. She did her best to avoid his gaze as she took a place at the end of the line.

Days passed at a grinding pace. Selene's anxiousness grew as they approached Maresbane. Ranur must know her secret. Part of her wanted to flee, though she knew that she would not get far. Cyprus was fast, but his stride was much shorter than that of Ranur's stallion. Even without the extra weight of the boy escape was not a possibility.

The body had become a bane to Selene upon the first night, and it had continued to fuel her frustration since. Unloading it was a chore. She preferred not to touch it even through the blanket, and the smell became worse with every hour that passed. Today it was nearly unbearable. Ranur and the others assured her that there was little scent to be noticed. It was the only conversation that they had all taken part in since before the murder of the boy. Perhaps it was true. The nights had been cool, slowing the advance of decay. Still, every once in a great while when the wind was right, she would catch that unmistakable smell. Selene glanced up at the partially clouded sky. Rotting or no, the boy deserved a proper sending. She was certain that he would never get one. Marked Ones rarely met the flames of a funeral pyre.

Selene glanced at Terran. On any other day she would not have dared lest he consider it an invitation to speak with her. It was safe today, distant as he was, raising his hand from time to time to touch the lashing scars upon his back. The closer they came to town, the more frequent his actions became. If the Tides were with them they would not receive a lashing. Ranur was the one who deserved it. None of the Riders had taken part in the killing of the boy. Selene knew that Praecyrs were not eligible for punishment, only for lessened pay, but that did not keep her from wishing that it could be so.

The clicking of Cyprus' hooves against the tiles of the Elders' Square served only to strengthen the nervous feeling within Selene's chest. A light breeze twisted from behind her, sending the scent of rotting flesh swirling around her face. She suppressed the urge to retch by concentrating on the wave-like pattern of colored tiles upon the ground.

Ranur came to a halt in the center of the square near where they had stood at the errand's beginning. "Settle your horses and clean yourselves. Meet me here when you've finished. There will surely be some silver to be given, perhaps a feast in our honor." He looked to Ormun. "Take Tarr and Dai with you. Be sure that they are properly cared for."

Ormun seemed content to follow Ranur's orders although they were technically no longer on errand. He nodded his head in consent and started off in the direction of the Hasana family home. He must have offered them a fair amount of coin; Lelyn Hasana was known to be choosy about whom she took in for boarding. Terran no longer rubbed his lashing scars, though he held a sour look upon his face as he turned his gelding towards home.

"Selene, with me."

Selene would have given anything to be allowed to leave. It seemed unfair that Terran and Ormun had been given that privilege and she had not.

She followed Ranur through the Square, past the carved wooden awning under which the Elders sat during council. She and Islyr had played there as children, under ocean waves and seabirds chiseled into weathered wood. They had taken the Elders' seats, sending each other on errand against Bloodsoul and shadeslight and having great feasts of bread and sunberries upon their successful return home.

Selene's gaze traveled past the Elders' place of council to a stout tree that grew between the awning and the Square. Its leaves were a deep red in color and its bark the perfect white of freshly fallen snow. Two short lengths of knotted rope hung from the largest branch, which grew out over the road so that anyone who wished to visit the Elders cottage would be forced to travel beneath it. *The Sending Tree…* Maye had not allowed them to play in the square while the tree was in use. More Marked Ones had lost their lives to that tree than Selene cared to think about. They had been cleansed of their curse. It was what was whispered as the Marked Ones dangled from that tree; as the ropes around their necks stole their breath.

It had been so long ago that the last One was punished. She and Islyr had run out to see him while Maye went to market and their father was out on errand. Islyr had suffered from nightmares for several months after. The man's face, the black emptiness where his eyes had once resided, still haunted Selene's dreams from time to time.

The path from the Square to the Elder's cottage was a short one. Its sandy surface faded suddenly beneath the tiles of the Elders' porch, pulling Selene abruptly from thoughts of the past. Driftwood walls came to life as the ocean's breath twisted the leafy vines that covered them. The entrance had been prominent when Selene was a child. It was now difficult to tell where the walls ended and the door began.

"Wait here." Ranur's voice severed her thoughts with ease. He dismounted and climbed the stone steps. The Praecyr knocked twice, centering his fist carefully in the only leafless spot upon the door's face.

Aged hinges screeched in complaint. Selene leaned forward in her saddle, hoping to catch even a few of the words exchanged between Ranur and the Elder as he was admitted. Her efforts were in vain. Ranur slipped inside.

Selene lowered herself from Cyprus' back. She untied the body and lifted it from him, trying hard not to breathe while it was near her face. Cyprus shook himself once he was free of it, as if to remove the scent from his hide. He lowered his head to pull at a ragged tuft of grass that had sprouted in the center of the path.

The body seemed heavier than it had been. Selene managed to get just to the edge of the porch before her stomach lurched. The smell of death gnawed at her senses. The body dropped to the ground and she to her knees. Bile burned her throat. It suddenly seemed more fortunate that she had not had any breakfast. Selene lowered her head to the tiles, letting the cold soothe her.

"Having some difficulty?" Ranur loomed over her.

"No, Praecyr," she stammered, searching his words for hidden meaning. "The smell of this thing is beginning to bother me, I suppose." She dusted stray sand from her clothes as she stood. Her feet held steady, though her stomach was far from settled. "I will be fine." Perhaps saying the words aloud would somehow make it so.

"Excellent. In that case you shall be pleased to hear that the Elders will see us now." He shot a steady look at the bundle. "With that as well. Take the feet."

Selene was not at all pleased to hear the news. The more time she spent outside the Elder's cottage, the less inclined she was to venture in. It was too late to run. She did as she had been told.

Selene's eyes were given no time to adjust as the door closed heavily behind her. The scent of musty cloth and beeswax candles permeated the air. Thick fabric covered each of the room's windows, blocking what little light crept between the vines residing upon the outer walls. She waded through the darkness, trying desperately not to stumble over anything as her vision returned. They traveled a narrow hallway, over creaking wooden floors and soft, threadbare rugs to the Elders' common room. A fireplace of smooth ocean stones encompassed one wall. The dying flames within it were the room's only source of illumination. The other walls were lined with light blue tiles, several of which held carefully painted ocean waves. A few wooden chests and glazed jars of pottery served as decoration, surrounding a single shelf of dust covered books all bound in various shades of leather. Three stuffed chairs sat near the hearth, though only two were occupied.

There were always three elders; one man and two women, or so Maye had told her. Selene recognized the closest one as Elder Prenn, the Father. He attended nearly all of the Elders' councils. A waterfall of white hair cascaded from his wrinkled face, ending just above the open tome that rested in his lap. Not one syllable of speech had ever escaped his gaunt lips, at least as far as Selene had heard. Elder Aldyn was always the one to speak when words were needed.

Elder Aldyn sat now by the hearthside, surveying Selene's progress with a look of careful consideration. Her face, with the fire's light casting shadows over its surface, looked much as it had on the day of her father's Sending. The Elder must have been a child once, long ago, though Selene found it hard to imagine that face without the mask of age covering it.

Nervousness washed over Selene as she realized that the third Elder was not present. *Out searching for a whipping branch, or worse.* She pushed the thought hastily from her mind.

"Set him here." Elder Aldyn said as she unfolded a blanket in front of the hearth. Her voice was the sound of sand ground against stone.

Ranur set his end upon the floor. Selene held her breath as the body's scent caught her once more. She stood quickly and bowed in Elder Aldyn's direction, as was proper. Perhaps they only wished her to aid in bringing the boy in. They might send her away now that the job had been finished.

"Now, child," the Elder said, peering at her from behind sagging layers of skin. "Explain to me why there is a dead boy on my floor when you were given explicit orders to bring him here unharmed."

All hope of leaving vanished like morning mist touched by the first rays of the sun. The thought of speaking to the Elder on the subject of Marked Ones made her skin grow cold. She eased her words out, taking great care not to show fear, and bending slightly at the waist to add formality. "With greatest respect Elder, perhaps the Praecyr could explain this better than I." It was the best plan she could concoct, short of taking flight.

Elder Aldyn turned at once to Ranur, who did not seem fearful in the least at becoming the focus of her attention.

"You certainly would have received the boy alive as you requested, were he found to be human." There was no hint of distress as he continued. "A Marked One, Elder. Mark of wolf. Death is the penalty for those bearing the Mark."

The Elder fell silent for a moment, as if considering what Ranur had said. The fire had dwindled, making it difficult to read her expression. Even so, Selene was certain it was hatred that crossed her ancient face.

"Show me his mark," she ordered.

Ranur knelt by the body's side. He pulled a small hunting knife from his belt and sliced easily through the ropes that held the blanket in place. Selene fought the urge to turn away as he uncovered the boy. *Concentrate.* She had managed to stay out of trouble thus far, but she was fairly certain that she had used up all of her luck for this particular errand.

"Turn him over."

The body was not nearly as rotted as Selene had thought it would be. She had wrapped it tightly, allowing no room for flies to crawl between the layers of fabric. Still, his skin seemed swollen and his eyes sunken. The closeness of the room left nowhere for his putrid scent to travel, making Selene wish she was anywhere else in the Ethereal Realm but where she now stood.

A rattling emanated from the far side of the cottage, followed by the now familiar complaint of hinges. The third elder had found her whipping branch, no doubt. Selene entertained the idea of pleading for a whipping on the rump rather than the back. Then she would not have to remove her shirt, bearing her mark for all to see. A bit of embarrassment was far better than a trip to the hanging tree.

"Are you listening, child?" The Elder's hand struck the back of Selene's head with surprising force.

"Yes, Elder," Selene replied in wonder. When had the Elder's attention turned to her? The blow had not been terribly painful, but it had been much more than was necessary to let her know that she was being spoken to. Years ago it would have been enough to draw her hand to her mark for comfort. Today, it merely angered her. "Forgive me, Elder," she added, making her best attempt at sincerity.

The Elder did not acknowledge Selene's words. She merely stood, her dark eyes passing along the length of the body, her scowl deepening with each second that passed.

Selene took Ranur's place. She grabbed the boy's tattered sleeve and rolled him over, taking great care not to glance at his face. It was troubling that the Elder had chosen her for the task. Ranur was just as capable, and he was certainly stronger than she.

"Move the cloth aside, so I can better see it."

Thick, rancid air filled Selene's lungs as she leaned down towards the body. She reached for the edge of the fabric that covered his mark. Her fingers slipped, touching not cloth, but rotting flesh. The burning pain of days before instantly returned. It was only a shadow of what it had been on the day of the boy's death, yet when combined with the smell of decay and the heat of the fire it became intolerable. Nothing mattered except ceasing the pain. Her hand moved to touch her mark. Realization of the mistake she had made came much too late.

"Are you ill, child?" The Elder's tone was just the same as it had always been, stiff and cold, but her eyes…

She knows.

Selene's mouth opened as if to speak, but no sound left her. The shock of what she had done settled heavily upon her.

Spirits protect me, she knows.

"Answer your Elder." Ranur placed a gloved hand upon his sword as he spoke, loosening the weapon from its scabbard. Dying flames illuminated its polished blade. He smiled as he had after killing the boy.

Selene's stomach rolled.

"A Rider should know better than to show such disrespect," Ranur said.

The Elder drew closer. She leaned in; her dark eyes searching Selene's face, delving through her skin to find what secrets were kept within.

Selene stood. She stepped back from the boy.

"Hold her."

Ranur's sword snapped as he pushed it roughly back into its scabbard. Selene reached for her weapon but found her wrists pulled securely behind her back before her fingers could touch its hilt. The Elder unbuckled the belt that held Selene's sword and set it, complete, into a metal chest that stood against the nearest wall. She locked it quickly, using a key that hung from a chain around her neck.

Ranur pushed Selene down. Her knees smashed against the wooden floor. Elder Aldyn stood over her. She could feel the fabric of her shirt being pulled back below her right shoulder, revealing the mark that resided there. *Death is the penalty for those bearing the Mark.* Natural patterns formed from the grains of the polished floorboards danced in the remaining light. The smell of the dead body engulfed her. It was stronger than it had ever been.

"Unbelievable," Ranur muttered. Fingers encased in leather tightened upon her wrists until it became painful.

"Mark of raven, and on you no less." There was an air of confusion in Elder Aldyn's tone.

"Turn it towards the light." Elder Prenn's voice was barely a whisper, but it held no less command than Elder Aldyn's. He rose from his chair and hobbled toward Selene.

Selene resisted Ranur's attempt to shift her.

"The Elder wishes for you to move." Ranur let go of her just long enough to drive his boot into her side. It was painful, certainly, but the pain was nothing when compared to the burning that had rushed through her mark as she had touched the boy's skin. She attempted to show no signs of anguish, though her left side now throbbed terribly and the urge to retch was strong.

Selene was now angled enough towards the fire to catch a glimpse of the boy. Her eyes focused upon the gaping wound that split his neck. Ranur had slain him without a second thought, without the slightest hint of regret. He would do the same to her.

The creaking of a floor board, the slightest of sounds, pulled Selene's gaze towards the hallway. She realized with horror that the scent that had trailed her from the woods had not come entirely from the boy. A Bloodsoul stood there, lurching dangerously from one side of the hall to the other as it attempted to keep its balance. The only Bloodsoul that Selene had battled had been found far from here, near the edge of the Barren Lands. Their group had come upon the thing merely by chance, and an unlucky chance it was. They had lost three Riders that day. The casualties would have been much greater had the Praecyr not called a retreat. That Bloodsoul had been ancient; made only of bleached bones. This one was considerably fresher. By the look of it the creature had been human not so long ago. Rotting clumps of flesh and bits of torn clothing clung precariously to its bones.

Panic gripped Selene. Ranur still held her wrists tightly, though his attention was now upon the Bloodsoul that was striding quickly towards them. She looked to the key which hung upon Elder Aldyn's neck. There was no chance of gaining her weapon in time for it to be of use.

Heat burst against Selene's neck. *The orb*. The sound of scraping metal came suddenly from behind her. The chest in which Elder Aldyn had placed Selene's sword moved as if thrown. It passed swiftly behind her, narrowly missing her head before striking Ranur with full force.

Selene's knees ached as she stood. She knew that items of magic were dangerous, yet she had still taken the orb from the boy. *Lucky I didn't knock my fool head off.* Perhaps the Tides were with her this day after all.

Hands of rotten flesh reached for Selene. The walls of the room seemed to press in around her. There was no known way to kill a Bloodsoul, and she had no weapon besides. A poker rested near the hearth. Its metal was warm to the touch. She forced the length of it through the creature's chest. The cracking of bones split the air of the room. The Bloodsoul did not seem hindered in the least, though portions of its ribs were now missing. Selene pulled the poker from between its splintered bones. She struck again, harder this time. The creature's arm separated from its shoulder. It hit the wall that stood behind it, shattering some pottery that rested upon a shelf. Selene swung back in preparation of a third blow, this time to the head. The pieces that she had knocked from the bloodsoul's ribcage flew up from the floor to reattach themselves to the beast.

Hard metal connected with bone. The creature's head cracked and splattered. Selene threw the poker down. Ranur had already begun to stir. His hands reached feverishly for his sword. Selene pushed past the headless body and ran. She burst out the front door, stumbling on the stairs but catching herself before she landed on the sand strewn path. Blinding midday light assaulted her eyes, pulling a curtain of white across the world. A knot of despair formed tightly around her stomach as her vision finally returned. The area before her was empty. She knew now why the third Elder had not been present. Cyprus was gone, as was Ranur's stallion.

Selene ran towards home, taking the back way so as not to pass through the Square. Word traveled fast when Riders returned from errand. By now a crowd of people had surely gathered there to witness the Elder's council. Terran and Ormun would be present as well, anxiously awaiting their pay or perhaps a lashing. Setting one foot upon the Square's worn surface would mean sentencing herself to death, unarmed as she was.

Selene glanced behind her as she reached home. There was no sign of either the Bloodsoul or Ranur thus far, but she did not expect her luck to last. It would take Ranur time to gather his party and the dogs, even if he managed to defeat the creature. She was certain that he would not waste a second of the time he had been given. She had injured his pride. That, combined with his hatred of Marked Ones, would cause him to seek swift retribution.

She pushed her front door aside, not bothering to close it behind her. "Maye?" Her voice echoed slightly as it forced itself through the silence of the empty room. She searched, only to find each room as devoid of life as the first. *The barn. She's there. She must be.* Selene's feet carried her out through the pasture and towards the barn. The tall door was open. Maye was not there. In fact, it looked as if no one had entered at all in the days since Selene had left.

Despair settled upon her. She could go back towards the Square. Perhaps it was not too late. If she found her mother on the path before it reached the center of town they might have a chance to leave without being seen. Selene started forward, but was stopped by the deep bellowing of Ranur's dogs. They were not far. It was frightening to think that he had dealt the Bloodsoul so quickly.

She would not be able to rescue anyone with Ranur's sword through her chest. Perhaps they would be much too concerned with her whereabouts to even think of Maye at all. She hoped desperately that her mother would manage to escape this place. *May the spirits guide her.*

The woods of Eiboren began just behind the pasture. An old path lay beneath the trees, overgrown with thick weeds and thorn bushes. What space remained was barely wide enough for one person on foot. It would certainly slow them down, perhaps even enough for her to lose them.

Pounding hooves joined the frenzied barking of Ranur's dogs. The forest's cool breath slid across Selene's skin as she stepped into its depths.

Lansfallow

Frigid water swirled around Selene's boots, soaking her feet and siphoning away what little warmth they still held. She had not been able to feel her toes for several hours. Still, it had been a good choice, walking the river rather than the faded pathway. Ennsea River was wide, yet its water was not deep. It came less than halfway to her knees and was swift enough to cover her tracks, yet not enough so to sweep her balance from beneath her.

Losing Ranur and his Riders had proved to be quite a bit easier than Selene had imagined, for they had not followed her more than a half hour into the woods. Selene had crossed the Ennsea's waters as she reached them, traveled nearly a quarter mile towards Eiboren and, after making sure that Ranur was nowhere near, she had doubled back and started upriver. The ploy seemed to have worked. The only sound to be heard over the constant, mesmerizing rush of water was the occasional rustle of some small creature navigating the brush and, every once in a great while, the call of an owl waking in preparation for an evening of foraging.

Night was falling around her. The same steady wind that had scattered her scent, making her difficult to track, now bit at her skin with chilled teeth and held the scent of an impending storm. She wished in vain for the soft warmth of her cloak. It was back in Maresbane in her saddlebags, along with a hundred other things she wished that she had been able to bring. *No use pining over things lost.* Her mother spoke those words often.

Selene's scowl matched the thunder that rumbled in the distance. She hoped that the weather would hold for just a few hours longer. She would be arriving in Lansfallow shortly if her sense of direction had not failed her. It was a bigger town than Maresbane, just large enough for a lone traveler to pass through unnoticed.

The voice of a wolf echoed between peals of thunder. Selene pulled her arms across her chest. A pack of woods wolves roamed this side of the forest. The largest one she had seen stood not much taller than farmer's herding dog, but the pack's number had more than doubled in the past few years. More than twenty some said. Given that, she would guess the true number to be less than ten. The darkness of night often stirred fear into frenzy, making one wolf seem like many.

Selene picked up her pace, though at the moment wolves seemed the least of her worries. An attempt to move her toes provided less than satisfactory results, and her feet ached from want of heat. She surrendered the idea of ever being able to feel them again and instead concentrated on sifting through the contents of her belt pouch. Luckily the Elders had not thought to take it from her. Seven copper pieces. It was little more than enough to get a decent room at an inn. Perhaps she could get something to eat while she made her plans to go back for Maye. Food had not passed her lips since yesterday evening, and then it had only been a piece of dried venison; left over rations from the errand with Ranur. The meat itself had been good, though the thoughts of Ranur and Terran that accompanied it had left a bitter taste in her mouth.

Distant flashes of light accompanied the soft, muddy sound her boots made as she climbed the riverbank. The light of day had completely faded and a half moon hung above, covered now and again by passing clouds. The storm was many miles off yet, though if the wind picked up just a little it could be upon her in a quarter hour, perhaps less.

Selene passed through edge of the woods and out onto a narrow strip of high grass that separated forest floor from hard-packed dirt. She paused near the road, listening carefully for even the slightest sound of horses' hooves or creaking leather saddles. There was no noise to be heard. Perhaps she had truly lost them. It was nice to think it, although she doubted that Ranur would give up so easily after what she had put him through.

Selene had been to Lansfallow only once, while on an errand a few years back. The Praecyr had ordered them onward within the hour. There was no chance that anyone would know her here.

Laughter and singing touched Selene's ears long before the inn's rickety wooden exterior came into view. The building's crooked sign depicted a shaggy donkey lounging atop an overturned cart. The words "The Broken Mule" had been crudely painted beneath the scene. She stopped as her hand touched the door. Doubt had sprouted within her and was growing quickly with nervous thoughts to speed it. Entering even the most reputable of inns without a weapon, or at the least a companion, was risky. Most people one could expect to find in a place like this would do anything for a few coins. A lone, unarmed female would be difficult to resist.

Lightning flashed once again, brightening the sky briefly. It was followed closely by a clap of thunder that rattled the inn's windows. The scent of rain hung heavily in the air. The storm was traveling more quickly than she had anticipated. She watched as clouds consumed the last of the moon. Eiboren was the nearest town to Lansfallow, and it was more than three days travel by horse. It was also farther from Maye.

Fat drops of rain began to fall, launching small puffs of dust where they hit the parched dirt road. Selene sighed. She reluctantly opened the door.

The Broken Mule's common room was a stir of noise and movement. Either Lansfallow had seen an unusually large number of travelers pass through on this day, or else every man in town had decided that tonight was a decent night for a drink. Three quarters of the chairs were occupied, and most of the men that filled them were either drunk or well on their way to being so. The scents of roasted meat, ale, and pipe smoke were strong.

Deep voices filled the room with an off-key version of a song she recognized as "Never a Lady Fair", successfully drowning out all sounds of the approaching storm. The men held their mugs high, sloshing them back and forth and spilling half of their drinks onto the floor as they belted the words. Not that it mattered. The moment a mug was emptied one of numerous smiling serving girls, their trays held high as they skillfully dodged quick hands and crude remarks, brought another. The girls were cleanly dressed, at least when compared to the scarred tables and ale covered floor.

Selene scrutinized the inn's patrons briefly. A good portion of them looked to be either merchants or farm hands. Not a single Rider sat amongst them. Perhaps it would not be as difficult as she had thought to rid herself of Ranur. No one had so much as glanced in her direction thus far. She was fairly certain that most of them would not remember her in the morning, or much else of the night for that matter.

A part of her longed to join in on the fun, to let singing and ale drown away the past few days. *I am not so tired yet as to let reason escape me.* She chose an empty table in the corner.

As she sat a serving girl approached. She had dark eyes and darker curls bundled high atop her head and held with a short green ribbon, to match the stained apron which hung from her waist. The girl held a tray of chilled mugs balanced precariously upon one shoulder. She set one in front of Selene, spilling a fair amount of its contents as she banged it onto the table. "Some food for you, Rider?"

Selene wondered momentarily at the fact that the girl had called her a Rider, but then remembered her hair and the metal pin that still held it in an altered Rider's knot. "A bit of that roasted meat," she said, straining to raise her voice above the din. She handed over two copper pieces. The dark eyed girl shoved them unceremoniously into her apron as she hurried off towards the kitchen.

Selene took a sip from her mug. It was not the worst ale she had ever tasted, but it was certainly far from the best. It had been watered down, yet the bitterness of it still clung to her tongue long after she had swallowed.

Selene pulled the orb from beneath her shirt and turned it to catch the light, admiring its beauty. It could prove to be useful if she ever figured out how to work it properly. Memories of the chest at the Elder's cottage careening only inches from her head kept her from attempting to reactivate the orb's power of levitation. She had fiddled with it for the first few hours of travel down the river, however, in case it had more powers than one. Magic items often did. So far her efforts had gained her nothing. With luck it would be something to aid her in fetching Maye. A pendant of invisibility would be ideal. Kailia, a Rider and friend though she had been eight years Selene's senior, had found one once on errand. Kailia had a penchant for items of magic. She had been more than pleased to explain the pendant's workings to Selene; how it did not really make one disappear but rather bent the way light flowed around them, making it seem like they had.

Selene took a second mouthful of ale in an attempt to still her rumbling stomach. It did not taste any better than the first. She wondered what Kailia would have done if she had found Selene to be Marked. Not that it mattered, for Kailia was gone; slain by a Bloodsoul years ago. Memories of that day; Kailia's screams over the sounds of tearing flesh and crunching bone, still made Selene's stomach clench even with what time had passed. The Praecyr had ordered a retreat, but Selene had begged to stay and fight.

You will do as I say. He had spoken calmly. *And you will live to thank me.*

Years of thought and regret had made the folly of her actions clear to her. She could not have aided Kailia by dying.

The orb began to glow suddenly; a bright, white light. Selene tucked it hastily back into her shirt, cursing that she had not been paying more attention to her actions. The inn's door swung open, allowing the storm that now raged outside to pull at the flames of the old stone hearth and the lamps of oil that hung from the walls surrounding it. Selene reached for her sword, a movement born of long years as a Rider. Her hand found only air. She sat up, ready, in case the need to flee should arise. *I lost them. I know I did.*

At first all she could see of the man that entered was a fine woolen cloak, the color of a midnight sky. She breathed a sigh of relief and sat back firmly in her chair. A mere glimpse of the cloak and the silver thread upon its edges was enough to know that this was not Ranur. This was certainly a wealthy man, much more so than the most talented Praecyr could ever hope to be. He must have been forced to stop here by the rain. No man with wealth enough to afford such attire would purposely lower his status by being seen in a place such as this.

Selene's stomach grumbled again as she took a large mouthful of drink. It was cold, at least. She could not help but wish that they would bring her food with a bit more speed. Ale did little more than water to soothe an empty stomach. She had intended to ignore the wealthy traveler completely, as he did not seem to be a danger to her, but she could not help but stare at the hills wolf that stayed at his side. It was a truly massive creature, as hills wolves commonly were, with a fine gray coat and large dark eyes that seemed to take in everything in the room at once without any effort. She would have wagered by its size and condition that it could have taken on both of Ranur's dogs at once and sustained little injury. The creature shook the rain from its coat, throwing droplets of water against the floor and the nearest wall. It then sat calmly and looked to the cloaked man.

Selene turned reluctantly from the unlikely pair. The dark eyed serving girl had finally returned. She balanced a steaming plate of meat and buttered potatoes on one arm and a full tray of mugs upon the other. The girl set the plate before Selene, banging it roughly against the table as she had with the ale. The food stayed in place for the most part, much to Selene's surprise. The sweet scent of roasted chicken made it seem like weeks had passed since her last meal. She skewered a potato with her fork and bit down before returning her gaze to the man and his wolf. Although there were several empty tables left in the room he seemed to think that the one nearest Selene was the best of them. As he sat his cloak shifted, offering her a quick glimpse of the sword hidden beneath it. Its hilt was inlaid with gold scrollwork, and the weapon was clearly well used. The man threw back his hood. His strong face held a firm, but not unkind expression. His wolf seated itself on the floor nearby. It could have rested its muzzle upon the tabletop had it thought to lower it just a little.

The serving girl was there setting ale in front of him in half the time it had taken her to get to Selene and without spilling so much as a drop onto the table. "What food may I fetch for you this evening, my Lord?" She eyed the wolf warily as if unsure that it was completely under its master's control.

Selene tilted an ear towards them as she bit into a piece of roasted chicken. It tasted nearly as good as it smelled. Likely that was due to the length of time that had passed since her last meal. Hunger seemed to make even the worst of foods more palatable.

The man's blue-gray eyes searched the room momentarily before settling back to the serving girl. "Just ale," he replied, handing her a silver piece. "You may keep what is left," he added easily, as if he had hundreds more and had no real use for pieces so trivial as silver in any event.

The girl's smile widened until Selene was sure it would crack her face. The sight of silver seemed to have banished all thoughts of being eaten by the man's companion. "You are so generous, my Lord."

"Xaiden," the man offered.

"Thank you so, Lord Xaiden." The girl lowered herself into a curtsy. She hurried to the kitchen, darting around drunken revelers with ease.

The man sat back and removed a pair of dark leather gloves. They matched his cloak perfectly down to the silver embroidery that graced their edges, which she could now see was composed of artfully stitched vines and tiny, galloping horses. He grasped the chilled mug that the serving girl had set out for him and pulled it to his lips. Part of a potato stuck in Selene's throat as her eyes caught sight of the back of his hand. A symbol was branded there; a serpent dragon coiled around a crescent moon. She recognized it at once from stories her father had told her as a child. The man was an Aranth; a member of the king's Elite Guard. There were nearly as many tales of them as there were of the Marked Ones, though Aranth were portrayed as dreams rather than nightmares. Never before had she actually seen one, though she remembered the stories with perfect clarity. Aranth were highly trained in weaponry as well as the assassin's arts. They were defenders of the innocent and guards to the royal family. They were killers of Marked Ones.

Long ago those with great talent would travel to the capital city of Evaria in hopes of being accepted into their ranks. Most returned without so much as gaining an audience with the king. It took more than strength and talent to be admitted. You had to have what was called an Affinity; the ability to form a bond of obedience with any undomesticated creature. It was also said that Aranth possessed inhuman powers, that some could kill a man without so much as raising a weapon. There was likely more rumor to that than there was truth. Other than his Aranth brand and the hills wolf that sat calmly next to him like a trained pup he looked like any other wealthy traveler. And most importantly, he did not seem to realize that she was marked.

Not all stories ring true to life. Selene thought as she watched the wolf settle its head gently upon its paws. Ranur had said that Marked Ones were able to change from man to beast at will, and that was something that she certainly was not capable of. Lansfallow was more than three weeks from Evaria at best. The man must be on errand for the king; tracking someone, most likely. *Pity that poor soul.*

Lord Xaiden's gaze met hers momentarily, bringing to light the fact that she had been staring at him while she thought. Selene quickly averted her eyes, casting them down upon her plate. She was surprised to find it empty save for a few bones. When she turned back the Aranth's attention had moved elsewhere, towards a fight that had broken out between two rather drunk patrons. One of the two, a sapling-thin fellow with mug still in hand, was doing well to stand let alone swing blows. He was struck at once by the other, a short-legged man, square in the jaw. The blow sent him back towards Selene. He collided with the chair that sat across the table from her, hurling it to the floor and knocking her half-empty mug onto its side. The man did not rise, though he did still take an occasional breath.

Perhaps it was best to find a room before trouble found her. Selene left the table, being sure not to look at Lord Xaiden or his wolf as she passed them. She hoped that he would not be staying the night.

The innmaster, a tall yet fleshy man with short cropped graying hair and a beard to match, was easily distinguished from his patrons by the troubled expression he wore as he surveyed the room. He had appeared from the kitchen as if by Mage's enchantment the moment the fight had erupted. He folded his arms above his bulging stomach. His eyes shifted between Selene and the unconscious man as if trying to decide who was responsible for the broken chair. She ignored the questioning glare he offered at her approach.

"Are you master of this inn?" she asked, making her best effort at a tone of formality.

"Indeed I am, Rider." Though his words were clear she could smell a bit of ale on his breath as he leaned towards her.

"I would like a private room."

"Alone, are you?" He glanced at her waist where her sword should have hung. Thick brows and plump skin wove into a puzzled expression. The man was quite blunt for an innmaster, and nosy besides. Perhaps he had consumed a bit more ale than Selene had at first thought. Though she had to admit that it must seem more than a bit odd; a lone Rider without a weapon or at least a set of saddlebags carried in from her horse. At least he had decided that she was not guilty of damaging the chair. She could not afford the few days of work it would take to pay it off.

"I leave early tomorrow and wish to rest before my journey continues." Selene handed him four copper pieces. She hated to part with so much coin, but it was better than sharing a bed with someone who might remember her well enough to give a description. That aside, she had not seen many women about. Sleeping in a room with several drunken men would likely cause more problems than she was willing to deal with on this particular night. The innmaster looked the coins over, his plump fingers turning them once before slipping them into his pocket.

"Up those stairs." He turned a short, pudgy arm to point at a narrow hallway that ran next to the kitchen. "Third room on the right. The door is marked with a lire leaf." He turned and strode towards the broken chair, rolling up his sleeves as he went.

The noise of the common room faded as Selene climbed the stairs. A single lamp of oil gave off just enough light to see the symbols that had been branded into the upper portion of each door. Selene passed a door with a fox and another with a five-pointed star before coming to one whose dark wood was branded with a rounded leaf.

Brief flashes of lightning illuminated the room's starkly furnished interior as she opened the door. A wooden bed frame with a large, stained mattress took up a great portion of it, leaving just enough room for a small fireplace, a bedside table topped with an unlit candle, and a round, threadbare rug of indeterminable color. She lit the candle from the lamp in the hall and set it back down upon the table. No need to bother with the fireplace. The room was not terribly cold despite the rain that pounded ceaselessly upon the window.

Selene sat down upon the edge of the bed. Her boots seemed welded to her feet. It took several minutes of tugging to dislodge them. She wrung the river water from her socks as best she could and draped them across the end of the bed. The clothes she wore would have to do for sleeping. They could come for her in the night. She lay down gingerly, shifting, trying in vain to find a comfortable spot. The mattress might as well have been filled with stones for all the luck she had with it.

Light from the candle and the storm danced together on the cracked plaster of the ceiling creating long, shadowed shapes across its length. Each flash of light was closely followed by thunder, the strength of which shook bits from the walls. She would leave the candle lit while she slept. It would be easier to find her way if she needed to escape.

Selene closed her eyes and laid back, letting the rhythmic drops of rain against the window's glass soothe her.

The tapping at once became louder. Selene opened her eyes. A second sound emerged from beneath it; one not at all like rain though drops still pelted the window. She pressed her hand to the windowpane in an attempt to shade the glare from the candle's flame. Her eyes found nothing but darkness. She unlatched the clasp and lifted the pane. Rain splashed onto the windowsill, forming tiny puddles that turned to pools of candlelight. A dark shape swept past her to perch upon the bedpost.

The rustle of the raven's feathers as he preened the storm water from them easily reached her ears. The bird's eyes, black orbs that reflected the candle's flame, were locked to hers. She moved closer, rubbing her eyes gently with her free hand. The creature was still perched upon the post as if it had grown there. This raven was no creature of dreams. Perhaps the Elders had been right. Perhaps she *was* cursed. To have a raven appear in your dreams was not a serious matter, but to have one come to you in life was quite different. There was no story known to her in which the appearance of a raven was considered a good omen.

"Cur-rruk," the raven said, tilting its head to one side.

With the bird's cry came a series of images. The first was of a grove of ancient trees growing along the edge of a vast sandstone cliff, their roots stretching out to soften the rock that composed it. Miles of forest stretched beneath them; a thick layer of green hues disappearing into the horizon. It was the raven's place of birth, the very center of the territory in which he and his family lived. The greeting was familiar, much like the sound of her mother's voice or the memory of her brother's laughter.

The next few scenes came with a sense of distress. A group of men galloped their horses through the deep mud of rain soaked roads. The sign that hung above the Broken Mule swung wildly in harsh winds. The last image nearly caused Selene's breath to cease. It was one of a group of men entering the inn, their sodden cloaks adding depth to the puddles of ale on the common room floor. She recognized two men at the head of the group as Ranur and Terran.

The first few images had been quite clear, as if she had witnessed them herself. The last one had been slightly foggy. They were not yet here, but they would be soon.

"Tukk," the bird said firmly as he turned his other eye to catch the light.

Time grows short.

He stretched his wings and swept back out into the storm.

Selene did not take the time to ponder what motive a raven may have for lending her his aid. The image of Ranur and Terran in the common room had been enough to stir her. Drenched woolen socks slithered over her feet bringing a chill that was akin to walking barefoot in the snow of full winter. Her boots were blocks of ice. She snuffed the candle between her fingers and headed out the door.

Selene glanced cautiously around the short wall at the base of the stairs. The common room was quiet compared to what it had been. She must have slept for far longer than she had realized. A few stragglers sat here and there, chatting quietly. One rather large man lay sleeping upon a table. His snoring was nearly loud enough to match the bouts of thunder that rattled what few empty mugs remained. The innmaster sat in the corner, engrossed in a game of cards with one of his patrons. He was losing, if the expression he wore was any indication.

The Aranth was gone. That put Selene somewhat at ease. She stepped around the corner, but had set no more than a foot into the common room when the inn's door burst open. She threw herself behind the wall, leaning only as far out from the shadows as it took to see into the room beyond.

A sodden group of men entered from the storm with Ranur and Terran at their lead. Ranur's dogs trotted in at his heels, wagging their short tails with excitement. Though they sniffed here and there, their noses grazing puddles composed of storm water and ale, they did not wander far from his side.

The Praecyr threw back the hood of his cloak. His eyes swept over the room's few occupants before coming to rest upon the master of the inn. He strode over to him, his stance mimicking that of a lord or wealthy traveler. His right hand, as usual, rested lightly upon the hilt of his sword.

"I am in search of someone," Ranur began. "A young female, well-favored, with long, dark hair. You will tell me if she has passed through this inn. If you speak honestly then no harm will come to you."

"Many girls have come through here," the innmaster replied. He seemed to perceive the Praecyr as more of an unwelcome interruption to his game than a threat, even with the number of men that backed him. "You've just described half of my serving girls and a good portion of my patrons," the plump man added with a laugh as he turned back to his cards.

Ranur drew his sword, pressing it between the rolls of fat that covered the innmaster's thick neck. A watery gagging sound escaped the man as the cards slipped lazily from his fingers to the floor.

Ranur waved a gloved hand at the group that stood behind him without once taking his eyes from his blade. Terran stepped forward and, much to Selene's horror, gave a most detailed description of her down to the way her eyes altered their color when she angered.

There would be no escape the way she had come in. She counted nine Riders not including Terran. The largest group of Riders she ever traveled with numbered merely seven, and that was including the Praecyr. It must have been the Elders' doing. Ranur would most likely have kept the group small to avoid spreading word of his embarrassment.

Selene entertained a thought of heading back to her room but dismissed it shortly. The second floor was high from the ground. With only packed dirt beneath her window the jump would be much too far. There would be no running from Ranur with a broken leg.

The innmaster's arm stretched back to point in the direction of the stairs. Selene lowered herself to the floor, leaning back against the wall as closely as she could manage. She glanced towards the kitchen. Suddenly the short length between its door and where she stood seemed like yards of open space. *This is no time to let fear bind me.* She steeled herself and ran, catching a glimpse of Ranur just as he noticed her. A cry of rage was cut short as the kitchen door closed firmly behind her. She grabbed one of several battered chairs that stood in the corner of the room and wedged it underneath the door's handle. *It will not hold for more than a few moments at the most.* Her thoughts rang true. At once the chair began to scrape its way slowly forward. Shouts and the barking of dogs pushed through the widening gap.

Selene scanned the kitchen, searching frantically beyond hanging pots and basins full of soapy water. *The Tides be with me. Please let there be a back door. There.* A lone serving girl stood in the kitchen's corner sweeping crumbs from the floor out into a darkened alley. She was a bit too thin for her height and was much younger than any of the ones who had served in the common room. Her eyes widened as she noticed Selene. There was no time for an explanation, even if Selene had been willing to give one. She pushed past the girl, nearly knocking the broom from her hand. A sheet of frigid water running from the inn's roof drenched her as she passed out into the storm. The clattering of falling pots found her over the sound of raindrops swiftly pounding the soil of the road into mire.

Selene sprinted through the alley and onto the main road. The mud there was slick and the passing of horses had deepened it. It pulled at her boots, threatening to suck them into its syrupy depths. Ranur and his Riders did not follow her as she crossed, yet his dogs were close on her trail. She pushed herself faster, speeding between two shops whose walls remained steady despite the storm's fury.

Rain turned to hail as Selene rounded a corner. Ice pelted her face, obscuring her vision. She slid to a halt just before colliding with the crumbling surface of a stone wall, the top of which stood more than a foot above her head. A brief flash of light illuminated its face just enough to find a suitable handhold. She struggled to grip the cracks between rain-slick stones.

Barks of rage echoed between buildings, drawing closer to where she stood. Selene pulled herself to the top of the barricade. She levered one leg over and was thrown to the far side in mid step. Rocks tumbled alongside her as the first dog struck the wall. She landed in a trench of freezing sludge. Large chunks of stone struck the ground near her head, throwing muddied water onto her face.

Mud worked itself up Selene's nose and mouth as she stood. It had a grainy texture and smelled of sulfur. She wiped at it with her hand and turned her head to the sky, letting the mixture of hail and rain wash away what it would. The wall behind her shook once again. Mud drenched paws clawed at the top of it as the dogs struggled to reach her.

The land beyond the wall was thick with trees and devoid of anything that could possibly be considered a pathway. The leaf-covered ground proved slick, though not nearly as much as the street. Travel was agonizingly slow. Selene was forced to use the brief flashes of light that cut through what few leaves remained overhead to avoid running into the trees that held them. Frantic barking faded, only to be replaced by the thudding of horses' hooves.

Selene pushed herself as fast as she dared. Branches reached out from the darkness to tear through her shirt, slicing the skin beneath. She looked back. Rain and driving wind pounded her face, forcing her eyes to close. Her next step touched only air. Rocks and broken branches assaulted her, cutting and bruising as she tumbled down the hill to land face first in the foul-smelling mud.

She sat up slowly. The fall left her head swimming. She was only vaguely aware of the stinging gashes that covered her, enflamed by mud and sweat. She cleared her eyes enough to open them, and then instantly wished that she hadn't. A horse's legs, covered in mud, were close enough to touch. Two riders blocked the path in front and one behind. She tilted her head up, scanning the darkness for recognizable features. Rain softened the mud on her face, allowing the grainy mixture to flow freely into her eyes.

"What luck," said the mounted man above her. "Act quickly now."

A sharp pain lanced through Selene's head. Darkness engulfed her.

Evaria

The chirping of birds led Selene from her dreams to awareness. Soft warmth surrounded her and willed her to stay in bed. Body and mind struggled momentarily before yielding to common sense. Her mother would be in soon to wake her regardless of her thoughts on early mornings. She eased her eyes open. Bright light assaulted them, forcing them closed. A second attempt yielded slightly better results; a dark sky with tiny silver stars. An unfamiliar ceiling wobbled into view. Deep blue paint was inlaid with tiny specks of silver. She turned. A wall of smooth, gray stones contained a small, arched window through which the light of the rapidly setting sun flooded freely. She propped herself up. The world spun and twisted. Throbbing pain washed through her head like storm-swept waves.

Memories of the past few days trickled unhurriedly into her consciousness. She pulled her hand from beneath the sheets. A thick metal band encased her wrist, pressing tightly against the flesh. A single seam cut through its otherwise plain surface. She slid her nails behind it and pulled. The band refused to yield. She struggled for several minutes, tugging at various places along its length, but gained no ground. Her head ached terribly. The pain had become worse in the few moments she had spent fiddling with the bracelet. Selene touched her hand lightly to the back of her skull, running her fingertips across the shallow wound she found there. The clean feel of it surprised her. It seemed that the skin had restored itself, healing the gash almost completely without need of her power. *How long have I been here?* The thought made her stomach roll. She pressed her palm to the back of her head and concentrated to finish the healing. Her mark tingled as flesh grew to cover the remaining space.

A quick scan of the room revealed a broad fireplace of limestone, a carved wooden wardrobe, and a stone pedestal upon which sat a silver pitcher, a porcelain bowl and several cotton towels. To her right was a skillfully crafted tapestry which depicted two unicorn stallions dueling for leadership of a herd of mares. The weaving came just to the edge of an arched stone window, through which the chirping of small birds could still be heard. Selene twisted around to look behind her. The tapestry that hung there was plain, woven in only two colors, yet it caught her breath all the same. Upon a background of midnight blue was a symbol woven in thread that echoed the silver of the stars above. It was a serpent dragon coiled around a crescent moon.

The Aranth had found her. But it made no sense that they had not simply killed her. And why was she in a room fit for a Lord or Lady rather than in the dungeon? Perhaps they had not seen her mark. Even as the thought crossed her mind it seemed more like wishful thinking than fact. Someone had washed the mud from her. The mark was nearly the size of her hand. It was impossible that they had not noticed. Regardless, she could not stay here long enough to find out the truth of the matter. Maye was awaiting rescue.

Selene stepped out of bed onto a rug of fluffed sheep's wool. It covered most of the highly polished wooden floor, stopping several feet before the base of the hearth. She picked up the silver pitcher that sat upon the pedestal and filled the porcelain bowl from it. The water was perfectly clear and held no scent that she could discern. She touched her tongue to it. No unusual taste. She gulped a large portion, then splashed some on her face for good measure. The cotton towel that she used to dry off was scented oddly of lavender.

Selene peered across the room. The hall beyond the open doorway lay mostly in shadow. The wardrobe opened easily, though she found its contents to be a great disappointment. A few clean nightgowns, much like the one she wore, were folded neatly upon the top shelf. The remainder was empty. She would have much preferred to be dressed while making her escape. A girl wandering around in her nightclothes would certainly draw unwanted attention. They could have at least left her boots. She groaned at the thought of walking back to Maresbane barefoot. Her captors may have planned it that way, thinking she would not leave without proper clothing. What little they knew. She was far too stubborn to let pride or pain bar her way.

Selene placed one hand on the polished stone blocks of the doorframe and peered cautiously around the corner. Flames from the few oil lamps that lined the hall flickered slightly as a slow current of air caught them. There was no other movement to be seen. She stood still a moment longer, listening for sounds of approach, but heard only silence. She should go now before the chance was lost. Selene bolted towards the hall, but was thrown down in mid-step. Her back struck the floor. She stared at the painted ceiling for a moment, attempting in vain to make sense of what had just occurred. It felt as if she had run headlong into a stone wall, though there was no obstacle to be seen between the hallway and the room in which she now sat. She smoothed her nightgown as she stood and stepped towards the door once more. *No running this time.* She rubbed her injured nose gently. It did not seem to be broken.

Her hand moved freely to the outer edge of the doorway where it came to rest against an invisible surface; cold, smooth, and as hard as steel. She moved closer, but could see only the hallway and the lamps of oil that lined it. Small ripples, like those formed when a pebble was thrown into calm water, crossed the doorway as she removed her hand. Selene pounded her fist on the clear substance in frustration. Long waves ran back and forth across its surface, yet it did not yield.

A grumble of frustration escaped Selene as she moved to the arched stone window and tapped lightly upon it. She breathed a deep sigh of relief when she found it to be blocked only by common glass. It swung out from the frame freely, much to her delight.

The sparrows that had been perched upon the window's sill flew off with cries of indignation. Salt scented air swept into the room. Selene pushed her head carefully through the opening. A lengthy patch of grass dropped off suddenly to the west. Tufts of it grew precariously at the cliff's edge, ready to fall at a single touch. The ocean stretched beyond it, shaded pink in places where its waves caught the light of the setting sun.

The room was quite a bit higher from the ground than she had imagined. There would be no jumping from this window if she wished to retain her life. She glanced at the bed. Both sheets tied together plus the down filled blanket would not come near to reaching the ground. *But perhaps torn in half...* She pulled the top sheet from the bed and ran it along the corner of the window frame to slice it. It would not be fast, but it would work.

"I would not continue to do that if I were you."

Selene's breath ceased at the sound.

"Queen Perfidia rather fancies those sheets. She had them sent for all the way from Eyrisa."

The sheet slipped from Selene's fingers as she turned in the direction of the voice. A man, quite close to her age by the look of him, stood causally just within the room. Fine quality leather armor covered much of his chest, leaving free the sleeves of the white linen shirt that lay beneath it. Ruffled golden hair had been cut short just above his ears. One hand hovered beside the hilt of a well-made sword. He regarded her with a scowl. The deep-water blue of his eyes immediately brought to mind the dead boy. Selene shivered despite the warmth of the room. *The orb.* She clutched at her neck. It was gone.

"Have you lost something?" he asked, placing his palm against the smooth stones of the doorway. The back of his hand was branded with a serpent dragon coiled around a crescent moon.

Selene was unsure of what to say. They could not possibly blame her for the death of the boy, for she was not the one who had slain him. He had not been Aranth anyway; at least she had not seen a brand upon him. Yet killing kin to an Aranth would no-doubt bring as much punishment. Were Marked Ones even eligible to become Aranth? She was fairly certain that they were not.

The Aranth moved closer. One hand now rested fully upon the hilt of his sword. He used his free hand to reach into a leather belt pouch that hung at his side while keeping his eyes locked to hers.

Selene's legs carried her back until they touched the side of the bed, forcing her to sit. The man was only slightly taller than she, yet due to the position that she was now in he had no trouble looming over her. He held something up to her face. It had been cleaned of blood and the leather cord replaced, yet she had no doubt that it was the same orb that she had taken from the boy.

Selene's mind raced to think of a suitable way to explain what had happened. She imagined that her face must be as white as the sheets of the bed upon which she sat. *Concentrate.*

The Aranth grabbed a bundle of cloth from atop the wardrobe and tossed it onto the bed. Selene wished that she had thought to check there earlier. She had foolishly assumed that any available clothing would be inside the wardrobe rather than above it.

"Dress quickly," he said, turning to face the hallway. "Xaiden awaits us. He will hear your story and discover the truth of it."

Selene was certain that her skin paled more upon hearing Lord Xaiden's name. His wolf companion came to mind, but she pushed it immediately from her thoughts. At least they were willing to hear her out. *Wouldn't expect that much from Ranur.* She carefully unwrapped the bundle, exposing a plain gray dress and matching slippers.

Selene glanced over at the Aranth, who now faced the hallway. She could tell from his stance that he obviously had no intention of leaving. A turned back would have to do. She dressed in silence and then moved to where he could see her.

He reached into his belt pouch once again and pulled out a straight black blade which stretched nearly the length of his palm. "Hold out your wrist," he said, pointing to the arm with the metal bracelet. "And be still. I do not wish to injure you."

Selene found it difficult to believe that to be true, though it did have some sense to it. The Aranth had been given ample opportunity to kill her, and yet they had not done so. It would not be advantageous to injure her before questioning, though during it was quite another matter. She held out her arm obediently. Blue light emanated briefly from both bracelet and blade as they touched. The metal fell easily from her wrist. The Aranth caught it halfway to the floor. He tucked both it and the blade into the leather pouch that held the dead boy's orb.

"Come with me." He headed out into the hallway but stopped halfway down its length when she did not follow.

Selene stood just behind the invisible barrier. How frustrating it was that he could walk freely through it when she had nearly broken her nose on the cursed thing. A moment of thought on his part seemed to bring about understanding.

"You may pass through. The metal band I removed from your wrist is what caused the doorway to solidify."

He spoke truthfully. The barrier was still in place, yet it gave in as her body pressed against it, allowing her to pass easily beneath the stone arch. It was like diving into water that had been touched by the first chill of winter. She ran her hands down the length of her dress as she reached the other side and was startled to find it completely dry.

"Come on, then," he said, turning from her.

The Aranth allowed her to follow him freely. He did not even bother to look back on occasion to be sure that she had not run off. She considered escape as they walked, but the maze-like sameness of the halls through which they passed pushed such thoughts neatly from her mind.

The Aranth slowed as he descended a set of stairs which led to a short, unornamented hallway. The dark stones that comprised its walls and floor shone so deeply that they held a reflection of both herself and her captor within their depths. At the end of the hall lay a single door.

The room that they entered was covered from floor to ceiling in the same polished stone as that of the hall. Large metal lamps of oil occupied each corner. The walls amplified their light, brightening the area considerably. Lord Xaiden sat at the center of the room on one of three thick wooden chairs. He not dressed quite as finely as he had been at the Broken Mule, yet his clothing was still of better quality than most. His sword hung sheathed at his side, though he held a short knife in one hand. Fear pressed its slick fingers into Selene, loosening its hold only a little when she realized that the hills wolf was nowhere to be seen.

"Please sit," Lord Xaiden said, raising a hand in the direction of the chair which was closest to him.

Selene did as she was told, and watched silently as the blond haired Aranth closed the room's only door. As the last glimpse of hallway disappeared from view a sound, the slightest escape of breath, emanated from the wall. Its ebony surface crept over the metal that comprised the door, leaving not so much as a seam behind to show where it had been. The closeness of the room brought memories of the Elder's cottage. *Only this time there will be neither Bloodsoul nor orb to foster my escape.* The Aranth's blue eyes narrowed as if she had actually voiced her thoughts of flight.

"Please answer each question in a clear and truthful manner," Lord Xaiden began. The words were spoken smoothly and with little effort, as if he had used the speech many times before. "Any falsification of fact or other willful act of deception shall be considered treason against the kingdom of Evaria. Do you understand?"

"I do," she said quietly, meeting his gaze.

Lord Xaiden did not turn away from her, yet it was to the other Aranth that he spoke. "The Stone, Felan."

The man stared at Selene for a moment before reaching into his pouch to retrieve the orb. He seemed to regret handing it over. Lord Xaiden moved the orb to where Selene had a clear view of it. "Are you familiar with this pendant?" he asked. His tone did not seem to hold any anger. In fact, his manner was rather serene.

"Yes, Lord Xaiden," she replied, casting her gaze towards the shadowy reflections trapped within the shine of the floor. His stare was much more piercing than that of the other Aranth. It roused guilt from within her.

"How did you come by it?" Lord Xaiden placed the hilt of his dagger beneath her chin. He tilted her head to meet his gaze.

"A boy," Selene's voice quivered slightly as she began. She fought to control her emotions. *Concentrate.* "A blond haired boy. I did not discover his name. His look was much like that of Lord Felan." Since one man was a Lord, the other must be as well. It was far better to give him a false title than to insult him by omitting it. The blond haired man gave no indication as to whether she had given him the correct title. She pulled her chin from Lord Xaiden's knife, but did not turn her gaze back to the floor.

"Where is the boy now?"

"He was with the Elders, last I saw him."

"Does he live?" It was posed as a question, though the look upon Lord Xaiden's face showed plainly that the answer was already known to him.

Selene suddenly found it difficult to draw a breath. "No," she managed.

Lord Xaiden nodded. "Were you present for the boy's death?"

She considered telling a tale, something short but believable. *He could have been dead when I found him.*

"Show honesty in this," Lord Felan said with a hardened tone. "Lord Xaiden's power is to know the truth of statements. No lie will pass undetected."

Lord Xaiden raised a hand as if to stop the flow of words with it. The blond haired Aranth fell silent, though not without first sending a disgruntled look in his companion's direction.

Selene drew a nervous breath and began her story from the moment she first saw the boy. She included as much detail as possible in its telling, paying particular attention to the part where she had attempted to heal the boy's wounds. Neither Aranth showed any signs of alarm as she mentioned her mark. For that she was thankful.

Lord Felan looked toward his companion in anticipation as the last word fell from Selene's lips.

"What she has spoken is true." Lord Xaiden said calmly as he handed the orb back to his companion.

The blonde haired man studied Selene in silence. She drew a breath as he unlocked his gaze from her.

"I shall meet you in the dining chamber," Lord Xaiden said as he stood. He crossed the room and touched a spot on the blank wall where, if it were still visible, the handle of the door would have been. Stone turned to metal for a moment, then was enveloped once again as the door closed gently behind him.

Unease crept up on Selene as his footsteps faded. Lord Felan's emotions had been anything but stable in the short time she had been here.

"Do you know what purpose this pendant serves?" His tone had begun to turn away from formality. Selene hoped that it was a good sign.

"Honestly Lord Felan, I do not," she replied slowly, searching his face for signs of the anger it had held earlier. "Something to do with moving things, I suppose," she added when he seemed to want more. That was what it had done at the Elders' cottage, at least. "I don't know how to control it. It grew warm once and has been silent since."

"Moves things, you say?"

Selene could not be certain, but she thought that she had seen the beginning of a smile creep onto his lips. It was gone in an instant. In truth it irritated her a little. Certainly nothing that she had said had been amusing. Why was he asking her at all? If it belonged to his kin then he should know its purpose.

"What is your name?" he asked, pushing the orb back into his belt pouch.

"Selene," she answered. Then, remembering her manners, she amended it. "My name is Rider Selene Valenne of Maresbane, my Lord."

"No need for a title," he replied. "You may call me Felan."

"You are not a lord?" He certainly seemed like one. She had been under the impression that all Aranth were lords.

"I am a lord, of sorts. But there isn't any need for you to use a title when speaking to me, or to Xaiden for that matter. Felan will do on its own."

Moments ago he had seemed ready to slit her throat, and now he was treating her as an equal. His easy tone went so far as to include combined words. The use of such words was considered to be highly impolite, at least when speaking to someone who was not well known to you. This man became more confusing with each passing moment. And how exactly could one become a lord of sorts? Either he was one or he wasn't.

"May I ask a question of you, Selene?"

"Certainly, though I cannot guarantee that I'll be able to answer it." If he could use combined words then so could she.

"Luca. The boy that Ranur killed…"

"He was your kin?" she injected.

"Yes. My brother."

The words brought Islyr to mind.

"Did he suffer long?"

She bit lightly upon her lower lip. It would not do to lie about such a thing, but how could she know the truth of what the boy had felt? "I don't think so. He lived for only moments after Ranur's sword found him."

Felan nodded. "He went missing a short time ago." He reached beneath his shirt and pulled out a pendant on a black leather strap. The center Stone was identical to the one she had taken, yet this one was enclosed in a maze of thin, string-like, silver metal. An opening approximately the size of her thumb had been left at its center.

"Luca was going to be Aranth. He did not have a chance to complete his training." Felan pulled Luca's orb from his pouch. He touched the two together briefly. His orb glowed with a deep burgundy light, and Luca's with white. He pulled them apart with a bit of a scowl. The light ceased.

An odd presence rested briefly within Selene's mind. It disappeared before her next breath.

"One gift given by these Stones is to find others like it," Felan continued. "But there are difficulties. The signal grows weaker as the distance between Stones increases. We did not expect Luca to be so far from Evaria. His Stone was bonded to mine, but that bond ceased when he was slain. It is near impossible to locate a Stone that is not bonded unless you are within yards of its location. Xaiden and I did not know who we were tracking to Lansfallow. We were shocked when we sensed you wearing the Stone at the Broken Mule."

I seem to send shock through a great many people of late. Selene thought in wonder.

Felan flashed her a partial smile. His timing was uncanny. "I'll take you back to the holding room," he said, standing. "You'll need to change before dinner. I doubt Queen Perfidia will approve of your attire as it is now."

Selene nearly said that she was not hungry in the least, though in truth her stomach felt ready to consume itself. She followed Felan back through the maze of hallways, walking beside him this time rather than behind. She really did not have the time to fool with such things as formal dinner. Then again, she had little money to speak of and not so much as a sling with which to hunt. These people did not seem to care that she was marked, unbelievable though it was. Perhaps if she stayed for the meal and ingratiated herself with them they might be willing to loan her a horse or weapon for her journey. This also might be the last decent meal available to her for quite some time. And she did owe them something for saving her from Ranur, even if they had not done it in concern for her welfare. *Thank the Tides for what luck they bring you, however small,* Maye always said. Selene's stomach clenched. She would leave directly after dinner no matter what came of it.

Felan's voice scattered her thoughts. "I knew of Luca's death long before we found you. Once a Stone is bound to someone no other may use it until their death. But death alone does not break the bond. The blood of the one bonded to the Stone must be cast upon it. This releases the Stone so that it can be used by another."

That must have been why they had thought her responsible for Luca's death. They assumed she had seen the Stone and known its purpose; that she had killed him to claim it for her own. But she had not meant to use it, only to keep it from Ranur. It should not have worked for her anyway since she did not have an affinity. *But Luca used it.* Perhaps it worked for Marked Ones as well. *I should have just left it on him. I could have rescued Maye and been a week from Maresbane by now. No*, she corrected herself. *I'd have been one week hanging from the Sending Tree or torn to bits by a bloodsoul without the orb. I should have listened to Maye. She could be dead because of my stubbornness.*

They came at last to the room in which Selene had been imprisoned. Her stomach had folded itself into a painfully tight knot from thoughts of what could have happened to Maye. "I am truly sorry for what Luca endured," she said, turning towards Felan. "I wish that I had been able to heal him. If only I had reached them earlier, perhaps I could have convinced Ranur to follow the Elder's orders."

"I have dealt with Ranur in the past," Felan replied. "Speaking with him would not have changed anything. He hates all Marked Ones and has sworn to slay any he comes across." His eyes met hers. "It is I who owe you an apology. I was distraught over Luca's death. I thought that you had killed him, and I found some measure of peace in the fact that you would be punished for it. I will come across Ranur again, someday. Then we shall see if he is willing to fight a match fairly met." The Aranth quickly changed the subject. "There should be proper clothing in the wardrobe. Xaiden said he would have something brought up."

Selene did not think that Xaiden had said anything of the sort. She opened the wardrobe. A fine dress of pale green hung there with a matching pair of slippers and a length of ribbon that she assumed was for use in tying back her hair. The edges of each piece were delicately embroidered with tiny vines and flowers in silver thread.

"I should also change," Felan said. He took no notice of the bewildered look she directed towards the dress. "I shall return shortly to fetch you."

"You aren't afraid that I'll flee?" Selene said, glancing down at her naked wrist.

"I'll know the instant you do," he replied causally.

That was certainly a disturbing thing to hear. Selene pulled the door shut. She puzzled over what Felan had said as she dressed. A fire burned brightly beneath the mantle, casting warmth into the evening chill of the room. How could he possibly be aware of her leaving? Surely he had only told her so in case the thought should cross her mind. After dinner, whether she could convince them to help her or not, she *would* leave. She had seen quite enough of the Aranth for one lifetime. Lord Xaiden's hills wolf had not shown itself thus far, but that did not mean that it would remain hidden. Whatever animal Felan controlled may be worse, though it was hard to imagine anything more intimidating than a hills wolf short of some sort of magical creature. *A dragon.* She shuddered. *At least he would be forced to keep that outdoors.* The jest brought a grin to her face.

Selene's reflection grinned back at her. The dress fit surprisingly well, clinging to her curves and then flaring out slightly just below her hips. She picked up a brush that lay upon the top shelf of the wardrobe and used it to pull back her hair. The ribbon was long enough, even after it was tied, to trail halfway down her back. She turned once, admiring the way the fabric flowed. One hand was all that was needed to count the number of times she had worn a dress at home. They just weren't practical for a Rider, or for doing farm work for that matter, though her mother always seemed to find them quite satisfactory. She opened the door to find Felan just rounding the corner at the end of the hall. He wore a dark, finely made coat embroidered in silver. It held the same leaves and vines of Lord Xaiden's cloak, she noted, though tiny wolves took the place of the galloping horses that graced the other. She was not given time to ponder on it.

"Ready?" he asked.

"I suppose." Selene realized quite suddenly that she had no idea of how one should behave when in the company of royalty. The Elders had demanded respect, surely, but they were far lower in status than the royal family.

"Follow my example," Felan said.

It seemed that he was always answering questions that she had not asked. Perhaps her expressions gave away more than she knew.

Felan led her through a short set of hallways, each more elaborately adorned than the last. Tapestries and paintings turned to shields and armor, then to weaponry and skillfully painted murals. In time they reached a set of stairs at the end of which was a darkened courtyard. The soothing scent of fresh pine needles filled the air. Smooth, flat stones formed a winding path between trees, the trunks of which were thicker across than rain barrels. The lowest branches hung several feet above her head, beyond which stars pierced the night sky.

Selene hastened her steps. She did not wish to let Felan get too far ahead for fear of losing her way.

Farther into the room the sound of falling water could be heard. A waterfall cascaded into a rounded pond, across the center of which stretched a bridge of stone. Multicolored fish swam back and forth across the pond's length, the shine of their scales illuminated by the light of the moon. They seemed unaware that night had fallen.

"This is called the Sky Room," Felan said, pointing upward. "The ceiling is composed of glass panes held in place by lengths of metal." There was a touch of awe in his voice, though he must have seen the room many times before this night. If she strained her eyes she could just barely make out several of the thin, silver bars. It was impressive now, but she had no doubt that it would seem even more so by daylight. *I am only staying for dinner*, she reminded herself firmly.

They passed from the Sky Room through one last hallway before reaching a set of wooden doors carved with scenes of a forest hunt. The carvings brought the Elder's awning to mind, though these were much more intricate than the ones at home.

A stonework setting of Evaria's Serpent Dragon was the first thing to greet Selene as she followed Felan through the doors. She had become so accustomed to seeing it coiled around the Aranth Crescent Moon that the wall seemed unfinished without it. Still, the work was extraordinary. Crafted marble blocks were set so closely that the seams, if indeed they existed, were not visible from where she stood. More stonework lay upon the floor; oddly shaped pieces of marble in black and many shades of brown, all of which came together to form an intricate pattern like that of a finely woven carpet. At the center of the room was a long table of dark, polished wood, upon each side of which sat matching chairs. There was room enough to seat at least fifty. Felan directed her to stand behind a chair at the far end. He then took a place next to her.

Silver plates, goblets, and utensils sat upon the tabletop next to pitchers of what looked to be chilled wine; both white and red. Only four places were set besides the ones that she and the Aranth occupied, and two of those were at the head of the table. *Must be for the King and Queen*, she supposed. *The other Aranth must be off somewhere*. Selene looked up from the place settings just in time to see Lord Xaiden enter the room and position himself across the table from Felan. He bowed his head in greeting, but said nothing.

A second man entered at Lord Xaiden's heels. He was sapling thin, and his skin looked as if the sun had not touched it in months. He held himself as if he were king of the Ethereal Realm, though Selene did not think it likely to be true. His light brown hair, which was nearly as long as her own, had been shaved upon both sides and left long down the center in the typical style of a Mage. The lengthy portion was held neatly at the nape of his neck with a short strip of leather. He was not Aranth, for neither of his hands held the brand. The man claimed the chair directly across the table from Selene. He turned to stare at her with eyes the color of ice at first thaw.

"Damaeus, I introduce to you Rider Selene Valenne of Maresbane." Felan seemed completely at ease beneath the man's unearthly gaze. "Selene, this is Damaeus Sarell, Mage to the kingdom of Evaria and thus the Ethereal Realm."

"It is an honor to make your acquaintance," Selene said. It sounded formal enough, leastways. One of the Praecyrs she had ridden for in years past had frequently used that as a greeting.

"Likewise," Damaeus replied. He inclined his head ever so slightly in her direction.

The doors opened once more, admitting two people Selene would have guessed to be royalty even if they had not been the last to enter. The woman had an air about her which was very much like that of Damaeus, though she was at least a good head shorter than he. Her mahogany hair had been cut just above her shoulders. Two tiny braids graced one side, each one of which was held at the end with several small beads of precious stone. She wore a dress similar in style to the one Selene had been given, though with so much embroidery as to be almost garish, and added seams along the skirt for elegance. A delicate band of braided gold crossed her forehead, resting above a face that had just begun to show the creases of age.

Her husband looked to be younger than she, for curly blond hair without a hint of grey covered his head. The gold band that he wore was much thicker, yet no less intricate than the queen's. They seated themselves at the head of the table. The king's eyes passed over her, but did not linger.

This time it was Lord Xaiden who spoke on her behalf. "Your majesty, I present to you Rider Selene Valenne of Maresbane." Selene bowed low, brushing her skirt back against the floor. "Rider Selene Valenne, I give you his Majesty King Graelen Elyon, ruler of the Ethereal Realm. At his side stands her Majesty Queen Perfidia Elyon."

"Thank you, Xaiden," King Graelen said with a nod. "You may all sit."

Servants wearing midnight blue and silver entered through a small door that was neatly hidden in the corner of the room. Each carried a platter piled high with food, the smell of which multiplied Selene's hunger tenfold. A tray of meat spiced with garlic and ginger passed closely behind her, followed by a long smoked fish and a sizeable bowl piled high with a mix of vegetables. The servants set everything down with amazing speed, covering the occupied end of the table with enough food for twenty Riders. They then scurried from the room like barn mice fleeing lamplight. It was not until the last had exited that King Graelen allowed them to begin the meal.

Selene watched the two Aranth for a moment before feeling comfortable enough to pour herself a glass of wine. It had a smooth, slightly sweet taste. The chill of it was soothing to her throat. She was suddenly much too nervous to think of eating. It felt as if every eye was upon her, though the only one she could truly say she had witnessed staring was Damaeus. He had turned away the moment she caught his gaze.

"Try one of these," Felan said, holding up a tray of gnarled, root-like vegetables. They had been sliced down the center to reveal pale, orange flesh. "They're very good, really." He added in response to her doubtful stare.

She took one, if only to avoid being rude. It looked as if sugar had been sprinkled upon it. Selene could not imagine what would cause someone to put such a rare thing as sugar on a vegetable. She took a small bite. It melted easily as it touched her tongue, leaving a sweet aftertaste. She decided firstly that the strange root had most certainly been covered in sugar, and secondly that she did not mind that fact nearly as much as she had before tasting it.

King Graelen and Lord Xaiden spoke at length while they ate, with Felan and Damaeus injecting comments as it suited them. Selene's presence did not seem to limit the subjects of their discussion, which ranged from the increased occurrence of Bloodsoul attacks between Aidenlyn and Kingsight to trade agreements with countries overseas, none of whose names she recognized. They even touched upon the caerim vows which were soon to be given by Lord Cedell of Miloren.

"But is he truly prepared?" Felan held a smile that seemed likely to bring trouble. "A woman's second braid holds fast a man's freedom." He looked to Damaeus. "How does the other go? I cannot seem to remember."

"With a woman's second braid comes man's penance to be paid," Damaeus volunteered with a smirk.

"But if there be only one she's half the work and thrice the fun," Felan added with a laugh.

Lord Xaiden seemed rather amused at the quip, to Selene's surprise, though not quite so much as King Graelen. In fact, the only one who did not seem to find Felan's words humorous was Queen Perfidia. Her expression could have warped the table's silver. The jest had certainly contained something off-color, if only slightly so. Selene had heard worse, no doubt. No Rider had ever held back crude jokes on her account. She might even find it amusing upon learning what it meant.

A mother weaves her daughter's first braid on the first day her hair is long enough to hold one. A woman's second braid is woven by her husband-to-be on the day their souls are joined as one by caerim vows.

Selene's eyes widened. She put her hand to her mouth as the sip of wine she had been attempting to swallow made its way down her windpipe. The voice had been inside her head, yet the thought had not been her own.

Felan threw her a sheepish grin. It had been him. She would have wagered on it if only she knew where they had taken her belt pouch. An uncomfortable silence blanketed the room, with herself and Felan at its center.

Lord Xaiden shot him a chiding look. "Felan," he began.

"My apologies," Felan said, cutting him off in mid-sentence. "My ability allows me to project my thoughts into other's minds as well as being able to hear what they are thinking if I so wish."

Selene wondered just how many thoughts of escape he had plucked from her head. Felan's honesty cleared her confusion on a few matters, but not all of them by far. Why had he taken her to Lord Xaiden for questioning? Surely he could have glimpsed her memories and known of her innocence.

"The only thoughts I can grasp are those at your mind's surface. I can catch pictures and thoughts from your memories only if you are reliving them as I read you. I attempted it as you slept, but could pick up nothing of any use. You are plagued by a fair number of nightmares for someone of your age."

Lord Xaiden cleared his throat, giving Felan a level gaze that would have looked at home on any Praecyr. It seemed that Felan had not been given permission to read her dreams.

"I suppose I should apologize for that as well," Felan added. "It was intrusive of me." His last words were stiff, unlike the first apology. He obviously did not think himself in the wrong on that. "It is difficult at best to read an unconscious person. Their thoughts are so scattered that you're lucky to find anything at all useful. My latent ability-" He stopped suddenly, as if he had been struck.

Backs stiffened across the table. Queen Perfidia looked as if she had swallowed a spinefish whole. *Latent ability*. Maye had used that term when speaking of Selene's Healing.

Selene raised her hand and pressed it lightly to Felan's cheek. A soft warmth spread through her mark. It was the same warmth she had felt whenever her brother's skin touched her own, yet this man was clearly not Islyr.

"You're marked." The revelation astonished her, though her mind told her clearly that it should not. Luca had been marked. It made perfect sense that Felan would be as well. *Aranth cannot be marked*. Her mind shot back. *They cannot be*. The discovery of a Marked Aranth would mean rebellion, if the rumor was spread and believed. Felan's cheeks colored. He pulled back from Selene's touch as if stung.

"It is of no consequence, Felan," King Graelen said, "Though I would like for you to use a bit more discretion in the future." He nodded towards Lord Xaiden.

"Allow me to explain," the Aranth began, sending a scowl in Felan's direction as if to keep his tongue in check. "Long ago the Ethereal Realm consisted only of scattered communities ruled by whatever man had the mind or power to control them. They warred often amongst themselves to gain possession of what land they could, slaying opposing bands of rogues as well as any innocents who happened to cross their paths. The country of Brenlen heard tell of the unrest and sent armies from across the Mortal Sea to cleanse the land and gather the people under a single ruler. That ruler was Sammeus Elyon, the first king of the Ethereal Realm." Lord Xaiden frowned at the less than proper yawn that escaped Queen Perfidia's lips. She had heard the tale many times more than she would like, by the look of it. He continued nonetheless. "King Sammeus' men came ashore near what is now the city on Evaria. They seized every acre of land between the valley of the Eldai and the Fallen Coast before returning to this spot to build the castle in which we now stand."

"Sammeus kept his secrets well, taking discreetly what Marked Ones he could find and forming the King's Elite Guard. Marked Ones were feared greatly at that time just as they are to this day. They were slain upon discovery although the animosity held towards them was mainly unfounded. Sammeus named his guard members Aranth and told all who enquired tales of animal affinity and the powers granted by it. He sent them out, always in pairs so that each could be seen with an animal companion. Some Aranth went on to win the trust of the people by slaying fiends and settling disputes. The best of them he kept at the palace to protect himself and his family. Thus you have the Aranth as we are today." Lord Xaiden paused. His eyes met Selene's with a dark expression that, for what she knew of him, seemed quite out of place. "We keep our secrets well to this day. Those who have stumbled upon them, blindly or otherwise, have been silenced. It is unfortunate, yet necessary."

His meaning was as clear to her as still water. "I will guard your secret as well as I do my own," she said. "If your true nature is spoken it will not be through my lips." Selene's mind was a jumble of questions, most of which she would never gain answers to for lack of time. Marked Ones and Aranth were one and the same. It was difficult to believe.

Perhaps the Tides would draw her here in the future, after she rescued Maye. Nowhere could be safer from Ranur than this place. He would avoid it as if it were plagued upon finding what it held.

"That brings us to an offer." Lord Xaiden's voice pierced her thoughts.

"An offer?" Selene echoed.

"You have three choices in the matter. Unfortunately for you, circumstance has crushed any others that may have been available to you in the beginning." He shot a disgruntled look towards Felan. "You may stay here to become a member of the Elite Guard. You will be given training and a room within the castle. We are paid quite well, though coin is rarely needed. All food, clothing, weaponry, and armor will be provided for you." He stopped to clear his throat. "If you do not wish to become Aranth you may stay in Evaria. You will receive a house in which to live and the means to set up a trade of your liking. You will come to us each day at dawn, and again at dusk so we can be sure that you have not strayed."

The two options given to her were not unpleasant ones, though neither would allow her to return to Maye. It was plain that they wished for her to join them.

I cannot stay here, no matter what the consequences.

Felan gave her a worried look. If she ever returned to this place she would speak with him on listening to others thoughts without their permission.

"You mentioned three choices. What is the third?" The strength of her voice surprised her.

"Hanging," Xaiden said plainly.

Selene leaned back in her chair, being careful not to form any thoughts for Felan to hear. "I suppose that is it then," she said lightly. "I cannot possibly battle all of you and expect to retain my life. I must choose the third. I cannot stay here." It was no lie, yet not completely truth; just perhaps enough like it to bypass Lord Xaiden's Latent Ability.

"Why is it that you are so eager to leave this place?" King Graelen asked, standing. "Most would consider it a great honor to become Aranth. In years past men abandoned their families and livelihoods to journey here. They trained their lives away only to be turned back at Evaria's gates. You cannot return to your hometown. Ranur, I am certain, will do everything in his power to see that your career as a Rider is through. Your ability would be of great use to us. Evaria has not had an Aranth with the power of levitation in nearly two hundred years."

Levitation? What in the name of the Spirits had given him that idea? "I have a personal matter to attend to," Selene said carefully. "Give me little more than a month. My errand may take me far from here, but I swear upon my father's ashes as the Tides swept them to sea that I will return to Evaria when I have accomplished my task. May the Spirits take me if I lie." The last part may have been unnecessary given Lord Xaiden's ability, but it could not hurt the others to hear it. Maye was all that remained of her family. She would rather die than leave her in the hands of the Elders.

"Perhaps we could compromise," Felan said suddenly. "You will stay here and train with Damaeus to become Aranth. Xaiden and I will travel to Maresbane to find your mother. I have seen her face often enough in your dreams to know it."

Xaiden did not look pleased in the least.

"That is with his Majesty's permission of course," Felan added, bowing his head in King Graelen's direction and receiving a nod in response.

Selene pondered a moment. The choice was certainly better than the first three she had been given, and what she had said earlier was true. She could not possibly battle against two Aranth and hope to survive. Yet it seemed somehow wrong to send them in her place. She was the one responsible for Maye's plight. Besides that, what would they do when she began training; when they found that she could neither levitate anything nor claim an animal companion?

Selene nodded her head reluctantly, and held out her hand to Felan. "I'll need an oath; a blood pact."

"I cannot give you a blood pact," Felan said without pause. "But may the Spirits take me if I lie."

"Myself as well, by my honor as an Aranth," Lord Xaiden added.

Selene considered for only a short time before shaking hands with both them both to seal their vows. Two Aranth would certainly be able to retrieve Maye better than she could alone. They could simply demand that the Elders hand her over if it came to that. She shivered a little as the warmth of each one's touch passed over her mark.

"Excellent," Queen Perfidia said as she stood. "Since that has been settled I believe I will retire for the evening." Her words were pleasant, yet her tone was like morning frost. "I bid you all good night." She stalked from the room like a barn cat with ruffled fur.

"I must see to my wife," King Graelen said as he pushed his chair beneath the table. "A room has been prepared for Selene in the West Hall. A pleasant night to all of you."

"Felan, please accompany Selene to her room," Xaiden ordered. "Meet us in the courtyard after you have changed clothes."

Selene followed Felan out, breathing the scent of pine deep into her lungs as they passed once more through the Sky Room. The fish had settled at the bottom of the pool to sleep. She made up her mind to return to the room tomorrow to see it properly. Perhaps she could explore the grounds a little as well. She would need to know her way around this place if she was going to stay here for any length of time.

"I'll arrange for someone to show you where everything is located," Felan raised his voice just above the sound of rushing water. "I would do it myself, but Xaiden and I must leave at first light if we wish to make decent time. Damaeus will inform you as to when your training will begin. He will need time to research your particular ability; to show you how to use it properly. Most likely you will have the next two or three days to yourself."

"Concerning that," Selene started as they came to rest before a wooden door carved with a serpent dragon coiled around a crescent moon. Selene glanced down the hall through which they had passed and up the next. Several doors identical to the first were scattered throughout the length of each roughly hewn stone wall, with mirrored lamps of oil and painted shields alternating between them.

"No need for concern," Felan said easily. "It's quite normal to be nervous about using your latent ability. It comes more easily each time. I learned to control my power well under Damaeus' training. So shall you."

He opened the door to reveal a room three times as large as the one Selene had been held in. It was decorated with fine furniture and contained a hearth carved from what looked to be marble. Carpets in Evaria's blue and silver tones lay upon floors of dark stone. Felan urged her forward. She could not help but feel awkward amongst such fine things. Two doors inlaid with glass as clear as calm water led to a small balcony through which the moon could be seen reflecting upon the ocean's surface.

"This will be your room," Felan said. "Xaiden's room is at the end of the hall on your right, and mine is around the corner several doors down."

"What of the other Aranth?"

Felan's smile faded. "I suppose you should be aware that as of this time there are only two Aranth that serve the kingdom of Evaria."

It was a jest, surely. "The entire Elite Guard consists of yourself and Xaiden?" Most tales of Aranth mentioned hundreds.

"There were more, not so long ago. Now there are only two. Three, once you have been properly trained. His majesty has not seen the need to recruit in many years; since the death of his first wife. Every Aranth admitted since that time has come to us by happenstance. Xaiden and I continue to press King Graelen on the matter. Perhaps soon we will have our way."

Quite an elite group indeed. Selene regretted the thought the moment it came to her. She hoped that Felan had not heard it. It was not her intention to insult him. *Serves him right for listening to my thoughts without permission.* She pushed that thought away quickly as well.

Felan turned to leave. "Xaiden and Damaeus will be waiting for us. Just head back to the Sky Room and turn right where the path splits. The door to the courtyard sits at the end of it. You will find something suitable to wear in your wardrobe."

Questions rolled about Selene's head in a most irritating fashion, but she supposed that there would be plenty of time to ask them later. *The rest of my life, by the look of it.* She sighed. Felan offered an amused look. At least they were going to retrieve Maye, something she would likely be killed attempting on her own.

"Bring a cloak as well," Felan called as he headed off. "Tonight is the night you learn to use your affinity."

Selene opened her mouth to protest, but he slipped away before she could utter a word. She closed the heavy, wooden door and headed for the wardrobe located in the bedroom. Though it was less than half-full it held more dresses and accessories as she had owned in her lifetime. Not a single pair of breeches was amongst them, much to her frustration. The dress she chose was plain, at least when compared to the others. She dressed as slowly as she could manage, grabbed a cloak from the wardrobe, and then headed from the room.

Selene found the door to the courtyard with little difficulty. It opened smoothly on well-greased hinges. Walking through it, however, proved more troublesome. Not for fault of the door, but for what she knew awaited her outside. A path formed of brick crossed the length of the courtyard between stretches of grass and short, broad-leafed trees. Trickling water echoed from the stone walls that enclosed the area, signifying the presence of what she supposed was a fountain, though it was far too dark to see.

Lord Xaiden, Damaeus and Felan sat upon wooden benches around a brightly burning fire at the center of the area. The night was not terribly cold, yet she shivered nonetheless. Surely the Aranth would be angry with her when they found that she did not have an animal Affinity. What if they refused their bargain when she could not hold her end of it?

Selene attempted not to form any coherent thought, concentrating instead on picking constellations from the starlit sky and listening to the soft sounds of her boots upon the stones. Felan caught sight of her before she reached the light of the fire and motioned for her to take a bench between himself and Lord Xaiden. Damaeus sat across from her, his white eyes nearly glowing in the firelight.

"I hope the room was to your liking," Lord Xaiden said as she drew near.

"It was. Thank you Lord Xaiden."

"You may call me by my given name," he said. "All Aranth are considered equals. It is only my length of service in the Elite Guard that charges me with responsibility for the other members." He did not mention that there was only *one* other member. Perhaps Felan had already told him that she knew.

"I must tell you something, Xaiden." It seemed odd to use only his name. Much worse than with Felan for some reason. "I am not sure that I possess what powers you think I do. My latent ability is healing." They sat silently, as if expecting her to continue. "Luca's orb was the cause of the incident at the Elder's cottage. It grew warm then; so much so that I thought it would singe my flesh. I do not have the power of levitation."

Xaiden stood. He reached to his belt and brought up a knife with a handle of what looked to be bone. The night suddenly felt much cooler. Selene held her breath as he pressed the blade into his palm. Blood dripped smoothly to the ground beneath.

"Use your Latent Ability," he said calmly.

It was a minor wound. Selene would have known it even if she had not seen him use the blade. She pressed her hand against his, ignoring the warming of her mark, and concentrated on healing; on flesh and muscle growing and re-forming. In seconds it was done. Xaiden wiped the blood from his hand. He scrutinized it a moment before holding it within Felan and Damaeus' view. Both men formed puzzled expressions.

"As for my Affinity," Selene shifted the thick cloak that she had brought from one hand to the other. "I was visited by a raven at the Broken Mule, but no others have approached me, dreams aside. I am not sure that I am able to bond one, or even that you will be able to teach me."

Felan looked away in a futile attempt to cover his amusement. Once again her mind stubbornly refused to grasp the reason for the humor.

Xaiden set his knife aside. "Speak it again. Deny that you have the power of levitation."

"I do not have the power of levitation," Selene said with uncertainty.

"She believes it to be true. What do you make of that, Damaeus?"

"A Marked female is truly an oddity; one in one hundred thousand," the Mage answered thoughtfully. "I suppose it is possible that she has two latent abilities. Only one female Aranth has graced the history of Evaria. A girl named Novalin. Her writings do not mention a second ability, but I would not discount it. Perhaps she found the first early and did not think to look for another."

An oddity. Some people had no manners at all. They spoke of her as if she were miles away rather than within an arms' reach. Selene held her tongue despite her irritation.

"It will require more research," Damaeus continued. "I may be able to find something, given the time. It makes little difference whether she has one ability or ten, for purposes of training at least."

"She seems to have a fair grasp on her healing," Xaiden said without so much as a glance in Selene's direction. "Start there. Bring it as far as you are able before moving on to levitation. We will be about a month to Maresbane and back. She should be sufficiently advanced by the time we return; enough so to redirect her efforts towards weapons and defense training."

Selene did not wonder at the fact that he sounded so pleased. Having a marked one literally fall at your feet after years of failed attempts to convince King Graelen to recruit; it must seem like the Spirits had taken up Xaiden's cause.

Both men fell silent as a servant appeared from the darkness. The boy looked to be nearing adolescence. His ears were still a mite too big for his head. "As you requested, Lord Xaiden," He flashed a lop-sided grin as he held out a tray topped with four polished mugs.

"Thank you Erud, that was very timely. Set it over there, please."

Erud did as he was told, placing the tray carefully on an empty bench. His crooked smile doubled in size as he scurried off with four coppers, given to him by Felan.

"Now we shall see what you can or cannot do, Selene," Xaiden said as the boy's footsteps faded to nothing. "You must trust my words and do as I say. Are you willing?" He posed it as a question, though she was sure there was only one answer that he would find acceptable.

"I am," It was too late for escape.

"Fine. There is a row of high hedges a short ways off. You must strip off all clothing, jewelry, anything binding. Cover yourself with your cloak and return to us."

Selene arched one eyebrow in the Aranth's direction. A smirk caught Damaeus' lips, but it was gone quickly; so much so that she could hardly be sure she had seen it at all.

"How will removing my clothing help me to form an animal bond?" Selene asked, not bothering to hide her suspicion. The comment moved all three men to laughter. Selene's face heated. She was not sure what the jest was, though she *was* sure that she was at the center of it.

"Aranth do not truly bond themselves to an animal," Xaiden explained patiently. "They become one."

Selene stood mute as shock passed over her. Was it possible that Ranur had been correct? She at once found her voice. "Perhaps I would be more at ease if one of you could show me how it is done,"

"Certainly," Felan offered eagerly, taking his cloak from the bench where it lay and heading to the area Xaiden had suggested. He returned quickly, the cloak his only covering, and stood in the light of the fire.

Felan closed his eyes. He slid his hand beneath his cloak at the right shoulder. A chill wind swept past Selene, dancing with the fire. Felan's face twisted painfully. His body contorted like a thing possessed by the Spirits. The snap of breaking bones overpowered the voice of the fire. He shuddered as if in great pain. Selene's body reacted in kind, but she managed not turn from the sight. The Aranth's face and limbs elongated. A wolf's legs, fangs, a tail, and pointed ears formed. Thick fur grew, swiftly covering bare flesh in various shades of gray. At last a hills wolf stood before her, its eyes catching the light of the fire in brilliant iridescence. The creature lifted one broad paw and set it upon Selene's hand. She nearly drew back before remembering that the wolf and Felan were one and the same. Warmth rushed across her mark.

An image, much like those the raven had brought, came to her mind. It was of the wide eyed look she had given Felan as he entered the Broken Mule's common room from the storm. Selene's mind extracted meaning from the next set of images without effort. She obligingly unclasped the cloak and pulled it from Felan's back. His fur was as soft as silk and cool against her skin. It did not bring warmth to her mark as the touch of his paw had.

Felan sprinted out into the darkness and back again. He took several laps around the fire pit, his broad paws kicking up sand as he went. Most of it landed on Damaeus.

"Enough, Felan," the Mage grumbled as he dusted invisible grains from his clothing. "Come here."

Felan bounded over, skidding to a hasty stop just short of him. A spray of sand cascaded over both Damaeus and the fire, leaving Xaiden and Selene miraculously clear.

"I said *enough*," Damaeus repeated. His words held an edge like that of fine steel. They were followed by a great deal of mumbling, the meaning of which was impossible to catch over the crackling of the fire. Felan, however, seemed to have no difficulty in understanding the Mage's words. His ears flattened against his head and a growl rumbled from behind pointed, white teeth.

"Reverse your affinity," Xaiden said serenely. Damaeus' muttering did not seem to bother him in the least. "Selene must be taught and the night passes us quickly. I would like a few hours of sleep before we depart."

Felan trotted back towards the hedges. He returned in human form and took his seat quietly, though not before sending a less than proper gesture in Damaeus' direction. The Mage showed no sign that he had seen it.

"Was that sufficient to ease your doubts?" Xaiden asked between sips from one of the mugs that Erud had brought.

Damaeus nursed his drink with a foul look.

"I'm ready." Selene headed for the hedges with cloak in hand. Her hands quaked. Her fingers fumbled with the laces on her boots, twisting in them and becoming caught. In what seemed like hours she had everything removed and placed in a hasty pile on the grass. She then covered herself in her cloak and started back to the Aranth. The soil beneath her feet turned to grass cooled by night air and then to warm sand.

"Here," Felan said, handing her a full mug. "Drink."

"This will help me use my Affinity?" Selene glanced into the shadowed liquid.

The Aranth's laughter filled her ears once again. Her words seemed to lighten even Damaeus' mood.

"It will, in a way," Felan replied.

Xaiden managed to stop laughing just long enough to explain. "This will be the first time you have used your Affinity. Felan suggested that you may want something to dull the pain."

Selene stared at him in silence.

"Best ale from here to the Fallen Coast," Felan said with a proud grin. "Xaiden and I brew it ourselves."

Selene brought the mug to her lips. *It would be rude not to drink it.* She really did not need the excuse, but her mind formed it for her nonetheless. She swallowed the contents of the mug quickly enough to gain the admiration of even the most seasoned Rider. What little touched her tongue she found tasteful, though strong.

Xaiden rose and took her hand in his. The warmth rushing through her mark brought with it realization of the situation she was now in. She was about to attempt something that she was not even sure that she could do, under the gaze of three men she barely knew, with only a cloak between herself and the night air. And that was not mentioning the mug of ale she had just downed. Maye would be furious if even the smallest part of this reached her ears. Strangely enough, Selene would have been pleased to hear her mother's voice no matter the tone.

"Do you trust me to aid you?" Xaiden's voice was calm, as it always seemed to be.

"Yes."

"Concentrate, then, on your mark."

Selene did as she was told. Her mark grew warm, as it had in times past when she had used her latent ability.

Xaiden's free hand slid beneath her cloak at the shoulder and came to rest upon it.

"You must concentrate harder. Push all thoughts away save those of your mark."

The warmth in Selene's shoulder grew to true heat. Xaiden's hand did not move, though he must feel it as much as she. The thought was fleeting. The fire and the Aranth disappeared into darkness. The heat of her mark grew to searing. It then turned as cold as water that lay beneath sheets of winter ice. Far away she felt Xaiden's hand shifting and being replaced with her own. The cold burn spread from her shoulder, carrying with it a thick pain. She stifled a cry of anguish as it moved to cover every inch of her skin. The sounds of the world faded to nothing. It was then that the true agony began. Skin divided. Muscle separated and rearranged. Bone fractured, losing much of its mass as it reformed. Suddenly, the pain snapped back. It melted away to nothingness. All feeling ceased to be. Darkness surrounded her. She gasped for air and felt soft sand beneath her feet. Felan's actions while in animal form were no longer a wonder. Energy surged through Selene's body, making her feel as if she could run the night through with no rest.

The darkness lifted, letting in light from the fire. Selene looked up at Xaiden as he removed the cloak from her and set it to one side. The colors of the world were somewhat brighter than she remembered. The smell of charred wood was strong, and underneath it a trove of other scents awaited her; green, growing things and bitter sea air; cured leather, sweat, ale, and a pungent, slightly sweet odor that her mind could not seem to place. Neither the chill of the air nor the heat of the fire seemed to reach her as she stood.

"What do you think, Selene?" Felan asked as he held a piece of mirrored glass down to her.

A raven met her gaze, its feathers reflecting purples and blues within the fire's light. Selene lifted one clawed foot, then the other. She spread her wings, tilting her head to scrutinize the mirror's image. She attempted to move forward, but managed only a few awkward steps before tripping. An attempt to spread her wings for balance landed her quite a bit closer to the fire than she would have liked. Xaiden lifted her to the bench on which Felan sat.

"Well-formed, indeed," said Damaeus. It seemed that he had finished pouting.

"Though not so graceful," added Felan.

Selene nipped at his arm without thinking.

"It's the truth," he said, rubbing the place where his skin had been pinched.

A few rather choice words slipped from her mouth before she could catch herself. What came out was not speech as she knew it, but rather several low, raven-like sounds.

"Barely two minutes as a raven and you've already taken up the temper of one," Felan said. "You would fit in well with the Woods Edge clan. They always seem to have some rather interesting words for any wolf in passing."

It was surprising, to say the least, that Felan had understood her. She would rather that he had not, considering what had been said.

"Wolves are closely bonded to ravens in nature. Wherever a pack of wolves is hunting you can be sure that ravens are close by. Even if that was not true I would have known what you meant by it. I can still read your thoughts, even while you're in your affinity."

Selene was quite thankful that ravens were unable to blush.

"It grows late," Xaiden lifted her once again. He carried her behind the row of hedges, setting her near where she had left her clothes. He then set her cloak beside her. "Reversing your affinity is much more simple, though no less painful. Your body always pulls towards its most used form. That is to say, if you had stayed in animal form most of your life it would be harder to transform from raven to human that it would be to switch from human back to raven. Do you understand?"

Selene nodded to show that she did.

"Fine. You must concentrate on your human form. Your body will return to it without aid of your mark." Xaiden headed off towards the fire.

Selene found her concentration reluctantly. She would have stayed in raven form all evening, perhaps tomorrow as well, if she thought Xaiden would allow it.

Perhaps some time would be left between Damaeus' lessons. He *had* said that he would need a few days for research.

She concentrated, holding her breath as pain encompassed her once again. The first transformation had passed in what seemed like hours, though in truth it could not have taken more than minutes. This one was over in an instant. She pulled her clothes carefully over sore muscles and headed back, nodding her head gratefully towards the Aranth as she reached them.

"You have my thanks," she said, "and my apologies for doubting your word."

"You are quite welcome," Xaiden answered as he began gathering mugs and placing them back upon the tray.

Damaeus parted with his mug rather reluctantly. It was nearly full, from what she could tell.

"Felan has arranged for a few ravens from the Ocean's Cliff clan to meet you here at noon on every second day. They will instruct you on the finer points of raven society, as well as the perfection of your actions while in Affinity, perhaps even some flying."

Flying? Perhaps it would not be so horrible to stay. Once Maye arrived this could be home. Her presence would make it so.

The moon hung high in the sky. It looked to be perhaps an hour or so past midnight. Damaeus passed one hand over the fire. The flames receded, leaving not so much as a wisp of smoke in their wake. Selene reached out to the charred logs. They were cool to the touch, as was the sand beneath them. Felan and Xaiden started off as if nothing out of the ordinary had occurred. Perhaps it was true for them. Damaeus nodded in Selene's direction, perhaps in appreciation of her expression of wonder. His ice colored eyes glowed even in the absence of firelight. He moved in the opposite direction of the Aranth, towards the far side of the courtyard. Selene was forced to sprint in order to catch up to Xaiden and Felan.

"Felan and I will have departed before you wake," Xaiden said quietly as they reached the door to the Sky Room. "We will keep our oath to you. Be sure that you keep yours."

"I do not break my oaths," she answered.

The thoughts of leaving that Selene had once entertained had vanished like morning mist the moment Xaiden had taught her to use her Affinity. She did not doubt his word. They would find Maye and bring her here, or else they would not return. Some tales of Aranth had turned out to be quite close to the truth. Felan turned back to meet her gaze, that trouble-ready look in his eyes once again. He was reading her thoughts, no doubt. *And some are not so close as they should be,* she amended. She would definitely speak with him about the polite use of his Latent Ability when they returned. Until then, she would train. Once she was Aranth then nothing could stop her from finding Islyr. The Tides were certainly with her on this day.

The Crimson Abyss

Thick fog filled the base of the Crimson Abyss, obscuring vast walls of red rock that led up to the surface. Islyr's eyes processed what little light lingered here as if it was the brightness of midday. His steps were cautious nonetheless. He would need the luck of the Tides to avoid the thorn-covered vines that snaked around his feet. The small, red, berry-shaped nodules that were clustered here and there along the length of them were of no danger to him. It was the needle sharp thorns hidden beneath each that would kill.

The base of the venomvine stood only a few feet away, set into a rocky crevice. Its bulbous body shuddered as it digested its most recent meal. A grin seized Islyr's lips. A more experienced plant would never have let him come so near to its base. He stepped aside as a partially digested boot catapulted past him to land in the sand of the dry riverbed. Several sets of bloody, thorn-like teeth protruded from the plant's gaping mouth. He hoped that the boot had belonged to some foolish warrior or perhaps a criminal in hiding. Few people traveled here by choice. Islyr held no pity for the ones who did. He merely watched as those seeking glory or obscurity met their untimely demise. He learned from their mistakes. Nearby towns as well as some from the farther reaches of the Ethereal Realm used this place to dispose of undesirables: thieves, murderers, those who committed treason. They were deserving of death and thus were of little concern to Islyr. Venomvine were swift killers, and shadeslight were near impossible to escape once the sun had set. Few trespassers lived longer than hours. The Ethereal Realm was a better place for it.

It was quite a different tale, however, when he came across those who had simply lost their way. Travelers attempting to cross the abyss, most often. Islyr made an effort to keep them from harm without making himself known to them. The land of the Kerell was far from this place. It lay across the Ocean of Tides, but water could not prevent word from traveling. The Kerell paid well for Marked Ones. There was never a shortage of buyers for those with the mark of a magical creature, nor for those with useful latent abilities. Islyr had both. The return of an escaped Marked One, especially one in high demand such as himself, could set a person with enough coin for life.

Islyr brushed his fingers lightly against his face. There was nothing to feel save skin, but that would not unmake the mark that his Kerell mistress had placed there. It covered a great portion of the left side of his head; black tendrils of imbedded ink that swept from beneath his hair to curl onto his cheek and around his left eye. They had completed the inking in just under a day. Mistress Nevane had held a mirror before him after wiping away what blood the artist's needle had drawn. She had repeated the ritual every morning before she sent him to kill other Marked Ones in the Pit. *To remind you,* she said in a broken form of his native tongue, *that you are now Rakaii; one meant only to serve. I accept nothing less than victory from my warriors. You may lose a match in the Pit and survive it, but you will certainly wish they had slain you when I am through.* She had held true to her words. Each scar held painful memories of battles lost. He had not looked upon his reflection in the three years since his escape.

Islyr glanced over the vine wrapped body beneath him. He was young, at least when compared to the others he found here. He was merely a boy. Not many men thought themselves capable enough to challenge this place after night fell, even to dispose of the worst of criminals. The cloaked ones who had brought the boy had shown no fear as they first set foot upon the sand of the dry riverbed. For that they had paid a high price. The shadeslight had feasted that night, leaving only one survivor. The fool had walked back up the path that led to the surface with no more speed than if he was browsing an open market. The Tides were with some more than others, or so it seemed.

Islyr pulled a pebble from his belt pouch and tossed it between writhing vines. Most Venomvine were rather sluggish during digestion, but it was always best to be certain in matters of life and death. *Only a fool assumes*. It was one of his father's sayings, and a rather useful one at that. The stone landed a carriage's length from where Islyr stood. A knot of vines curled lazily up to engulf it, but let it fall immediately upon finding that it was not edible.

The boy's body had been pulled a great ways towards the plant's base. The dead falcon, the boy's companion, was held closer still. The bird's presence was much more of a mystery to Islyr than that of its master. Its color, along with the fact that it was unusually well trained, proved it to be an expensive animal. It was not something that any sane person would leave with a criminal to be disposed of.

Islyr had guessed early on that the boy might be marked, for he and his bird had lasted longer in this place than most. Shadeslight rarely consumed creatures of magic, Marked Ones included. They had followed the boy, yet kept a respectable distance. They had not attacked him even in the darkened hours.

Islyr watched patiently as a vine slithered through the boy's sandy colored hair. He looked to have seen at least fifteen years pass. It was plenty old enough to get himself into trouble with the law, though what he could possibly have done to earn a trip to this place was beyond Islyr's comprehension. Marked Ones were hung, most usually. The boy's captors must not have been aware of what he was. The vine slipped beneath the boy's neck, pressing into his flesh now and again as if checking to be certain that he was dead. The lad had the Tides on his side in more ways than one. The Venomvine had eaten recently. It had no need of the nutrients his body held as of yet.

Islyr inched closer to the plant. It would be best to free the falcon first. Thrashing vines could easily shatter the bird's hollow bones. Islyr grasped the falcon's body gently in his free hand, carefully avoiding the vines that held it. He pulled a rust covered knife from his belt, drew his arm back, and launched it in one smooth movement, aiming for the center of the plant's mouth between rows of thorny teeth. The weapon struck perfectly.

The plant screamed; a high-pitched, metallic sound that made Islyr's ears ache. Vines splattered as pieces of rock fell soundlessly from the cavernous walls. Islyr's arm erupted in pain as a fist sized piece of rock bounced from it. The plant's hold on the bird loosened. Islyr pulled the falcon free and sprinted towards the boy's body, moving with care between open patches of sand. The plant grasped frantically within its gullet in attempt to remove the blade. The thick vines which held the boy at his neck and legs released and retreated towards the venomvine's base. Islyr grabbed the boy's arm and began to drag him. A deep, burning pain shot through his mark. The lad had been dead less than an hour, by the feel of it.

Metal struck stone a few feet behind him. The plant had freed itself from his knife. Thrashing vines rose up on all sides, twisting the boy from his grasp. Islyr threw the falcon to one side, counting on the thick layer of sand to cushion its landing. A tendril tightened around Islyr's ankle. His feet were swept from beneath him. Needle tipped vines thudded against the sides of his leather boots in attempt to push their poison through to his flesh. The plant would quickly realize its error and move up his leg. He drew a deep breath and allowed his body to go limp. The thudding slowly ceased, and the venomvine relaxed its hold. It surely thought that it had won. He lay still until most of the tendrils had pulled away. The plant left only two upon him, perhaps to be sure that no other creature of the abyss could steal its latest catch. Islyr reached his bruised arm down towards his belt pouch. The falling rock had not shattered any bones, as far as he could tell, but the movement brought pain. It was nothing, in truth. He had endured much worse than bruised flesh and pulled muscles while under Mistress Nevane's care. To be *Rakaii* was to ignore pain, no matter how severe.

The plant dragged him over sand and weathered bones, closer to its open, bloodied jaws. A series of angry clicks, sounds like that of a lock being thrust open, bounced from the walls of the abyss as the plant searched for any further intrusions upon its territory. Islyr at last found what was needed. He slid the blade out slowly and struck. He slashed the vines that had taken hold of his legs. The plant roared in agony. Vines slithered away like shadeslight at dawn. The boy's body fell to the sand with a soft thud.

The boy's slight weight told of the many days that he and his falcon had spent wandering the abyss. Food was beyond scarce in this place, though few souls lived long enough to be taken by starvation. Islyr pulled the stopper from a flask that he had tied to his belt. He poured half of the spring water within it over the boy's open eyes to rinse away the sand that clung to them. "Your expression is thanks enough, little one," he said with a laugh as he dragged the body to the opposite side of the riverbed and out of the venomvine's reach.

The falcon still lay where he had thrown it. The few tendrils that had been slithering towards the bird quivered and drew back at Islyr's approach. The venomvine would not risk further injury for such a meager snack. Islyr folded the falcon's wings gently against its side and placed the bird in his satchel, then went back to where the plant had ceased its attempt to drag him to its maw. A thicket of tendrils now blocked the crevice within which the venomvine lay. It would take no more chances this day. Two of the pieces that Islyr had severed from the plant lay in a puddle of viscous red juice. They flung clumps of sticky sand here and there as they writhed. He wrapped both in a worn piece of leather and placed them snugly next to the falcon. In moments the boy's body lay heavily over his shoulder.

Multiple sets of crimson eyes followed Islyr as he made his way down the dry riverbed. The creatures' presence did not worry him. Shadeslight could survive only where shadows lay. The sheer rock walls and constant mist that shrouded the abyss made it possible for them to venture out during most hours of the day, but they rarely appeared before night fell unless hunger drove them to it. It had taken only a year to earn their deference. After three they had come to consider him one of their number, if low in rank. Even those above him would not challenge him directly. They would wait until his attention was elsewhere to thieve his catch.

Islyr smiled as he thought of the stories that the Elders had told so long ago. Maye had not wanted Selene or himself to hear them, for they were tales of living shadows which concealed themselves, patiently waiting for the cover of darkness to suck every ounce of flesh from the bones of little children who misbehaved. The last of it was truth, at least in part. Yellowed bones were scattered throughout the dry riverbed like seashells upon a long forgotten shoreline. Most of them belonged to those who had committed some act of treachery or deceit, but shadeslight did not care what shadows men's souls held. They were much more interested in the flesh that covered them.

Fifteen and a half steps from the marked stone to the beginning of the pathway. Fifty more to the cave's entrance. The measurements were no longer needed since his eyes had adjusted to the gloom of the abyss, but using them brought familiarity to this forsaken place. A rocky outcropping materialized suddenly from beneath layers of smoky white.

The cave that Islyr now claimed for his own had once belonged to a shadeslight, which kept the less manageable creatures at bay. Shadeslight preferred shallow cracks and fissures when they could find them. The more open the area, the more chance that sunlight would be able to reach them. The subordinate had given up its resting place without a struggle, much to Islyr's pleasure.

The fire had dwindled during his absence, leaving only a few dimly glowing embers. A low growl issued from the cave's murky interior upon his approach. It was a youngling. He often found one or two slithering about upon his return, but only when he had been absent long enough for the light of the flames to wither.

"Be gone," Islyr snarled. "This territory is mine."

A set of crimson colored eyes appeared. They narrowed as the creature slipped like warm oil between the fallen rocks at the cave's mouth. Shadeslight observed what creatures they could find and then formed themselves to match, usually in bits and pieces. The creature's body paled as light touched it. Had the day been any brighter it would have disappeared completely. Its eyes melted into shadow and were replaced by several rows of dark, pointed teeth mimicking those of the venomvine. The creature hissed in fury before sliding out into the mist beyond the cave.

"Welcome home, my friend," Islyr said as he propped the upper half of boy's body against a curved portion of the cave wall. It stayed well enough, though his head hung awkwardly to one side.

A few breaths of air upon the embers of the fire, along with a handful of dead grass, returned it to a useable state. Islyr moved the cloth of the boy's shirt upon his back, nearest the right shoulder. His mark was that of a magical creature, certainly, but it held no familiarity to him beyond that. It was curious that the boy had not changed shape in the time he had been here. *Perhaps he does not know how*, Islyr reasoned. Most Marked Ones had need of another to show them how it was done. Islyr had learned from his uncle, just before the man's untimely disappearance. His father had become furious upon learning of it. He had forbidden him ever to use his mark again. The Kerell had forced Islyr to sever the promise he had kept so faithfully throughout his youth. He continued to hate them for it.

Islyr untied the satchel from his belt. He pulled the now lifeless pieces of vine from it, but left the falcon. It would not do for the boy to see it before the time was right.

Three venomvine nodules with needles removed, five leaves of fogstalk, a pinch of powdered filea root and a hand's length of nightflower vine. The last he had gathered from one of several springs that ran within the abyss. It was the only spring he dared to drink from, for nightflower grew only near pure water. He placed the ingredients into a large stone bowl, which he set at the edge of the fire. A bit of water from one of the few wineskins that he kept within the cave and a smooth, palm-sized rock aided in crushing the ingredients. It had taken him several tries to perfect the concoction. The first few experiments had been disastrous, to say the least. He preferred not to think of them even in passing.

Islyr waited patiently as the mixture warmed. When it was heated enough to be easily poured he knelt down beside the boy. He placed both hands upon the boy's head and closed his eyes in concentration. The body's skin was cool at first, but grew warm as Islyr's concentration deepened. The boy quivered. His eyes opened and then rolled back into its head. He drew a ragged, hacking breath. Islyr held the boy's mouth open with one hand and took hold of the stone bowl with the other. He poured the still-warm mixture down the throat, being sure to leave enough for the bird. He then placed a hand over the boy's nose and mouth, forcing him to swallow. Convulsions wracked the boy's body as Islyr dragged him to the cave's exit. He reached it with no time to spare. The boy wobbled to a stand and promptly vomited up everything that Islyr had forced into him. It did not matter. The nightflower was added to ensure that the concoction would soak quickly through the lining of the mouth or throat.

The boy bent over double, clutching his middle, then stared groggily at Islyr. "Cael?" He sounded as if he had downed a half bottle of rum.

A bit of disorientation was typical for those brought back by Islyr's latent ability, though he was most often mistaken for a family member rather than a pet. The boy's vision must be blurred.

"Cael?" he said again, staring Islyr full in the face. He wobbled to his feet, but lasted only seconds before falling.

Islyr gripped the boy beneath his arms and dragged him back into the cave, laying him near the fire. The heat would speed his recovery. The boy bent over once more, heaving up air. He then sat back against the cave wall.

"Your falcon is safe, and you will see him soon." The language of the Ethereal Realm lay strangely upon Islyr's lips. He had been forced to speak only the twisted words of the Kerell for too many long years.

"My falcon?" The boy's brow furrowed. His red-rimmed eyes held no glimmer of understanding.

"What is your name?"

He received only a few retching noises in response.

Islyr filled a dented metal cup with spring water from his wineskin. "Drink this," he said, placing it carefully into the boy's quivering hand.

"What is it?" the boy asked, eyeing the cup suspiciously. The drunken slur of his voice was beginning to disappear.

"Only water. It will help wash the bile from your throat."

The boy studied it momentarily before taking a small, cautious sip. After a second of thought he gulped down the rest, seemingly satisfied that it truly was nothing more than water. He held out the empty cup. Islyr made no move to refill it.

"Enough for now. Your stomach will not tolerate any large amount."

The boy stared blankly into the fire. His eyes widened as they settled upon Islyr. "What is this place?" Panic touched his voice. "What right have you to bring me here?" He attempted to stand, but failed miserably.

"Easy," Islyr said, placing his hand upon the boy's shoulder in attempt to keep him seated. "My name is Islyr. You will not come to any harm while under my care. Neither you nor your falcon."

He received only an anxious stare.

"The needles of the Venomvine are deadly. I trust you've learned your lesson. I may not be able to call you back a second time." He pulled a few semi-dry twigs from a pile in the cave's corner and threw them onto the dying fire. "I would be more civil to a man who had given me back my life. You could at least provide me with your name, to save me from having to ask for it again."

"Devren," the boy said with uncertainty. "Just what did you mean by-" His words were replaced by an expression of horror. Islyr turned to see his satchel on its side. The tail of the dead falcon was hanging from it. The bag must have been toppled by the boy's thrashing.

"Cael," Devren managed a few staggering steps towards the dead bird. The empty cup dropped from his hand. "You've killed him."

"No," Islyr said calmly. "The needles of the Venomvine killed him, just as they killed you."

"The mist of this place had addled your mind," the boy snapped through his tears. "I am obviously not dead."

His temper alone could have landed him here if offered in the wrong company. Few nobles took kindly to words used against them. Islyr rallied his patience.

"You are not dead now, but you were moments ago."

"You'll pay for this with your life!" Devren shook the bird in Islyr's direction.

"You'll want to be a bit more careful," Islyr said, reaching out in an attempt to stay Devren's arm. "I can't bring him back with a broken neck."

Devren lowered himself awkwardly to the cave floor, still gripping the bird tightly in one hand. "You can bring him back? How is that possible?"

"My latent ability works to call souls back from their time with the Spirits and bond them to the body from which they came." Islyr hoped that his few words would be explanation enough.

"You're marked?"

"I am."

"You ask me to believe that your latent ability brings people back from the dead?"

"There are limits, but yes."

"What sort of limits?"

"Things don't always turn out as I would like," Islyr sighed. "I would rather not speak of it."

"I believe I have a right to know, seeing as you've used your latent ability on me."

It seemed that the Tides had abandoned him on this. Islyr picked up the dented cup from the cave floor, filled it with water, and handed it back to the boy. Devren gulped it down as if he had spent a week in the Barren Lands. He then looked towards him expectantly.

Memories of horrifying failure dried Islyr's mouth. He took a few sips from his wineskin. The water seemed to slide down his throat without ever touching his tongue. He began slowly. "If the body has been poisoned, such as you were, then I must nullify that poison directly after bringing the soul back. Otherwise death will occur once again, usually within moments. Also, there are complications if the body is damaged too severely, if the poison cannot be nullified, or if more than several hours have passed since the time of the body's death." He pulled the moist air of the abyss deep into his lungs. "I am still able to bring back the soul in such cases but there are unpleasant consequences."

"Such as what?"

Prying should be the boy's given name. Islyr continued, if somewhat reluctantly. "Have you ever heard tell of a creature called bloodsoul?"

With one look at Devren's face Islyr was certain that the boy had heard of them. More than that, he seemed as if he had come into contact with a bloodsoul before, perhaps on more than one occasion. The boy scrutinized the skin of his arms.

"I haven't turned you into one," Islyr said patiently.

"I didn't think that." Devren's cheeks reddened enough to be seen even by the fire's light.

"Of course you didn't."

Devren thrust the dead bird towards Islyr. "You said you could bring him back. I would like you to do it now, before it's too late."

Cael had a short while left, by Islyr's calculations. The passage of time was difficult to surmise without the aid of the sun, but with years of practice he had learned to come close. Then again, there was no need to push the Tides' luck. The last thing he needed was a falcon bloodsoul on his hands, small though the creature was.

"Give him to me."

The boy handed Cael over obediently. Islyr stirred what little of the mixture remained in the stone bowl and set it near the fire to heat. The falcon's head disappeared beneath his hand. The other he placed upon the bird's back. Its soft feathers yielded easily to his touch. The warmth that came before the soul's return spread more rapidly than it had with the boy. It happened that way most usually with creatures of smaller size. Islyr poured the venomvine antidote into its mouth. The bird's body shook violently. It stretched its wings out and fell to the floor, where it stumbled in circles with one wing held aloft.

"He's acting strangely." Devren said, watching the bird as it continued to work its way around the cave.

"He will return to normal, given a few moments." Islyr grabbed the thrashing falcon by the feet to hand him to Devren. A feeling of warmth washed over his mark. The shock of it nearly caused him to drop the bird.

"He is a Marked One." It was not at all what Islyr had meant to say.

"Yes," Devren replied simply as he took Cael from him.

Islyr knew well that feathers and fur masked the burn of a Marked One's touch, but it had caught him off guard all the same. "Why is he not in human from? Surely that would be safer in a place such as this."

"Neither of us are able to transform. He has been trapped in his animal form, and I in my human form. To tell the truth, I'd hoped that the spell would have worn off by now."

So the boy had angered a Mage, or someone with enough coin to employ the services of one. It was not a difficult feat. Both Mages and nobles were known to have rough tempers.

"It's my fault that we found ourselves here." Devren looked down at the bird. "I was eavesdropping, which was wrong of me. My stepmother and her brother, they were plotting against my father. I heard them talking about it. They were trying to convince Cael to help them, but he said he wouldn't. Then they caught me listening in." Devren stopped suddenly, as if choking back a sob. His voice shook as he continued. "Cael told me to run and get father. I wasn't fast enough. My head started to ache and then everything went dark. I woke up here."

The bird uttered a short, screeching noise. It began to preen its ruffled feathers.

"We've spent all of our time searching for the path to the surface, though I'm not sure what good it will do when we find it. My father trusts my stepmother. It will be our word against hers. Besides that, her brother is a master of the Mages' arts. Even if Cael and I were to face them together with our affinities in working order we would be no match for Damaeus' magic."

Damaeus? Memory snatched Islyr from the present. The steel of the cage was cold and damp upon his bare skin. Dried tears lay stiff upon his cheek and fresh ones threatened to follow in their wake. He lay still, breathing even, shallow breaths. They would not continue to beat him if they thought he was asleep.

"Three hundred platinum pieces, no more." The man's shrill voice cut into his throbbing head, deepening the ache.

"This One is worth much more than that," a woman's soft voice argued. *"I would accept three hundred for an average Marked One of magical affinity, but this one's*

mark is unusual beyond that. His latent ability is unheard of and he was difficult to capture. He is worth seven hundred."

"I don't care if you did have to kill his father to get him. Nor does it matter to me how many men you lost for it. Four fifty, then. You'll not get a copper more. I've got at least two more to see tonight. Take it or be on your way."

Islyr choked back a ragged sob. His father had fought to his dying breath; a valiant effort against six armed men. The cool night breeze sent shivers across his bare skin. Pain lanced through his chest at each breath.

"Speak to this man, Damaeus. He will not see reason." The woman's voice seemed to brush the edge of true anger. *"I tire of this idiocy."*

"You will get one thousand platinum pieces at least for the boy at open auction. We demand at least half that, or we take our business to another."

The cage tilted slightly, causing Islyr to slide across its length. He concentrated on the soothing sound of waves lapping the shoreline.

"Hold there. No need to leave. You drive a rough bargain, for sure. Five hundred it is. Make sure he's out good, though. Don't want any mishaps." The clinking of coins rose faintly above the ocean's roar. *"Rest is on the ship."*

"Do you have a Circlet?"

"I've got a few, but no Mage for attaching them. It gets messy if I do it myself. Better to have someone with magic see to it once we reach Khnum. Sure not to lose any that way."

"I will do it for you, free of charge. I find the process to be quite gratifying."

"You have my thanks, Lord Damaeus. You're a great man, for certain. Be sure and leave the bond open, though. He'll be transferred quickly enough."

"Yes, yes. The Circlet?"

"This one will do for him. Size looks about right."

Islyr's eyes snapped open with the squeal of rusted hinges. The barred door swung back. Long, dark hair fell forward as the Mage leaned in. A cold hand reached out, gripping his throat so hard that he thought it might collapse.

"Don't move boy or you'll anger me. I have no patience for your kind."

The light of a full moon glinted from the arched, silver band. Islyr choked back a fresh sob upon seeing the long spikes of metal that protruded from it.

"This will cause you more pain than you've ever felt," Damaeus said with a smile. *"I guarantee it."*

"Islyr?" Devren stared across the fire at him. "Are you even listening? I've explained everything to Cael. He seems to think that we owe you something for what you've done, though we don't really have anything with us."

Islyr ran his hand across his forehead from temple to temple. The metal points of the Circlet had pressed though the bone of his skull like a fine blade through flesh. His skin had healed over long ago, leaving no visible trace of the round, boneless spaces left beneath, yet a wave of sickness washed over him each time his fingers touched one. He lowered his hand thoughtfully. Damaeus was not a common name, at least in any part of the world Islyr had visited, and Mages were far from plentiful in the Ethereal Realm. It may not be the same man, but who could foretell the turn of the Tides? The possibility of revenge settled sweetly over his thoughts. "I understand that you have nothing," he said carefully. "So, in exchange for returning your lives to you I ask only a simple favor."

Cael, who now perched upon Devren's shoulder, eyed him questioningly.

"We will travel together to your hometown. Once we reach it I will consider your debt repaid. I will stay on to help you meet with your father if you have need of my aid."

"It would be safer with the three of us," Devren agreed. "But Cael and I wandered around this place for ages and couldn't find the way out. I think we're stuck here for a time."

"I can take you to the surface," Islyr replied. "I could follow the paths of the Abyss with blinded eyes."

"If you know how to get to the surface then why in the name of the Spirits are you still here? This place is just as bad as the stories portray it to be. It's worse if you *aren't* killed. We've been eating nothing but mushrooms and rat flesh since we arrived." Devren screwed up his nose in distaste. "If we hadn't found that spring with the nightflower we would have been dead long since. I have only Cael's years as a Praecyr to thank for our survival."

The boy shut his mouth suddenly. He furrowed his brow and looked to Cael, as if he had said something that the falcon would disapprove of. Islyr could not imagine what it may have been. He did not care what they were, or from where they came, so long as they led him to Damaeus.

"Do you accept my offer then?"

The boy looked to Cael. "What do you think of it?"

The bird nodded his head.

"Then we leave today," Islyr said, ignoring the puzzled look the boy gave him. He rummaged through one of the pouches that hung at his belt and produced a handful of smoked meat strips. "You should eat something. You're beginning to look half bloodsoul."

Devren's cheeks colored once again at the mention of bloodsoul. He took the strips of meat and handed one to Cael. The bird accepted it with a nod of thanks, then glided to the floor and began tearing it into easily manageable pieces. Devren was more cautious in his tasting of the meat. He sniffed it several times before warily pressing it to the tip of his tongue.

"You've been feasting on rat flesh for two weeks and now you're worried about eating something that's freely given to you?" Islyr popped several small pieces into his mouth.

The boy frowned.

"It's only rabbit. I journey to the surface once in a while when supplies are needed. I smoke everything I catch there so that it will stay fresh."

The boy glanced down at Cael once more before placing a small piece into his mouth. "Are you certain you wish to leave today?" he asked between wary bites.

"Why waste daylight hours? I have all the supplies we will need."

Islyr stepped to the back of the cave, where the fire's light was dim. A shallow recess in the cave wall served as storage for his supplies. He had collected all that was useable from the bodies that lay scattered throughout the length of the abyss. He could lay claim to what parts he wanted if he arrived there before the others. Weaponry was most easily found, for the shadeslight were not able to dissolve that as they did flesh. Clothing was harder to come by, as were most other objects not made of metal or glass.

"Are you able to use this?" Islyr asked, pulling a wide bladed sword from the shadows. It was mildly rusted, but that was to be expected in a place constantly blanketed by mist.

"Of course I am able," Devren said with a scowl. "Just what do you take me for?"

"No need to anger." The boy definitely needed help in managing his temper. "I thought it best to ask. I hope you're being honest with me. It would be a shame if you were to slice yourself open for foolish pride."

"My father taught me swordsmanship." Devren pulled the sword from Islyr's grip. "He is the best in all of Evaria."

"The capital city. I've always wanted to see it." He handed the boy several wineskins full of water. It was a lengthy journey to the nightflower spring, one he made only at the end of each week. "A dangerous place, Evaria, for Marked Ones at least. Not that I'm saying anywhere is truly safe for us, but the home place of the Aranth would be a most difficult place to live, I would assume." He pulled a long leather belt from the pile and began to string it with tattered pouches. "That wouldn't be who left you here, would it? Last time I heard it was hanging for Marked Ones, but that was years ago. Things may have changed by now."

The falcon stopped suddenly. A small piece of smoked meat hung from its beak.

Devren's mouth opened as if he were about to speak. It hung that way momentarily. "I have met a few Aranth," he began at last. His words were cut short as the falcon bit into the flesh of his leg. "Owww!" Devren shot an offended look at the bird. "You didn't have to do that!"

"Are you certain that he's tame?" Islyr asked through laughter. It must have been the Aranth that had dropped them here, along with Damaeus. The bird's actions nearly confirmed it. They had made powerful enemies indeed. Perhaps Cael was afraid that Islyr would not help them if he knew of it. Aranth could be no worse than shadeslight or venomvine, of that he was certain.

"Kii-reeh," the falcon said, spreading its wings.

"I am not going to tell him that," Devren replied with wide eyes. "My mother's ashes would boil if half of those words passed my lips."

The bird had the attitude of a Praecyr if the few Islyr had come into contact with were any indication. "You understand him," he said thoughtfully.

"Cael taught me some falcon speech. It is rather difficult to learn. Some sounds are very close, too much so to distinguish with human ears. I know enough to get by. What he said is not important, honestly." He looked down at Cael, who was swallowing the last chunk of meat with zeal.

"What weapon does he use?" Islyr picked up his staff from where it lay in the corner. He had not had any cause to wield it in quite some time. Standard weapons were of no use against most creatures of the abyss.

"He is proficient at many, though he usually carries a sword."

Islyr uncovered a second sword from beneath a metal breastplate and a hole-filled length of leather that may have at one time been a vest. Initials had been carved upon the weapon's blade, though they were much too worn to read. He slid it through his belt and snatched up a filled wineskin along with the one he had used for the concoction he had created earlier. Devren lowered his hand for Cael. The bird climbed up to sit upon the boy's shoulder.

"Fetch some sand to throw over the fire."

The boy did as he was told, using a rusted bucket Islyr kept near the cave's wall. Someone had taught him to follow orders, at least. Islyr would lay bets that it had been Cael. It seemed that he functioned almost as a second father to the boy; an elder family member at the least.

The boy was quiet as they left the cave and traveled to the base of the Abyss. He followed Islyr closely after reaching the dry riverbed, giving uneasy looks to each pile of human remains that they passed.

"Where did you get these things?" Devren asked suddenly, turning his sword from side to side in attempt to read the lettering that had been etched upon its center.

"You came down the northern path, I believe," Islyr said, ignoring the question. He may answer it later, when more trust had been built between them. Devren had nearly ended up as a source of plunder, though in truth the men that had brought him here had not left him much. It was near a miracle that Islyr had found the two of them in time.

He started up the northern path. The rocky edges that marked either side of it blended perfectly into the rock of the abyss with the mist to aid them. Islyr followed the inclining path and came shortly to a place where it split into two. The mist hung more thinly here, allowing an amazingly clear view of the few feet ahead of them.

Islyr pushed the end of his staff into the soft sand. "I am not sure which one they carried you down. It may be best to simply choose one now and correct ourselves with the aid of the sun once we reach the surface. It will cost us a few days at the most."

"There's no need for that." Devren reached down to pick up a piece of rock that had fallen from the walls. He folded his fingers around it and closed his eyes.

"What are you doing?" Islyr hoped that he had not addled the boy's mind when he had used his latent ability upon him.

"Here, I'll show you." Devren touched his hand to Islyr's arm. "This wasn't of much use back there. Everything looks the same, what with the mist and all. I couldn't seem to find anything of us passing." The boy scowled at him. "You'll have to close your eyes or it won't work."

Islyr did as he had been asked. Images flooded his mind, all of them shrouded in the ever-present mist of the abyss. A view from the ground, so it seemed. The scene was as silent as a bat's wings. Days and nights passed in seconds. Blye spiders, shadeslight, and abyss rats passed over and around him. Time slowed as a group of cloaked men traveled warily down northwest path. They carried with them an unconscious, sandy-haired boy and a snow colored falcon. Something must have startled them, for four of the men drew their swords. The fifth one raised a hand to still them. He was their leader, most certainly, for his was the only cloak with embroidered edges and the leather of his boots was mostly clean. The man that carried the boy threw him down roughly and turned to run. He stumbled to the ground less than ten paces from the group, with no cause to be seen. All of the men's faces, much to Islyr's dismay, were obscured by darkness and the thick wool of their hoods.

Islyr remembered looting the bodies. The one that had fallen was the most fortunate of them. Better to die from a broken neck than to be eaten by shadeslight while you still lived. The plunder had been light from this group. Several swords, metal buttons and a few coins. Islyr always saved what coins he found in case he had need of them someday. It was interesting as well; something to pass the time. You could tell what place a person was from by the mark of the coins they carried.

A knife appeared from the leader's hand. He bent down to slice the boy's forearm, then reached into his robes and produced a small pendant on a leather cord. He pressed it to the boy's bleeding arm, and then tucked it carefully away. The man did the same to the falcon, pricking its leg first with the tip of the blade. One of the remaining henchmen, a tall man with dark, matted hair that hung out beyond his hood, picked the boy up from where he had been thrown. The group started out once again. The image faded away quite suddenly. Islyr opened his eyes. Devren had thrown the rock back to the sand.

"We go northwest, then." Islyr started up the path. The scene must have been difficult for Devren to witness. No matter. The boy's pain would be avenged in due time.

Mage's Return

Selene glowered at the patch of stone that led from the castle's side entrance to her feet. The puddle upon it had grown considerably in the past few hours, much to Damaeus' vexation. A sharp, metallic sound rang out as Damaeus forced the empty tin cup back onto the castle steps. There was hardly a smooth place on the thing, due mostly to his abuse.

A month of time had passed like swift autumn winds between lessons with the ravens and Damaeus' teachings on using her affinity. Selene had improved greatly since her first session with Damaeus, but that did not diminish the frustration that came from being under his authority.

He snatched up one of several pitchers that sat upon the steps and filled the cup once again to the brim. Selene had emptied four pitchers worth of water onto the road thus far. They would soon be forced to call for more.

Concentration is the key, Damaeus told her before her first lesson using levitation. *Your Latent Abilities hold more power than this kingdom has seen in three hundred years, and that is without the use of a Stone. But power is worthless without control. You will remember that, if nothing else.*

"Again," he snapped. "Properly, this time."

Selene held back the look of displeasure she so desperately wished to give him. He acted as if she drew such great pleasure from his lessons that she deliberately botched the most simple of teachings in order draw them out indefinitely. In all her years as a Rider she had never met anyone more disagreeable than Damaeus. He was stubborn, selfish, and narcissistic. He aggravated her in ways that

Terran had never dreamed of. Worst of all, he was her superior. One by one, the pitchers of water began to shake.

"It would not be prudent to damage any more of my sister's property," Damaeus said. "She has a temper much deeper than your own. I doubt that I could convince her of anything less than physical punishment for your next offense."

Selene grasped for control of her power. It was much like attempting to ladle soup with a slotted spoon. Damaeus had learned quickly what it meant when Selene's eyes turned from green to gray. He took advantage of it to the fullest. Selene managed a few shallow breaths, but they did nothing to calm her.

"Recite the words as I taught you." He sipped at the cup of tea that he had been nursing for the past few hours. It did not seem possible that the liquid was still warm.

Selene closed her eyes. She had repeated the words so often that they passed her lips with no effort. "I will not let anger control my actions. I open my mind to the winds of tranquility." She levered her eyelids open just enough to see that one corner of Damaeus' mouth was curled up condescendingly. It seemed that he took every opportunity to lord his power over her. "My thoughts are pure serenity. There, are you satisfied?"

"Again," Damaeus said evenly. "And it would be wise to resist adding extra words between rounds."

Selene considered using her latent ability to pour the remaining pitcher of water over Damaeus' head. He deserved it, surely. She pushed the thought away. The only thing it would gain her was more time training with the horrid man. *That* was something she certainly did not want.

Selene repeated the words until the last of her anger drained away. She could not decide which was worse, the fact that it had actually calmed her, or the knowing look that Damaeus was now giving her because of it. He nodded his head for her to begin. The tin cup lifted evenly from the step. Selene sighed.

Damaeus returned to his seat; a carved hardwood chair cushioned in green velvet. He had ordered it brought out and placed beneath the awning that shaded the top of the steps so that he would not be forced to sit on cold stone. Selene was given no such luxury, even between teachings.

Her lessons were held in the common room to begin with, and she was allowed to sit while learning. She and Damaeus worked on perfecting her healing ability as Xaiden had instructed. The indoor lessons ended promptly once they began work on Selene's levitation ability. It was troublesome to control, especially when her thoughts turned to anger. Anger was a certainty as long as Damaeus was in charge of her training.

When Selene became angry, things shifted. Her power acted as it pleased. Pieces of stone loosened from the walls and launched themselves across the room. Furniture lifted into the air. Decorative swords and armor clattered to the floor. Queen Perfidia was forced to order three new common room chairs, one table, several bowls, and a sizeable slab of black marble for one of two large hearths that heated the room. The last put the queen in a nastier mood than was usual. Apparently marble of that particular type was rather hard to come by. It took some negotiation on Damaeus' part to keep the things from being subtracted from Selene's pay. He could be agreeable in rare instances, whenever the notion took him. The bargain that Damaeus and Perfidia reached seemed fair, the greater part being that he and Selene practice outdoors from then on. Perfidia also insisted that they take a break from learning healing to focus upon control of levitation.

"Excellent. Much better than expected."

The tin cup hovered only inches from Selene's nose. True shock came when she realized that all of the water Damaeus poured into it was still present.

"You may take it," he said, his stony expression unchanging. "We will attempt this lesson again to be sure you have mastered it. If you manage to complete it perfectly five times in succession then you may have the remainder of the day as free time. Three additional flawless executions of the feat will be required for each failure."

It was a fair enough deal, considering who it was coming from. Selene folded her hand around the cold tin cup and released her latent ability. She sprinted up the steps and placed it next to Damaeus' chair before returning to her spot.

She used greater caution this time than she had in previous attempts. She did not dare to believe that her ability was finally under control. The cup lifted smoothly, gradually closing the gap between the steps and where Selene stood. It floated easily over tan paving stones darkened to auburn by fallen water. A few moments of leisure in the Sky Room would be quite pleasant. The jewel-colored fish always swam close when they sensed her presence, their mouths gaping in hope of a snack. They were especially fond of the plump, white worms that could be found under loose rocks near the edge of the west cliff. Selene pushed all thought from her head. *Concentrate.* A single drop of water upon the pavestone would mean failure.

A flash of white caught the edge of her vision. She turned her head slightly, being sure to keep the cup steady. A black and white horse galloped down the pathway towards her, its hooves ringing loudly upon the paving. The bony creature came to a sudden stop. The cup dropped to the path with a clink.

Damaeus rose from his chair, cursing her failure. Selene paid him no heed. His words seemed far from her.

"Cyprus!"

The horse's ears swiveled. He saw her then, and in a moment was at her side. Selene pressed her cheek against his neck, ignoring the warm sweat that dampened her skin. The horse's body shook with each labored breath.

"What happened to you?" Selene breathed, stepping back for a better look.

Cyprus followed, pushing his muzzle against her.

"Steady, now. Be still." She placed both hands upon his side and closed her eyes, using her latent ability to search for wounds as Damaeus had taught her. There was really no need to come into contact with the flesh when healing, nor to blow upon it as she had done when she was a child. Still, she found the habit difficult to break.

A cracked rib sealed easily under her touch. Bruises and shallow cuts faded to nothing. Cyprus pawed at the road impatiently. He had never been one to hold still for long, even when injured. His skin twitched as the last bruise was found and healed.

"Easy," she said as she guided him towards the stables. He was not wearing any tack, yet he followed eagerly when she placed one hand upon his neck and began to walk.

A brief glance at Damaeus found him glaring from his seat. His arms were folded heatedly across his chest. This would cost her ten more repetitions at least. It did not matter. She would do what he asked of her as soon as Cyprus was taken care of.

The barn was only a short walk from where they had been practicing. It was a massive structure built to hold over one hundred and ninety horses, though at the moment less than one quarter of the stalls were occupied.

King Graelen had promised Selene a stall here, as well as first choice from next year's foals. She had been given a horse to ride in the meantime, a spirited black gelding named Trinine. The horse once belonged to a former Aranth, a member of the Elite Guard for many long years. The man's name was Cael, and he was gone. No one would say more about him than that. In fact, people grew quite irritated at her prying. The few members of the castle staff that she questioned about him suddenly remembered that they had something urgent to do in a place most conveniently far from her.

Slanting rays of light reached down through the barn's interior, glancing off motes of dust that hung causally in the air and forming puddles of brilliance upon the well-swept wooden floor. Trinine's stall stood empty. Most of the horses spent their daylight hours grazing in the pasture beyond the barn. Selene opened a stall near to Trinine's and ushered Cyprus in. The stable-hands made certain that all of the stalls stood clean and ready, including those that were not in use at the moment. You could never tell when someone of importance would stop in unannounced.

Selene brought Cyprus a bit of hay and half of a bucket of water. It would not do to allow him too much to drink, as winded as he was. The stable hands would refill it when they came to settle the horses in for the evening. She brushed her fingers lightly against Cyprus' still damp neck. He flicked one ear in her direction over a mouthful of hay. "I'll be back to see you. Soon, I hope." It would be soon as long as Damaeus was not terribly irritated with her.

Selene slipped out of the barn and headed back towards the castle. She hoped that Damaeus would not force her to practice through dinner. He never seemed hungry, regardless of how late her lessons ran. An odd sight greeted her as she crested the hill near the castle's side entryway. Damaeus had risen from his seat. Stranger yet, he was out in full sun conversing with two mounted men. Selene quickened her pace.

Xaiden dismounted smoothly, followed closely by Felan. Selene broke into a run, her eyes searching frantically for any sign of Maye's presence. Xaiden had given his word that they would not return without her. She expected a smile as she approached, from Felan at the very least. He refused to meet her gaze. Xaiden nodded in greeting, but said nothing. It was then that she caught sight of Felan's horse. A long bundle, wrapped in dark blankets bearing Evaria's crest, was tied behind the saddle.

Selene's heart plummeted. Despair slithered its way around her lungs, constricting the space within to nothing. She found herself by the horse's side with only a vague awareness of how she had come to be there. She reached out to pull back the layers of blanket. Xaiden's hand caught her wrist.

"I think it is best that you do not see her as she is now," he said softly. "Felan will show you parts of our journey, if you wish."

Selene turned to Felan. He offered her a questioning look. She nodded in consent.

"Close your eyes," he said.

Selene found it difficult to take her gaze from the bundle. She forced her eyes to close. The blanket's crescent moon and serpent dragon crest slowly disappeared. All was dark for a moment.

The path to Maresbane appeared in her mind. The image felt similar to the one sent by the raven at the Broken Mule. It was indistinct in some places, as if pulled from the depths of his memory, and as clear as fine glass in others. The scene altered suddenly. A charred piece of ground stood before her, surrounded by battered portions of a wooden fence. Singed grass reached up around open gate. Selene recognized it, eventually, as the house that she and Maye had shared. The hearth that once occupied one wall of the kitchen now reached to the sky alone. Selene's stomach clenched. She hoped that Maye had not been inside when it burned.

The vision shifted to show the back path to the Elder's cottage. Cyprus was tied there, a few feet from the road. His head was held as low as the rope would allow. His eyes were half-closed. Dried blood covered his neck where the tightness of the rope cut into his flesh. His skin stretched taut against protruding bones. No doubt he had been stubborn with the Elders. He had always been wary of strangers. They probably tried to break him with cruelty, and then with starvation.

"Are you certain you wish to go on?" Felan asked, placing his hand upon her arm. Her mark warmed.

"Yes," she heard herself reply. "I wish to see her."

A fresh image filled Selene's mind, turning her stomach to ice. Blood red leaves against pure white bark. *The Sending Tree*. Her eyes ran up its trunk, across the broad branch that crossed the sandy path to the Elder's cottage. It was there that she found Maye. Bile rose up in Selene's throat. Breath rushed from her hollow chest. It was her fault. Tears that had been hovering just out of sight flowed freely down her cheeks. If only she had stayed home from the errand like her mother wanted. She had been so selfish, for she continued to go on errands when she knew that discovery would be the end of them both. Maye paid for Selene's disobedience with her life.

One by one the silver pitchers rose from where they sat. Damaeus's chair tumbled down the stone steps, crashing to the road below. One of the massive stone pillars that supported the awning began to quake, then to crumble. An Aranth called her name. She did not turn to see who had spoken. Selene ran into the castle. The walls trembled. Tapestries and paintings fell as she passed them. She paid them no heed. Selene found herself at once in her room. Hinges screamed and a door slammed. She threw herself upon her bed. There she stayed, and wept, until sleep took her.

Aranth Duty

Selene sipped carefully from her cup of tea. It was pleasantly strong and carried a light aftertaste of mint. She popped the last bite of fresh bread into her mouth and laced her shirt. The view from her balcony was truly spectacular, though it was more so in the evening than at morning's light. The town of Evaria stretched below her and the ocean lay beyond it. Townsfolk were steadily filling the Seller's Square, setting up multi-colored tents from which to sell their wares.

The pain of Maye's death lingered with Selene, returning to shatter her calm when some small and unexpected thing brought her to mind. Maye was given a Sending fit for royalty. King Graelen paid all expenses. It was a private affair, with only Aranth and members of the royal family attending. Selene insisted on singing the Sending Hymn on her own, though Xaiden and Felan offered to aid her. It would not have been right. Only family or friends of the departed should perform the Sending Hymn save when no family or friends were left living.

This morning's breakfast was the first full meal Selene had eaten in a little over two weeks. They brought them to her, three a day, regardless of how little food she consumed. She pulled on her boots. They were crafted of fine, smooth leather which felt odd upon her feet. Her old ones had been well worn. They had been patched until most of the original leather was no longer visible, but they were comfortable and truly hers. Perfidia had ordered them disposed of. Selene was given back the contents of her belt pouch, few as they were, but none of her clothing had been returned. The new items were all of high quality, which made it that much more difficult for her to accept that she owned them.

Selene wrapped her belt around her waist, looping it through the metal link at its end. It felt light with no sword attached. She still reached for her weapon every so often.

Xaiden promised her that she would receive a sword when she was ready. Perhaps they still did not trust her fully. Selene trusted the Aranth as well as she could for people she not known for any real length of time. Xaiden and Felan had done exactly as they had promised. She could not fault them for that. She had no one but herself to blame for Maye's death.

She pulled her hair into a Rider's knot and headed out into the hallway. It was empty, much to her pleasure. She had not spoken to anyone since Maye's return aside from Felan, and that was only yesterday afternoon. He informed her that he and Xaiden were planning to travel into town this morning and that she was invited to join them. She did not reply at the time. Guilt crept up on her afterward. She should have responded somehow, even if it was simply to decline. It took her half the night to decide whether she would go.

Sunlight assaulted Selene's eyes as she stepped from beneath the awning that shaded the castle's side entrance. Aranth were discouraged from using the front entrance hall unless properly dressed, which meant Aranth-marked light leather armor, a vest over a standard cotton shirt, matching boots, and wrist guards, at the least. Selene felt rather silly donning such equipment just to go into town, especially as she had no sword. Thus she decided to stay away from the main entrance and the throne room. She would not willingly disobey one of King Graelen's orders. Damaeus' orders, however, were a completely different matter. Selene scrutinized the new stonework. The pillar had been expertly patched. Even so, there were several places where the damage she had caused was evident. She hoped that Perfidia would not think to pull that from her pay.

Selene started down the steps. Once she was a full member of the Elite Guard she would finally be allowed to pass the walls that surrounded this place. She would then renew her search for Islyr. A smile came with the thought.

Felan and Xaiden waited by the main door of the barn. Both were already mounted. Trinine stood idly nearby in his saddle and bridle. They must have known she would come. It was likely that Felan had been reading her again. Felan did not need to be within eyesight to do so as long as he used his Stone, according to Damaeus. The thought unsettled her.

"I am pleased that you could join us," Xaiden said as he patted the neck of his iron-gray gelding. The horse's name was Requiem, and Felan's bronze colored mare was called Daea. The stable hands became so uncomfortable after she asked about Cael's gelding that she found it necessary to ask of something else as well. Questions concerning the other horses seemed to ease their fears a little. She could not remember half of what she had been told, though a few of the names stuck with her.

Trinine stood steady as she swung up onto his back.

"What is our plan for today?" Selene asked as they started downhill, passing from formed paving stones to tightly packed dirt. She hoped that the errand would be interesting enough to keep her thoughts from straying.

"You and I are to pick up a few things for King Graelen," Felan replied. "Xaiden will be off by himself for a while, solving petty disputes and the like. He has a fairly short list compared to the usual."

Selene closed her eyes for a moment, enjoying a cool breeze that held the scent of the ocean. It felt good to be outdoors once again.

"We'll catch up with him as soon as our part is finished," Felan continued. "That way you can see how everything is done. It is part of our duty as Aranth to keep peace. You'll be handling things by yourself sometimes, seeing as there are so few of us."

The steep path turned once again into paving stones, this time of a deep red hue. They passed beneath a stone archway and onto the main road, which was lined on both sides with taverns and all manner of shops. Most were constructed from the same multi-colored stone as the Aranth barn. The familiar scents of incense, animals, sweat, and roasting meat embraced her.

"May I ask something concerning the Aranth?" She looked to Xaiden.

"Certainly," he replied as he perused the short list of names that King Graelen had given him.

"I mean no disrespect. I am certain that you are quite capable in your leadership, but shouldn't one of us be…" She stopped herself, at once remembering where she was, and rephrased the question. "What I mean to say is that perhaps it was foolish of us to leave our *animal companions* behind?"

"Do not worry." Xaiden laughed. "The people of Evaria are accustomed to seeing us both with and without our animal companions. In time you will learn where precautions are necessary and where they are not."

"You'll find it difficult to sway people from what they believe to be the truth." Felan added as they reached a half wall that marked the edge of the Square. "What would you have done if I approached you before your time here and revealed the true story of the Aranth? If I had explained to you then what we truly are would you have accepted my words?"

"No. I suppose not."

"You began to believe the true way of things when you were confronted with unyielding evidence," Xaiden added. "Even then, you retained some doubt. You questioned if what you had found could possibly be true because beliefs you had held since your youth were being challenged. It is natural for the mind to resist change."

"But what of those who work and live in the castle? Surely they must know the secret of the Aranth."

"The castle is ancient," Xaiden explained, "as is the magic that protects it. You will find that most people are unable to recall a majority of events which occur within its walls once they leave them. It does not work on our kind, however, nor does it work upon those of the Graelen line, whether they are members by blood or caerim vows."

"None have slipped past unnoticed?"

"A few have done so. It is part of our duty as Aranth to be sure that they are properly dealt with. There is always a Mage on the castle grounds for that reason. If Damaeus is unable to alter their memories then they must be put to death. It is unfortunate, but entirely necessary to preserve our ways." Xaiden urged his horse into the crowd.

The Seller's Square was a great source of entertainment due to the plethora of interesting things that one could find for sale there. The massive ships that arrived at Evaria's docks throughout the daylight hours and at times well into the night always brought new and exciting items for the peddlers to vend.

Today, as every day, the Square was alive with movement. Every inch of it seemed to be covered with either merchants or their wares. A dark-haired lady to Selene's right, whose nose was hooked like an owl's beak, held up lengths of brightly colored silk for a woman with beautiful, copper toned skin. They seemed to be haggling over price, a common occurrence and a subject of some interest to Selene when she had time to spare. To Selene's left was a well-dressed merchant selling tiny, round, stone beads like those that the women of Evaria wore at the end of their braids. The beads were kept in tightly woven baskets, and were sorted by quality and shade.

Selene once asked Perfidia of hers and had been told, in a rather haughty tone, that they were all carved of precious stones, not at all like the false ones that most townsfolk wore. On the first braid the Queen wore one of sapphire, her birthstone, and two of onyx in memory of her mother and father. On the second was a bead of emerald, which was King Graelen's birthstone, and one of blue-green iridescence to represent her caerim vows. Selene excused herself shortly thereafter by saying that Damaeus had ordered her to practice her latent ability. In truth she only wanted to escape from Perfidia. The woman's tone was quite condescending whenever she spoke to Selene, which was not something that she could tolerate for any length of time.

The horses were forced to walk single file as they squeezed through the narrow aisles that had been left between peddlers, but none of the animals seemed to be bothered by it. They were well used to crowds. Xaiden turned his gelding to the left just before a rather round old woman selling animals of every sort. Rabbits, geese, and chickens were held six or so to a pen. As Selene drew closer she could make out several wooden cages full of pigeons and a few squat goats tethered to a post. In the corner of the peddler's space was a long, wire cage full of creatures labeled as scrub pigs, though they did not look much like any pigs Selene had ever seen. Their bodies were shaped like that of a plump, tailless rat. They had a smooth coat of fur that grew in patches of black, white and tan except for upon their ears, which were bald. The old woman held one in her lap. She was petting it like one would a cat. The little creature chattered at each touch. It seemed to enjoy the attention she gave it.

"Buy a scrub pig!" The woman bellowed with more than enough strength to cut through the noise of the crowd. "They come all the way from the Barren Lands. Great pets for the little ones and mighty tasty too."

Selene screwed up her nose. Well enough to keep one of those things as a pet, but to eat one was a completely different, rather disturbing, matter. She wondered momentarily how one would cook a scrub pig. There could not possibly be any decent amount of meat on the little things.

With a little butter and some spice I'm sure they would be quite tasty. The words echoed through her head.

She looked up to see Felan staring back at her with a rogue's grin upon his face. She sincerely hoped that he was joking.

This is where we split off. Follow me. Felan led her out of the square and down a series of narrow roads lined on both sides with shops and fine homes. They stopped in front of a well-kept store. One side of the street was open, which allowed a perfect view down to the shore, though the drop was blocked off with a length of chain strung between wooden posts. A neatly painted sign swinging just above the shop door bore the sword and shield symbol for weaponry, but no name.

Selene reached into her belt-pouch to feel the few platinum coins that sat at the bottom. King Graelen had given her the first month's pay as an Aranth only two weeks after she had arrived even though she was still in training and had not gone through the acceptance ceremony. She had never before seen platinum, in coin form or otherwise. It was far more money than she could have made in years as a Rider, even if she happened upon some item of great value during an errand. She had more than enough to purchase a fine sword, though Xaiden would not be pleased with that. She promised to obey him and she intended to honor that promise, even if it meant a few more weeks without the comfort of a weapon at her side.

Felan dismounted, leaving Daea untethered in front of the store. Selene supposed that it did not matter, for she seemed well trained and not many would dare to steal a horse with the brand of Aranth upon its side. She followed him closely as he stepped up to the storefront. Metal chimes, which had been attached to the door's handle, sounded pleasantly as they passed into the shop's dark interior. Selene's eyes adjusted slowly.

"Selene, this is Meiun of Northlight," Felan said, gesturing through the darkness. "Meiun, Selene Valenne. She is to be the Aranth, after her training has been completed."

Selene barely managed to hold in a gasp of astonishment. It was nearly human, the creature that stood behind the chiseled slate counter. His well-muscled chest was bare, leaving scattered clusters of pearl-white scales exposed in places where skin would naturally be. His eyes, the color of fresh blood, rested upon her from behind locks of long, white hair.

"A pleasure to meet you, Selene Valenne," he said in a voice that seemed much too human, given his appearance. "And it is always fine to see you, Felan Hadrian. I have readied the weapon King Graelen requested. One moment." He turned, and just before he left the room Selene's gaze moved up to find a pair of massive, yet lightly folded wings sprouting from the upper portion of the creature's back beneath his shoulder blades. They were much like the wings of a dragon or bat. Light scales faded into flesh, which covered the skeleton beneath.

The ceiling was high here, she noticed, as if they had left out the floor of the second story. Perhaps Meiun had requested for it to be built that way. His wings would certainly reach far above his head when he opened them. Felan's voice scattered her thoughts.

Meiun is of the Khaloc race. He was exiled from his land for the lack of pigment in his skin, which is considered a curse amongst his kind. He came here a little over one hundred years ago to seek sanctuary at the hand of the royal family.

Selene found it difficult to believe that so much time had passed since Meiun's arrival. He looked to be no older than she, at the most.

They age as all magical creatures do, slowing considerably during their prime years.

"All magical creatures?" Selene said aloud, forgetting for a moment that Felan could hear her thoughts. "Are Aranth included as well?"

"Yes. Aranth are not considered to be fully human. We are magical creatures."

"How old are you, then?"

"Me?" He seemed surprised that she had asked. "My day of origin is quite close to yours, a little over twenty-two years ago, but in the second month of Awakening rather than the first month of Returning. Your appearance should reach its locking point late this year." He smiled. "You ought to ask Xaiden about his day of origin. It is truly interesting. That is if you can convince him to admit to it."

Selene was about to ask just how old Xaiden was, and also how Felan knew of her month of birth, but she was interrupted by Meiun's return. The Khaloc carried a bundle of royal blue cloth held in place with several lengths of matching ribbon.

"Many thanks," Felan said. He placed a full bag of coins into Meiun's clawed hand. Each dragon-like talon was tipped with silver leaf. "From King Graelen, along with his gratitude," He unwrapped the bundle, inside of which was a newly made sword. It was a beautiful weapon with silver inlay upon its grip. Letters in a language unfamiliar to Selene were etched down the length of the blade. The symbol of the Aranth lay just below the hilt.

Felan turned the sword from side to side, inspecting it. "Beautiful work, Meiun, as usual. I am constantly in awe of your skill."

The Khaloc nodded. Felan handed the sword to Selene and picked up the matching scabbard, which Meiun had placed upon the counter. The weapon felt wonderful in her hands. It was a bit longer than any sword she had used, but it was lighter as well and perfectly balanced.

"What do the symbols mean?" she asked, casting her eyes down the length of it.

"He who holds the spirit of honor shall always find victory," Meiun replied. "Those words are etched upon each Aranth sword in the Ancient Language."

Selene pointed the sword's tip to the ground and turned her wrist out, as if inviting Felan to spar.

"You'll have plenty of chance to spar with me later," he said. "With Xaiden as well. Weaponry is a large part of our training. This sword will become yours, but not until after your acceptance ceremony."

Selene's mark burned with excitement. Never had she imagined owning a weapon so fine. She raised the sword's point from the floor and reluctantly handed it back to him, hilt first. He slid the weapon into its sheath and re-wrapped it. "I thank you again, Meiun. I shall see you soon."

"May your wings forever touch the sky." the Khaloc said, bowing his head.

"May the earth keep you lightly," Felan replied.

Selene followed Felan out of the shop, storing the formality carefully away in case she had cause to use it in the future. She was just settling herself onto Trinine's back when a scream pierced the air. She turned to see an elderly woman running towards Felan from the direction of the Square. A Bloodsoul lurched closely behind her. It uttered a deep, vibrating groan at the sight of Felan, but did not slow its chase of the breathless woman. The clatter of its yellowed bones against the road grew louder as it picked up speed. It was an aged creature, completely devoid of the bits of flesh that clung to a young Bloodsoul's form.

Felan drove his horse between the two. Windows rattled with the Bloodsoul's cries. The creature clawed at Daea with its bony fingers, tearing bits of flesh from her hide. The horse's eyes widened, showing the white around them, but she stayed true to Felan's command as he backed her just out of reach. Selene did not dare come close enough to attract the creature's attention. The thing could easily kill her, unarmed as she was. The Bloodsoul dodged each swing of Felan's sword with amazing agility. It grabbed at his blade. Metal scraped against bone as Felan pulled his weapon from the creature's grasp. The Aranth moved with more speed than the most skilled Praecyr. Still, the Bloodsoul retained the upper hand. A second creature rounded the corner. It ignored both Felan and the elderly woman, who was rising from the road where she had fallen, and headed straight towards Selene. Felan's mare screamed in fear as the first Bloodsoul pulled at her saddle. Selene forced herself to concentrate. The second creature stopped only inches from her. It tilted its head up. Though devoid of eyes it seemed to show curiosity all the same. *Impossible. Concentrate, for Spirits' sake!*

A skeletal hand reached slowly out to her, so different from the swift, cutting movements of the creature's companion. Trinine did not move, though he snorted in warning. Cael had trained him well. Memories of Kailia's bloodied face visited Selene. Kailia's dying screams echoed through her. She would not leave Felan to such a fate. The creature lifted suddenly from the ground. She forced it swiftly through the air towards its brethren, who had a hold upon Felan's leg and was attempting to pull him from Daea's back. The wooden posts that lined the open side of the road shook violently at the sound that came from the bloodsoul's empty skull. Both creatures toppled over the edge of the road to the sand beneath.

Selene trotted Trinine over to Felan, who had since dismounted and was limping towards the cliff with a few short lengths of rope in one hand. Blood soaked through the fabric of his breeches in several places.

Selene climbed down from Trinine's back and peered over the chain to the sand below. The two Bloodsoul lay at the bottom, their bodies separated by the fall. She watched as the bones began to quiver then to pull towards each other, leaving sandy trails in their wake.

"What now?" Selene asked. "I suppose it's too much to hope that the Aranth have discovered a way to destroy them."

"No such luck," Felan replied as he stepped over the chain to the edge of the wall. "Can you hold them down with your ability?"

"I hope so. I'll have to wait until they're formed more completely. There are too many separate pieces right now."

"Keep them from moving as best you can so that I can tie them. After that we should search for others."

Selene waited until the bloodsoul were mostly formed, then forced their torsos down against the sand with all of the power she could muster. It required a larger amount of concentration than she anticipated. Never before had she worked with two separate entities at once. "Ready," she said hesitantly.

Felan lowered himself over the edge of the wall and dropped down to the beach below. He climbed atop one of the Bloodsoul and bound its hands to its feet. The tiny bones of fingertips and toes slid up to join with the creature as he worked. "Alright," he called when both were properly tied, "Lift them up to the road."

Selene did as Felan had asked, then lifted him up behind them. She released her concentration with no small amount of relief. The familiar ache of her latent ability came upon her with full force.

Felan tethered both bloodsoul to the nearest wooden post. Selene eyed the two creatures doubtfully as they struggled against their bonds. Glass and loose paving stones shook with their cries.

"Are you sure that they won't free themselves?" Selene asked, attempting to place her words between the creatures' screams and the pounding in her head.

"Fairly certain," Felan replied. "Their brains have long since rotted. They haven't enough wits about them to untie a knot, and they aren't able to break their own joints apart, as far as I've seen." He mounted Daea with a grunt of pain.

Selene ran over to Trinine, who had wandered down the road a few paces, and trotted him back to where Felan and Daea stood. She closed her eyes. The wounds of horse and rider closed in upon themselves. Her head ached all the more for the effort.

Felan nodded in thanks. "The woman?"

"She did not seem injured," Selene replied. "She ran off, anyway."

"We'll ask the guard to watch for her." Felan tapped Daea to a trot. "I've spoken to Xaiden. He has three Bloodsoul in the Square. We're to meet him there."

Selene followed him, but not without one final, doubtful glance back at the two groaning creatures.

The Square was thick with chaos, though there was much more of a silence about it than Selene had ever experienced. People were running in every direction, herding escaped animals and collecting wares that had been strewn about. Several children wailed in fear, though none of them looked to be injured. Three Bloodsoul were tied in the center of the area.

Xaiden rounded a corner between shops with one more in tow. He dismounted and untied the rope he had used to drag the creature, and then placed it with the others. Selene's excitement grew at the thought of weapons training under his watchful eye. Felan's swordsmanship was far better than any Praecyr she had known, yet he had found trouble with one of the creatures. Four had fallen under Xaiden's hand and he had no more than a gash upon his forearm to show for it, freely bleeding though it was.

"This is a worrisome occurrence," Xaiden said as he approached. He tied a strip of torn cloth around his arm as he rode. Selene could have easily healed the wound, yet she did not dare attempt such a thing without his permission. "Six Bloodsoul, including those which you and Selene subdued. Attacks have increased greatly since the beginning of the year."

"Should we send them to the Holding?" Felan asked.

"I will take them," Xaiden replied. "Inform Damaeus that we will need fifty members of the Standard Guard; thirty for patrols, and ten for each gate. We must be certain that no Bloodsoul remain within the city."

"Shall I fetch the other two? We left them tethered by Meiun's."

"That will not be necessary. They can harm no one while tied. The standard guard will bring them to me." Xaiden removed a square of cloth from his belt pouch and used it to clean the blade of his sword. "You will report to King Graelen on what has happened here." He coaxed Requiem to a trot, but stopped only a short distance away.

"Selene," he said thoughtfully.

"Yes, Xaiden?" Perhaps with some luck he would ask her to accompany him to the Holding. Curiosity had pulled at her unmercifully since the moment the place was mentioned.

"You will accompany Felan."

Her hopes fell like a stone through water.

"Damaeus mentioned to me this morning that you owe him several hours of practice. You will spend as much time with him as he deems necessary, after which you will have weapons training with myself."

Selene wished desperately for Xaiden to change his mind, yet she knew that any argument would be futile. She could count on one hand the number of times she had challenged a Praecyr's command. None of those instances had turned out anything near the way that she had wanted. Xaiden did not look like one to compromise, as much as he claimed himself to be equal with the other Aranth.

"As you wish," she said simply.

Felan was already half-way across the Square, but he was not moving with any great amount of speed. A moment of trotting allowed her to pull Trinine in beside his mare. "I wouldn't worry over it too much," he said as she closed in. "You'll have plenty of chances to see the Holding. Especially if these Bloodsoul attacks keep up the way they have been."

"You really shouldn't read people's thoughts without their permission, you know?" Selene snapped. Half of her irritation was for Xaiden's command, and half for Felan's discourtesy.

Felan's brow furrowed. "It's not as easy as you might believe. My Stone amplifies my latent ability, which makes it more difficult to control. Some days I pick up bits of thought without meaning to."

"You could at least make an effort to allow me some privacy. If I want to tell you something then I'll say it aloud. Don't intentionally pull things from my mind without asking."

"My apologies." He sounded as if he truly meant it. "I will do my best to keep from reading you."

"I have your word, then?" He had given in much too quickly for her liking. Then again, she did not truly know the man. Perhaps his temper was more even than she had at first thought.

"I suppose you do."

Felan reached into his belt pouch and brought out a small, dark-handled hunting knife. He ran it lightly across the palm of his hand right hand, drawing a small amount of blood.

"You cannot form a blood pact with me," Selene said with suspicion. "I am not Aranth."

"You are training to be Aranth. Thus I am not breaking any of my vows. Xaiden would not be pleased by it, but he won't know unless you tell him." He moved Daea closer to Selene's gelding and handed the knife to her. She accepted it graciously, for she had performed the ritual countless times before. Selene pulled the blade across her palm, glancing over the slightly puckered lines of everyday pacts and the dark ruts that marked promises with deeper meaning. They could be gone with the lightest touch of her latent ability, yet she would never consider healing them. To heal a pledge-wound, whether by herbs or magic, would bring great dishonor to a Rider and, she supposed, to an Aranth as well. Selene handed the knife back to Felan.

"May the Spirits bind me to truth," he said.

"May the Spirits bind me to truth," she answered. She twisted towards him, balancing carefully upon Trinine's back, and placed her palm flat upon his. The meeting of their hands sent a curiously strong warming through her mark.

"It's from the blood," Felan explained as he removed his hand. "Aranth are not permitted to form a blood pact with any other than their fellow Aranth, those in training to be Aranth, or those of the royal family. It is done to ensure that the secrets of our kind are kept." His eyes narrowed. "I did not read your thoughts," he added. "Did you know that your eyes turn to gray when you anger, even in the slightest?"

Selene nodded, ignoring the obvious jab. She was satisfied that he was being truthful. No one with any sense about them would break a blood pact. She removed her hand, ignoring the mix of dark blood that now covered it. It could not be wiped away until it had completely dried.

"Would you stable Daea for me?" Felan asked as they reached the barn. "His Majesty has a very small amount of patience when it comes to waiting, especially when the report concerns important matters such as Bloodsoul attacks."

"Certainly," Selene answered. Damaeus could wait a few moments while she took the horses in. She had no great desire to see him, truth be told.

"Thanks," Felan yelled back as he hurried towards the castle entrance. "Enjoy your lessons," he added with a sarcastic grin. "With the grace of the Tides you may be done before dinner."

Selene dismounted and took Daea's reigns. She would need more than the grace of the Tides. It would take a blessing from the Spirits themselves if she expected to be done any time before midnight.

Meeting Viverr

Islyr raised a hand to his brow in a futile attempt to shade his eyes. The short trips that he had taken from the base of the abyss to the surface each week had not properly prepared him for the unrelenting brightness of the midday sun.

His irritation grew steadily as time passed. Each day that he traveled with the boy was a test of his patience. They would reach the town of Vale soon, or so Cael had said, and he seemed to be correct more often than not on matters of distance and direction. Islyr was not certain that his serenity would last until then. Mistress Nevane had not often purchased Rakaii of less than twenty years. What few children Islyr had come into contact with had been fully trained Battle Rakaii; young in body but not in demeanor. Devren was badly in need of proper guidance, and Cael was ill equipped to deal with him while in falcon form. The boy was headstrong. He acted as if those around him should simply comply with his every whim.

Islyr watched Devren with half-closed eyes. The boy ambled slowly, eating a handful of sunberries that he had found growing near the path. He walked as if he had never been made to cover any great distance in his life. He also complained often of aches in his feet, and had goaded Islyr into stopping prematurely on each of the past three nights.

"When will we stop next?" Devren asked between berries. "It's past noon. Cael could catch us some rabbit or quail. We could rest while we roast it."

Cael glided above as they walked, never straying so far that he could not keep a proper eye on the boy.

"We will stop a half-hour before dusk. Any respite before that time would be wasteful. You want to reach Evaria soon, am I correct?"

"Yes, but," Devren began.

"Every minute we squander is another minute of danger for your father," Islyr said. "The next time you complain we will walk on past dark with only berries and a few strips of dried meat for our dinner."

Cael landed gracefully upon the boy's shoulder. The bird seemed amused by the words that passed between them.

"So where *did* you get these things?" Devren asked, lifting his sword in Islyr's direction. He often changed the subject of conversation suddenly when the Tides were not flowing his way.

"Looting," Islyr replied.

"Looting," Devren echoed. "You mean from dead bodies?"

"Yes. That is exactly what I mean." Islyr was not in a mood to be bothered by such things. The boy was old enough to know the ways of the world.

Devren dropped his sword with a disgusted look. Cael nipped his shoulder, after which the boy retrieved it from the dusty path, if somewhat reluctantly.

"Why leave things to rot away when they could be of use to me?" Islyr said. "Dead people have no need for weapons or armor."

"You should bring them back to life like you did with me and Cael." The boy looked thoughtful for a moment. "At least the ones that you are able to."

"I can't just go around raising every dead thing I see." Islyr said, shifting his staff between hands. "A delicate equilibrium exists between living creatures and the dead. It would not be wise to upset that balance. I made an exception for you because of circumstance. Don't give me cause to regret my decision."

"I'm sure you would want someone to bring you back if you'd been sent to the Spirits," Devren muttered.

"There are far worse things in this world than death," Islyr replied calmly. "In fact, I've witnessed quite a few of them first hand. I could show you one or two, if you'd like."

Devren scowled for a moment before wolfing down the rest of his berries. Cael lifted from the boy's shoulder to scout the path ahead. He returned rather quickly amidst an agitated torrent of screeching noises. Devren's expression changed suddenly from irritation to worry.

"Trouble?" Islyr asked. Cael and the boy had been teaching him falcon speech, but the few noises he had memorized were not near enough to glean anything useful.

"Maybe. Three members of Vale's guard and one prisoner. They're readying rope for a hanging." He stopped for a moment to listen to the falcon. "No spectators, though. Just the four of them."

"We'll go around," Islyr said. "Through the woods. We don't want to draw any attention to ourselves." Nothing in the forest could be near as horrific as the creatures he had dealt with in the abyss.

"Kii-reh," Cael said as he flew over to perch upon Islyr's shoulder.

Islyr understood that particular sound perfectly. "Then what would you suggest?"

The falcon made a few low noises, none of which he could form into anything even mildly comprehendible.

"He says we should help the man," Devren relayed, though he did not seem to agree. "If it is a hanging then he may be marked."

Islyr's foul mood vanished in an instant. "Little wonder that you two ended up as you did," he said with a laugh. If Cael did not worry for the boy's welfare in a fight then why should he? "Fine. I'm always prepared for battle."

He still longed for the pit at times. Every Marked One he slaughtered created a hollow in his soul, yet every win thrilled him in a way that was difficult to convey. Mistress Nevane had trained him to kill without remorse. Perhaps that training would never leave him. "We should listen in first," he suggested, at once returning to his senses. "He may not be marked, though the chance is small. I won't risk my life for a common criminal."

"Sounds reasonable," Devren replied as if he had any choice in the matter. "They're just past the next bend in the path."

Cael said nothing. Perhaps it was sign of his approval.

"You will stay here." Islyr handed Devren the sword that he had brought for Cael. "There is less chance that I will be noticed if I go alone. I'll return momentarily."

The boy sat down by the side of the road with a grateful expression upon his face.

Islyr followed the path until it began to curve. He then moved off to one side, settling himself down behind a cluster of tine bushes. There were indeed three guard members ahead. They wore light leather armor which had been dyed in deep red and dusky grey to form a pattern of squares upon their vests. The first restrained a trussed prisoner, who stood beneath largest branch of an aged sablewood tree. A second stood behind him, holding a coil of rope with an eager expression. The last looked to be the one in charge, for he gripped a rolled piece of parchment.

"Unbind me," the prisoner demanded in a sharp northern accent. He was short for a man, most especially for a northerner. His hair hung loose above mismatched clothing which was heavily soiled and torn. "Double-dealing bastards. We had a bargain." The man twisted his wrists. "You'd better hope that these ropes are good and tight, or your next breath will be your dying one. Fine to slay a child, but a man isn't so easy to silence, eh? The Spirits will have you for that."

The guardsman forced the prisoner to his knees with a heavy hand.

Building his own Pyre, Islyr thought irritably. *They should have gagged him as well.*

The man who held the rope moved forward to throw it over the branch beneath which the prisoner knelt. The mix of heated pleas and empty threats which spewed from the man's mouth increased tenfold. Islyr inched closer to get a better view.

The guardsman who held the parchment carefully unrolled it and began to read. He was older than Islyr had at first thought, with wisps of gray running through his otherwise dark hair. His voice was dry and rasping, like wheels grinding in a mill. "Viverr Templain," he began as one of the others tied a ragged strip of cloth around the prisoner's head to cover his eyes. The name stirred something in Islyr's memory, though he could not seem to draw the thought completely to the surface of his mind.

"We, as members of Vale's Standard Guard, bring you here on this day in the presence of the Spirits to see that justice is properly served in the name of the Lady Tynalin Middale and the righteous citizens of Vale. A private execution by way of hanging has been most civilly granted by the Lady Middale in exchange for information regarding the whereabouts of One Aurin Fetlask." It was another name that pulled at Islyr's memories. With a few more moments of thought perhaps he could free it.

"I should've expected as much from your type," Viverr said as the hanging rope was fitted to his neck. "A whoremonger has got more honor than you lot combined."

He received a strong kick to the stomach for his troubles.

"The Spirits keep you!"

"Speak again and I'll do worse," said the guardsman to the rogue's right. "You'll beg Emel to hang you before we've finished." He drew a hacking breath and launched a mixture of yellow mucus and chewing tobacco onto Viverr's face.

The guardsman with the rope, who Islyr assumed must be Emel, chuckled. "Thanks a bunch, my good fellow," He gave the rope a playful tug which caused the rogue to gasp for air. "Couldn't have gotten by without you."

Viverr remained silent as the spittle oozed its way down to his chin.

"Enough now. We've got to do this official." The elder guardsman offered a knowing smirk to his companions before continuing. "The prisoner who stands before us has been tried and rightly accused of: Fourteen counts of thievery in the major degree, three counts of thievery in the minor degree, nine counts of illegal use of a weapon within the city's walls, one count of assault upon a city official, sixteen counts of disorderly behavior whilst under the influence of intoxicating substances, three counts of forgery, five counts of consorting with persons of an objectionable nature, and one count of murder of an innocent child."

Islyr stood silently, preparing to leave. This man deserved to be hanged, even if he was marked. *Not hanged,* he corrected. *Drawn and quartered, or perhaps left in the abyss for the shadeslight to do with as they please.*

"What happened? You said you'd be right back."

Islyr dropped his staff. He grabbed the back of the boy's head with one hand and covered his mouth with the other, knowing that it was most likely too late.

"Who goes there?" the elder guardsman called out.

Islyr released Devren's head and retrieved his weapon, all while cursing the boy's inability to follow what he considered to be a rather straightforward command.

"Eavesdropping upon official business of the Vale Standard Guard is considered a heavy offence. Show yourselves immediately and we may be lenient."

Islyr moved slowly to where he could be seen. He retrieved his staff from the leaf litter, but kept it out to one side. Devren stood with him, his hands held away from his sword. He seemed to know exactly what the guardsman expected of him. Islyr was not at all surprised by it, especially with what he had learned of the boy's history.

"Over here, where we can see you properly."

The other two guardsmen had drawn their swords. They scrutinized Islyr with expressions that held varying degrees of displeasure. He walked cautiously towards them, motioning for the boy to follow. "You act when I do," he whispered. "Not a moment before."

Devren nodded shortly.

"Stand there," the old man said, motioning towards the base of the sablewood tree. "Unhand your weapons."

Islyr placed his staff upon the path and stepped back. Devren dropped his sword, but with a much deeper glower of irritation than he had ever held for any of Islyr's commands.

"What business do you have here?"

"We have no business in this place, in truth," Islyr began carefully. "We are merely traveling towards the fine city of Vale. We wished to be sure that whoever lay ahead would do us no harm. My friend and I will quickly be on our way, if you would be so kind as to allow it."

The guardsman looked Islyr over. His gaze lingered for a long moment upon the tattoo that swept from beneath his hair onto his face. A flash of white caught Islyr's eye. Cael had perched himself on the lowest branch of a dead lireleaf tree that stood across the path.

"Be on your way," the elder guardsman said at last.

Islyr retrieved his staff. He watched as the boy slid his sword back into place. He then stepped carefully around Viverr, who knelt with the hanging rope still fastened around his neck.

"Be quick of it," the guardsman added. "We could easily prepare more rope."

Islyr's mark grew warm suddenly. He looked down to find the prisoner's bound hands clutching his wrist.

The rogue's mouth dropped open. "Brother," he whispered. "Have pity. Don't leave me to these wolves."

"What's this?" The elder guardsman levered his sword once again from its scabbard. "You are acquainted with this scoundrel?"

"Never seen him before," Islyr replied as he pulled his wrist from Viverr's grasp. "The ramblings of a condemned man, I expect. Some will say anything when they know their life is forfeit." He grabbed the boy's arm and pulled him along. They could come back for Cael's weapon after night fell.

"Hold up," the guardsman said, pointing the tip of his sword towards Islyr's throat.

Emel dropped the hanging rope and moved swiftly to aid in blocking their path.

"Check them."

Emel grabbed Devren's wrist.

Islyr brought his staff up beneath the guardsman's chin with full force. A satisfying crack issued from the man's jaw as the bone shattered. The guardsman released Devren and stumbled backwards, providing Islyr the room he needed to swing back. His second blow struck the back of the man's skull.

The clang of metal weapons sounded behind him. Islyr hoped that the boy had not lied when telling of his swordsmanship. He was given no time to worry on it. The eldest guardsman surged towards Islyr, raising his sword evenly with both hands. Islyr blocked the strike just before it descended upon his chest. His wrists jolted back painfully as the blade struck near the center of his staff. Screeching noises pierced the air. Islyr's eyes darted in the direction of the sound. Cael had sailed down from his perch and was clawing at the guardsman who fought Devren. Blood dripped from the man's forehead and into his eyes as he lashed out wildly with his sword in attempt to dodge the falcon's blows.

Islyr stepped down upon the foot of the elder guardsman and pushed him back hard, thus releasing his staff from the man's sword. The man stumbled slightly, but kept a firm grip upon his weapon. He then lurched back in preparation for another blow. His halting movements left him wide open to Islyr's attack. It was difficult to believe that Vale's guard was so poorly trained. Battle Rakaii in the first year of instruction had better weapons skills than these men. The guardsman doubled over in pain as Islyr's staff struck him squarely between the legs. Islyr took the opportunity he was given, bringing his staff down upon the man's sword arm with enough force to fracture the bone. The guardsman issued a grunt of pain and dropped his weapon. Islyr kicked the sword out of the man's reach, then pounded the blunt end of his staff into his temple. The guardsman collapsed. Blood pooled in the dry grass beside the road.

The clanging of metal had ceased. Islyr turned to search for Devren. He found sitting in a miserable heap, tears leaking from his eyes to his chin. Apparently his swordsmanship was decent enough.

Islyr thought idly of his first kill. He had never learned the man's name. True names were not meant for slaves. The Kerell had called him Ursus, for Ursus meant bear in the ancient language and his mark was of a large mountain bear. Not all slaves were named for their mark, though all slaves' names were given in the ancient language. Ferir was the name Mistress Nevane had given Islyr after his battle with

Ursus, for his ability to strike quickly, or so she had said. Before that he had simply been known as Novus de Nevane; the newest from the house of Nevane. The battle had continued for nearly an hour before Islyr's bladed staff came crashing to his opponent's temple. Ursus had bled to death engulfed by the cheers of nearly three hundred spectators. Mistress Nevane had gained one hundred and twenty gold pieces for his victory. It was a fair prize for a beginner's match. Islyr's reward had been his opponent's heart, which he had been forced to consume while it was still warm. That night he had cried until sleep took him.

Islyr plucked the boy's sword from the dirt. He wiped the blood from it upon a patch of dry grass that grew near the road, then tucked the blade into his belt.

"You alright?" He offered a hand to Devren. The boy accepted it as he stood, wiping his cheeks with the back of his free hand.

"Yes. I'll take my sword back."

Islyr slid the weapon out, holding the hilt in Devren's direction. He had not expected that the boy would want to handle his sword so soon after what he had done. Devren grabbed it with a rather stubborn look upon his face.

Cael cried out suddenly. He lifted from Devren's shoulder and flew to perch upon the sablewood tree, near the center of the largest branch. The rope still hung there, drifting slightly with the breeze. Viverr was no longer beneath it.

Islyr's eyes found him shortly. The man moved on his knees, shuffling clumsily towards the forest with no small amount of haste. His hands and feet were still loosely bound. The rogue's blindfold had moved down from his forehead to hang to one side, barely covering his eyes. Islyr caught up to him with little effort. "Journeying, are we?" He grabbed the man's dirty collar.

"I'm innocent!" Viverr whimpered. He flailed his bound arms in an attempt to writhe from Islyr's grasp.

Islyr pulled the blindfold from the rogue's head and tossed it aside. Viverr stared up at him. It was clear by the look of shock upon his face that he had expected Vale's guardsmen to triumph over a scruffy looking man and a boy with a rusted sword.

"Brother," he muttered. "You sent them where they belong, eh? You fellows did a fair job of it, though I might have done it better. I'd have been gone had you come upon us a moment later."

"Don't call me that," Islyr said sternly. "I don't care what else you've done, but no one who murders children is any blood of mine. That aside, you almost had us both killed. Were you attempting to add a second child to your conscience?"

"I am not a child," Devren called out from across the road.

Spirits, the boy recovered quickly.

"Anyone who cannot follow simple orders is a child by my logic," Islyr shot back.

Cael watched with interest from his perch on the sablewood tree.

"Shall we haul you back to Vale, then?" Islyr asked, turning his attention back to Viverr. "I wonder what bounty the countess gives for escaped prisoners. A fair amount, I suppose, since you've just killed three of her guards." He had no intention of turning the man in, but Viverr could not possibly know it. He dragged him to the side of the road, then pulled the hanging rope down from the branch and used it to tether his legs to a fallen log that lay nearby.

"Don't act 'till you hear the truth," Viverr pleaded. "Emel and his guardsmen murdered the girl." His bound hands moved to his throat in a cutting motion. "Slit her throat straight through. I didn't have anything to do with the killing. Swear it on the Spirits."

That did fit with what Islyr had heard the guardsmen say, but only a fool would put their trust in the word of a rogue. "Go on," he said simply. It was more difficult to lie when the questioner offered you no words upon which to base your falsehood. He did not want to provide Viverr with any advantage in altering his opinion.

"Her name was Laridane." Viverr's bottom lip twisted as he spoke. "An urchin. A drifter girl. Her type is plentiful in Vale's lower parts. She asked Emel for coin. Worst mistake of her short life. That man's got the temper of an injured bull. Emel has-" Viverr glanced down at the man's body with a nervous smile. "I suppose I should say that he *had* no patience for beggars, eh? Laridane learned that hard. A pity, with what talent she had for thievery."

Islyr would take from the dead with no guilt, but to steal from those still living was unfathomable. He nodded his head for Viverr to continue.

"I was in the alley on business that night."

"What business?" Islyr asked.

"Meeting my friends is all."

Islyr decided that he most likely did not want to know what business Viverr would have in an alley at night, and so he let the subject drop. He could force it out of him later, if needed.

"Saw the whole thing," the rogue continued. "Then Emel and his buddies got it in their heads to catch me and offer a deal in return for my freedom. They said if I took the blame for Laridane's death they'd ask the Lady Middale for a private hanging. They promised to let me off once we were outside the city. I had no choice, really, so I went along with it. Put me to question first." Viverr lifted his shirt to reveal a layer of purple and yellow bruises. "There's worse down below, but I'm sure you don't want to see that, eh?"

Islyr was certain that he did not.

"Lucky for me they didn't strip me before they beat me. Never crossed their minds that I might be marked, I guess. Then they found out that I was already a wanted man. Not sure if that changed their plan or not. Likely they had no intention of freeing me in the first place."

"Finish your story."

"You know the rest," Viverr replied. "That's guessing you were watching things for any length of time."

Either the man was being truthful or he had quite a talent for creating convincing stories. Islyr tore off a piece of Emel's shirt and wet it from his wineskin, then held the cloth out to Viverr. The rogue clutched it between his bound hands and wiped away what spittle remained on his face, then threw the cloth aside.

"Thanks," he mumbled.

"So all of the things that they accused you of, I suppose that none of them are true?"

"Oh no," the rogue's cheek twitched into half of a smile. "They're all true, except for the last one. I would never murder an innocent girl, nor a not so innocent one, just so you know."

Cael flew down from his branch to perch upon Islyr's shoulder. He uttered a few low noises. Islyr's mind translated what it could. Cael thought that the boy should decide Viverr's fate.

Why not? It would be entertaining, at least.

"Devren, come here a moment."

Islyr had no doubt that Devren had heard the entire tale, for he stood no more than a few paces from the path. The boy ran to Islyr's side, anxious to be a part of what was happening.

"I offer you a chance to prove your adult nature. You will choose our good friend's fate." He slapped Viverr heartily on the back. "I will abide by your decision without question." Islyr seated himself upon the dry grass a few steps away. This would likely turn out to be the best part of his day.

Devren looked more joyful than Islyr had ever seen him. He circled Viverr with an air of importance, straightening his back and putting a hand to his chin as if to pull thoughtfully at a beard he did not yet have.

"Please," Viverr began. "I ask humbly for mercy, my tiny lord."

"Be still!" Devren commanded. "Every word you speak from now until I have made my decision will earn you nothing by my wrath."

Viverr sat back in stunned silence.

Islyr worked hard to keep a smile from creeping onto his face.

"We have four options, as I see it," the boy said as he continued to pace around Viverr's kneeling form. "Two of those I will dismiss at this moment."

The rogue watched him with wide eyes.

"I deem killing you to be improper given the circumstances. However, it would not be fair to Islyr and myself, given what you have put us through, to set you free."

It seemed as if the boy had suddenly matured. He was wholly at ease in his actions.

"That brings us to the third option: turning you over to the city of Vale to do with as they will."

Viverr drew an audible breath.

"That I also consider inappropriate seeing as they will likely hang you for being marked, something which I do not consider to be a crime."

Islyr found that he did not care in the least what the rogue thought of him. Of all of the things that had happened in the past few weeks, this was by far the most amusing.

"You owe us twice; once for almost getting us killed, and again because we freed you from your captors." Devren bent down in order to look Viverr in the face. "You shall travel with us. You will help us fight until your debt has been paid. You'll have to abide by our rules as long as you are with us." He threw a glance in Islyr's direction. "What do you think?"

"Very reasonable," Islyr replied.

"Can I speak now, Master Devren?" Viverr asked.

"Don't start with that," Islyr said. "The boy's quite full of self-importance as it is."

Devren rolled his eyes.

"Alright. Devren it is, then. Could you possibly untie me? Since we're to be partners now, I mean. Can't go around with my hands and feet bound, eh?"

Devren reached down to him.

"Wait," Islyr said, approaching the rogue. "I want you to know that we are releasing your bonds on good faith. If you should run from us and I happen to find you, which I will, your life will not be spared a second time. I will not turn you in to the guard of Vale, but you will certainly wish I had before I am through with you." Islyr's stomach tightened as similar words, those Mistress Nevane had spoken to him so long ago, slid through his mind. He untied Viverr from the log, then took the hunting knife from his belt and set the man's hands and feet free.

"You can start by helping us search the bodies," Islyr said with a furtive glance towards Devren. The boy did not seem terribly disturbed by the prospect. A good sign. They would need all the luck of the Tides in order to avoid more killing on this journey. "Don't take anything that is marked with Vale's colors, none of their swords or personal items that may be identifiable. And be quick about it. We need to get rid of these before someone comes along and sees them."

"You've got my oath, upon my mother's lost ashes, that I'll do my best to aid you on your journey until my debt is paid," Viverr said, rubbing his wrists. The skin was red and torn in places from the tightness of his bonds. He reached into the Emel's belt pouch and began to rummage through it. "I haven't seen my last partner in ages, you know. A great man, Sir Aurin Fetlask."

"So what exactly did this *great man* do to earn a betrayal of his location to Vale's guards?" Islyr asked as he pulled the elder guard's money pouch from his belt. It contained five gold pieces and several copper. The city of Vale apparently paid them well. "I hope you don't treat all of your companions in such a way."

Viverr's brow furrowed. "So you heard that, did you?"

"I did."

"It wasn't like it seemed," Viverr said, holding up a short knife. It was well used, but the quality of its making was evident. Islyr nodded in approval, and the rogue handed it over.

"It's easy to convince someone that you're being truthful. You just need to tell them what they want to hear."

"And what did they want to hear?"

"That Aurin was in hiding. In Falnea, no less. He isn't there, of course, though I have heard some rumors to that effect."

"That was smart," Devren said with a laugh. "It'll take them the better part of a month to get there." He pulled a small, green gem from the guardsman's coat and held it up to the light. Cael had taken his place upon the boy's shoulder and seemed to be advising him on what to keep. "I imagine they'll be in quite a foul mood when they return. You had better get yourself far from Vale by that time."

"That shouldn't be a problem. I'll be traveling with you three now. I don't plan on going back there for as long as I can help it."

"Your plans will have to change," Islyr said sharply.

Viverr opened his mouth as if to protest, but Islyr cut him off before he had a chance to begin complaining. "We are in need of a void-charm; therefore we require the aid of a Mage. You will show us where to find one. Vale is the largest town for miles, and we're near it now. The closer we come to Evaria, the more chance there is that we will run into trouble. We may need Cael's help in the next few days."

"A void-charm, eh? You've been cursed, have you?"

"Not exactly," Devren cut in. "Cael and I have had our affin-" He winced as Cael snapped at his head, but recovered quickly. "Neither of us can transform. He's caught in animal form and I'm stuck as a human. We'll get the void-charm, and then Cael will try to change to human form while touching it. That will reactivate the spell, giving the charm a chance to soak it up. He'll be ok then, and better able to help us. We'll have to wait until we reach my father to get one for me, though. I'm sure that we don't have enough money for two."

"Oh, really?" the rogue said, opening a pouch of what looked to be pipe tobacco and giving its contents a tentative sniff. "And just what do you plan on saying to the Mage when you reach him? You can't possibly tell him the truth."

"We don't need to explain everything to him," Devren replied. "We'll just tell him that we need a void-charm, he'll give us one then we'll pay and be on our way. How hard can it be?"

"I've never met a Mage who sold anything without twenty questions to the buyer," Viverr said knowingly. "It just isn't done."

"No more quarreling," Islyr said suddenly. He was quickly tiring of Viverr's attitude. "We are going to Vale. We could drop you at the guard station on our way in if you still wish to argue on it. Help me clear these bodies. We've wasted enough time already."

The rogue did not protest any further.

Islyr and Viverr carried the dead men and their weapons a few yards into the woods and covered them as well as they could with brush and fallen leaves. Devren did not offer to help, but instead chose to stay and sweep the blood soaked dirt from the road with a branch. Islyr did not push him. The boy had endured enough for one day, even if he did not choose to show it at the moment. They returned to find him resting idly upon a log. Cael's sword lay upon the ground nearby. The area looked much the way it had before the struggle, with the exception of a few small pools blood that lingered upon the grass at the far side of the path.

"How far to Vale?" Islyr asked.

"Not as far as I'd like," Viverr replied. "But you can't just pass through the gates dragging me behind you."

"That may be true, or it may not be. Either way we are going." Islyr thought for a moment. "What is your mark?"

"Ferret," the rogue said reluctantly.

"Perfect. You will tell us how to get to the Mage's place of residence, then you will transform. You can stay in my belt pouch until we leave Vale. No one will pay any extra notice to a man with his hunting ferret."

"Perhaps you could catch us a few rabbits as well," Devren added with a laugh.

Viverr did not seem at all amused, nor did Cael.

"What about my things?" the rogue griped.

"Devren will carry them for you."

A scowl crossed the boy's face.

"Do as you're told." Islyr said sternly. "Unless you do not wish Cael to return to human form?"

The boy offered no further argument.

"What errand are you three on, anyway?" Viverr asked cautiously. "It's not something that'll get me killed, is it?"

"We will tell you of it later, perhaps," Islyr replied. "But only if you keep to your word."

Viverr stood silent for a moment. He did not seem to be enjoying the situation. "Once you pass the second wall head up the main street," he said at last. "Turn down the third road on your left. Turn left again when you reach The Fat Sow. It's hard to miss, as it's the largest butcher's shop in Vale. Madame Covern's is down the alley there. It's the fifth shop on your right. That's where you want to go."

"Are you certain?" Islyr asked. "That doesn't sound much like any Mage's shop I've heard of."

"Well, you could wander Vale for a couple days searching for something you'll never find, if you'd rather. There are three Mages in Vale, all spread out to separate corners of the city. Ask someone for directions to a Mage's shop and you'll not only attract attention to yourselves, but you'll get a different answer from each person you question."

"Fine," Islyr said reluctantly, "but if you betray us, the Spirits help me I'll-"

"No need to worry," Viverr put his arm around Islyr's shoulder. "We're comrades now, eh?" The rogue smelled of sweat and stale blood. "We've got to protect each other's interests, am I right?"

"Use your mark." Islyr pulled from Viverr's grasp. "We have stayed here much too long."

Viverr transformed as if he had done it a thousand times; quickly and with no hint of the pain he surely felt. Using your mark was agonizing on a regular occasion, yet when the body was damaged it became excruciating beyond belief. It pained Islyr to watch. He turned to the boy in an attempt to keep old memories from surfacing. Devren looked to the rogue with envy.

Islyr turned back to find Viverr crawling from beneath his clothes, which now lay in a jumbled pile on the path. He looked much like the hunting ferrets Islyr remembered from Maresbane; a long, weasel-like body and short legs covered with a coat of brown that darkened to black at his feet and tail. His pointed face was rimmed in white, in the center of which was a mask of sable colored fur.

Islyr plucked him easily from the path and held him up so that Viverr's dark, rounded eyes were level with his own. "No trouble." A strong, earthy scent emanated from the rogue. "You remember to act like a ferret, or we'll all be in line for the hangman's noose."

Viverr nodded. Islyr opened his largest belt pouch. He moved several items to the side and placed Viverr into it. The ferret peered out from beneath the flap.

Islyr gathered Viverr's things and rolled them in the rogue's shirt, securing the items with a length of the hanging rope. He handed the bundle to Devren, then took Cael's sword from the boy and pushed it down behind his belt.

The distance to Vale was indeed short. Within moments Islyr found himself looking up at a set of massive iron gates and the dark, rusted spikes that ran the length of them. The colossal structure was set into a rough-hewn stone wall that surrounded the entire city.

"Be still and let me handle this," Islyr said as they drew closer. The comment was meant as much for Viverr as it was for Devren.

The ferret crouched down into Islyr's pouch as they neared the guard station. Four guardsmen stood beneath the partially raised gate; two men on the right to examine those entering the city, and two on the left for those leaving. They were dressed much like the guardsmen that had been with Viverr, save for the left side of the dyed leather armor that covered their chests, upon which a bounding stag was embroidered in black thread.

Islyr leaned heavily upon his staff as they approached. He lifted his right leg carefully, as if to avoid putting pressure upon it.

"Your names?" The guardsman was a short man whose cheekbones stood out slightly from the rest of his face, giving his eyes a sunken appearance. He regarded Islyr's tattoo with a look of vexation. Islyr silently thanked the Spirits that the man did not recognize it for what it truly was.

"My name is Arcis," Islyr said calmly. "This is my brother, Rumel." They were names from a story Islyr had been told while in the service of Mistress Nevane. The Marked Ones whose minds has not become addled by days of endless slaughter and repeated blows to the head spread tales amongst themselves to pass the time before matches. It was a good way to take one's thoughts away from the sure fact that for some of them, the match would be their last.

The story, as Islyr remembered it, told of two brothers and their attempt to sell an aged bull to a dim-witted merchant. The boys managed to convince the man, through the course of the tale, that the animal was a prized milking cow. It was not at all a story suitable for children.

The guardsman dutifully wrote the names in a thick book that sat on a wooden pedestal. He did not appear to give them a great deal of thought, much to Islyr's relief.

"Family name?"

"Forthtine."

"Town of birth?"

"Kylinn." It was close to Maresbane, but not close enough for anyone there to recognize his name. There was not much of a chance that anyone in Maresbane would know him by description, especially with the tattoo that the Kerell had placed upon his face, but Islyr would not take any chances. Selene and Maye were safe in Maresbane, and he would like very much to keep them that way. No one would believe that his sister was a Marked One unless it was shown to them. Marked females were simply unheard of in this place. His family would be protected from the Elders and the Kerell as long as he did not return to them.

"State your business here."

"We are traveling towards Belamun on family business. We've stopped here to purchase supplies for our continued journey."

"Length of stay?"

"Two days, at the most."

The information was recorded in a hurried hand.

"That is quite an unusual falcon." The guardsman eyed Cael suspiciously. "Must've cost you."

Islyr could feel Viverr shivering through the leather of his belt pouch.

"Thank you, sir," Devren said before Islyr had a chance to speak. "Our father gave him to me. He trains falcons to hunt quail and the like. We sell most of them, but the white ones always stay in the family. Father says they're good luck, so that must be the truth of it."

Islyr was not sure what profession Devren's father followed, but it certainly had nothing to do with training hunting birds. He subdued a smile. The boy picked things up quickly as long as they were of use to him. It would be best to keep an eye on him while he was around Viverr, lest the rogue teach him any irritating habits that could not be easily broken.

"You'll need to bind that sword," the guard said, handing Devren a cord of leather. "Yours as well," he added with a cautious glance in Islyr's direction.

It seemed that Devren's story had been accepted.

The second guard suddenly spoke. Monotone words exited his mouth in an orderly fashion. "No weapons shall be drawn whilst in the city of Vale. Any man caught with a weapon unbound within the walls of the city shall be detained in the reformatory for a period determined by the Lady Tynalin Middale. They shall then take punishment according to the Lady's judgment. Is that understood?"

"Yes, sir," Islyr said, nearly in unison with the boy's response. It seemed that the ruse with his staff had worked as well. They had not made any mention of him binding it, at least.

The guardsman helped Devren tie his sword, wrapping the leather cord around the hilt, then around the boy's belt. He pulled a second length of leather from his pouch and tied the sword they had brought for Cael in a similar manner.

"Be on your way then," the guardsman said.

Islyr kept his eyes forward as he limped down the road, so as not to draw suspicion. They passed beneath a second wall which, like the first, was equipped with a large, spiked iron gate, then traveled up the main street until they came to the road Viverr had mentioned. Shops with gray slate roofs and large glass windows to display their wares were dispersed evenly between similar looking houses. Narrow alleys ran between each, though most were stopped dead by a fence or wall within a few yards.

Vendors working out of wheelbarrows and small, wooden hanging trays moved up and down the street hawking everything from roasted meats to hair ribbons. The crowds moved lazily aside as the occasional team drawn carriage or lone rider pushed through.

Soon they came to the third true road on the left. It was nearly as wide as the main road, and twice as crowded. Islyr ushered Devren down it, steering him away from an unkempt man who had been pushing the boy to purchase a rather dodgy looking meat roll. Islyr found it increasingly difficult to keep his composure as they sidestepped shouting vendors, stray dogs, and shabby looking children playing games of fox and mouse. This city reminded him much of the city of Khnum, though the aroma of the ocean was not amongst the heavy scents of food, sweat, and waste. It was in Khnum that he had first been put up for auction. It was there that he had been trained for battle.

The Fat Sow came upon them shortly. It was indeed one of the largest butcher's shops Islyr had ever seen. Its green and white striped awning stretched the length of three standard shops. Cuts of beef and venison hung beneath it alongside skinned rabbits and plucked geese. The cries of live chickens and ducks could be heard, though the bins which held them were obscured by the crowd. The front of the store was engulfed in a sea of bodies struggling to gain entrance. The wave of haggling shouts and bickering was nearly enough to deafen him.

Islyr slipped through the narrow space left by the crowd, dodging more than a few angry women who assumed that he had come to muscle his way into the line. The language of one rather rotund, graying lady was enough to make a Battle Warden blush.

Islyr pushed his way around the corner and into the relative silence of the alley. He pulled the boy down the road until the roar of the mob was reduced to naught. Cael launched himself from Devren's shoulder to perch upon a nearby lamppost. Viverr stuck his nose out from Islyr's pouch to scan the area.

"Hold still." Islyr grabbed Devren's arm. He freed the boy's weapon, and then retied it with a careful hand.

"How does it look?" he asked.

"Just the same as before," Devren replied, rolling his eyes. "It wasn't loose. We're wasting time."

"You're a fine one to tell me that I'm wasting time," Islyr growled. "Draw your sword."

"Are you daft? You just fixed it so I can't."

"Just do as I say for once. But be discreet, if you can manage it."

The boy levered his sword from his belt with no difficulty. His jaw dropped in shock. Islyr pushed the sword back before anyone had a chance to notice.

"You should teach me how to do that." There was awe in the boy's voice.

"You should learn to trust me," Islyr answered. "Now close your mouth. You look like a netted fish."

The boy complied without comment. Islyr started off down the road, not bothering to wait for him. "Don't remove it unless your life is in danger," he warned as the boy sprinted to catch up.

Madame Covern's was indeed the fifth shop on the right, just as Viverr had said, though it did not look at all as Islyr would have liked. Three level stone steps led up to an old wooden door painted in a garish lavender color. A sign with a tailor's needle and spool hung quaintly above a window filled with bolts of cloth as well as pre-made dresses, shirts and breeches.

"This doesn't look much like a Mage's shop," Devren said with a frown.

Islyr was inclined to agree. He slid down the nearest alley, dragging the boy behind him. Devren wrinkled his nose as they entered. The area smelled strongly of rotting meat and emptied chamber pots.

Islyr pulled Viverr from his pouch. It was difficult to resist the urge to squeeze the breath from him. "My patience is growing thin," he said as calmly as he could manage. "You will transform, and explain to me exactly why you've given us directions to a seamstress' shop. Then you will take us to a place where we can get what we need. Do you understand?"

Viverr nodded his head slowly. Islyr placed him upon the ground. Within seconds he was back in human form. The rogue brushed the dirt from his skin, then dressed using the bundle of clothes that Devren had carried for him. Every inch of his skin, save for what could not be covered by clothing, was taken by a blanket of colorful bruises and partially healed wounds. A branding mark in the shape of a bounding stag stood out in raised, irritated flesh upon his side.

"I meant no harm," Viverr said as he finished dressing. "I just thought you might want to get some clothing for your friend before we fetch the void-charm. A naked man wandering the streets will attract attention for sure."

"You lied to us," Devren grumbled.

"No," Viverr replied. "I said this was where you'd want to go. You weren't listening."

Islyr took a few deep breaths in an attempt to calm himself. The silence was broken as a few of the Fat Sow's customers strolled by Madame Covern's with their newly acquired cuts of meat. "Fine, but there will be no more of this. No more lies. No half-truths. We'll get Cael some clothing, but then you take us someplace where we can get a void-charm. Agreed?"

"Nowhere else until we fix their predicament," Viverr agreed.

Islyr followed the rogue back out into the street.

"Madame Covern is a good friend of mine. No need for worry."

Best to start worrying when a rogue says something like that. Islyr gripped his staff with both hands.

Viverr led them up the stone steps at the front of the shop. A bundle of harness bells rang out as Devren shut the door behind them. The dry air smelled slightly of clothier's vinegar. The area was quite a bit smaller than Islyr had imagined. Narrow tables spanned from one side of the room to the other, each covered from end to end with neat stacks of bolted cloth. Draped fabric hung from every wall, as well as from the counter and the back of the chair that sat behind it. Islyr turned his gaze to the floor in attempt to give his eyes respite from the stomach-churning mass of color. Long, multihued rugs ran between each aisle, allowing him no relief. He looked up to find Devren pulling at a loose piece of pea green material, the end of which protruded from a rather unstable looking pile. Islyr pushed the boy's hand away from it and ushered him up to the store's gaudy counter.

"A pleasure to see you, Madame." Viverr bowed graciously as a well-proportioned woman with close cropped, dark hair sauntered out from behind a velvet curtain. The fabric of her dress, which was a painfully bright color of orange, clung tightly to her body at the waist. It was cut so low at the bosom that Islyr was certain that her breasts would fall out of it at any moment. He forced his eyes away and stepped closer to the counter, partly in attempt to block the slow grin that had begun to spread across Devren's face. Viverr lowered his head to kiss the jeweled ring that graced the woman's right hand.

"Viverr." Madame Covern's voice was low and soft. "How wonderful it is to see you as well." She smiled at Islyr, then moved around the counter to where Devren stood. She leaned down to him. The boy's gaze shifted quickly to her face. "I see you've brought some friends."

"This is Arcis," he said, gesturing towards Islyr, "and his brother, Rumel."

At least the rogue had enough sense not to use their true names.

"You are a handsome one, aren't you?" She laughed a little as she put a finger to Devren's cheek. "A bit too young for me, but I do have a few girls about your age. I'm sure they would be delighted to have your company."

Devren's face colored. Islyr realized at once why the shop seemed so small. It was split into two with the back half holding a different, no doubt much more lucrative, business.

The boy's smile grew suddenly, as if he had just made the same realization.

Cael watched silently from atop an unused dressmaker's dummy that stood near the door. He did not

make a move to stop Madame Covern. Perhaps he did not
consider Devren to be in any danger, though what the boy's
father would have thought of that Islyr could only guess. Islyr
would not consider allowing a marked boy to visit a brothel to
be a first-rate idea, which made him wonder exactly how
Viverr had become acquainted with this place. He decided
that the rogue's reason for frequenting Madame Covern's
could not possibly be what he had first assumed.

"Or have you actually come to me for clothing?"
Madame Covern asked, turning back to Viverr.

"Sorry to say that we have," the rogue answered,
"and we're in a bit of a rush."

"Pity. The girls will be horribly disappointed." She
drew her finger down Islyr's chest, then leaned forward to
press her lips to his neck. Her touch sent pleasant shivers
down his spine. "You could stay for just a little while," she
whispered in his ear. "There will be plenty of time for other,
less important things when we're finished."

"Perhaps we could stay," Devren began hopefully.
"You know, just for a while."

"No." Islyr stepped back a pace. "I think not." He
was not about to fall into whatever trap the rogue had laid for
them.

Devren crossed his arms over his chest.

"We may come back to visit you later," Islyr
amended. "After our business is finished. For now we'll take
a set of men's clothing. A shirt and breeches." He looked over
at Devren.

"About your size, a little taller maybe," the boy said
without looking up.

"Some boots too, if you've got them," Viverr
added. "I know your patrons sometimes leave things."

"You're certain that I can't convince you to stay?"
Madame Covern said with a frown.

"Not today," Islyr replied.

"I'll see what I can find." Madame Covern sauntered back around the counter and through the curtain.

Islyr's eyes followed her well-formed body until the curtain obscured it. Her shape reminded him somewhat of Mistress Nevane. His former Mistress had taken him to her bed often. It was common for Rakaii to be called upon to perform such duties. Some were trained solely for the purpose of giving pleasure. But it was unusual for a battle Rakaii to be consistently brought into his Mistress' or Master's bedroom. It made Islyr ill at ease to think of it now, but during his time as Rakaii it had been a matter of great pride that Mistress Nevane had asked for him most often.

"It's been a pleasure traveling with you fellows," Viverr announced suddenly. "Unfortunately, Aurin is expecting me. Can't have him thinking I'm dead, eh?" The rogue moved himself quickly between Islyr and the boy, who had wandered over to the far corner of the room. He placed his hand upon Devren's shoulder. A sharp sound, like steel striking stone, penetrated the air. The boy crumpled to the floor. Cael let out a distressed cry.

Islyr started towards Viverr, cursing the tables of fabric that stood between them.

"This makes us even," Viverr said as he sprinted over to place his hand upon Cael's struggling form. The bird dropped to the floor with a dull thud. "I hope our next meeting will be on good terms." He bowed in Islyr's direction and slipped out the door.

Islyr raced towards the opening, skidding across a small area in the center of the room that lay uncarpeted. "Viverr!" he called out the partially open door. The street was empty save for a ragged looking tabby cat, which fled at the sound of his voice.

Islyr hurried back to where Devren lay. He uttered a deep sigh of relief when he found that the boy was still breathing. He removed Devren's sword from his belt and propped the boy up against the counter.

Devren's eyes fluttered open. "Islyr. Did you catch him?"

"No," Islyr growled. "He disappeared. I didn't want to leave you here."

"Forget Viverr. He is certainly long gone."

Islyr turned. An unclothed man stood near the doorway. Broad shoulders sat over a body that would put even the most costly of pleasure Rakaii to shame. Wavy, brown hair fell over the man's dark eyes as he leaned down to grab the nearest bolt of cloth. He unrolled the wine-red fabric from it and tore off a short strip to wrap around his left hand. He used what remained to cover his lower half.

"Cael!" Devren cried out. He pulled himself up, grabbing his sword as he stood. "I can feel my mark."

"The rogue turned out to be good for something," Cael replied. "May as well give up on catching him. He knows Vale as well as you do the abyss. It could take days to find him. We don't have that much time to spare." He smiled at the boy. "Thank the Spirits that he did us a favor before deserting us."

Islyr nodded in agreement. He was not certain what Viverr had done to them. He supposed that it did not really matter, as long as they were well and the spell had been removed.

Mistress Covern pushed back through the curtain at that moment, carrying an armful of men's clothing. A look of delight crossed her face as she noticed Cael. "What have we here?" She did not bother to hide her eyes as they took in the whole of him. "The clothes are for you, I assume." Her cheeks reddened under his gaze. "Well I'm just not certain that I have anything that would do you justice." She did not seem to notice Viverr's absence, or perhaps she simply was not concerned by it.

"Anything you can give me will be fine," Cael replied. "But I would like to have it as soon as possible, if you don't mind."

"Of course." Madame Covern handed the clothes to Islyr, who in turn handed them to Cael. "I have some boots as well." she smiled. "I'll be back in just a moment."

Cael dressed quickly, keeping his back, and thus his mark, to the wall in case Madame Covern should return. The fit of the clothing was close enough that he would not look out of sorts. Islyr handed Cael the spare sword, which he tucked expertly into the leather belt that he had just lashed around his waist.

"Most all of them act like this around him," Devren said with a look of envy. "Even when he has clothes on. It's something to do with his latent ability. At least that's what he always says. I'm hoping it's not, personally. That way he can teach me how it's done. He says I'm too young yet for that sort of thing but I don't think that's true."

Cael raised one eyebrow in the boy's direction. Devren fell silent immediately, making Islyr at once thankful that Cael was back in human form. He could deal with the boy's tantrums from now on, leaving Islyr to concentrate on what he would do to Damaeus when they finally came face to face.

"You're injured?" Islyr said, gesturing at his wrapped hand.

"It's nothing," Cael replied. "A small wound."

"Here we are," Madame Covern said cheerfully as she flung the velvet curtain aside. "I'm certain these will suit you." She wove her way carefully around piles of gaudy fabric to hand Cael a fairly new looking pair of soft leather boots. "Lythan will never miss them. He hasn't been around here lately. Wife's been keeping a closer eye on him than usual."

"Thank you," Cael said evenly.

"What do we owe you?" Islyr asked. It did not matter much, seeing as they were would no longer need to purchase a void-charm.

"Consider it a gift." She eyed Cael. "For brightening my day."

"We appreciate your kindness."

"Perhaps you boys will visit me the next time you are in Vale?"

Devren looked hopeful.

"We will certainly stop in next time we are in town," Cael said.

"Certainly," Devren echoed.

Islyr nodded in Madame Covern's direction before following Cael and Devren out into the street.

"Plan on making this a regular stop?" Islyr asked.

"We will visit if we ever find ourselves in Vale again, but that's not to say that we'll utilize Madame Covern's services other than for clothing."

Devren did not look pleased.

"I'll think on it," Cael amended. "It will require some discussion with your father. Disease often thrives in those places. Better to go to a town in which the practice is legal. And I assume that I need not mention the vast difficulty that utilizing such a business would present for our kind."

"You should've just said no," Devren said miserably. "It wouldn't have raised my hopes."

"He has no idea what he's attempting to get himself into, does he?" Islyr said.

"Not the slightest," Cael replied with a laugh. "He is just very used to getting what he wants."

Devren cleared his throat noisily. "I'm still here. Don't speak over me."

"We should purchase supplies before we leave." Islyr found it much easier to ignore Devren now that there was someone else to converse with.

"True." Cael fingered his sword's hilt. "We have more than a few days of travel before us. We'll need every advantage to survive an encounter with Damaeus." He glanced at Devren. "First, though, I believe we should find a barber's shop. We don't want to attract too much attention to ourselves, and we all look like mountain hermits. It is a pity that we cannot hide your tattoo, though I don't think that anyone here will recognize it as a mark of Rakaii."

"What do you know of Rakaii?" Islyr touched his hand to his face.

"*I was a Praecyr, long ago,*" Cael replied easily in the tongue of the Kerell.

"*And what has that to do with Kerell slaves?*" Islyr asked in kind.

"One of my regular Riders was a Kerell escapee," Cael responded, returning to the language of the Ethereal Realm. "His tattoo was similar to yours, though not identical. Each house has its own pattern, so he said." Cael paused thoughtfully. "I've heard that only one in ten thousand manage to escape the grasp of the Kerell; that those who do break away are changed greatly by what they have endured. Am I correct?"

"You cannot possibly know pure truth of what you have spoken." Islyr gripped his staff tightly, and entertained pleasant thoughts of using it to shatter Damaeus' skull.

Cyanna

Cyanna sat cross-legged near the edge of the Sky room bridge. Her eyes followed the mass of jewel-like fish that had clustered in the water beneath her; their long fins trailing behind them like banners of the guard. She reached into the tin cup that sat by her side and pulled out a plump, white grub. Its smooth body writhed between her fingers as she held it out beyond the edge of the bridge, several feet from the surface of the water. Grubs were plentiful in the castle gardens any time of year save for winter. Miss Lacey, the Mistress of Gardens, had looked at Cyanna strangely when she'd asked to have them, but in the end she had allowed it. She seemed content to be rid of the creatures no matter what the manner. The fish seemed even more content to eat them. A large fish whose body was made up of patches of white and red as bright as a tent in the Seller's Square leapt from the water. It snatched the grub from her fingertips and plunged back into the depths of the pond. Cyanna laughed as droplets of water sprayed her face.

"A proper Princess would not allow herself to be seen playing with dumb animals."

Cyanna turned and stood in one smooth movement, sliding the tin cup behind her back as she did so. She was met by Erud's lop sided grin. *Should have expected as much,* she thought with a scowl.

They had played fools games on each other since Erud's first day within the castle walls. Unfortunately for her, he had quite a talent for replicating the voices of others, her mother included. Erud's parents had been gem merchants; a dangerous profession at the best of times. They had been slain by rogues in the middle of his seventh year. Cyanna's father had always had a soft place in his heart for wayward children. Any child found without a parent was brought to the castle grounds and put under the care of Mistress Vera, who was head of the kitchens and whose own children were grown. When they reached a proper age for work they were given training and offered a position in the castle staff or guard. Erud was nearly fourteen, if what Cyanna remembered as his day of birth was true to fact. He had spoken to her of joining the Standard Guard. She hoped that if he did he would receive a place within the castle, rather than out in town. His presence usually cheered her, though at the moment she was doing her best not to strangle him.

"Got you, didn't I?" he said, beaming. "For sure you thought that was your mum." He removed a small bone handled knife from his belt, knelt down, and leaned over the side of the bridge. Cyanna recognized the knife as the one she had given him during the Festival of High Tides two years past. It was just like him to add insult to her loss.

"What a fine day this is turning out to be," Erud continued as he scratched a small mark beneath the weathered boards.

Cyanna could not see it from where she stood, she would have to hang over the edge for that, but she knew that he was winning. The count was now thirty one to her twenty-nine.

"I didn't even have to travel far to add to the tally," he added gleefully as he stood.

Cyanna gave him a firm shove with her free hand. He stumbled back, coming precariously close to the edge of the bridge, but gained his balance quickly.

"No need to douse me," he said as he edged closer to her. "I'm clean already. Mistress Vera made me bathe just this morning."

"Do you want something?" Cyanna asked with a scowl. "Or have you just come here in an attempt to scare my wits out?"

"A little of both." He produced a palm-sized bundle wrapped in cloth of forest green and tied with a gold ribbon. "I'd surely be much nicer to someone who'd brought me a gift. Don't they teach you royal people any manners?"

Cyanna laughed a little in spite of herself. "From watching my mother you wouldn't think so."

"True," Erud responded. "Your brother as well, I'd say."

"I suppose," she answered, setting the cup of grubs a good foot from the edge of the bridge to be sure that it would not fall in. "But it's hardly Barrik's fault. He's only six. Mother hasn't let him out of her sight for a second since Devren…" Her smile faded for a moment. "Well, I mean since he's gone missing."

Devren was the best friend a person could wish for, aside from Erud. He understood how it felt to never have a moment outside the castle walls without several stone-faced guardsmen hovering over your shoulder. Not once had he told their father about her nighttime travels to the Seller's Square and the docks, or to go riding on the beachside by herself. He had always been ready for a game, and several times he had taken the worst of her mother's temper in her stead. Cyanna looked up to him, even though they shared only her father's blood. Devren's mother, the Queen of Evaria for only three short years, died giving birth to her only son.

"You'd think she'd want to keep an eye on you instead of Barrik, seeing as you're the heir to the throne and all."

"I am *not* the heir to the throne. Devren is. Say that again and I'll toss you in the pond for true."

"Alright, you're not," Erud said, rolling his eyes. "Whatever makes you happy." He offered her the bundle once more. "Open your gift already. Your day of birth will be over before you get around to it."

Cyanna took a moment to scowl at him before accepting the package from his outstretched hand. She unwrapped it carefully, looping the ribbon through an unused buttonhole on the front of her dress and tying it into a small bow. It looked quite pretty against the dark blue of the silk.

Beneath the cloth was a finely carved wooden box and within it, a smooth, silver ring. A bird's feather was etched onto its surface between various curves and lines, which she supposed were letters of some sort. The letters altered their shape as she attempted to read them. They were symbols of magic, she was certain of that. The language of magic never held its place to an untrained eye. Her uncle Damaeus taught her that during one of his more generous moments. He also told her that items of magic were never sold cheaply. Her father paid Erud for the services he provided, but nowhere near enough to afford something like this. Cyanna stared down at the ring. She was unsure of whether to thank him for the gift or protest it.

"I wanted to get this for you," Erud said suddenly. "You're my best friend. Besides, your father raised my pay a few months back. And the Aranth have had lots of extra jobs for me since the Lady Selene came." He closed her fingers around the ring. His cheeks flushed suddenly. He dropped her hand as if it had caught fire. "Anyway, I still have some money left, not that I'll need it as long as your father lets me stay here. The Mage who sold it to me said it would bring you protection. I figure you need it, what with all the trouble with the Aranth."

Cyanna turned the ring over thoughtfully within a slim beam of light that had slipped through the pine branches that hung overhead. Its etchings shone where the light touched them.

"I brought it to your uncle just after I got it, seeing as it's magic and all. Caught him in a good mood, luckily. He said it's ok, so it must be."

"Thanks, Erud," she said, pushing the silver ring over her left thumb. That was the proper place for a ring of friendship, whether it was magic or not. It slid easily into place. She moved her hand back and forth experimentally. It felt as if it would stay.

"It's beautiful. Beyond price." She leaned over to kiss him lightly on the cheek. He seemed more content with that than he had been with the fright he had given her earlier. Boys were so odd at times. You never could tell what would please them.

"Want to stay with me a while?" Cyanna said in attempt to break Erud's strange silence. "I was going to sneak out for a ride through town as soon as I finish with the grubs."

"Can't," he replied with a sigh. "I'm in the kitchens today. Mistress Vera said that if I helped her I could have tomorrow as a free day. It'll be worth it, no matter how much I hate scrub work."

"You need some help?"

"The heir to the throne, scouring away at greasy pots in the kitchen. I can just imagine the look on Mistress Vera's face. *That* would be beyond price."

Cyanna ignored that he had once again named her heir to the throne and smiled as she placed the wooden box and cloth wrapping into her belt pouch. Her mother was quite fond of reminding her that belt pouches were not well worn with a dress. Cyanna did not often heed her mother's warnings, at least not until she was within sight of her. After all, she was old enough to make her own decisions. She had worn a belt pouch every day since her sixth year and was not about to give it up now. She certainly did not want to know what her mother would think of Erud giving her expensive gifts. You could never tell what she would raise a temper about.

The velvet cloak that her father gave her this morning would more than cover the belt pouch and the ring in case she should run across her mother somewhere in the castle halls. The day was cool enough by far to warrant wearing one. She would say that she was on her way to the courtyard, if she was asked, and then she would go there for a short time so that her words could not be considered a lie. It sometimes seemed that Cyanna's father purposely provided her with ways to slide from her mother's grasp. She had no proof, of course, but then she really did not need any. As long as it worked to her advantage she was satisfied.

"Oh, I almost forgot," Erud said, scattering her thoughts. "Selene and Felan want you to come to the Hollow. They have something for you, I think. Xaiden won't let them off until dinner and they wanted to be sure they saw you today."

"Thanks," she replied as Erud wandered off through the pines. "Good luck with the pots."

"I'm telling you, it'll be worth it come tomorrow."

Cyanna tossed the last of the grubs one by one into the pond, and then made her way through the castle's familiar halls. She lingered a while in the Hall of Ancestry, whose oil paintings of long deceased Royalty and the Aranth who served them would continue to be of great interest to her so long as her mother remained uneasy beneath their steady, timeless gaze.

The castle seemed so empty now that most of the Aranth had disappeared. Galt and Relen were the first two to go, at least in Cyanna's mind; for she was just old enough at that time to understand what happened. She remembered her father's infuriated stare as he spoke of them. She was simply happy that his anger was not directed towards her.

He had ordered the two Aranth to Seral on errand. The city of Seral not terribly far from Evaria and the errand was not a treacherous one. Neither returned. The next to go were Wesh and Jevelir, with Arlen, Teve, and Retilus following close behind. Luca was the first that Cyanna had wept for. He had not truly been Aranth, but he was her friend. He was the only one of whom they had been able to find even the smallest trace.

Then there was the incident with Devren and Cael. Cyanna would not believe what Damaeus said of Cael, even if everyone else seemed to. She knew him as well as she did Xaiden, for both men had been Aranth since long before her birth. Cyanna had heard a story, near to the beginning of her fifth year, of blye spiders as large as a wagon wheel. They hid in dark places, waiting for the lamps to be extinguished so they could paralyze their victims and drag them away to feast upon at their leisure. Her mother smiled condescendingly at her worries and told her not to be silly. *Grown girls don't fear such things*, she said. *I'm much too busy for your games today, Cyanna.* Cael found her crying outside of her room that night, too scared to enter for fear of being eaten. He checked beneath her bed and within her wardrobes every night for a good part of her fifth year. It did seem silly, now that she thought back upon it, but at the time she was terrified and Cael was the only one who understood. She would always remember his kindness. He would not have harmed Devren, she was certain. He would have given his life to save him.

Cyanna slipped down a narrow hallway and through the servant's entrance into the cool air of the training courtyard known as the Hollow. It was one of the largest courtyards in the castle, half of which was taken up by a great area of bare earth used only for Aranth weapons training.

Selene stood at the edge of the Hollow, her unusually long hair up in a form of Rider's knot. Cyanna recognized the style from the Riders that came to the castle for an audience with her father. Though most were male, all of them had their hair up in a similar way. She pulled at the ends of her own hair, which fell to just below her shoulders. She wondered idly if it was long enough to put into a knot. After all, Selene got away with it. Then again, Selene got away with many things that a princess would never be able to do. If Cyanna were to put even one toe into a pair of breeches her mother would very likely throw a fit to rival the Spirits' wrath. Yet there Selene was, in breeches and what looked to be a men's cotton shirt, and no one so much as mentioned the impropriety of it all.

"Empty your mind of all conscious thought," Felan said calmly. He and Selene stood several paces from each other with the points of their wooden practice swords aimed to the ground. Their wrists were turned out and their eyes closed.

"Let your instinct control your movements."

Cyanna seated herself upon one of the stone benches that lined the sides of the rectangular patch of ground. Not so long ago it had been used for the other Aranth to watch their brethren training. From her new vantage point she could see that the soil of the Hollow had been watered down slightly to prevent any more dust than was necessary.

Cyanna always enjoyed watching the Aranth spar. Especially Felan. She would have done just about anything to get some proper weapons training. Since Devren was gone there was little chance of that. Selene had offered to teach her a few techniques when she had time, but her free days were few and Damaeus seemed to grab her for latent ability training whenever he caught sight of her.

"Ready." Felan's voice rang out across the courtyard.

Cyanna was anxious to see Selene's improvement. Her father had not permitted recruiting since Devren's mother died, much to Xaiden's displeasure. The few Marked Ones that had been allowed into the Aranth since that time had shown up purely by the luck of the Tides.

"Begin."

Both Aranth's eyes snapped open. Their swords met in a torrent of fluid movement. Felan fought with the force and skill that his few years of training had given him, but Selene's steps were swift and sure.

They moved so quickly that Cyanna's eyes had trouble keeping pace. Felan taunted his sparring partner, tapping the edge of his sword to hers then drawing back quickly before she could strike him. He dodged each graceful blow with the confidence of one that was well used to having the upper hand. He had cause to be sure of himself. When they first began Selene's training he bested her every time. Cyanna remembered how Selene's forest colored eyes turned to gray as she stormed from the Hollow with a defiant look upon her face. It must have been hard for her, Cyanna surmised, being a Rider for so many years and fighting to earn her pay, then learning all at once that she was not as good as she thought; that one of the Aranth could have killed her in less than a shadow's breath.

Selene's skill had improved greatly during the past few months. Cyanna could now say that the two were fairly matched, though neither of them came at all close to Xaiden's skill, nor to that of Cael. Her father always said that a well-trained Aranth was a match for ten men. The first time Cyanna watched Cael and Xaiden spar she believed him. Age had a great deal to do with it, but even young Aranth were nothing to be trifled with.

Selene's sword swept through the air, barely missing Felan's head. They were supposed to keep it low. At least that was what Xaiden always said. When he was not around the rules tended to become a little bent, especially so since Selene arrived. She and Felan thought up more ways to get themselves into trouble than Devren had even in his younger years, and she had to assume that she had not heard all of it. Damaeus at one point suggested to Cyanna's father that they should separate the two Aranth. He said that they were worse than children and that he should be paid more for having to deal with them. Cyanna had little trouble understanding his anger, seeing as most of their fools' games were directed towards him. That being said, at times he certainly brought it upon himself with his ill temper.

Felan's sword came down upon Selene's left arm with a sickening crunch. Cyanna winced at the sound. It was a sign of superiority, to wound on the left rather than taking her sword arm. Xaiden used the move on occasion to show that he could have ended the match in his favor yet had decided against it. Though Xaiden had never struck anyone so hard as to splinter bone, at least not while sparring.

Selene showed no sign that the weapon had touched her. She quickened her pace, as did Felan. She met Felan's next thrust with ease and then pulled her sword low, as if to hit his leg at the knee. He moved his weapon down to block her. She lifted hers in mid swing, striking him hard in the side. Their movement stopped as suddenly as it had begun.

"Fatal strike," Selene called out between labored breaths.

"Fair enough," Felan replied, tossing his battered sword upon the nearest bench. He was breathing nearly as hard as she. He pulled up the edge of his shirt to examine his side. "That's really going to bruise."

"I think that's only fair," Selene replied with a smile, "considering that you've broken my arm."

"I suppose so."

Selene laid her sword down and took a seat on the bench next to Cyanna. "You were watching. Do you have anything to say?"

"You've improved. But you're supposed to stay low."

"I was staying low," Selene replied with a wink.

"I don't think that Xaiden would consider Felan's head to be low. Aren't you afraid that he'll find out?"

"Xaiden does have a habit of appearing exactly when you don't want him to." Selene's breathing had nearly returned to normal. Her left arm was bent at an unusual angle and the flesh was beginning to swell.

Felan smiled one of his characteristic smiles as he took a seat on the bench. "I guess we lucked out for today. You're the only witness."

Cyanna could feel her cheeks heat into a blush.

"You won't tell, will you?"

He was so close. Her voice refused to work.

"How about a bribe?" He had obviously mistaken her silence for refusal. "A small gift, perhaps? It is a day to celebrate, after all."

"I wouldn't tell," she managed. "Even without the gift." She forced her gaze from his deep blue eyes towards Selene, thinking at once of how the two of them were nearly always together. It was difficult, at times, not to be jealous of Selene even though she was sure that they were nothing more than good friends.

Cyanna would be of a proper age for Felan soon enough. Marked Ones aged differently than ordinary people. He had only recently reached his slowing. That meant that in six years, when Cyanna reached twenty, he would look just the same as he did on this day. He treated her like a child now, but in time he would surely return her feelings. Her mother and father could do nothing about it then, because she would be grown and able to decide for herself. After all, she could not marry anyone but an Aranth. They were the only ones who would not judge her for what she was. What *would* her mother think of her marrying Felan?

Felan offered her questioning look.

She released her thoughts suddenly, hoping that his expression was on account of her silence and not because he had been reading her. Her cheeks heated all the more upon realizing her folly.

"It's up in my room," Selene said as she prodded her swollen arm with interest. She seemed to consider wounds of any sort, even her own, a learning experience. She also seemed to have more tolerance for pain than most, perhaps because of her latent ability. "You can come up if you like. That tapestry I ordered was delivered this morning. It's beautiful." She met Cyanna's gaze. "Or would you rather I bring your gift to you?"

"I'll come up," Cyanna said decidedly. She really did want to see the tapestry. Word was that it had been costly and tremendously difficult to weave.

Selene stood. The wooden swords that she and Felan had been using, as well as pieces from some that Cyanna supposed they had broken earlier, lifted from where they lay strewn about the Hollow. They floated to the opposite side of the courtyard, forming as neat a pile as was possible in an empty spot near the wall.

"You're really going to like this, I think," Selene said as she headed off across the bare patch of ground.

Felan lifted himself from the bench to walk with them. Cyanna took a place to Selene's left, pushing herself between the two Aranth. Neither Selene nor Felan seemed to notice.

Doors opened obediently as they neared them, allowing the three to pass through the halls with ease. Cyanna knew it was Selene's doing, though she was not showing off by any means. Damaeus' orders were that she should use her latent ability as much as possible. Selene confided to Cyanna that she obeyed Damaeus' command mostly to keep him from pestering her further.

Selene's room was nearly as massive as Cyanna's. It had been furnished, at first, in the standard manner, but had not stayed that way for long. Each Aranth was allowed to change their room as they chose. Selene had recently removed everything she considered to be gaudy, which was apparently almost everything. She redecorated it with simple yet costly things that were more to her liking. It was not shabby by any means, but rather held an air of simple elegance. Cyanna rather liked it.

Selene also had a penchant for tapestries. Cyanna recognized the unicorn tapestry from the holding room in which Selene had been imprisoned, the one of ravens in flight that Xaiden and Felan had given her a few weeks past, and the Aranth symbol tapestry, which still hung above Selene's bed. Her newest acquisition took up most of the north wall. It showed a bird of fire, its wings spread gracefully against a starlit sky. Cyanna was forced to agree with Selene about its beauty, though she had no idea what the creature was.

"It's a phoenix," Felan said, rubbing one corner of the tapestry between his thumb and forefinger. "Excellent craftsmanship."

"Why did you choose a phoenix?" Cyanna asked as she leaned in closer to admire its fine stitching.

Selene's gaze became distant. "Reminds me of my brother." She turned and headed into the bedroom.

Cyanna opened her mouth to ask his name, but Felan's voice echoed through her mind. *It upsets her greatly to speak of him. I will tell you his story later, if you wish.*

He used formal speech, as he was prone to do whenever he was speaking seriously about something. Cyanna nodded her head silently and followed him into the bedroom.

"Would you push my bone back into place?" Selene asked, holding her broken arm up for Felan. The swelling suddenly lessened, revealing a small lump where the break was centered.

"Of course." Felan placed one hand on either side of the split. Selene winced a little as he forced the bone back into place. She finished the healing, then lifted her arm this way and that, testing its strength.

"Remove your shirt," she said finally. "We'll both be in trouble if Xaiden sees that once it begins to bruise."

Felan complied, plopping himself down onto Selene's bed as if he belonged there. A few light scars ran across his well-defined torso. Selene pressed her hands to his side. It pained Cyanna to see her touching him. She suppressed a scowl. *Good friends can fast become lovers.* Her mother had been speaking of Cyanna's relationship with Erud at the time, but the saying could just as easily be applied to Felan and Selene.

"I seem to have cracked a few ribs," Selene said with a rogue's smile.

"Don't worry on it. A real foe would have done much worse."

Cyanna watched with interest as Felan's bruises faded to nothing. She hoped that her own latent ability, when she found it, would prove to be half as useful as either of Selene's.

"Better?"

"Enormously, thanks." Felan rose from the bed and pulled his shirt back on. He turned towards Cyanna. "Ready for your gift, then?"

Cyanna nodded numbly. She attempted to push thoughts of Felan's shirtless chest from her mind with little success.

"Ok. Close your eyes."

She could hear Felan's footsteps and the squeal of the balcony door as he opened it. The hinges sounded in dire need of oil.

"Alright."

Cyanna opened her eyes slowly. Felan knelt before her holding a palm-sized, furry creature. It was possibly the most darling thing she had ever seen. The scrub pig looked up at her with large, dark eyes. Cyanna took it from Felan and held it up, admiring its soft, calico colored coat. The tiny thing squealed in pleasure. She realized at once that the noise she had heard had not been the door to the balcony.

"I saw you eyeing them at the Seller's Square last week," Selene said with a grin. "It's a female. They're supposed to be easier to train."

Selene and Felan took her to the Square every so often. Cyanna looked forward to such days, for it was the only way that her father would let her go out without an escort of twenty guardsmen.

"This is for you as well," Selene added as she handed Cyanna a hard leather pouch with silver accents upon its edges. "You can string it onto your belt. She loves to sit in it. I carried her around a bit yesterday."

Felan shot her a questioning look.

"She was lonely," Selene said defensively. "She's just small you know."

"She's adorable." Cyanna placed a kiss upon the creature's furry head. The pig nuzzled against her. She seemed content just to sit in Cyanna's arms. "I wanted one, but was afraid mother wouldn't allow it." She smiled at them both. "She can't possibly make me give up a gift from the Aranth."

"True," Felan said. "We'll have her crate brought up to your room. I would do it myself, but Xaiden will be back soon. If he catches either of us up here instead of in the Hollow it may well be months before we get our next free day."

"What will you call her?" Selene asked as she passed back into the living room.

"Novalin," Cyanna said decidedly. She always enjoyed reading the journal of the first female Aranth. It seemed only proper that her first animal companion should be named after her.

"That reminds me," Selene said as they stepped into the hallway. "I have a free day at the end of the week. Would you like to practice using your mark?"

"I would." Cyanna said immediately. She had once tried to climb a loose section of the paddock fence. It had toppled beneath her small weight, and she had ended up with a wooden pike through her leg. Using her mark hurt a hundred times worse than that, but it was worth the pain. She had never before imagined that she would be able to sneak out of the castle with such ease. A princess was someone to be noticed, to be guarded and pampered and followed. At times it seemed that a simple sneeze brought the entire First Quarter of the Standard Guard running to see if she was still in one piece. A striped barn cat, on the other hand, was no more noticeable than a grain of sand upon the shore.

The first time Selene offered to help Cyanna with her mark she was uncertain. Both Cyanna's mother and her father had instructed her repeatedly not to use it under any circumstances. Her father amended his statement at Selene's urging, saying that he only wanted Cyanna to wait until they could find someone proper to instruct her. No doubt he was opposed the idea of a male Aranth training her in the use of such an intimate thing as her affinity. Cyanna briefly considered arguing that Felan could show her how it was done, but thought better of it almost immediately. Her father eventually deemed Selene suitable.

"Meet me here at midday," Selene said as the door to her room swung shut.

"Alright," Cyanna replied. "I'll bring Novalin too. I'll have taught her at least a few tricks by then."

"I look forward to it." Selene flashed her a half smile before sprinting to catch up with Felan.

Cyanna slipped Novalin's pouch onto her belt as the Aranth disappeared down the hallway. She then headed off towards her room. She would take the upper hallway. The Queen's sitting room was the only room that was occupied in that section. Her mother ordered it built there for privacy and quiet. It was not used often, and even when it was the door remained closed.

Cyanna climbed the steps that led to the upper hall with care in order to avoid jostling Novalin. Dimly burning lamps were spaced evenly across panels of lacquered redwood. There were no windows in this section of the castle, and the lamps were not mirrored, so they gave off precious little light. The thick, flowered carpet that covered the stone floors muffled Cyanna's steps.

Her mother's muted voice drifted unexpectedly though the silence of the hall. It was raised in such a way that Cyanna knew her to be irritated. Her first thought was to flee. There were several other ways to get to her bedroom, none of which passed near this hall. Her mother would never have to know that she had been here. She pondered it until curiosity overwhelmed her. A few careful steps brought her close enough to understand her mother's words.

"I told you that he would not join us, but you refused to listen. She is willful, just as he was, and has the potential to become dangerous. We should dispose of her before she is fully trained."

Cyanna moved closer. She beseeched the Spirits that Novalin would stay silent. She did not like the revulsion that shaded her mother's words, nor the odd nervousness that played beside it. It was disrespectful to listen in on a private conversation, yet she just could not seem to pull herself away.

"We must have her if we expect to succeed," came her uncle's low voice. "Or perhaps you know of another with such an unusual gift?"

A knife's edge of light stretched from beneath the door. Cyanna stood to one side of it just in case they should happen to glance her way.

"There is no way to be certain that the foretelling speaks of her. I will not put everything we've accomplished at risk based solely upon an assumption."

"Ander's journal has not been wrong in the past. My interpretation of it is certainly not wrong. She is the only one who has the potential to control them."

Glass clinked, then came the sound of liquid being poured. Who was Ander? Most likely an Aranth, since all of them were required to keep journals. But why had she never heard of him?

"You should not be near her, most especially if what you have read is true," her mother said softly. "Everything we have done will be obliterated because you think yourself invincible."

"This news should warm your heart." Her uncle was the only one who could ignore her mother's words without facing her wrath. "Those who were taken to the abyss, may the Spirits keep their prying souls, have departed this plane."

"That is fine to hear," her mother agreed. "I assume that you have some evidence to show the truth of it."

"The proof lies here."

Cyanna wished that she had the courage to look through the keyhole.

"Once a Circlet is placed upon the girl we will have no difficulty with her. Trust in me and have patience, Perfidia. You will not be disappointed."

"I have no reason to doubt you, I suppose, though it pains me to say it. It simply makes me nervous knowing that so many of them still run free. We have done what we can, but I feel that it is not enough. Each delay in our plans means one more day that the common people must live in fear. It is your duty as a Mage, as one of higher power, to protect those who cannot protect themselves."

"Indeed," Uncle Damaeus replied. "You have my word that it will be done in due time. It would serve us well if you were to act agreeably towards the girl until then. Try to earn her friendship if you are able. It is true that they can be dangerous if handled improperly. It will be easier to catch her unaware if she believes us to be allies."

Uncle Damaeus said something more, but it was spoken much too softly for Cyanna to hear. This was by far the most interesting conversation she had heard in ages, though a bit difficult to follow. She pushed her ear against the cold wood just below the handle. With a few more minutes of listening she might be able to figure out exactly what they were speaking about.

The door swung in without warning. Cyanna stumbled forward. She looked up and was met by her mother's angry glare. She prepared herself for the punishment she knew she deserved.

"Stand up." Her mother grabbed her roughly by her upper arm. "I won't have you lying about on the floor like a commoner."

Uncle Damaeus sat at the center of the room in one of two burgundy velvet chairs. A bottle of red wine stood upon the gilded table between them though only one half-empty glass was visible. Cyanna assumed that it belonged to her mother. Uncle Damaeus rarely drank. He said that it was hazardous for a Mage to indulge in beverages that altered the mind.

"Yes, mother." It terrified Cyanna more that she had not struck her. One thing that had always been constant was her mother's wrath. Knowing that her mother only grew angry because she feared for Cyanna's safety did not make the bruises, nor the pain, fade any faster. Perhaps it was because uncle Damaeus was here. Her mother did not punish her as much when others were within viewing distance, especially family. She considered it to be undignified.

"Sit," she ordered, pointing to a stiff wooden chair. It was the only one in the room that did not look the least bit comfortable. "Your uncle Damaeus wishes to hear what you have been busying yourself with on this day."

Uncle Damaeus' ghostly blue eyes followed Cyanna's movements. His face held its usual impartial expression. Cyanna seated herself obediently upon the chair. It was every bit as hard as she had imagined.

"Father wanted to give me a gift, so I went to him." She could feel Novalin shifting in her pouch. "I never left the castle grounds. I swear it."

"You were with the Aranth." uncle Damaeus said calmly as he refilled her mother's glass.

Uncle Damaeus always seemed to know when she had been around the Aranth. It was a vexing problem, to be sure.

"I assume that you did not use your mark without proper supervision. You know how your mother feels about such dangerous pastimes. You certainly would not wish to upset her, as much as she cares for your welfare."

"No, uncle. The Aranth were in weapons training, so I did not use my mark at all today." It was a simple question coming from him, like someone asking of the weather. So why couldn't she keep her legs from shaking? It seemed that the more she tried to control them the worse they became.

"Very good," he said, rising. "In that case we have a gift for you."

"A gift, sir?" Her uncle rarely gave her anything, even on her day of origin. Gifts were generally given to her by her father, though he always reminded her that the item was from both himself and the rest of the family.

Uncle Damaeus rose and reached into the black leather pouch that always hung at his waist. He pressed something cold into her outstretched hand. Cyanna lifted it up for examination. It was flat, with a rounded edge like that of a gold coin, yet the entirety of its surface was the near-white color of a hen's egg. A phoenix was carved into one side, like the one in Selene's newest tapestry. Upon the other side was a raven perched on a lifeless tree. Looking upon the coin made her stomach numb. She did not like the way it felt against her skin; the way it sucked the warmth from her like frigid water.

"It will protect you," uncle Damaeus said. "Be sure to keep it near you at all times. Do not show it to anyone, under any circumstances. It is meant only for you."

Cyanna pushed the thumb of her free hand between her fingers, rubbing the ring that Erud gave her. She wondered why she would possibly need two items of protection. *Perhaps this one is stronger,* she reasoned. Strong objects of magic often gave her a peculiar feeling.

"A very fine gift, indeed," Her mother's brow furrowed. "Where are your manners, Cyanna? Thank your uncle."

"Thank you, uncle," Cyanna said haltingly. "I appreciate your concern for my welfare." She slipped the coin into her old belt pouch, happy that she would no longer be forced to touch it. With the uneasy feeling of the coin gone it was now much easier to notice the tingling in her legs from where the poorly crafted chair pinched into her flesh. She shifted to one side in attempt to return the flow of blood to them. Novalin squealed with interest and pushed her head out into the room. Cyanna moved her arm to block her from view, hoping her mother would think it was just the chair's aged wood that had made the sound.

"Is that an *animal* in your pouch?"

Cyanna cringed.

"Bring it out."

"Yes, mother." Cyanna lifted Novalin gently into her hand. The little creature busied herself with licking Cyanna's fingertips. She would have laughed at the antics had she not been so worried about her new pet's welfare.

"What in the name of the Spirits is that horrid thing?" Her mother screwed up her nose in distaste. She looked as if she would like to take Novalin from her, but did not dare for fear of touching the little creature.

"She was a gift from the Aranth."

"A rat is not an acceptable gift under any circumstances." Her mother was not at all fond of small creatures, especially rats and mice. "Disgusting. Get rid of it at once or I shall see to it myself. It will suffer much less in your hands, I am certain."

"Novalin is not a rat, mother. She's a-"

The force of her mother's hand knocked Cyanna's head painfully against the back of the chair. Her eyes stung with tears. She barely managed to keep from dropping Novalin, who was now quaking with fright.

"You will not speak back to me, child. Show some reverence for your mother."

Cyanna righted herself. Her cheek stung horribly where she had been struck. The back of her head began to throb. "My deepest apologies, mother," she managed, lowering her gaze. "I should not have been so disrespectful. It will not happen again." She should have known better than to speak to her mother that way, but she had insulted Novalin. It was a terrible thing to do; especially as she was half from Felan.

Cyanna turned her gaze towards her uncle. He had returned to his seat and was idly strumming his fingers on the arm of his chair. By looking at him one would think that nothing at all had occurred. Her mother's expression reminded her otherwise.

"See that it does not," her mother said as she lowered herself into her chair and retrieved her glass of wine.

Uncle Damaeus appeared suddenly by Cyanna's side. It unnerved her that she had not witnessed him crossing the room. He tilted her head with icy fingers. "Compose yourself, Perfidia," he said, keeping his eyes upon Cyanna as he spoke.

Her mother did not seem to be aware of his words.

The sting in Cyanna's cheek subsided, as did the ache in her head. "Thank you, uncle," she heard herself say.

"Any time, my dear." He wiped a tear that had leaked onto her cheek, and then moved over to the chest of drawers that sat in the corner. "Now, I have a bit of an errand for you. I am certain that if you manage it successfully your mother will allow you to keep that new pet of yours. After all, it was a gift from the Aranth." He glanced towards her mother, who nodded her head in reluctant agreement before turning to scowl at her wine.

Uncle Damaeus pulled out a small pouch of black, silken cloth. "You must take this to your father," he said, crouching down to Cyanna's level so that his eerie eyes met hers. "I would see to it myself, but I have a few vital items of business to manage before the day is through. It is very important that he gets it in a timely fashion, so you mustn't allow yourself to be distracted by anything until it is delivered. Do you understand?"

"Yes, uncle," Cyanna's mind began to churn. She wondered what this thing could possibly be. She could not discern anything at all just from looking at the pouch, much to her dismay.

"It is for your father's eyes alone," Uncle Damaeus added sternly.

Cyanna knew that it was impossible for any Mage to have powers like Felan's. Her father had told her so. But her uncle sometimes said things that made her believe otherwise. His bright, penetrating eyes only served to further her suspicion.

"When you hand it to him, you must tell him that your uncle Damaeus sends his deepest condolences." He reached out to stroke her hair. She found his touch to be more than displeasing. "You may take it now, as long as we have an agreement."

"Yes, uncle. I will tell father exactly what you've said." She yearned to be far from him and her mother, and her bottom was becoming numb besides. She wished that her uncle had chosen to ignore her this day, or to shoo her away from his work as he nearly always did. She wished most of all that she had chosen a different route to her room. Novalin chattered a bit as Cyanna pushed her gently back into her pouch. At least one of them had regained their confidence.

Cyanna took the bag gingerly between her fingers and thumb, just in case the item inside should be breakable. There was no telling what her mother would do if she damaged something of importance. She was certainly searching for any excuse to dispose of Novalin. Cyanna was not about to allow her one.

"You may go," her uncle said firmly.

Cyanna did not need to be told more than once. She walked carefully towards the hall, being sure to keep her shoulders back and her head high in case her mother was watching her posture. She often berated her about it, saying that the way she held herself reflected upon the entire royal family. The last thing she wanted was to be called back into the sitting room.

Cyanna picked up her pace immediately upon hearing the quiet bump of the door. She ran straight to the Hall of Ancestry. It was not quite on the way to the library, where she knew her father to be, but it was not horribly out of her way either.

Cyanna sat gratefully upon the thick, embroidered carpet. Someday, when she was grown, she would burn that chair and all others like it. She felt carefully around the outside of the silken bag in attempt to determine its contents. It was only one item, of that she was sure. It was slightly rounded, and hard. Cyanna crossed her legs as she passed the bag from one hand to the other. Why would Uncle Damaeus feel the need to send her father his condolences?

What could it hurt to look? Just one, short glimpse and then she would bring it straight to her father. It could not be anything dangerous, otherwise Damaeus would not have entrusted her with its care. Cyanna pulled open the drawstring and upended the bag above an unadorned section of carpet. She stared numbly at what fell from it. It was a Stone, like those that the Aranth wore to amplify their latent abilities.

There had once been hundreds of Stones. The method of their making had been lost through the years, allowing time and use to take a toll on their numbers. Some had become worthless when the Aranth they were linked to passed on to their next life. Less than one hour after their death the Stone became clouded and could not be set to another. It was because their blood had never touched the Stone. Only eleven functional Stones remained, and all of them were property of the royal family. The best of the Aranth were allowed to choose one. Devren was an exception, as he was neither Aranth nor in training to become one.

Cyanna lifted the pendant by its leather cord. Silver, feathered wings held the clear, rounded Stone in place. They touched each other at the top and bottom, leaving a thumb-sized opening at the center. The Stones themselves were identical when at rest, yet the setting that held each was unique, as was the color they glowed upon being used. The user's affinity and latent ability determined the color in some way, though no one seemed to know exactly how. Her half-brother's color was bronze, but Cyanna did not need to see the glow of color to know this Stone. It belonged to Devren.

Cyanna's throat felt thick and dry. Uncle Damaeus had made a mistake. He must have. Why else would he send his condolences to her father with Devren's Stone? Her uncle must have given her the wrong bag. She should go back, tell him of his error, and take whatever punishment she deserved for disobeying his instructions.

I could find out. The idea squirmed its way into her mind. *It would be so simple.* She needed only to touch her flesh to the open part of the stone. If Devren was still living and she touched it, nothing would happen. She would know for sure, and no harm would be done. But what if something *had* happened to Devren. Cyanna's stomach turned queasy at the thought. If his blood had been shed upon the Stone and she touched it, then it would be set to her. Her father would be furious. He did not anger easily, but when something did manage to bring his wrath it was a fearsome sight.

Devren is alive. She decided at once. *He has to be.* Touching the Stone would confirm it. Cyanna pushed her thumb against its smooth center. The Stone remained clear.

She breathed a sigh of relief and moved to place it back in the silken bag, but something caught her eye. A thin trail of lavender colored smoke swirled about the Stone's center, followed by one of dusky blue moving in the opposite direction. Her hand stilled.

"No…" she whispered into the quiet of the room.

It had to be wrong. She touched her flesh to it once more. The Stone glowed shortly. The color was lavender.

"No!" she screamed. "It's not fair!"

Why would the Spirits allow this to happen? Why would they take him from her? What had she done that they should punish her so?

"Bring him back!" she shrieked into the emptiness. The eternally placid faces of her ancestors offered no condolences. Tears cascaded down Cyanna's cheeks. "I'll do anything; I swear it, if you'll just bring him back." Her voice faded to a choking sob.

Her father appeared in the doorway, his face ashen. He looked formidable, even so. The sword that he always carried was drawn. His eyes surveyed every corner of the room in attempt to determine the cause of her distress. He seemed puzzled at finding no immediate threat. His gaze landed upon her face.

"Cyanna?" He sheathed his weapon and came towards her, passing a warm hand along the side of her face. His touch was as soothing as Uncle Damaeus' was unsettling. "Whatever is the matter?"

Cyanna folded her hand around the Stone. She rested her head against her father's chest and allowed his burly arms to surround her. It would have comforted her, if not for guilt she harbored. Not only had she had disobeyed a promise to Uncle Damaeus, but now yet another Stone was gone. It would be useless until her death. She would never outlive the shame of what she had done.

Cyanna levered herself from her father's grasp. She ignored his confusion and pushed the leather cord over her head. The Stone was hers now. She would tell her father the truth. She would accept whatever punishment she was given.

*   *   *   *   *

Damaeus leaned back into the plush velvet of his chair. His mind was finally at ease.

"Are you certain of this?" Perfidia asked between minuscule sips of wine. "The girl may have a penchant for trouble, but she usually follows direct orders."

He had always been much more intelligent than Perfidia, though without a doubt she would rather die than confirm the fact. "Not only am I certain that it will work, but I am certain that it already has." Damaeus thought idly of forcing the rest of the liquor down his sister's throat. She was remarkably more manageable when she was inebriated.

"And how do you know this?"

"I know it because I have seen it, of course. I placed a viewing spell upon the ring that Erud so kindly brought for my inspection. It was an origin-day gift for your beautiful daughter, and a costly one at that. I believe the boy may have feelings for Cyanna, much like the feelings she has for a certain one of your Aranth."

Perfidia's expression darkened.

Damaeus could not help but smile. "Not to worry. Felan's thoughts towards Cyanna are not more than those of an older brother for his sibling. And if that alone does not comfort your fears then there is this; I am certain that Selene will be more than ready to tend to Felan's needs before Cyanna has grown enough to gain his interest."

Damaeus tipped his head to one side as Perfidia's glass rushed past him. It shattered as it struck wall. Damaeus did not flinch, lest it give her some pleasure. He lifted one hand while whispering a spell of restoration to bind the broken shards. "Retrieve it," he said.

Perfidia wrinkled her nose in distaste, but obeyed his command. She had always been one to want her own way, no matter how much it inconvenienced others. Their father tried everything from chiding to beating to cure her of it. Damaeus had little patience for such foolery. He was her superior, and expected her to treat him as such.

Perfidia held the glass out to him. He gestured towards the table, weaving a calming essence into her mind as he did so. It was the simplest of magic to cast, yet he found it immensely useful.

Perfidia poured what was left of the wine into the mended glass and seated herself once again. "My apologies, brother. Certainly you know that I never meant to harm you."

"Of course," Damaeus replied evenly. He was well acquainted with her tantrums. Speaking of the Aranth wore away at her patience. There were several blemishes to be found in every soul; subjects that ignited love, hate, or some deeper yet equally unsound emotion. They worked like a flame upon the dry tinder of the common mind. He found it immeasurably rewarding to unearth the flaws in each soul that he dealt with, for only when that subject was discovered could you truly gain higher ground. Only then could you achieve complete control. The first of Perfidia's flaws was the Aranth; Felan in particular. Damaeus only occasionally used the knowledge for pleasure. He was not completely without pity, after all.

"Your daughter has set Devren's Stone to herself, as I knew she would," he said, altering the flow of the conversation.

Perfidia pressed her lips together impatiently. "And that means?"

"Stones can be read, in a way, though you must be in possession of another Stone to do so. They arbitrarily absorb the feelings, thoughts, and actions of the Aranth that is bonded to them. If another Aranth, say Xaiden, or perhaps your beloved Felan, were to read Devren's Stone then our necks would more than likely be upon the execution block before morning." Damaeus rose from his seat to place his hand upon her shoulder. "That is why I allowed Cyanna to carry the Stone to her father. Now when they gain access to it they will find only the thoughts of your daughter. All will be well, just as I promised."

"You risked our lives upon the assumption that Cyanna would not do as she was told. She is headstrong, I agree. Yet what if she had not set the Stone to herself? She could have taken the bag to my husband without so much as a glance at its contents."

The corners of Damaeus' mouth turned up in a smile. His answer, he knew, would truly irritate her. His Mage's abilities had been a blemish upon Perfidia's soul since he began to develop his talents, near to his eighth year. Her jealousy only served to prove his superiority.

"A simple coercion spell." The spell was not at all simple to concoct, in truth, though it required only seconds to cast. It had taken him the better part of three weeks to prepare for it. But there was no need for Perfidia to know that, and no chance that she would ever find out on her own due to her incomprehensible aversion to reading. "I placed the spell, along with the other, upon the ring Erud gave her."

"You can control her?" Perfidia's eyes narrowed in disbelief.

"No. Gaining complete control of a person's actions by aid of a spell is not possible. The magic simply gives her consciousness a small push in the direction of my choosing. An impulse, if you will, though it is quite limited."

"You seem more certain of your magic than is warranted."

It was a vain attempt to antagonize him, which was not uncommon for her. "As long as the victim is unaware of the spell it will work as cast. It pushed Cyanna's thoughts towards disobeying my orders. I set it to dissipate once the Stone was bonded to her. No trace of my magic will be left to find, if that is your concern."

"And the coin? You are certain that it is secure in her hands?"

"As certain as the rise and fall of the tides." The truth was that he simply could not keep it close any longer. The magic of it was starting to affect him. It was information that he would rather not share with Perfidia. "I have cloaked its true magic. Any Mage who attempts to discover its purpose will see only a totem of protection, though such precautions are hardly necessary. His Majesty trusts me most completely."

"And if it is lost?"

"Do not worry so." Damaeus handed her a fresh bottle of wine. "Drink, and have faith."

Damacus' Room

Selene pressed her stomach against the balcony railing, levering her upper body out above the west courtyard.

"What in the name of the Spirits is taking so long?" she called into the room behind her.

She lowered her feet to the sand-colored tiles then turned and shifted her balance, leaning her arms back against the railing. Being grounded was making her restless. The more often she used her affinity, the more she longed to be in animal form. Xaiden said that it was to be expected, and that it would pass in time. Selene was not so certain. Most activities seemed quite ordinary when compared to flying.

"Would you like me to help you look?" she asked, peering past the balcony door.

"No need," Felan replied. "Found it."

He rounded the corner holding a bone-handled knife. Its blade would have easily reached from his wrist to the tip of his fingers. "I lark about for your sake. To give you a proper chance to back out." He used the knife to gesture in the direction of a nearby chair. "This can't be undone," he added in a mockingly somber tone.

Selene smiled despite her irritable mood. "I was afraid you had lost it. Xaiden would be livid." She dropped into the chair that Felan had offered.

"That, he would," Felan agreed. He lowered the knife behind her head. Its blade was crafted from the same metal as the Aranth standard sword, and thus held a much finer edge than any weapon of ordinary metal. Xaiden had allowed Felan to borrow it on the condition that he return it as soon as he was finished.

"You're certain, then?"

"You had best do it now, before I have a change of mind."

Felan's movements brushed air against the back of her neck. "Stay still," he warned, though in truth there was no need for it. She knew better than to shift while a weapon was held so near to her flesh.

The pull of the blade through her hair was whisper soft. Felan handed her a small piece of mirrored glass with a silver frame. Selene turned it to catch her reflection. The clarity of the images such glass held never ceased to amaze her, though she had several large pieces of it in her room. It was not at all like the wavered images of the polished steel mirrors she had become used to back in Maresbane. Every detail of her face was visible. Selene turned her head to one side. Her hair now ended more than an inch above her shoulders. She had been growing it out since her seventh year. It was gone now, and any connection to her hometown had been severed with it. In less than two weeks' time she would be Aranth.

"What do you think?" she asked, standing and turning to face Felan. Her head was a great deal lighter without the weight of her hair behind it.

"Nice," he replied. "But there's something missing." He handed her a miniature leather bag. Inside were three beads of precious stone; two of onyx and one of emerald. There was also a short strip of soft, silver metal.

Felan held the mirror for her as she created a small braid on the left side of her head. She slipped the onyx beads on first, as she had seen in Perfidia's braid, and then added the one of emerald, securing the three by bending the soft metal beneath them.

"Now you look like a proper Evarian."

"Thank you, Felan," she replied, pulling him close.

He stood silently for a moment as she released him. A peculiarly sober expression lingered upon his face. She found it strange. Felan was not the type to show embarrassment.

"Perfidia mentioned that you asked about hers," he said.

Selene found it difficult to hide her surprise. She did not think that Perfidia would have remembered the conversation let alone relayed it to Felan, though the queen had become rather friendly towards her of late.

"I'm glad that you like them so well," Felan said at last, returning to one of his characteristic grins, "because I have a favor to ask of you."

"What sort of favor?" she could not keep the suspicion from creeping into her tone, no matter how hard she tried.

"Consent first, and then I'll let you in on it." Felan motioned for her to follow him back into his room, to a settee which stood beneath a tapestry of delicately stitched wolves and bare winter trees. He closed the doors to the balcony and took a seat next to her. "You're the only one I can trust with this."

Selene was not sure that she liked where this conversation was headed. She and Felan had developed a solid reputation for waywardness amongst those who lived and worked within the castle. Their antics were not enough to turn annoyance to anger in most cases. Still, it seemed that the most daring of their adventures started with Felan confiding to her that she was the only one he could trust.

"If you would just tell me what it is beforehand," she began.

"Please, Selene? This is important, honestly." His mouth pulled into an amused grin. "Remember the specter?"

She did indeed remember it. The incident was one of their first transgressions. It began with Selene realizing that her levitation ability, combined with Felan's telepathy and a good sized piece of cheesecloth borrowed from the kitchens, made for a rather convincing specter. It continued with Perfidia passing out cold on the floor of the Hall of Ancestry, and ended with Felan and herself scrubbing much of the castle's laundry for the next three weeks. Xaiden insisted that it had to be done between their regular training, leaving little time for sleep. Perfidia did not take kindly to being at the center of a jest, no matter how harmless. The plan was Selene's to begin with, and thus Felan figured that she owed him. It did make sense, in a way.

"Fine, if it means that much to you. Now will you at least tell me what sort of crime we'll be committing?"

"Of course," Felan leaned towards her. "We'll be breaking into Damaeus' room."

"Absolutely not," Selene said, rising. "That sort of thing could get a person killed." She started towards the door. "My initiation is in less than two weeks. If Damaeus' magic doesn't slaughter us then Xaiden surely will."

"Selene, wait," A soft warmth washed over her mark as Felan grabbed her arm. "It has something to do with Cael and Devren."

Selene turned to face him. "What do you mean?"

"I picked up a few of Damaeus' thoughts. It was just before he left on his journey to collect spell ingredients, three days past."

"Didn't Xaiden forbid you to read Damaeus' and Perfidia's thoughts?"

"He did, yes, but this was accidental, I swear it."

Selene could not bring herself walk out now, though her conscious warned her against remaining.

"He has Cael's stone."

Her thoughts stilled as the shock of his words passed over her. Everyone was quite distressed over the finding of Devren's Stone. It seemed that the king's eldest son was no longer living, and that Cyanna was now the heir to the throne. She had also heard it mentioned that Cael's Stone had not been found, though why that was of importance she could not surmise. She had thought the man to be dead. Selene lowered her voice as she spoke.

"But he told King Graelen that he was unable to find it. Why would he lie about such a thing?"

"I don't know."

"What happened with Cael?" Selene asked. "People act strangely when I mention his name." She was certain that Felan knew a great deal more of the story than most, and now seemed an opportune time to pry it from him.

"I should not tell you. King Graelen has forbidden us to speak of it."

"But you haven't taken a vow on it."

"No, I haven't," he agreed.

"Please, Felan?"

Even the ladies' maids knew more of it than she. It was horribly unfair.

"You won't tell anyone what I've said?"

"Of course not," she replied. "You know as much."

"Fine, then. Better to hear it from me than from Xaiden, I suppose."

Selene grinned, to which Felan rolled his eyes.

"Cael joined the Aranth long before my time, but sometime after Xaiden," he said finally. "He was forced into service as you were, though the circumstances were not nearly as clean as those which brought you here."

"What do you mean by that?"

"I can't tell you. You can ask Xaiden if you truly wish to know, but I would advise against it."

Selene suppressed a sigh. No doubt he would leave out most of the interesting parts. "Go on, then."

"Cael was a good friend of both myself and Xaiden, or so we were led to believe. He was quite loyal in his service to the Ethereal Realm despite his past."

"I suppose that you can't tell me of that either?"

"No, I can't. But I can tell you the most important bit; that Cael is responsible for the death of King Graelen's eldest son. Xaiden thinks himself at fault, at least in part, for he is the one who convinced Cael to join the Aranth."

"But the Aranth vow," Selene said. "I thought that it was not possible to break it."

"I'll explain it to you as Xaiden did to me. An Aranth is not supposed to be able to kill a member of the royal family directly or his brand would take his life. But the magic is ancient. The effects of any spell will deteriorate over time. This is part of the reason that the castle always has a mage in its employ."

"To repair magic?" She found it strange that such a thing was necessary, or even possible.

"Sort of. The spells that come with the Aranth brand, as well as those that protect the castle, are terribly complicated. They are in dire need of replacement, but none of the Mages who have served the castle in recent years have been talented enough to do so. Thus the spells have been patched instead. The spell that keeps others from being able to remember that we are marked is one of the few that has not yet been compromised. Its magic seems to be quite a bit more durable than the rest."

It was a frightening thought. Selene resolved not to dwell on it.

"Anyway, that's not what's important. If Damaeus truly has Cael's Stone then he must know where he is and whether or not he lives. Either way, he has no reason to keep that information from King Graelen."

"Why don't we just have Xaiden question Damaeus about the Stone? That way we won't have to risk getting ourselves killed."

"Can you imagine me asking Xaiden to put the Queen's brother to question?" Felan asked incredulously. "Someone who has never done anything even remotely disloyal in all of his years here? Someone King Graelen trusts with his life? It would be my word against his. That's why I need to get into Damaeus' room. I need to find some proof of his deception. I need to find out why he lied about Cael's Stone."

Selene breathed a deep sigh as she sat back down upon the settee. "I'll go with you."

"I knew you would."

"I assume you've thought of a way in?" She hoped that he had not. Everyone in the castle knew that the entrance to Damaeus' room shifted. Many members of the castle staff had happened upon it by accident at least once while going about their chores. There did not seem to be a pattern to its movement. It could be in the West Courtyard one moment and in the upper hall the next. The door blended into its surroundings, taking on the look and texture of the wall adjacent to it, much like the door of the room the Aranth used for questioning. A touch to its surface would reveal it for what it truly was, though it usually moved only moments after being found.

"I happen to know for a fact that it was most recently seen on the north wall of the Common Room," he said proudly. "I accidentally plucked that bit of information from Perfidia earlier today."

Selene chose to ignore his blatant misuse of the word accidentally. "And how do you suppose we get past the lock?"

Felan held his palm out to her, exposing a rounded ball of black glass approximately the size of her thumbnail. It reminded her of the marbles she and Islyr played with as children.

"I don't see how a marble is going to help us."

"It's not a marble."

"Then what is it?"

"A latchstone. Observe."

Selene followed him out into the hall. Felan closed the door behind them, removed the key from his belt pouch, and locked it. He pressed the latchstone against the keyhole. The stone wobbled slightly, losing its glossy appearance before melting into an oozing puddle that clung to the door. It slithered into the keyhole like a miniscule black snake. A series of short clicks emanated from inside the lock. The stone then slipped back into Felan's hand and returned to its former, rounded shape.

"Try it," Felan said.

Selene turned the handle. It opened easily.

"It cost me more than I would have liked, but there's no way we'll be able to get in without it." Felan pushed the latchstone back into his pouch. He held one hand out, inviting Selene back into the security of his room. She entered gratefully. It would not do for someone to hear them speaking of their plans. Damaeus may have gone, but Perfidia surely hadn't.

"And the magic?" Selene asked. "There are certainly spells protecting his room from forced entry. I don't want to open the lock only to be roasted alive by some sort of magic flames, or have my flesh suddenly melt from my bones." She did not know much about the Mages' arts, but what she *had* learned was enough to turn her stomach to knots.

"I've already thought of that," Felan said much too cheerfully. He searched through a chest of drawers which stood on the far side of the room and pulled out several small items. The first of the two, which he handed to her, was composed of a smooth, cream colored stone which had been carved into the perfect likeness of a raven. The other, which he kept for himself, had been shaped into a wolf.

"Void-charms," he said. "Each one has two charges. I hope that will be enough. It was the most I could find on short notice."

Void-charms could be easily found at most independent Mage's shops, though they were costly and most often held only one charge per piece, which meant that they became useless after absorbing a single spell. Selene had seen them carved into a myriad of tiny shapes; animals, people, coins, weapons, even food items and furniture. It was common for people to collect the used ones. It would have been nice to have had one during her days as a Rider, though she would never have been able to afford such a thing at that time. It was thoughtful of Felan to purchase one shaped like her Affinity. She could keep it in her room afterward to serve as a reminder of today, though the chance that she would want to be reminded of what they were about to do was slight.

"And you're certain that Xaiden and Perfidia will be occupied?"

"Positive. She wanted to go to the Square for a few things. Today is Xaiden's day."

King Graelen had not allowed the members of his family to go anywhere outside the castle grounds without an Aranth escort since the last Bloodsoul attack. Each Aranth had been assigned days of the week for such duties in order to leave them all with a bit of free time. Selene was included, though she was not yet truly one of them. She had found that she did not mind taking the children anywhere they wanted to go when her days came around. Escorting Perfidia, however, was a different matter. The queen had been acting strangely of late. She was much friendlier than she had been in the past, and seemed oddly delighted about her days with Selene. She took her shopping in town, bought her food and drink, and insisted that Selene call her by her given name. Selene found their time together to be awkward, at best. She tried her best to be companionable, though she had almost nothing in common with the woman. Perhaps her Majesty was lonely. She supposed that a queen did not have much chance to find friends.

"I should return this before I really do end up losing it," Felan said, grabbing Xaiden's knife from a nearby table. "And I'm going to check and make sure that they're still out. Meet me in the Common Room in ten minutes?"

"Alright."

Selene made her way slowly towards the Common Room, dallying a moment in the Sky Room though it was out of her way. When she finally reached her destination she found Felan sitting by the north wall in one of the room's plush chairs.

"Took you long enough," he said, raising an eyebrow in question.

"I promised that I'd help you," she replied, "but I never said that I'd be quick about it."

"True enough. Are you ready, then?"

"As much as I'm going to be, I suppose."

Felan stood and reached out, touching a finger to the side of a polished oak panel near the center of the north wall. Dark iron spread from the tip of his finger. It grew outward to reveal a studded metal door.

"You have your void-charm? Your flesh must be touching it for the effect to work."

"I know that."

Selene realized that she was gripping it so tightly that the raven's beak was digging painfully into the palm of her hand. She loosened her hold on the carving.

Felan pressed the latchstone to the keyhole. It slithered obediently inside. The door clicked and groaned in protest, then all was silent. Selene thought that perhaps one of Damaeus' spells had rendered the latchstone useless, but her fears eased as the slender river of black glass returned to Felan's hand.

"Ready?" he asked as he took hold of the iron handle.

"I suppose." She did not bother to keep the nervousness from her voice. "You realize that you owe me greatly for this."

"Don't fret," he said with a rogue's grin. "If we're burned to ash when I open the door then I promise I'll never ask you for another favor."

"If we're burned to ash because of you then you'd better hope that whatever body you claim in your next life is quick as well as clever," she replied.

Felan pushed the door inward.

The Common Room flashed with blinding, white light. Selene's void-charm took on the chill of full winter as it soaked up the spell that had been protecting the door. Magic crackled through the air around her. It left a misty haze within the room as it dissipated. Selene blinked several times. Only when the colored spots that danced around her vision had ceased was she able to see Felan.

"Good thing I thought of these." He brandished his void-charm before heading into the room. The stone carving had turned from cream to stormy grey. "One charge left." He seemed rather pleased with himself.

Selene was greatly relieved that only one spell had been cast upon the door. She did not think that her heart or her vision could handle another. She followed Felan into the darkness, staying as close behind him as she could manage. It would do no good to remain in the Common Room at this point. The longer they lingered, the greater the chance that they would be found.

A familiar odor seeped into Selene's lungs. It made her eyes water. The scent was wholly unique, as if someone had mixed rotting flesh with daffodils, and it was one she associated solely with Damaeus. She could smell it most times when he was near, though it was strongest when she was in raven form.

Selene once attempted to discover exactly what it was that caused Damaeus to smell so horribly foul. She decided, after much thought and a long discussion with Felan, that it was probably best not to know. Felan then suggested purchasing a bar of scented soap from the Square and giving it to Damaeus as a gift. He even offered her ten gold pieces to go through with it. Selene declined after thinking the matter through. Damaeus worked her mercilessly at lessons, more so when he was angry with her. He did not have his sister's temper, but the jest may not have been taken lightly. Selene drew a shallow breath, wrinkling her nose in distaste. With the way the odor permeated Damaeus' room, she doubted that a single bar of soap would have been nearly enough.

Mirrored oil lamps erupted into flame as Selene closed the heavy iron door behind her. The room was unlike any she had ever seen. No windows graced the black, marble walls. It gave the space a suffocating feel much like that of the Elder's cottage. Damaeus' living space was composed of only two areas that she could see; a bedroom and the room in which they stood. There was no door to separate one from the other. Damaeus probably had no need of one. Felan said that the Mage never entertained any visitors.

Heavily loaded wooden shelves lined each of the walls from floor to ceiling. Most were filled with jumbled stacks of books whose titles twitched as Selene's eyes ran across them. Others held glass containers piled on top of one another in a seemingly careless manner. Jars of dried herbs, powders of every color imaginable, and oily liquids sat precariously atop those containing bloated, white creatures in clear preservative. A hastily scribbled label hung crookedly from the front of each. The letters upon them did not shift, unlike those of the books, though the words were in a language which was frustratingly unfamiliar to her.

A glance towards the ceiling provided a clear view of several dead animals which had been stuffed and fitted with glass eyes. An owl looked down upon her from its cobwebbed, wooden perch. A dusty raccoon stood upon its hind legs, like a dog begging for scraps. Selene waded farther into the room, stepping mindfully around piles of tarnished silver, stone carvings, and one of the largest skulls she had ever seen, the top of which ended just above her knee.

An expertly stuffed saltsnake lay between two shelves in an otherwise empty corner on the far side of the room. Its tan and white patterned scales stood out easily against the aged wood. Saltsnakes were quite dangerous in the wild, where their colors blended perfectly with the ocean salt that crusted around dried tidal pools. Many lived around the town of Maresbane, and Selene's mother had warned her repeatedly not to play near the salt beds for fear that she would be bitten. Though the snakes were small, their fangs held enough poison to kill a man in less than five minutes. Selene leaned closer. She wondered what in the name of the Spirits had possessed Damaeus to stuff one of the creatures.

The snake struck without warning.

Selene jumped back, only to witness the creature knock its head on a disturbingly clear pane of glass. Her latent ability slipped, causing several books to topple from the nearest shelf to the floor. She drew a frantic breath, grasping for control of her power.

Felan made no attempt to hide his laughter.

"That was not at all amusing," Selene mumbled as she used her latent ability to return the books to their places.

"You can't be cross. You would have laughed if it had been me."

She could not argue with the statement. "Let's get this over with. The smell of this place is making me sick."

"Right," he agreed. "You start on the left side. I'll take the right."

Selene was more than happy to do so. Part of the left wall was taken up by a sizeable desk, leaving fewer shelves for her to search.

"Be sure to put everything back just where you found it," Felan reminded her.

"Yes, yes. I know," she replied irritably.

Selene moved cautiously towards the desk. It was made of wood, though a dark lacquer had been applied so thickly to its surface that the grain was no longer visible. A matching chair with a seat of worn velvet sat crookedly beneath it. The desk was the only piece of furniture in the room that was not blanketed with Damaeus' possessions. In fact it was empty aside from a glass topped, wooden case which held a delicate spiral horn the color of fine porcelain and three books, which had been stacked with unusual care. Selene pushed the glass panel aside. She lifted the top book gingerly from its place, flipped it open, and attempted to read. The words shifted and blurred, making her eyes ache. She closed it in frustration.

"Language of the Mages." Felan looked up from the dilapidated chest through which he had been rummaging. "Can't read it unless you're one of them. You may as well give up. You'll only succeed in giving yourself a headache."

Selene set the book back down as close to where it had been as she could manage.

"Cael's Stone isn't going to be in a book," Felan added, turning back to the chest. "Quit wasting time."

Selene took a moment to stick her tongue out at the back of his head before pulling on the first of three drawers which had been built into the front of the desk. It was locked.

"Throw me the latchstone, will you?"

Felan dug through his belt pouch and, upon finding it, tossed it to her. Selene caught it easily with her free hand. She would have used both hands, for fear of losing the catchstone in the sea of items beneath them, but the other hand held the only thing protecting her from Damaeus' magic, though only one charge remained. She wasted no time in pressing the latchstone to the keyhole. There was bound to be something interesting inside, seeing as it was locked.

The drawer opened easily, though its contents turned out to be rather disappointing. *Another book.* Selene lifted it out nonetheless, opening it where a thin strip of leather protruded between pages. The words held steady as she read them.

The Healer shall arrive in the Aranth's decline, as the lands prepare for winter's sleep. And with the passing of the one she believes to be the last of her own shall she be promised to the ranks of the Aranth against her will; thus shall she battle for their cause, which she believes to be just.

On the day of her bond shall the journey begin, as a raven's flight into darkness.

By the given title of Aranth shall she discover the nature of trust in others, and thus shall that trust be forsaken. She shall unknowingly lay herself, in either body or soul, before those four who she considers to be constant, their true motives mixed of love, power, greed and honor, thus allowing them to betray the faith she has offered.

She is the one to whom kingdoms may fall; in whose hands lies the unification of the Army of Shattered Souls. She, given a choice between honor and darkness, with the unwilling aid of her living flesh and blood, shall be inexorable in her rule; for she is the one who commands the flesh, the air, and the lost souls of the walking dead.

She shall be the hope of the many, or the ruin of all, for she is a creature in which evil may thrive.

Selene thumbed ahead. The text continued on for several pages before breaking. She turned the book over to read its title.

Daxun, Ander. It was an Aranth journal.

"Do you know anything of an Aranth named Ander Daxun?" she asked Felan hesitantly.

"A little. I've never been much on foretelling. The future is always changing, as I see it. There's no way to truly know what is going to happen before it happens. Even in the off chance that some of it does come true, I've heard that it's never in the way that you think it will be."

"Ander Daxun could tell the future?" Selene slid her thumb over the book's leather binding where the letters of his name and the Aranth symbol had been pressed.

"Crazy fellow, from what I heard. His real name may have been Ander, but everyone called him Elmaen. That means 'prophet' in the ancient tongue. Most of the Aranth of old didn't go by their given names. They preferred to use a name that matched their latent ability or affinity instead. His latent ability gave him dreams of the future, though I can't tell you how much truth was in them."

"And where did you learn of this?"

"From Damaeus. He just loves talking about prophecy, even to those who don't wish to listen." Felan rolled his eyes. "I'm surprised that he hasn't bored you to death with tales of Ander Daxun like he did me."

"He never mentioned him."

It seemed narcissistic to believe that the foretelling had anything to do with her. After all, there had been at least one other female Aranth. Many females would join the Aranth in the future as well, for all that she knew.

"What was Novalin's latent ability?" Selene asked through the lump in her throat.

Upon receiving no answer she looked up from the journal to find Felan in the far corner of the room. In his left hand he held a worn leather sack. In his right was a hunting knife with a dark wooden handle. His face was as pale as morning frost.

"What's wrong?"

Selene made her way towards him. She beseeched the Spirits that he had not come across one of Damaeus' spells while she was pondering that idiotic journal. She should have been looking for Cael's stone instead of wasting time with Damaeus' books.

"Felan?"

He turned to her then. His eyes held a distant look. "This was Luca's." He clutched the knife so firmly that his knuckles were pale.

"Are you certain?" She knew that he was, even as the words crossed her lips.

"I gave it to him just after our father died, for protection. He had it with him when he disappeared. He always carried it with him."

"He had no knife on him when he…" She found that she was unable to say the words. "He may have lost it. Perhaps Damaeus came upon it, around the castle I mean. Perhaps he meant to give it to you when he returned."

Felan stared down at the weapon as if seeing the spirit of his brother within it. "I suppose," he said doubtfully.

"Wait for a few days after Damaeus returns, and then you can mention it and see what he says. If you take it now then he'll know that we've been here."

Felan nodded absently. "It's strange though, Luca's knife wasn't engraved the last time I saw it. Maybe Damaeus did it, but it doesn't seem to be in the Mages' language. The letters don't shift, but I can't read it."

"May I see?" She did not want to upset him any more than was necessary, yet getting the knife away from him seemed prudent.

He handed it over reluctantly.

Selene's thoughts began to drift as she gazed upon the writing. The words did hold a strange familiarity. Her mind converted them into recognizable letters. She began to read. The vibrating whisper began in her chest. It pulsated upwards, soothing her and calling her home. Her soul yearned to submit to the pleasure of its song. She hated that which was keeping her from it, though her mind could not determine what it was that betrayed her.

In the distance, jars fell from the shelves and shattered. Far away, Felan brought his hands to his head in agony.

Selene longed to tear herself away from the body that held her. She longed to give in to the calm warmth of the words. She longed for freedom. She longed for power and knew that she could have it, if only she would surrender.

Felan's hand striking her face brought her back in a horrifying rush. The breathtaking words slipped from her grasp. Reality engulfed her, holding her soul to its place like a leaden weight. Her skull felt as if it might collapse from the pain.

"I told you not to let go of the void-charm!" Felan seemed much closer than he had been. His words were deafening. "We need to get out of here." He pushed something cold and hard into the palm of her hand.

Selene's thoughts were clouded and heavy. She puzzled over Felan's expression. It was different, somehow.

"It must have been your touch that triggered it," he said. "But why would Damaeus think to set a hidden spell upon Luca's knife?"

Realization came to her at once. He was terrified.

"Perhaps because my flesh was touching the void-charm and yours was not," he muttered, seemingly to himself. "Perhaps the spell knew it."

It had been the most wonderful sensation. Selene could not begin to guess what troubled Felan so. Thinking came with such difficulty. "I'm sorry, Felan. We can stay. I'm fine now, really."

He did not seem to hear her.

"The Spirits keep me if that didn't sound just like a Bloodsoul's cry." He returned the most glorious knife to its sack and grabbed her wrist with his free arm.

The warming of her mark swept away what was left of the mist from her mind. Still, she glanced longingly towards the sack that held the knife as he pulled her to the door.

He stopped suddenly.

"Is something wrong?"

"We're in trouble." Felan replied.

Selene looked down at the bits of broken glass, books, and various unidentifiable objects that now covered what little empty space there had been on the floor. She thought Felan's worries to be largely unfounded. "Everything will be fine. We'll clean up as well as we can. Damaeus can't possibly keep track of everything in this refuse heap he calls a room. He'll never even know that we've been here."

Selene knelt down to retrieve a sizeable piece of shattered glass while attempting not to touch the bloated, tentacled creature that lay next to it. She straightened to find herself face to face with Perfidia. Her Majesty's expression looked as if it could scald stone.

Nothing can worsen this situation, Selene thought. She would be doing chores long after taking her Aranth vows. That was if she was allowed to become Aranth.

It was then that Xaiden entered the room.

"I am pleased to see that your Aranth have found something worthwhile to occupy their time while my brother is absent," Perfidia said in a smooth, icy tone.

Selene shifted her eyes towards Felan. He remained silent, which she believed to be the safest course of action given the circumstances.

"So it seems," Xaiden said with his own sidelong glance at Felan. "It was foolish of me to think that they could conduct themselves in an acceptable manner without my constant guidance."

"The fault does not lie with you," Perfidia replied.

"You need only name what you would consider to be a suitable punishment, Majesty. I shall see to it that they abide by your word."

For the second time this day the conversation was not going at all in the direction that Selene would have preferred. It was obvious by looking at Felan that he shared her opinion. She fully expected to be working in the kitchens tomorrow morning, if not scrubbing the privies on hand and knee.

"No punishment is necessary," Perfidia said simply.

It took a moment of reflection to be sure that she had heard the queen's words correctly.

"No punishment?" Felan echoed.

Xaiden shot him a chiding look.

"However," Perfidia continued, "I do recommend that they be separated until Selene's initiation into the Aranth two weeks hence. I am by far too busy to be bothered with matters such as this."

Selene's joy evaporated like morning mist. She should have known that Perfidia would not let them off as easily as that.

"It will be as you wish, Majesty." Xaiden's voice was calm, yet his casual demeanor did not cover the disappointment that shadowed his words.

It made her feel all the worse for betraying his faith.

"Do you have anything you wish to say?"

Felan stepped forward. "I would like to offer a sincere apology. I shall be more mindful in the future."

Felan would be mindful, that much she was sure of, though it was most obviously of being caught rather than of respecting the privacy of others. It was Felan who had taught her that Xaiden's ability did not have the power to distinguish between such things.

Xaiden scowled. No doubt the thought had occurred to him as well. "And you?" he asked Selene.

"My deepest apologies to each of you. I assure you that it shall not happen again."

Xaiden seemed more satisfied with her answer than he had been with Felan's. "Would you like them to replace the belongings that have been broken?"

"That won't be necessary, though I thank you for the offer. My brother is not likely to miss anything that they have damaged, in all honesty, though I will question him on the subject when he returns."

Selene could not imagine Damaeus taking any of this calmly.

"You should speak at length with your Aranth on the importance of trust and on the honor of the bond he accepted for the Kingdom of Evaria," Perfidia added. "Selene, you will come with me. I wish to speak with you privately. We will go to my sitting room."

Selene placed one hand behind her back as she made her way around the piles of objects towards Perfidia. She crossed her first two fingers so that only Felan could see. It was the sign that they had agreed upon to let him know that he had permission to enter her mind. She would be bored to death without his company, especially if she was forced to spend any amount of time with Perfidia or perhaps, Spirits forbid, Damaeus. It was fully worth the intrusion upon her privacy.

Good luck with Xaiden, she thought, knowing that he would already be listening.

I think you have the best end of this deal, he replied as Xaiden led him away. *Guess the Tides are flowing your way today. I'll contact you when Xaiden is finished with me. That's if I'm still living.*

Selene followed Perfidia to the upper hall in silence, though her mind sprinted through every possible scenario as they walked. The queen ushered her into the sitting room immediately upon reaching it and gestured for her to sit. She perused the labels of several bottles of red wine before choosing one and pouring both Selene and herself a glass. It was a very old vintage, dry, and not nearly as enjoyable as the ale that Xaiden and Felan brewed. Selene sat stiffly. She attempted to seem grateful for the drink, though her stomach was nowhere near settled enough to accept it. She found Perfidia's hospitality troubling.

"I beg your forgiveness, Majesty," Selene said as Perfidia closed the thick, wooden door. "Neither Felan nor I meant any harm by our actions."

Perfidia's face was as still as the portraits that hung in the Hall of Ancestry. "I know why you entered my brother's room," she said between careful sips of wine.

This was worse than Selene had at first thought. It was now obvious why Perfidia had not wanted Xaiden to punish her. She intended to do it herself.

"Majesty, I assure you-"

"No need for formalities. I asked that you call me Perfidia. Have you forgotten?"

Selene had not forgotten, though the fact that Perfidia had given her permission certainly did not make her any more comfortable with using her given name. "No, Perfidia, I have not."

The braid in the queen's graying hair swung forward as she leaned towards her. Fresh wine scented her breath. "I want you to know that you have my approval."

It had to be a ruse. Surely Perfidia would only say such a thing in order to make her betray the true reason that they had entered Damaeus' room.

"In fact, you have my blessing."

"I'm sorry," Selene said before thinking, "I'm not certain I heard you correctly." She realized at once that she had just insulted Perfidia. She knew that she should use formal speech when addressing a member of the royal family. Cyanna was only excluded because she was young, and because she and Selene were companions. *Common speech is only acceptable amongst friends in this place,* Xaiden had informed her, as if it was somehow not true of everywhere else. He, for one, seemed to use formal speech all of the time. Not a single combined word had ever passed his lips, as far as she could tell. Felan said it was because of his age.

Perfidia did not seem to notice. "You have my blessing," she repeated.

"I really am so sorry," Selene began again. "We were merely curious. Damaeus never allows anyone into his room. We wanted to see the living quarters of a Mage." She had never been happier that Xaiden was not nearby, though the thought that he may be questioning Felan at this very moment set her on edge almost as much as Perfidia's pleased expression.

"I have always felt a special kinship with you, Selene." The corner of Perfidia's mouth lifted into a rigid smile.

The situation was quickly getting out of hand. Selene was not certain that she and Perfidia were engaged in the same conversation. In fact, she had no idea what Perfidia was speaking of. Perhaps her Majesty had consumed a bit of hard liquor while at the Square.

"I know of your feelings for Damaeus. I thought that you may need someone to speak with on the subject. I assure you that it is nothing to be ashamed of. I will not betray your confidence."

Selene could not believe that Perfidia actually expected her to say aloud how much she hated Damaeus. She gulped the rest of her wine and searched for a place to set the glass. Upon finding none close by she settled for gripping the stem nervously in one hand. She did not think that she had ever been more uncomfortable than she was at the moment, trapped within Perfidia's merciless stare.

"Well," Selene began. She knew that she should say something, yet she was not at all sure what that something would be.

"No need to be timid," Perfidia interrupted. "It was clever of you to convince Felan to aid you in your crime. He has always had talent for such things."

Selene would not let Felan forget how much he owed her for this.

"I understand your pain. I, as well, am unsure of what to do with myself in Damaeus' absence." Perfidia placed her hand upon Selene's shoulder. "Your love for my brother is no secret to me."

The wine glass slipped from Selene's hand. She snatched it with her latent ability just before it hit the floor. She stared at Perfidia in disbelief, silently thanking the Spirits that she had not revealed her true thoughts. Selene's mind struggled to work out what she should say. It would not be prudent to anger her. "I beg your pardon, Perfidia, but you are mistaken. There is nothing between Damaeus and myself." She couldn't wait to tell Felan of this. The look on his face would be absolutely priceless. It was a pity that she would not be able to see it.

"Of course," Perfidia answered.

"I speak the truth," Selene said more forcefully.

"I see," Perfidia said after a moment of contemplation. It was obvious that the queen did not believe her. "Tell me this, then, if you will. Is there a possibility that you may become involved with him in the future?"

Selene had endured near as much of this as she could take. She wanted to tell Perfidia that under no circumstances would she ever feel anything short of aggravation towards Damaeus; that he was one of the most self-centered, abrasive men she had ever met. The Queen's expression told her that any answer that strayed too closely to the truth would be highly unacceptable. Selene silently thanked the Spirits once more for Xaiden's absence before speaking.

"I suppose it is possible." It was not a complete falsehood. Perhaps even Xaiden's ability would not have proved her wrong. It *was* possible that she could at some point have a relationship with Damaeus, though the likelihood of such a thing was nearly nonexistent. She would have to be either heavily drugged or at least a hair's breadth past insanity to enter into such a thing willingly.

Perfidia seemed pleased by Selene's words. She raised the bottle, offering her more wine.

"No, thank you," Selene said as politely as she could manage. "It has been quite pleasant speaking with you, yet I have a several chores that I must finish before dinner. I would not want to anger Xaiden. He is not pleased with me at the moment, as you know."

"Very well," Perfidia replied. "I shall see you at dinner. Perhaps we could go for a short walk afterwards. I would like to go down to the shore. Although it is Xaiden's day to watch over me, I am sure he would appreciate some leisure time. Perhaps that would improve your standing with him as well."

Selene suppressed an irritated sigh. "Yes. It would be my pleasure to accompany you." It would be a very long night. She rose from her chair and headed for the door, walking as quickly as was possible without seeming hurried. "I will see you at dinner," she called from the relative safety of the hall.

"I do not believe that it is healthy for you to be spending so much time around Felan." Perfidia called from the doorway. "He is drawing you down a dangerous path."

"Thank you for your honesty, Perfidia." She continued to back away from her as she spoke. "I will certainly consider your words."

Selene paced herself as she headed down the stairs. She was searing with anger by the time she rounded the corner. If the queen thought that her words would sway Selene into rejecting a friend then she was sorely mistaken. She would obey Perfidia's orders as an Aranth in training, but her personal life was her own. Suits of armor and mounted weapons rattled in place as Selene passed them. She drew a deep, calming breath while reciting the words Damaeus had taught her.

My thoughts are pure serenity, she finished at last. The objects stilled.

Perhaps some time in meditation would serve her well. Xaiden required at least one hour of meditation each day, split into three twenty minute sessions, as part of her training. She may as well do the last of it now in case he asked her about it later. She could go to the Hall of Ancestry. Perfidia hardly ever visited there. Afterwards she would think up some believable chores with which to occupy herself before dinner. Selene would gladly scrub the privies if it would keep her away from Perfidia. She hoped that Felan was having better luck with Xaiden.

Becoming Aranth

The Holding was not at all what Selene had envisioned. It floated upon the ocean, for one; a massive, cage-like structure of steel bars secured to a wooden base. They were still quite far from it, yet the cries of angered Bloodsoul carried easily across the water.

"How many are held within at the moment?" She glanced at Xaiden and Damaeus, who sat at the front of the tiny boat discussing some subject of little interest. They did not seem to notice that she had spoken.

Ninety and some, I think. Felan ran his fingers over the handle of Luca's knife as his words entered her mind. Damaeus had given the weapon to him shortly after his return. The words of magic were no longer upon it. In fact, there was not so much as a mark upon its handle. Felan carried the knife everywhere despite the pitying looks he received from those who knew its story.

Xaiden was fond of saying that a person must make their peace with the past in order to succeed in the future. She hoped that Felan would soon take that advice to heart.

Damaeus caught Selene's gaze as it moved over him. The smile he attempted looked greatly out of place beneath such severe eyes.

I'd be more cautious if I were you, Felan thought to her. *He'll be sending you more gifts. Who knows what it will be this time.*

Very amusing, she replied, touching her words with sarcasm.

Selene had received at least one gift per day from Damaeus ever since he returned from his journey. The items included everything from candied apples to armor. Her theory was that he had no idea what she was fond of, and thus had decided to send one of everything.

Flecks of white darted around the top of the Holding, which was open to the air. *Seabirds*, Selene realized as they drew closer. Hundreds of them dove down in attempt to pull pieces of flesh from the ambling Bloodsoul beneath. A hand of yellowed bone snatched a bird in mid-flight and pulled it into the cage. Loose feathers floated gently down, coming to rest in the water below.

You shouldn't put too much faith in that journal, Felan thought, perhaps noticing her expression. *I've told you how prophecy is.*

I want to do this, Selene answered. *Just distract Xaiden and Damaeus for a minute. It shouldn't be too hard for someone as talented as yourself if what Perfidia says of you is true. I'll test it quickly and then, when it doesn't work, I'll have proved you right and we can forget about the whole thing. You owe me for-"*

I know, Felan replied, cutting her off mid-thought. *Just figured I'd share my thoughts on prophecy once again beforehand.*

The vibrating cries of Bloodsoul rose in pitch as they approached. Xaiden tied the boat to the docking post. Selene hopped up on the deck that surrounded the cage before Damaeus had a chance to stand.

Felan pounced upon the Mage immediately. "Wouldn't you say that it looks a bit rusty over there?" he asked, pointing to the far side of the cage. Damaeus frowned, but his eyes followed Felan's hand as it gestured. "Is that a hole?"

That, of course, attracted Xaiden's attention, allowing Selene a chance to slip around to the opposite side of the cage. She had to give Felan credit. He was quite talented in the art of half-truths.

The outer railing was not nearly as steady as she would have liked, and not quite as thick as her wrist. Selene pressed herself against it nonetheless. She wanted to leave as much space between herself and the Bloodsoul as possible. Skeletal arms reached out to her, yet the pathway was wide enough so that a small distance was left between her body and their fingertips. Several of the creatures stopped their cries suddenly as she drew near them. Bare skulls turned to follow her movements.

Selene searched through the group. Her gaze came to rest on a disconcertingly fresh looking fellow. The man had not met with a pleasant end, if his injuries had been caused before his death. Stringy wisps of hair hung precariously from what skin was left upon his skull, one side of which had been smashed inward. His left leg jutted out at an odd angle and one eye was missing, probably taken by the seabirds. The remaining eye dangled from its socket, brushing up against his cheek as he swayed to and fro with the push of the waves.

The foul scent of decay and seabird droppings wafted around Selene. She beseeched the Spirits that the prophecy was nothing more than an odd nightmare of an Aranth of old.

"Sit," she said to the Bloodsoul. It was the simplest command she could think of.

The creature watched her silently.

"Sit, I command you."

It wobbled into one of its brethren as a particularly strong wave rolled past. The creature's loose eye swung like a pendulum. Selene was at once more thankful that none of the other Aranth were with her. She was beginning to feel rather foolish. One more try, just to be sure. She could have chosen poorly. Perhaps some of them were more obedient than others. "You," she said to an ancient, sun-bleached Bloodsoul that clung to the side of the cage. The creature turned its head towards her. *Happenstance, surely.* "Sit," she attempted again.

The creature strode towards her. It stretched an arm between the bars.

It was then that Damaeus rounded the corner. "Foolish girl!" he said as he moved himself between the Bloodsoul and Selene. "Do not draw so close. Must I watch over you every moment?"

The Bloodsoul struck out, tearing at Damaeus' arm with its bony fingers. He smashed the creature's hand back against the bars with surprising strength, splintering them against the steel.

The damage had already been done. Damaeus clutched his injured arm with a sour look.

Selene reached out to him with her healing ability. The blow smashed down upon Selene's mind like a forge hammer with the force of ten men behind it. She brought her hands to her temples in agony as her latent ability bounced back, striking out in the direction of the cage.

Nearly one month ago Selene had dropped one of the castle's porcelain tea cups upon the Common Room floor. The sound she heard now was similar, though much louder. It lasted for only a few seconds before being engulfed by pure, strange silence. Selene opened her eyes. Damaeus, Xaiden, and Felan were all staring at the space where the Bloodsoul had been. All that remained of the creature was a haphazard pile of splintered bone fragments.

The wind passed over the pile, yet the fragments did not stir. The only sound to be heard was the lapping of waves. Selene looked up. Not a seabird remained in sight.

Damaeus' face contorted with anger. He took hold of Selene's shirt and pulled her to him. "Do not *ever* use your latent ability upon me without my permission!" He released her with a shove and stormed back towards the boat, pushing past Xaiden and Felan without apology.

Selene was left speechless. Damaeus had been angry with her before on more occasions than she could count, yet none of those times compared to the rage he showed this day. She looked to Xaiden for aid.

"What have you done?"

"It was an accident," she answered quickly. "Damaeus was hurt. I attempted to heal him. He reflected my latent ability, I think. It must have struck the bloodsoul."

Xaiden scrutinized the pile of shattered bones. "I never would have thought of such a thing, though I suppose that it does make some sense."

Selene could not see how what had happened made the least bit of sense, though she would not dare say so. "I'm sorry, Xaiden." Her head was still reeling from Damaeus' magic. "I should know better than to use my latent ability upon another person without asking." She had become so used to healing Felan and Xaiden on whim that she had not given it a second thought. She supposed, thinking back on it, that it *had* been rather rude of her. Much like before she and Felan had made the bloodpact; when he had used his latent ability to read her thoughts any time he had the notion.

The bone fragments shivered and began to piece themselves together.

"You need not apologize to me," Xaiden said, showing surprisingly little concern for Selene's disrespect towards Damaeus. "Your healing ability obviously has a rather negative effect on the walking dead. I would like you to try it on another. A fresher one, perhaps."

Selene would have been content not to use her latent ability for days with as much as her head ached, yet she did not want to upset Xaiden seeing as he was in such a pleasant mood about the whole thing. She reached through the pain and took hold of her healing ability. After searching briefly for the Bloodsoul with the dangling eye, she pushed her power towards it with full force. It splattered, creating a nauseating pile of flesh and fragmented bone upon the wooden floor of the cage.

Felan muttered something unintelligible. His face, which had been splashed by bloodsoul remains, held a nauseated expression.

Within moments the pieces of bone shivered and began to re-form. The viscous mass of flesh that surrounded them stayed mostly where it had fallen, though a few rogue pieces of skin and muscle swept up onto the slowly forming skeleton where they hung like tattered festival ribbons.

"Perhaps we will work on this later," Xaiden said, noting Felan's expression as he dipped his hand into the sea to clean his face. "Let me show you how to gain entrance to this place, after which we should head back to the castle. You must prepare for your induction ceremony."

Selene followed Xaiden and Felan to the front of the Holding with only a short glimpse back at the Bloodsoul. The first was now fully formed, and was once again wandering aimlessly throughout the cage. Damaeus was seated at the front of the little boat. He did not acknowledge her presence.

Selene listened carefully as Xaiden explained the workings of the entranceway. It was a set of enclosed gateways, the inner of which could be raised only while the outer gate was shut, allowing bloodsoul to be added as they were captured, yet preventing accidental escapes.

Felan had obviously heard the speech before, and so chose to spend his time on the opposite side of the cage taunting bloodsoul while Xaiden's back was turned. He put his hand between the bars, withdrawing it just as the creatures reached for him. Their vibrating grumbles of frustration joined the squawks of returning seabirds. Selene found his antics to be rather distracting, especially during Xaiden's lengthy speech on the levers and gears that controlled the doors.

Xaiden continued to speak about the Holding as they sailed back to Evaria's docks, which suited Selene quite well as it gave her a reason to ignore Damaeus' sulking. The Mage disappeared instantly upon reaching land. Selene wanted to apologize to him, but she supposed there would be time for that later. Only a few hours remained before she would become Aranth.

The ceremony was always performed at dusk; a tradition from times of old. She would certainly see Damaeus there, though she doubted that he would show himself at the celebration that Felan said was to follow. Damaeus was not much for large crowds of people, and Selene had heard that all of Evaria would be a part of the festivities. She imagined that it must have been exciting living in Evaria when the Aranth were great in number. Xaiden, she knew, would like nothing better than to see their ranks grow once more.

Xaiden gave Selene permission to leave as they reached the horses. The single, rather bored looking Standard Guardsman who had watched over the animals in their absence perked up immediately upon noticing their return. It was not soon enough, unfortunately for him, to escape Xaiden's notice. Selene mounted Cyprus as Xaiden gave the guardsman a stern lecture on keeping up appearances while in public, with Felan looking on in amusement. She started back through town, leaving the unlucky man to his fate.

Many of the shops that she passed were closed, and the center portion of the square was roped off in preparation for the dancing that would later occur. There were several areas in which Selene counted herself as talented. Dancing was certainly not one of them. Xaiden had given her some lessons, yet she would only consider herself decent on a good day. Her hope was that by the time the dancing began it would either be too dark for anyone to see her mistakes, or else they would be too intoxicated to notice them.

The wonderful smell of baking bread mingled with that of roasting meat and spices, which caused her mouth to water. There would be a great feast after the ceremony, as

Felan told it, and the festival would most likely last until morning's light. Selene passed several open booths selling some rather tempting sugared pastries, and a few smaller vendors hawking crystal candies. Jugglers, musicians, story tellers, and puppeteers were practicing on street corners. The small crowds that gathered wherever they stood would surely grow before the evening's end.

Selene stopped first at the Aranth bathing quarters upon reaching the castle. A tub of heated water scented with extract of roses was quickly prepared behind the curtain of fabric that sectioned one half of the room from the other. She removed her bloodsoul splattered clothes and slid gratefully into its warmth. It was not likely that Xaiden and Felan would enter the room while she was bathing, especially with the way the ladies' attendants hovered about the doorway, but Xaiden insisted that the curtain be there in case an accident should ever occur.

Several weeks ago Perfidia had insisted that Selene had need of ladies' maids to assist her. The queen swore that the magic of the castle would keep the girls from remembering Selene's mark for more than a few seconds even if they were to see it, but Selene remained doubtful. The first time that she requested a bath they attempted to help her wash as a mother would a child though Selene was their senior by at least five years. She put an end to that as kindly as her patience would allow. The girls continued to heat and mix her bath water for her. That was one area in which they would not yield.

Selene left the water reluctantly though it was beginning to turn cold. She pulled one of several robes that hung upon the wall near the hearth over her shoulders, then pushed the curtain aside. Mera and Sedna were still there, just as she expected. She handed the girls each a silver piece.

"Go and join the festivities."

"But Lady Selene, you will need help dressing." Mera objected.

"I have been dressing myself for over twenty years, thank you. I guarantee that I can manage on my own."

"As you wish, Milady," Sedna said with a curtsy. "But we must come in to turn up your bed later in the evening."

Selene considered it a small victory.

"Fine, but please lock my door when you are finished. I do not wish anyone else to gain entrance."

They both giggled at that, for they had seen the gifts and knew that she was speaking of Damaeus. "Yes Lady Selene," they replied at last.

When Selene finally entered her room she found Perfidia waiting for her. The Queen was clothed in a fine velvet dress of deep blue. Her face had been powdered and her graying hair had been set with tiny gems the color of a midnight sky. The band of braided gold that always graced her forehead had been polished to a lustrous shine. "I thought that you may need some aid in preparing for the initiation ceremony," she said, motioning towards the garments that lay upon Selene's settee. It was obvious that Damaeus had not spoken to his sister since his return from the Holding. The Tides had granted her that much luck, at least.

"Thank you, Perfidia. This is most considerate of you." Guilt eased its way into Selene's thoughts. The Queen had been so pleasant to her of late, and yet she found it difficult to accept what kindness she was given. "I would appreciate any aid that you are willing to lend." She pulled the undergarments from the neatly laid pile and began to dress.

"I had hoped that we would be able to spend more time together before you became Aranth," Perfidia said as she helped Selene into a fine cotton shirt and then a leather bodice of midnight blue. The symbol of the Aranth was embroidered in silver thread upon the left side. "I have come to miss your company over the past few days," the queen continued as she laced a black leather cord through the eyelets that lined each side of the bodice. It was clearly made for the female form, for it clung to Selene's curves in all of the proper places, yet it was thick enough to be armor nonetheless. Selene wished that she could have had something like it during her time as a Rider, though it most likely would have caused her more trouble than good considering the type of men who often rode with her on errand.

"There are several more of these in your wardrobe. Some with the symbol of the Aranth and some without, in case you should have need of them." Perfidia stepped back as she finished tying the cords. "The design was quite difficult to come by. It seems that Novalin first formed the idea. She became weary of wearing armor designed for men."

Selene finished dressing and moved to the mirror. The bodice lent a definite air of femininity to the Aranth formal armor.

"I thought that it would suit you well," Perfidia said. "I believe I was correct.

It was truly a kind gesture. So much so, in fact, that Selene became slightly uneasy at the thought of it. Perfidia did not seem to treat anyone, not even Cyanna, with such care. She pushed her concerns aside. The queen was obviously trying her best to be pleasant. What type of person was distrustful of someone who had been nothing but kind to them?

"We will still be able to see each other after I am Aranth," Selene said. "I am certain that I will have some free time to spare." Selene's only true friends were Felan and Xaiden. She had not had any female companions since Kailia's death other than Cyanna, who she thought of much like a younger sister.

"I thought these would go well," Perfidia said, offering two lengths of deep blue ribbon. "Sit."

Selene did as she was told.

Perfidia spoke to Selene of the honor of becoming Aranth as she wove an intricate braid through her hair, entwining the ribbons and the braid which held the beads that Felan had given her within it. The setting sun bathed the town of Evaria in crimson and ocher as she finished. Selene pulled on her breeches and boots. She looked into the mirror one last time before embracing Perfidia. An odd smile touched the Queen's lips as they parted. "My husband awaits you," she said. "We shall see each other again in good time."

Selene made her way quickly to the throne room. She recited the calming words that Damaeus had taught her before pushing the twin doors aside.

Intricately woven Eyrisian carpeting led her over marble floors as white as pure snow. Ahead lay Evaria's throne; a creation carved from a dark, unfamiliar wood inlaid with silver. The sight of King Graelen seated upon it made Selene's stomach clench. His left hand rested with ease upon the pommel of his sword. His eyes held a commanding gaze. She had spoken with him many times before, and had supped with him nearly every day since she found herself here, yet he had never looked so much a king as at that moment. A lesser chair had been placed to his right, upon which Perfidia sat. She must have taken a shorter passage to the room, for she did not look winded in the slightest. Damaeus stood to the King's left, wearing a white Mages' robe of softly flowing fabric. His face showed no discernable emotion. Perhaps he would not see fit to hold a grudge, or perhaps he simply knew better than to show his temper before King Graelen. Either way she was safe from his wrath for a good part of the evening.

Xaiden and Felan stood just beyond Damaeus. Selene marveled at their appearance, for it encompassed what she had always believed to be the essence of the Aranth; a lethal combination of power and splendor. It was a spell which was only temporarily broken by the smile Felan offered upon meeting her gaze.

"Kneel before your King," Xaiden's voice was hard with the authority of his position.

Selene knelt, turning towards King Graelen. She and Xaiden had gone over the ceremony a hundred times, yet she still feared that she would make an error; that actually repeating the words of the Aranth before the Spirits and the King would turn out to be much more difficult than she had anticipated. Selene had allowed the Aranth to train her. She had made them her companions, all while ignoring the impossibility of her position. Aranth were the heroes of stories; pleasant dreams to counter the evils of the world. She would become a warrior of truth, an apparition of fireside tales to some, when for so long she had been nothing more than a nightmare.

King Graelen stood. "For what reason do you approach me on the dusk of this day, as the Spirits and the earth meet as one?"

Selene found her voice with less effort than she had expected. "I, Selene Valenne, request permission to join the ranks of the Aranth," she replied, bowing her head, "to offer my life to the Spirits and the Ethereal Realm."

Xaiden's voice echoed across the vast space. "Speak sincerely the pact of the Aranth before the Spirits and his Majesty, and they shall judge the merit of your request as the sun makes its decent."

Selene's heart pounded against her chest. She formed her words carefully. "I vow before the Spirits and the throne of Evaria, upon my life as I devote it to the Aranth in whole, to uphold the law of the Ethereal Realm and to strive to meet the ideals of society. I vow to lend aid to the innocent where it is needed and to strike down those whose souls have been corrupted by the evils of the world.'

King Graelen nodded his head, as if encouraging her to continue.

"I vow to keep the secrets of the Aranth, to reject those family and friends who have known me, and to shed my blood in pact only to my kinsmen. I reject my right to form the bond of caerim vows, though it may mean that love is forever lost to me. With these words I vow to exterminate those that come to learn the truth of the ways of the Aranth and those who would seek to harm my kinsmen, whether their souls be of innocence or evil."

"I vow to remain true to King Graelen's authority and to those who follow in his reign. I will protect the lives of my King and his kin as I would my own. May the Spirits keep my soul from the lives which shall follow if they find these words to be false."

Selene returned her gaze to King Graelen. His Majesty glanced at Xaiden, who nodded in the slightest. The King then pulled an ivory handled knife from a black silk bag. He drew the knife across his palm and then handed it to Selene. The ivory was cold against her skin. She pressed the knife's razor edge into her hand, forming a pact-line.

"I accept your vow as truth," King Graelen said as he held his pact hand out to her. "Do you willingly give your life to my service?"

Selene accepted his hand, pressing her blood against his, and stood. "My life is yours. Do with it what you will."

Xaiden came to her then. She handed the knife to him, watching closely as he made his pact-line.

"My life for yours," she said, pressing her already bleeding palm against Xaiden's freshly scored flesh. A fierce warming crossed her mark.

"My life for yours," he replied in kind.

She repeated the ritual with Felan, thinking of what Xaiden would do if he was ever to find out that this was not their first blood pact. "My life for yours," she said, attempting not to ruin the terribly formal moment by smiling.

"My life for yours." Felan kept his composure well.

Damaeus approached Selene as Felan withdrew. The Mage held a branding iron with the symbol of the Aranth in one hand. Selene tried to read his expression, but could not discern anything other than a look of concentration. He muttered a few unintelligible words of magic. The branding iron began to glow with soft, white light. "Your left hand," he hissed. Selene held it out to him. Damaeus gave her no warning before pressing the iron against the back of her hand. Freezing pain blossomed where iron touched flesh. Selene remained calm, allowing him to do what he would. She would not play his games. Damaeus muttered to himself as he released her and returned the branding iron to a gilded chest. Selene wondered whether they were Mages' words, or a curse that she had not shown a hint of pain as he had branded her. She found that it made no difference. Her hand now held the sign of the Aranth. She would forever be one of them.

"Rise," King Graelen commanded.

Selene stood.

King Graelen held out the Aranth sword and matching scabbard that Meiun had made. "This is my gift to you, as the newest member of my Elite Guard. May you use it well."

"I accept this token with deepest gratitude." She lowered herself into a sweeping bow. "I shall serve Evaria and the Ethereal Realm with honor."

"I welcome you, Selene Valenne, to the ranks of the Aranth," King Graelen said with a pleased smile. "And I grant all Aranth freedom from what duties they might have this night, so that they may participate in the festivities."

Selene embraced both Xaiden and Felan before heading up to her room to change into something more suitable for the festival. Upon her desk she found a gift from Xaiden; a knife of the same metal as the Aranth swords, much like the one she and Felan had used to sever her hair. No doubt Xaiden had paid one of the servants to deliver it upon seeing her leave. A note was attached, explaining how it was tradition for each Aranth give a gift to the newest member on the night of his or her initiation. Selene could not help but laugh. It was so much like Xaiden to combine lesson and gift into one.

She placed her sword upon her bed with more than a bit of regret. She did not think she would have need of a weapon tonight, though one could never be completely certain. The knife that Xaiden had given her would do for defense, she decided after some thought. It was difficult to dance while wearing a sword, and she had trouble enough with dancing. Selene changed clothes quickly, for she was eager to see what the festival had become.

Xaiden and Felan were waiting for her just beyond the castle's side entrance, as they had promised. The air was crisp with the coming of winter and tiny flakes of snow, the first of the year, descended as they started towards Evaria proper. Xaiden congratulated her on how well she had done with the ceremony as they walked. Felan, in his standard lighthearted fashion, poured over what they should do upon reaching the revelry. He decided that dancing should be first, much to Selene's dismay, followed by drinking and perhaps a few shows.

Maresbane's Festival of Low Tides seemed like an evening with close friends when compared to what Selene saw before her as they reached town. More people filled the Square than she would have thought possible; their faces just visible in the glare of torches and hanging lanterns. Speech mixed with the music of fiddles and flutes, laughter, and the occasional scream of delight. Applause erupted from the fair-sized crowd that was gathered before an Aureus displaying his arts. The audience gasped as he pressed a burning torch past his mouth and into his throat. They returned to applause as he exhaled fire above them. The scents of food and fire mingled thrillingly with those of sweat and ale.

"Perhaps the drinking should be first," Selene protested as Felan dragged her through the crowds towards the area that had been roped off for dancing. "If I'm going to make a fool of myself I would rather not remember it."

Her words moved both Aranth to laughter.

"Nonsense," Xaiden replied. "You will do well, I am certain."

Selene had never seen him so much at ease.

"You would not break a promise to your fellow Aranth, would you?"

"Ah, no." It was difficult not to seem taken aback by his jovial demeanor. "I suppose I would not." She had promised them each a dance, though she had hoped that they would have forgotten about it by this time. Felan lifted the ropes, pulling her behind him.

Selene stayed true to her word, perhaps more so. She danced several rounds with each Aranth as the moon crossed the sky, taking only a few short breaks for food and drink. They did not seem to care that she hadn't any talent for it, nor did anyone else for that matter, though she figured that their indifference was due to the multiple kegs of ale that had been provided by King Graelen for the festivities.

In the end she did not want to leave, though sparse clouds had gathered and the air had turned chill. Xaiden, who did not seem the least bit inebriated despite consuming as much ale as she and Felan combined, headed off towards the nearest tavern with a few of the Standard Guardsmen to play Forces; a game of war in which colored stones used to represent armies were moved across a piece of cloth upon which the continents of the world had been drawn. Selene had played Forces against Felan and Xaiden several times. She managed to win about one game of ten, on average, which was why she politely declined when Xaiden asked her to come along. She went with Felan instead. He insisted that she should see the view from the top of the Aranth barn, for there was not likely to be another initiation festival for quite some time.

Felan pulled himself easily from the top of the haystack inside the barn and through an upper window. He led Selene around to the far side of the roof, which faced the Square. The tiles were mostly flat there, which made a perfect area for viewing. He sat, and Selene settled herself nearby. Evaria lay far below them. Its beauty was striking. All sound was diminished to nothing by the falling snow, and the lights of the festival glowed like faeries against the darkness, echoing the cloudless patches of the midnight sky above.

Selene leaned back against the roof, enjoying the faint, dizzying warmth of the ale. "Are all of Evaria's festivals so splendid?" she asked.

"Not all," Felan replied. "The festivals of Aranth initiation are the grandest by far."

"Have you been to many?"

"Only my own. I was the last before you."

"Do you think that we'll live to see another?" She slid closer to him; to rest her head upon his shoulder. "I know Xaiden wishes it, despite King Graelen's feelings on the matter."

"Perhaps not," Felan answered distantly. "Luca's would have been the next."

"I'm sorry, Felan." She had not meant to upset him.

"I knew that you would appreciate the beauty of this place," he added suddenly, changing the subject and producing one of his characteristic grins.

Selene could not help but smile back. It was clever of Felan to find his way up here. The window that they had climbed through looked much like any of the others that lined the upper part of the barn. It opened a fair bit wider, however, allowing a person to access the roof. "How long have you known of this? You've never spoken of it."

"No. I wouldn't have," he replied. "I come here often when I need to think on things. It's perfect for when you don't want any company."

"My being here sort of ruins the effect then, doesn't it?" she offered in jest.

"Not at all," A slight color crossed his cheeks, perhaps from the ale.

The wind circled softly around the eaves of the barn, gathering snow in a gust as it went.

"I have something for you."

Selene's mark warmed pleasantly, adding to the dizzying effect of the drink, as Felan took her hand in his. He released some small object into her palm. Moonlight glinted from its surface. She recognized the object, after a moment, as Luca's Stone. The silver talons had been polished and a new length of leather held it.

"I can't possibly accept this," she said as she attempted to hand it back to him. Felan rarely released the Stone since its return. If anything of Islyr's was left she would certainly keep it as close.

"Of course you can. It's already set to you, anyway. Just channel your power through it. Be careful though, Stones amplify your latent ability much more than you would have thought possible. They're hard to control on occasion. Sometimes it seems as if they have thoughts of their own." He took it gently from her hand and fastened it around her neck, looking amused at her doubtful expression. "Xaiden agreed that you should have one, if that's what you're worried about. He said that you've learned enough to earn one."

"No, it's not that, but there are other Stones and this one-"

"Please," he said, his eyes firm. "I want you to have it."

"Felan," she protested, "I just can't-"

Felan leaned in, pressing his lips to hers. The kiss caused a pleasant shiver of warmth to cross Selene's mark. It was unexpected, yet she found that she had no wish to escape. He slipped his arms around her waist, pulling her against him. The thrill of his embrace pushed all doubt swiftly from her mind. She delighted in the wave of heat that flourished at his touch. She had been kissed before, yet never by one who was marked. The heat of her mark grew to an exhilarating burn. It spread downward as she pressed herself closer.

"I hope that I am not interrupting anything of importance."

Selene turned abruptly from Felan's embrace. The caressing burn of her mark ceased, yet the fluttering feeling inside her remained. Damaeus scowled down at the two of them. His eyes matched perfectly with the flakes of snow that landed on his robes.

"What are you doing here, Damaeus?" Felan's tone was as close to irritation as Selene had ever heard it. "King Graelen gave us leave for the evening, in case you've forgotten."

"And it seems that you are making good use of the time you have been given," Damaeus replied bitterly. "But then you never were one to waste an opportunity, Felan. Always a step ahead of the other fools."

Felan's cheeks colored as Damaeus crouched down to him.

"It is not I who wishes to see you," the Mage whispered. "It is my sister."

Felan's anger softened ever so slightly. Selene would have missed it completely had her gaze not remained upon him. Felan levered himself from the roof, dusting the snow from his clothing. *I'm sorry, Selene. I should go.* His words filled her head in a soft rush. She had not given him the signal to allow what she had previously considered an intrusion upon her privacy, yet she found that she was not angered by it in the least. *I hope that the next time we meet will be as pleasant as this night.* He disappeared around the side of the barn, heading towards the window through which they had come. Damaeus' acid stare lingered upon Selene for a moment before he followed.

Selene took a deep breath, drawing the frigid air into her lungs. She leaned back against the roof, tracing the moon's steady path from clouds to starlit sky and waiting until the headiness that had come from the ale and Felan's touch gave way to clear thought. When she was certain that Damaeus had made his way far enough into the castle for her to avoid him she headed back to her room, thinking on what had occurred as she walked. Felan had not given any indication of his attraction to her until tonight. *Could it be the vow?* she wondered silently as the murmuring sound of the Sky Room river soothed her. She sat upon the bridge and watched the shadowed forms of sleeping fish waver beneath the water. Perhaps Felan could not show his feelings earlier because she was not truly Aranth. But the vows only forbade the taking of caerim vows, and he had not balked at bending the vow of the blood pact. *Or was it because of Damaeus?* It was common knowledge amongst the castle staff that Damaeus was vying for her favor. Felan may have wanted to avoid upsetting the Mage at first, but perhaps over time he had changed his mind. He had never been one to spare Damaeus' feelings. And the whole thing had ended miserably, if that was in fact what he had been attempting.

The why of it does not matter. Selene realized at once as she climbed the stairs that led to the Aranth hall. For the first time in her new life she was free to choose a path that pleased her. Felan knew her for what she was and he did not judge her for it. Indeed, he could not judge her, for they shared a curse between them.

Selene paused with her hand pressed up against the smooth metal handle of her bedroom door. Her eyes caught movement at the far end of the hall. Few lamps had been lit there since her room, Xaiden's, and Felan's were all at the end where she stood. She squinted against the darkness in attempt to make out a recognizable shape. Shadows danced in the flickering lamplight. Surely that was what had caught her eye. She started to push the handle once more, but heard a shuffling sound, much like that of footsteps, and turned her full attention in the direction from which it had come. There was nothing to see, yet a slight, foul odor caught her senses.

"I am not of a mind to play games with you at this hour, Damaeus," she said with more than a hint of irritation. "I will speak with you tomorrow, if you wish."

The form stepped from the shadows, swaying as if caught in a breeze. Selene was not given the chance to wonder how it had entered the castle. The bloodsoul came at her with a vibrating roar that rattled the hanging lamps, sending several of them crashing to the floor and leaving the area in near darkness. Two others appeared suddenly behind it, the white of their tilting skeletal forms made them visible even in so little light. Selene stared in disbelief. Five more came at once from the direction of the stairs, blocking off her escape.

A sickening realization came to Selene as the creatures bore down upon her. She had no weapon save for Xaiden's knife, and her levitation ability was not strong enough to encompass all of them at once. She pushed hard upon her bedroom door. With her sword she would stand a chance. She could hold them off for a few moments, at least. The door refused to open. For once Mera and Sedna had followed Selene's orders, and now she would die for it.

Selene threw open her belt-pouch, grabbing her knife with one hand and searching frantically for the key with the other. She ducked beneath the bloodsoul's grasping arms and reached out with her latent ability, sending the creature careening down the steps behind her. The few Bloodsoul that she had hoped to hit with the creature moved swiftly out of its way. Shock washed over Selene. These Bloodsoul were much quicker to react than any she had fought before.

The others reached her then. Selene lashed out with her knife, slicing easily through the wrist of one. Its hand slid across the floor, stopping at the wall for a moment before shuddering and returning to its proper place upon the creature. The Bloodsoul whose hand had been severed paused only inches from Selene's face. It cocked its head as a dog would upon seeing some small, curious animal of prey. It was as if something akin to thought rolled around in its brainless skull. The possibility pressed Selene's stomach into knots. Death-scented air brushed against her face as the Bloodsoul leaned in. The respite lasted only a moment's time. The others came at her. Arms composed of bone and rotting flesh grabbed at her suddenly from all sides, tearing flesh and clothing alike. Selene tried to pull away, but their putrid bodies shadowed her every move. There were too many, and a knife was of no use against creatures who could not feel its blade. She attempted in vain to shield herself. Pain flashed through her forearm as bony fingers sliced its flesh. Selene's ears rang with their vibrating screams.

Luca's Stone warmed against her chest suddenly. Memories of the Holding rushed into her mind. Selene channeled her healing ability through the Stone, amplifying and bending it to match her needs. She pushed her power out, willing it to surround her. It swept across the bloodsoul, stifling their screams of anger with a sound like the waves of a storm against the shore. Selene's healing ability filled the hall, traveling the length of it with impossible speed. She fell to her knees. A throbbing ache engulfed her mind. She released her power. Silence reclaimed the Aranth hall.

Selene opened her eyes slowly, frightened of what she would find. The hallway was as black as Alchemist's pitch. She held her breath, straining to hear the scraping of gathering bones. The sound did not come. She reached into her belt-pouch then, her hands slick with warm blood, and found the key which had eluded her with such ease only moments ago. The smooth wood of the door slid easily beneath her fingers, ending finally in cold metal. She pushed the key into the lock and turned, opening the door. The gentle glow of the fire that Mera and Sedna had prepared in the hearth crept past her. The dull, aching pain of her head gained strength as her eyes adjusted to the light. The sight of the hall astounded her. A few scattered shards of bone were all that remained of the Bloodsoul. They did not stir. The walls were coated in a white, powdered substance. She ran one finger through it. The powder clung to her skin. It smelled of decay.

Selene wiped her bloodied hands upon her breeches and entered her room. She took her sword from where it lay upon the bed and looped her belt through its scabbard. The weight of it gave her comfort. She healed herself enough to cease the bleeding in her forearm, threading her power through the Stone to do so. The use of her healing ability, slight though it was, made her head feel as if it might split open. Rest would cure it, when there was time for such things.

Selene sprinted from her room, heading in the direction of the Imperial Hall where the royal family's bedchambers were found. Cyanna and Barrik would be there by this hour, perhaps Perfidia as well, if she had finished speaking with Felan. King Graelen was an excellent swordsman, though he was not Aranth. There was no doubt that he would be able to hold his own against a bloodsoul, perhaps two for a time. It was his family who would need Selene's protection. Perfidia was beyond terrible when it came to weaponry of any sort, and Cyanna and Barrik were simply too young to learn it to the point of being proficient.

An unnatural stillness greeted Selene as she entered the Imperial Hall. Only the two lamps which hung next to Cyanna's door were lit. Their meager light did not allow Selene to see nearly as far as she would have liked. She headed towards Cyanna's bedchamber first, for the door was open ever so slightly. She did not want to frighten the girl if it was avoidable. It was possible that the bloodsoul Selene had encountered were the only ones that had entered the castle, but it was not likely. She pulled a lamp from the wall and set it upon the floor, tilting the mirrored back so that light shone into the room, then pushed on the door. It slid evenly at first, but caught upon something solid half-way in. She peered around the corner. Shelves of books had been toppled. Cyanna's writing table and chairs lay broken against the far wall. White feathers, most likely from the bed in the other room, covered the chaos like fresh snow. There was no movement to be seen.

A muffled sound came from Cyanna's sleeping chamber. Selene drew her sword. She reached through the ache in her head to find her healing power and crossed the room, stepping carefully over the crumpled rug that was wedged beneath the door. She breathed a sigh of relief upon entering, for she found neither Cyanna's body nor any bloodsoul within. Everything had been destroyed, however, just as in the living area. A cloying odor wafted from the carpet, where smashed bottles of perfume lay. *Strange behavior for Bloodsoul.* Selene thought as she stepped over the remains of Novalin's crate. The little scrub pig was nowhere to be seen.

The sound came again, allowing Selene to isolate its location; a wardrobe which rested in the far corner of the room near the window. Shards of glass crunched beneath her boots as she made her way towards it. She levered doors open with the tip of her sword. It was empty. Odd, she was certain that the noise had come from within. The muffled sound came again, as if the wardrobe itself was speaking. It was then that Selene noticed a small hole in the corner of the base, near the back. She pressed one finger into it and lifted. The panel of wood pulled away with little effort. Something squirmed beneath. She moved closer. Barrik pulled his arms tight to his head, screaming with fear.

"Barrik, it's alright," Selene said, sheathing her sword. "Are you hurt?"

Barrik looked up at her then, shaking his head. His eyes were red with tears. He looked to be unharmed for the most part, though a shallow gash crossed his forehead. A rivulet of dried blood ran from the wound to his jaw. Selene healed the wound, heedless of her throbbing head.

"The bloodsoul," Barrik whimpered.

"They're gone," Selene said softly, beseeching the Spirits that it was the truth of the matter. She lifted him up. He clung to her as if letting go would be the end of him.

"No," he insisted, bursting into fresh tears. "They caught sis."

Selene's stomach knotted once more. "Come, let's find your father." She attempted not to let her fear show as she carried him from the room.

She came upon Xaiden first. He was standing over two tethered bloodsoul in the north hall. The creatures' rattling groans caused Barrik to bury his face in Selene's shoulder.

"Tell me of what occurred," Xaiden said.

Selene told her story, beginning with the attempt to enter her room. She left out the portion where she had thought the first of the creatures to be Damaeus, as it was not completely necessary and also mildly embarrassing.

"What of Cyanna?" Xaiden asked when she finished.

Barrik burst into tears once again upon hearing his sister's name.

"Barrik seems to think that she was taken." Selene wished for Xaiden to tell her that Bloodsoul were not capable of planning such a thing as kidnapping, let alone executing it with success.

"I see." His short response did nothing to allay her fears. In fact, it made them somewhat worse.

"Dispose of them," Xaiden said, motioning towards the struggling Bloodsoul. "The rest of the castle is being searched by the Standard Guard. I have warned them not to travel in parties of less than ten men. They should be able to handle what bloodsoul remain." He paused, and his expression hardened. "There is trouble, Selene. The bloodsoul are the least of it. King Graelen has ordered us to gather in the Throne Room. I will take Barrik."

Selene passed Barrik to him. She wondered what could possibly be worse than a Bloodsoul attack within the castle walls.

"Do not linger," Xaiden said, rubbing a hand across Barrik's back in attempt to calm him.

Selene waited until Xaiden had rounded the corner with Barrik before disposing of the bloodsoul. She did not want to frighten the boy any more than was necessary. Her healing came to her more easily than it had in the Aranth Hall. The ache in her head had faded slightly since she had healed Barrik, but it returned in full force the moment she touched her power. The struggling Bloodsoul crumbled to dust. She watched the piles of bone powder for a short time, to be certain that they would not reform.

An unexpected sense of nervousness encompassed Selene as she entered the Throne Room. King Graelen stood in the center of the vast, white marble floor, with Xaiden and Damaeus nearby. Rows of Standard Guardsmen, at least fifty by her hastened count, stood at attention near the east wall.

Fifteen more stood at each side of the main doors. Selene could not remember ever seeing so many of them in one place. Barrik was nowhere in sight, much to her surprise. Perhaps Perfidia was watching over him in a place of safety.

All conversation ceased as Selene entered, and the three men turned to her. King Graelen did not look at all pleased. "Is it too much to request that my Aranth come to me in a timely manner?" His demeanor put her in mind of a rapidly breaking storm.

"My most earnest apologies, Majesty," Selene replied, taken back by the expression of loathing that crossed his face. He had always been pleasant with her. Often, when she had crossed Perfidia and Damaeus, or even when she had angered Xaiden, though raising the Aranth's fury was truly a difficult feat, King Graelen had taken her side of things. Perhaps the stress of this evening had worn away his patience.

"I do not wish to hear your apologies," he growled. "I wish to hear an answer to my question. I accepted you into my Elite Guard with open arms. You have devoted your life to my service, and you cannot come to me when I am in need of you?"

"Majesty," Selene stammered. "I assure you that I came here as quickly as possible. I disposed of the bloodsoul as Xaiden asked. Using my healing power in such a way is new to me, so I stayed an extra moment to be sure that the creatures would not return to form. Surely Xaiden relayed his orders to you."

"So he did," King Graelen drew so close that Selene could smell the light scent of festival ale that traveled with his breath. "But, in truth, I do not care what occurred after you met up with Xaiden. I am much more interested in what you were doing before that time; between the time that Xaiden left you in the Square and when you came across him once again in the Imperial Hall."

Selene faltered for a moment, attempting to think of what it was that she had done wrong. The constant throbbing of her head certainly did not help matters. She could come up with nothing. None of her actions that night could possibly be considered a breech in her vows. King Graelen's eyes met hers. It was clear to her that silence would not do for an answer.

"Felan and I," she began, mindful of Damaeus' contemptuous stare. "He brought me to the top of the Aranth barn. He wanted to show me the festival lights from above." Her mark warmed at the thought of what had occurred there. She did not wish to tell King Graelen of it. She did not wish to tell anyone of it. "He wanted to give me my initiation gift," she added at last.

King Graelen's expression darkened. "And what was that gift?"

"Luca's Stone."

"Where are they?" he roared.

His hands were on her throat. They pressed hard, crushing it. She moved her lips to ask him who he meant, but found herself unable to draw a breath.

"You are the most powerful amongst the Aranth. With a Stone you may well eclipse the strength of the Spirits themselves. That is why he befriended you. That is why he chose you for his lover. You are the only one capable of destroying the bloodsoul. He knew that you would be safe amongst them while he abducted my family and destroyed my kingdom. He left you here to finish what they could not."

Selene's still throbbing head reeled as King Graelen pounded her back against the wall. His arms held her with much more strength than she would have believed him capable of.

"He left you to take my life!"

She tried to tell him that he was mistaken, that she would never think of harming him. She struggled for breath.

Blackness crept in, obscuring her vision and threatening to claim her consciousness.

"Traitor!" he screamed with rage. "You know where they are and you *will* tell me of it!"

Xaiden rushed towards them then, whether he meant to grab her or King Graelen, Selene did not know. Either way he was too late. Her Stone heated, and King Graelen's hands were ripped from her throat. He slid back across the pristine floor to strike the marble platform that held his throne. Selene dropped to the ground, gasping for breath. Her Aranth brand turned chill, and her chest began to ache. The blackness ebbed like evening tides.

King Graelen rose slowly, his eyes filled with disgust. A wound ran from his forehead to his cheek, marking the place where his face had collided with the edge of the steps. He made no attempt to wipe the blood away as it flowed from the gash. When he finally spoke it was not to Selene, but to Xaiden.

"You trained this monstrosity," King Graelen said, motioning towards Selene. "Is this what my ancestors have wasted their lives to create?" Blood dripped from his cheek, marring the pristine white floor. "Unrivaled nightmares? Death honed to precision?"

Selene recognized the look that King Graelen's eyes held as they rested upon her. It was the same look that Ranur had given to Luca on the errand she had taken so long ago. It was a look far beyond hatred. King Graelen wished for nothing else more than he wished for her demise. More than that, he yearned to be the one responsible for it.

Selene pushed herself carefully from the floor. She had not meant to use her latent ability to harm him. Her hand came, unbidden, to settle upon the hilt of her sword.

"You need rest, Majesty," Xaiden said softly. "We will begin our search for Perfidia and Cyanna at morning's light. I will-"

"Be silent!" King Graelen commanded.

If Xaiden was taken aback by the king's outburst, and Selene was sure that he must have been, he did not show it.

"I accepted you into my service. I befriended you, as my father did, and his father before him. I lost my son, my heir, to the Aranth yet still I trusted that you would not betray me. My losses are much greater this day. I will end the treachery of the Aranth tonight." He looked to the ceiling, as if begging the Spirits for aid. "But even now, at the worst of my days, you will find that I am not completely without compassion. You will leave before morning's light. Any Aranth found upon the castle grounds when the sun crests the eastern sky shall be brought to death by my hand." He drew his sword, pointing the tip towards Xaiden's throat. Xaiden made no move to reach for his own.

"You may redeem yourself by no means save one," King Graelen continued. "I do this for you alone, Xaiden. A master cannot be responsible in whole for the crimes of his students. You must punish your brethren. Slay Felan. Offer me proof of his death. Redeem Selene or destroy her. Bring my living wife and daughter before me. If you should return without meeting my conditions your life, and the lives of any that follow you, shall be forfeit."

Xaiden stood in silence for a moment.

"As you wish, Majesty," he said at last, bowing deeply. "My life for yours."

Selene remembered how she had felt upon losing her mother. The scar within her would never fully heal. A much deeper scar would have been created had she lost Maye through the treachery of a friend. Cael had taken King Graelen's son, and he now thought that Felan had taken his wife and daughter. Selene pitied him for all that he had lost, but at the same moment she hated him for holding the Aranth responsible. "I honor my vows," she said, watching his unchanging expression. "I will return to you, not with Felan's body, but with proof of his innocence." She turned her back to him then, heading out of the throne room and towards the Aranth Hall.

No less than fifteen standard guardsmen followed Selene as she walked. She did her best to ignore their presence, instead thinking over the day's events and those of the passing week in attempt to find something Felan had said or done against the royal family. She came up with nothing. Selene knew that he had met with Perfidia before the Bloodsoul attack. Surely Damaeus had told King Graelen that Felan was the last known person to see her. Felan had been troublesome at times. The Spirits knew that Selene had as well, but it was never more than a few harmless jests. The look that crossed his face when Damaeus spoke of Perfidia upon the Aranth roof was odd, indeed, but far from a showing of murderous intent.

Selene's latent ability slipped, causing the decorations of the hall to rattle. She found that she did not care to bring it under control.

Only a few hours remained until daylight. Selene had no doubt that King Graelen would hold to his word. She would need to leave this place alive if she wished to clear Felan's name.

The guardsmen stood in her room as she packed clothing and the few small personal items she possessed. She worked quickly, but with an air of calm about her movements. The guardsmen would remember the dignity she kept in her remaining hours, if they remembered anything of her.

At last she was ready. Her favorite cloak lay heavily upon her shoulders. It was the warmest one she owned, and was a beautiful deep black with tiny silver ravens embroidered around its edges. She secured the platinum clasp at her neck before heading out of the castle.

Plump, white flakes of snow drifted lazily through the air, pushed by frigid winds. Several inches of snowfall lay upon the castle steps, obscuring the stone and resting heavily upon the branches of the leafless trees that lined the road. The guardsmen left Selene as she reached the Aranth barn. She was certain that they would be waiting for her at the castle's entrance, should she attempt to return.

The interior of the barn stood empty save for the horses, whose coats had thickened considerably during the past few weeks in preparation for the descending temperatures of deeper winter. Selene woke Cyprus gently. Several of the other horses nickered softly at the sound of her footsteps. It was a pity that she would no longer be able to see Trinine. She hoped that he would be well cared for in her absence.

Selene had just finished placing Cyprus' saddle blanket upon his back when a foul odor reached her. Selene drew her sword in the blink of an eye, only to find Damaeus' neck at its point. Exasperation, caused mostly by the night's events, erupted to the surface.

"The next time you sneak up on me like that," she said irritably, sheathing her sword, "I may just kill you."

Damaeus watched her silently.

"And for the Spirits' sake," she added, "find some time for a bath. A few moments, at the most, and you would be done with it."

"I understand your pain," Damaeus said, seemingly undisturbed by her biting words. "It is quite a lengthy fall from Aranth to exile."

"You understand nothing," Selene replied, levering Cyprus' saddle onto his back. "Pity will not change the events of the past. Therefore I am not in need of any, least of all from you."

"I did not come here to bestow the gift of my pity. I came to offer aid. Danger awaits those traveling in small numbers. You should know this, having once been a Rider."

Selene considered the Mage for a moment. His concern for her welfare momentarily eased the biting hatred she felt for him.

"I appreciate that Damaeus, but you should not be seen in my company. Xaiden will see to my safety, and I to his." She was partially to blame for Xaiden's exile, and she would not let herself forget it. Besides that, she had rather been looking forward to finally escaping Damaeus' attention. She considered it one of the few rays of light that could penetrate the darkness of recent events. Still, there was no need to insult the Mage. "King Graelen's anger is quite long lived, from what I have heard, and I would hate to think that I caused yet another of Evaria's force to lose their livelihood."

The Mage's white eyes glowed against the darkness. "Not to worry. His Majesty has already given his consent."

"Is that so?" Selene frowned and turned away from him under the guise of making sure that Cyprus' saddle bags were properly balanced.

"Indeed it is. He said that I should do as I wish. Perfidia is my sister, lest you forget. It is in my best interest, as well as that of the Ethereal Realm, that she is found soon and in good health."

"Be that as it may, I believe that we will be better off following separate paths."

"And I believe that you are wrong," the Mage replied, placing a hand upon her shoulder.

Selene pushed him away, glaring. Her patience was at an end. "I do not need your help, Damaeus, nor do I want it." Never in her life had she been forced to resort to such blunt discourtesy with anyone else save for Terran, and he had usually grown sullen at her words or ignored them completely. Damaeus did neither.

"You are angry, but it will pass. You will come to realize in time just how much you are in need of my aid." A smile crested his lips. "Your fellow exile has come to terms with the severity of your situation. He has agreed to let me accompany you. Therefore, whether you are agreeable or not I shall do so." He leaned closer to her, lowering his voice to a whisper. "You would do well to obey Xaiden's wishes. I believe you owe him that much courtesy."

Xaiden appeared then, leading Requiem and a well-tamed mare named Sable. The horse was exceedingly gentle for her age, and thus was used most often with untested riders. It was hardly a secret that Damaeus had no talent for riding.

"Do what you will, then." Selene suppressed a sigh of frustration as she loosened Cyprus' tether. The Mage was right, much to her chagrin.

The wind came in rapid gusts, swirling snow around Selene's face as she led Cyprus out of the Aranth barn.

Xaiden handed Sable's reigns to Damaeus before settling himself onto Requiem's back. He turned to Selene then, his expression unreadable in the pre-dawn light. "Lead the way," he said.

Selene regarded him with puzzlement. Her tracking abilities were passable at best. Praecyrs were expected to be exceptional at such things, but for Riders such skills were not necessary. To track someone through a snowstorm in the dark was far beyond her capabilities.

Xaiden's brow furrowed.

Selene wished that she had paid more attention on the few hunting trips she had taken with her father. He would have been able to find Felan in this weather. She would have bet her life on it.

"Your Stones are bonded to each other," Xaiden reminded her with less patience than was usual.

"Are you certain?" Felan had not mentioned that he had bonded the Stones. Their conversation had ended rather abruptly, however. Perhaps he had not been given the chance.

"When one Stone is touched to another it forms a bond between the two," Xaiden explained. "The bond enables the wearer of one Stone to be able to find the other, no matter how much distance stands between them. Felan inadvertently set his Stone to yours on the first day you came to Evaria. He did not want to believe that Luca was truly dead. He touched the Stones to each other, hoping that the Stone you had taken would continue to glow with Luca's colors. He told me of it, for the Stone glowed white instead, a color which is rarely heard of."

"And your Stone is not bonded to Felan's?" Selene asked.

"My Stone was bonded to one person only, long ago," Xaiden replied. "That person is no longer living." His tone kept Selene from pushing the matter any further.

"I would gladly use my Stone to guide us," she offered. "But I haven't a clue how to do so." Time was growing short. They should leave soon if they wished to be gone from Evaria by the time the sun began to rise.

"Simply concentrate on Felan and you will be able to feel his presence."

Selene did as she was told. White light flashed from beneath her cloak. She was amazed to find that she did indeed know where he was headed, though he seemed much farther away than should have been possible. Perhaps she did not fully understand the feeling it gave her. It was, after all, her first attempt.

"Southeast." She tapped Cyprus gently with her heels.

"I know of a place where we can stay for the night." Xaiden offered as he followed. "There is a decent campsite a few miles from Evaria's limits. We can get some rest there before continuing our journey."

Selene was somewhat relieved at his words. The night was beginning to wear on her. Thoughts of her forthcoming initiation ceremony easily kept sleep at bay for the past few nights, and the excitement of the festival had long since faded.

Selene looked back to find Damaeus thumping Sable's sides several times in a clumsy attempt to make her move. The mare took it in stride. Selene pulled the hood of her cloak up against the wind. The Aranth barn faded behind her, and she turned to the path ahead.

Lystonne

Damaeus smiled to himself as he dusted away layers of snow and dead leaves to reveal a solid bronze ring. The problems with voyage rings were few, and the benefits were innumerable. It was well that he had thought to put one here. He could be back amongst the Aranth long before they woke. True, placing the rings cost him much more time than he had anticipated, but his journeys were easily explained away. Mages were always in need of ingredients of some sort, and the spell components for finding a person's location were exceedingly difficult to come by. Especially when that spell did not truly exist. Graelen had been more than willing to fund Damaeus' expeditions so long as he believed that it may bring some proof of Devren's survival. The hope of a parent paid death no heed.

Damaeus stepped into the ring. "*Acleiu imedimun reaulei,*" he whispered. Darkness folded around him and he found himself at the edge of Lystonne behind a long abandoned barn near the edge of the Magden Woods. He could not afford to be overconfident. The spell that he had placed upon the ring would prove quite lethal should a fool attempt to use it without the proper words, but another Mage would certainly be able to meddle with it, changing portions of the spell to take it for his own.

Damaeus began his trudge through the underbrush, cursing the dead branches that snagged his robes and the inches of leaf litter that lay beneath them. It was not far to the main street, where paved stones locked together in a wonderfully flat sprawl, but the distance was enough to make him want to burn the forested area clean. He could not fathom why anyone would choose to spend their time outdoors when any number of perfectly decent pastimes could be carried out in the warmth of one's home.

Trees grew more sparsely as Damaeus walked. Dirt became paving and scattered farm houses gave way to the long rows of connected residences that were unique to the towns nearest the Crimson Abyss.

Featherlarks had already begun to herald the approach of morning. There were very few places within the Ethereal Realm that their shrill voices did not sound. Xaiden and Selene were guaranteed to sleep for a few hours at least. The events of last night had fatigued them better than any spell could. He would be back with plenty of time to spare, assuming that Perfidia could manage what he had asked of her.

The windows of the unopened shops were dark, yet the smell of baking food emanated from several. He quickened his pace. It would be best if his passing went unnoticed.

Each of Lystonne's houses and shops were numbered, which made Damaeus' search particularly simple. Fifty-seven was the one that he and Perfidia had agreed upon. He entered without knocking.

Damaeus' eyes adjusted to the darkness of the hall without difficulty. His vision had grown considerably better over the past few years, in contrast to most of his other senses. The bodies of a man and woman lay before him, their blood seeping unhurriedly into the hewn planks of wood that composed the floor.

"Perfidia!" He made no attempt to hide his irritation.

She appeared at the far end of the hall, silhouetted by the light of what appeared to be the kitchen.

"These were to be disposed of."

Perfidia's green eyes narrowed with displeasure. "Perhaps they would be if you had come to my aid earlier."

"And what do you suppose would have occurred if I had disappeared as you did?" Damaeus asked. Perfidia had an irritating tendency to forget the wellbeing of others when her own was concerned.

"I do see your point," she replied as she crouched down to retrieve a woodsman's axe from the floor, "though you could have offered me something more than this with which to accomplish it. You know that I have no talent for weaponry."

"You seem to have talent enough." Damaeus eased the tip of his boot beneath the dead woman's head. He lifted it slightly, meeting her vacant stare. She was not well-formed by any standards, which made him feel somewhat better about her untimely death. It pained him to see anything of splendor destroyed, though at times it was regrettably necessary. True beauty was difficult to come by.

"They did not fall to me." Perfidia drew the sharpened edge of the axe anxiously along the floor, tracing one of several crooked boards. "With another to assist us these could be moved before you leave. What of Felan? He could be useful, if only for lifting."

Damaeus removed his foot, allowing the homely woman's head to drop to the floor with a pleasing thump. Perfidia's true intentions had become as clear as finely crafted glass. She was not concerned by the lack of aid. She wanted use of her Aranth. Once again Perfidia insisted on exposing that which fouled her soul.

"You may visit your pet later, if time permits," Damaeus offered with a smirk. He would control her completely as long as he held Felan. Only a Mage could command a Marked One wearing a Circlet. His sister knew that it was so. Perfidia placed both hands upon her hips, as if to begin with one of her bothersome tantrums.

"You must treat any Marked One, even one who is held by a Circlet, as an untamed beast." Damaeus closed the gap between them, pressing one hand to the smooth skin of Perfidia's cheek. "They may obey you without question one moment and tear the flesh from your throat in the next. It is a danger to keep him unconfined when I am not nearby, as he has not yet been trained to submit, but I have taken pity on you and allowed it. It would be foolish to remove the spell at this time. I must return before Xaiden awakens, therefore I will not be here to protect you in the event that something unforeseen should occur."

"We had an arrangement, Damaeus. Felan is mine to do with as I see fit. And when we take the harlot she is yours. I have done everything you have asked of me, and more." Perfidia pressed the blade of the axe idly into the dead man's leg. "Wake Felan. He will not harm me."

"Now is not the time." Damaeus was quickly becoming irritated. Perfidia believed that she felt something akin to love for Felan, and she believed that because of her love Damaeus would not use the Aranth as he had planned. He considered both assumptions to be beyond absurd. "We have many things to do and only a few hours in which to accomplish them. Use the dissolving potions I provided you." He beseeched the Spirits that Perfidia had not misplaced the potions. He did not have the patience to deal with such idiocy, nor the time to make new ones.

"I did use them," she said, pulling her free hand nervously down her hair. "There were more living here than I at first thought. Two older children and an infant."

"I assume that they were disposed of without incident."

"They were, mostly."

"Mostly?" Damaeus scowled. There was something else she wanted, he could tell, but she was fearful that asking would anger him.

"Yes, well, I used the potions on two of the children, the older ones. The first as he slept so there would not be any chance that he would betray my presence. The second child I slew first before using the potion upon him, to spare him any more pain than was necessary. Ranur and Terran dealt with the parents. You were wise to choose those two. They are capable Riders and quick assassins."

"And the infant?" Damaeus asked, ignoring her disgustingly transparent attempt to win his favor with flattery.

Perfidia lowered her gaze to the bloodstained floor.

"You did not kill it."

"He will sleep for the next quarter hour, at the most."

At last she had come to it.

"I specified that all within the house were to be disposed of."

"You did say so," Perfidia replied, "but I thought perhaps we could keep him. I could hire someone to care for him so that he would not trouble you."

"Is he marked?"

"He does not carry a mark at this time. But there is no way to tell that it will not appear later. You know that as well as I."

"He is of no use to us."

"Damaeus, please," she begged. "Take a moment to consider it at least."

"You may have either Felan or the child. I would say that Felan is the better choice, were you to ask." Perfidia cared nothing for children. She would order the child sent off the moment he became too old to gain her the envy of others. Damaeus had her interests at heart as well as his own. The child would certainly be a burden.

Perfidia rolled her eyes. "Fine then, do away with him if you think that it is best. But I do not wish for him to suffer."

"Where are Ranur and Terran?" Damaeus asked, hoping to distract her.

"Ranur is in the cellar, digging. We are in need of a place to dispose of these two and I did not think that it would be wise to leave him alone with the Marked Ones."

"Terran is with them?"

Perfidia nodded.

"Fine, then. I shall speak with him." Damaeus made his way over the bodies and climbed the stairs. Perfidia followed, stepping with care over what blood lay upon the floor as if to avoid ruining her boots.

"Where are you keeping the Marked Ones?" he asked as he reached the second floor landing. Their souls were flecks of ecstasy blossoming at the edge of his consciousness, but he could not determine in what direction they lay.

Perfidia motioned towards the northernmost door. "Tonight, before you go back to the Aranth? Perhaps you could leave a potion of some sort that will calm him?"

It was so much like Perfidia to expect that a potion could be made for every occasion. She simply had no understanding of the work that went into preparing such things.

"Perhaps," he said wearily. "I suggest that you check on Ranur's progress. I would like the house to return to the condition in which you found it. Find something to cover the blood in the hall if you cannot remove it."

"Of course," Perfidia replied, heading obediently towards the stairs.

It was astonishing that a single Marked One could cause such a change in her demeanor. Damaeus pushed the door aside. A shelf holding a few tattered storybooks and a group of wooden soldiers sat between two small beds with quilted covers. Felan lay unconscious upon the first. The twisted silver metal of his Circlet caught what light slipped through the flawed glass of a single window. Cyanna lay upon the other bed. Perfidia's genes were not strong. The child's look was much like that of her father despite her strikingly feminine features.

Damaeus' gaze fell at last upon Terran, who sat contentedly at a child-sized desk, pressing a bit of tobacco into his fine meerschaum pipe. The pipe was only affordable through Damaeus' generosity. Terran was by no means poor, but a pound of meerschaum held the same worth as a mid-grade Marked One of late. The Rider was not in his employ for coin, however. He wanted Selene. It was not yet clear exactly what he wanted from her, and so Damaeus was not yet certain whether he would allow it when the time came. At the moment Terran was useful for many reasons. He had talent with a sword, he followed orders well, and he knew Selene on sight. The Rider's temperament was also somewhat more stable than Ranur's. Terran despised Selene, but he held no great hatred for other Marked Ones. It made him the perfect guard for Felan and Cyanna. He would be able hold his own against the drugged Aranth long enough for practical purposes.

"Lord Damaeus," Terran said, bowing his head accordingly. "I hope you are well."

"They have not stirred?" Damaeus asked. He had no time for idle chatter.

"No, my lord," Terran replied, seemingly undeterred by Damaeus' short words. "They sleep like the Spirits have taken them. It's rather unnerving."

"And yet you stay?"

"It will take more than a bit of sorcery to be rid of me, my lord." Terran grinned. "You pay far too well."

"I assume, that being the case, that you are not opposed to running an errand in my stead." Damaeus pulled a platinum coin from his belt pouch and offered it to Terran. "I think you will find the task pleasant, especially when compared to what I have asked of you thus far."

"I would travel the Crimson Abyss at your word, my lord," Terran said, accepting the coin. "What you have promised is far beyond the value of any coin."

"Well enough." Damaeus watched Terran place his pipe upon the tiny table. "You will visit the Winsome Lady every night for the next two weeks. Gamble at dice or cards, drink, do whatever else you wish, only make yourself well-liked by those who frequent there."

"You would pay me to visit the tavern?" Terran asked, furrowing his brow. "My lord, surely you jest."

"It is no jest. You are to aid Perfidia and Ranur in moving the Marked Ones to Greyridge Keep tonight. You shall live at the Keep during the day and return here each evening. Do you recall the password for the voyage rings?"

"Yes, my lord. You ordered that we commit it to memory."

"So I did, for it is of the utmost importance that you speak it correctly. Any error, no matter how slight, will mean your death."

"Yes, my lord. I have not forgotten."

The slightest bit of boldness touched Terran's tone. Damaeus chose to ignore it, for it was most likely caused by youth rather than disrespect. He had come to know the difference while working with Selene.

"Two weeks hence you will visit the Winsome Lady one final time to meet with a man named Aurin Fetlask. It should not be difficult to locate him as he frequents the establishment. He is taller than most and strong of build. You would think his lineage to be of the giants of the Levaril Hills by the look of him."

"I am a Rider, my lord. I could find him with half the description you have provided."

Damaeus untied a small pouch from the belt of his robes. He pulled a glass vial from its depths, no more than half of a finger in width. The clouded liquid within it held a touch of iridescence. "Aurin believes that the meeting has been arranged for the sale of ill gained spices rather than for what I truly have in mind. I have sent word that you will be in town beginning tomorrow evening. He will no doubt send a man beforehand to witness your character." Damaeus opened his palm, offering the vial to Terran.

One corner of Terran's mouth turned downward. "I see. You wish me to poison him."

"You doubt my wisdom?"

Terran regarded the Damaeus for a moment before snatching the vial from his hand. "Consider it finished."

It was well that Terran's loyalty had held. It would be a shame to slaughter someone of such potential. "What that vial contains will not kill him," Damaeus revealed at last.

Terran's gaze was questioning, but Damaeus would not risk furnishing him with any more information than was necessary.

"Aurin's drink is Pyrewood whiskey. Use what coin I have given you to buy him some if he wishes. The rest is yours to do with as you please. You will do whatever is necessary to gain Aurin's trust, but remember to be discreet. He is an intelligent man, and is not easily taken in by charitable gestures."

"I don't know many Riders that can hold more than a shot of Pyrewood whiskey. That stuff is twice as foul as dragon's blood and ten times the strength of it." The Rider's eyes grew distant. "Selene could drink a full three rounds with no ill effects. She won money on it more times than I can count. I asked her once how she managed it." He turned his head to spit. "She never offered me an answer."

"It is so with Marked Ones," Damaeus whispered. "They are deceptive. If you complete this task to my liking it may earn you more time with her."

"You can be certain of it, Lord Damaeus." Terran slipped the vial into his belt pouch. "I will not fail."

"That is why I chose you for this. Do not prove my trust to be false. Go now and aid Ranur with digging. I will renew the spell upon the Marked Ones so that they will sleep until tomorrow's light."

"Yes, my lord." Terran made his way silently out the door as if he feared to wake them.

It was a pity that Damaeus was forced to risk wasting such a powerful Marked One as Aurin Fetlask. But to be rid of Xaiden he knew nothing less would suffice.

Damaeus sat lightly upon the bed near Felan's chest, his hand lingering over the sleeping Aranth's wheat-blond hair. The slightest touch of his flesh to the warm metal of the circlet sent a wave of pleasure through him; perhaps like the feeling one Marked One gained when touching the flesh of another. He longed to feel such a bond with Selene while he was still able.

"She has granted you the highest honor." He drew close to whisper in Felan's ear. "To earn her love is not a thing so simply done." Felan had managed with ease what Damaeus could not. It was truly a pity that he did not have another male Marked One suitable for breeding. Thoughts of the union Felan and Selene would share pained Damaeus, though surely his pain was nothing compared to that which Perfidia would endure upon hearing what must be done. Ah, but when the Marked Ones came together, a Circlet upon each and each bonded to him, then he would know the true meaning of pleasure.

The hideous screeches of a waking infant swept through the hall, breeching the silence of the room and returning Damaeus somewhat to his senses. He stood awkwardly, cursing the Spirits while wrenching the needed words from his mind's recesses. To end a person's life with magic required the most complicated of spells, the words of which must be spoken with absolute precision. One careless slip could turn it back upon the caster.

The infant's cries rose in volume, filling the whole of the upper hall. The words of magic did not come to Damaeus as easily as they had months ago; a fact which would have worried him somewhat more had he not been intent on finishing what Perfidia had not. Why would anyone would wish to keep a child so close at hand? If the urchin's screaming did not cease soon then the neighbors would become wary.

Damaeus pulled the spell components carefully from his pouch. He repeated the spell's phrasing several times in his mind to be sure that it was correct. The child would feel no pain. He made his way hastily to the cradle, thankful that Perfidia still lingered in the cellar.

*　　　*　　　*　　　*　　　*

Cyanna did not know where she was, though she knew it was far from home. She lay motionless upon the bed, warm tears leaking from her half-closed eyes. The tears themselves were a danger, for tears would show that she was not truly asleep. She had waited for what seemed like days while uncle Damaeus spoke with Terran.

The frightened cries of a babe carried swiftly in the early morning stillness. She pitied the child, but could not help but be thankful for the distraction. It had caused uncle Damaeus to leave. It was noise enough to cover any sound she might make.

Cyanna's jaw pained her terribly. She had been too surprised to cry out when her mother struck her. Tears came anew with the thought. The strike was nothing compared to what had come after. *Keep her awake*, her uncle had ordered. Her mother had done so, with cold cloths and water, while she held her to the floor. Then came her uncle's nauseating smile, his pale blue eyes, and sharp metal points passing through the bone of her forehead with no more effort than a fish through water, creating pain greater than any she had known. Cyanna thought she would die then, but the Spirits had not been so kind. She lived, though blood ran into her eyes and her head felt as if it might split from the pressure. The pain had eased somewhat since then, though it returned in full force when uncle Damaeus was near. She was thankful for her life now; just as she was thankful for the chance that she had been given.

Precious little light filtered through the window and onto Felan, who lay unconscious upon a narrow bed. Cyanna wobbled as she stood. Her arms and legs ached with the stiffness of long suffered immobility. She stumbled to Felan's side, clutching the fabric of his shirt in desperation. He would help her. Together they could make their way back to Evaria, to her father. She shook him as hard as she dared, beseeching the Spirits that he would wake. His eyes, half open and eerily unmoving, stared through her. Cyanna's breath came in painful gasps as the world closed in around her. Felan could not protect her. She would have to escape on her own, or lose her chance to do so.

She pulled several deep breaths, easing the air in slowly as her father had taught her. She willed herself to remain conscious. They would not harm Felan, though the fact did little to calm her. Her mother had ordered Terran to be careful while carrying him. Cyanna released his shirt, leaving stained fabric standing where her hand had been. Felan was a fully trained Aranth. If he could not escape then he would at least survive. Her father would send someone for him at once, she was sure of it. He would send Xaiden. Her uncle would stand no chance against him. It had to be so.

Cyanna crept to the doorway. She could see the whole of the hall from where she stood. The way to the staircase was clear. One door, from behind which the babe's cries came, stood open a finger's width. Cyanna slipped out of the room, using the wall for support as she made her way to the stairs. The descent was difficult. Her legs wobbled and the banister creaked beneath her slight weight. Muffled voices drifted towards her as she reached the bottom landing.

One was her mother's, and it was coming closer.

Cyanna searched frantically for a place to hide, but her eyes refused to adjust to the darkness after the lamplight of the upper hall.

"The keep can hold over five hundred men at full capacity. The barracks are in good condition though they have been abandoned for many years."

"And the pay?"

Cyanna recognized Ranur's deep voice, and placed one hand over her mouth to stifle a sob. Fresh tears coursed down her cheeks as the memory returned to her. Ranur had killed Novalin.

The fault was her own, for she had refused to reveal where Barrik was hidden. Novalin's murder was carried out as punishment for her disobedience. The pain in her chest increased tenfold at the thought of what they may have done to Barrik had they found him. Cyanna did not know what they wanted of her brother, for she had heard her uncle say that unmarked children were of no use to them, but she knew that she must do everything possible to keep him from them.

"I know a great many who will join us, if that is truly the price you are willing to pay. It will be of no difficulty to gather them. Give me little more than a few weeks." Ranur's voice crept around the slowly opening door.

"That is well," her mother responded. "Damaeus will certainly be pleased."

Cyanna scanned the hall in a panic, searching once more for any small place in which to hide. Time slowed to an agonizing crawl as Ranur turned to face her. She crouched down, laying her body flat against a damp, somewhat sticky liquid that coated the floor. She found herself at once glad that the hall was much too dark to see. It was then that the babe's wailing abruptly ceased.

Ranur's gaze was pulled towards the stairs.

A dull, yellow light emanated from the far side of the hall. Cyanna ran towards it, heedless of the noise her feet must be making upon the hardwood floor. They did not speak of needing her as they needed Felan. They might even slay her if they caught her before she could escape. The light of the kitchen, brought by a single narrow window and a flickering lamp, blinded her nearly as much as the darkness of the hall. Some unsteady thing of wood struck her leg. A chair, she realized in despair as it tumbled to the floor.

Footsteps filled the silence. Cyanna pulled open the door nearest to her, neither knowing nor caring where it led. She closed it as carefully as she dared.

The room was barely large enough to fit her, standing as she was. It was a pantry, by the smell of flour and dried foods that came from it. All was silent for a moment, but then came the tapping of leather boots upon the wooden floor of the kitchen. The sound left her shivering in fear. Surely they could see her feet in the sliver of light that ran near the base of the door, or hear her heart beating through its thin wood.

"It is no fault of mine," Terran said defensively. "Damaeus ordered me to aid you in digging. He meant to renew the spell that caused them to sleep, so I left him to it. She must be within the house still. There is only one door out, and it's still locked."

"Over there," Ranur's voice struck Cyanna's soul with panic. She stepped back without thinking, pushing herself against jars of preserves. The sound of small, hard objects hitting the wood of the floor came unexpectedly. She jerked forward. Her belt pouch pulled her back. Terror took her breath. The door was open in less than a beat of her racing heart and the smooth, leather gloves that Ranur always wore surrounded her throat.

"Thought to escape, my cursed one?" he said, pulling her so close that she could smell the oil of his leather and the cloves on his breath.

"No," she started. She was too afraid for tears.

Ranur loosed one hand from her throat. He struck her so hard that the room tilted. Cyanna's neck felt as if it might tear from the base of her skull. She prayed to the Spirits that she would pass out. Her prayers went unanswered.

"I mean no disrespect, Praecyr," Terran's words reached through the ringing of her ears. "But perhaps it would be best not to damage her. She is part blood of Lord Damaeus, after all."

"She is a Marked One," Ranur growled. "Thus she is no kin to any human, lord or otherwise." He leveled his eyes with Terran's. "Question me again if you wish to be buried in the basement with the others. You will think that they have gained the luck of the Tides, for I will not do you the favor of killing you first."

Terran said nothing more as Ranur dragged Cyanna up the stairs, grasping her still by the neck. The blessed haze of unconsciousness hung back as if it did not dare to encompass her while Ranur was so close at hand. She tried her best to climb with him. They reached the top much too soon. He pushed her to the floor with such force that it seemed as if the wooden planks had lifted up to strike her. Her neck burned from Ranur's grip.

Uncle Damaeus' crouched down to her level. His breath smelled of rotting things. "You struck her," he said absently. His eyes closed, and he shivered as his hand neared the metal that gripped her forehead.

"Yes, lord Damaeus. She was attempting escape."

"We cannot have that." Her uncle looked thoughtfully away. "I suppose that we could begin breaking

Felan early, though only a short time remains before I must leave. I can give you one half-hour. He will have little strength while the effects of the spell dissipate, and there will be ample time for me to renew the magic when you are finished with him. I am sure that you will not be heard if you take them to the cellar."

Ranur smiled. It was the first time that Cyanna had truly seen him do so. It made her wish beyond anything that she had the strength to run.

Felan staggered into the hall as if summoned.

"We begin the lessons now," her uncle announced with glee. "It will do Cyanna some good to know for what reason we keep her. Perhaps Felan will learn what is expected of him as well."

Felan noticed Cyanna then. He attempted in vain to keep his balance while reaching for a sword that was not there. "King Graelen may be lenient with you if you return her now." His speech was slurred.

"She is of my blood." When her uncle laughed it carried a dark, vibrating sound. "I will use her as I see fit. And you will learn not to question me."

Felan's hands flew to his forehead, clutching at the metal band that uncle Damaeus had buried there. He fell to his knees and a moan of pain escaped him. Of all the times that Felan had been injured Cyanna had never heard him cry out. It terrified her, for Damaeus had not so much as touched him. She did not dare to move, lest her uncle do the same to her. It ceased as quickly as it had begun, leaving Felan on all fours with his head touching the floor.

"Will you resist me?" Damaeus asked.

"Yes."

"If that is how you wish it to be." Uncle Damaeus nodded in Ranur's direction.

Cyanna did not expect to be pulled to her feet, nor did she know enough to ready herself for Ranur's gloved hand striking the bone of her jaw, just beneath where her cheek had begun to swell. A fresh wave of pain swept across the bruised flesh. Felan bolted towards her but stopped within a pace, clutching at his Circlet once again. He remained there for what seemed like an eternity, while Cyanna's face throbbed and Ranur held her on her feet. She dared not look away for fear of angering her uncle further. Blood began to trickle from Felan's nose. It was then that Damaeus released him.

"You will go willingly to the cellar?" Damaeus' words were clearly not meant as a question.

"Yes," Felan replied weakly.

"You will address me as lord from this point forth. Do you understand?"

"Yes, my lord."

"Take her downstairs," Damaeus ordered.

Cyanna looked to Felan, but he would not meet her gaze. Her uncle pressed one finger deep into her injured cheek. She turned her head willingly towards him to ease the pain.

"And now we shall see how well your Circlet was placed, my little one."

The last of Cyanna's hope vanished, leaving only despair in its wake.

The King's Wrath

Evaria was much as Cael remembered it, with cobbled streets and close set houses built of beach stone weathered smooth. They camped as close as they dared, in a patch of forested ground called the Glade. It had been used to train Aranth in the ways of tracking in a time when there were Aranth to train. Few men visited it these days, mostly because there was nothing of note left in the place. Despite that, its familiarity was comforting. Cael still considered Evaria and the area that surrounded it to be his home. It struck him as odd that he was now unable to enter the town that he had once traveled through so freely.

"Your hand has not healed," Islyr said with a troubled look. "It should have done so, or perhaps festered, with what time has passed." His appearance still shocked Cael in the slightest, for he looked nothing like he had when Cael first met him. He was clean shaven, for one. Islyr did not need much in the way of shaving, it turned out, for his family line was of the lowlands. What little hair he had removed served to reveal fine features accented by the curving black lines of his Rakaii inking. He was dressed in the latest fashion as well; a fine cotton shirt of a deep gray color and matching breeches. Cael insisted on decent clothes for each of them so that they would not stand out should they be forced to enter Evaria, though he had let them choose what color they thought would suit. Devren had selected the deep blue of the Graelen line, much to Cael's vexation. The boy was never one to be subtle.

"I have a small pouch of ground maidenslip." Islyr's ebony, shoulder length hair had the subtle gloss of fine silk now that it was clean. It was tied into a club at the back of his head, which was the style of Kerell nobles. A bit of irony, perhaps. "Less than a week worth of applications would restore the flesh to new."

Devren, who was seated against a nearby tree, looked up at them with interest. He had taken it upon himself to repair a small hole in his belt pouch, to Cael's surprise, and would accept no help with the task. The young prince was finding a rather rough time of it, having never sewn anything in his life, and so took every opportunity to seem as if he was merely interested in the conversation rather than frustrated with what he was attempting.

"I thank you for your concern," Cael replied as he rubbed the cloth that covered his Aranth brand. "But it is an old injury reopened and not likely to respond to such things."

"As you will, then," Islyr said easily. "But perhaps you would be willing to answer a question."

"I may, depending on what you ask." Cael and Islyr had developed something of a friendship in the time they had traveled together, but he had not forgotten that the man was once Rakaii. He could not be certain what Islyr would do when he learned that Cael was Aranth. "There are some things I will not speak of." Cael was sorely in need of someone to guard Devren while he searched for King Graelen. He had come to respect the talent Islyr displayed in a brawl as well as his character.

"I showed you honesty in the matter of my latent ability," Islyr began.

Devren's hand hovered over his work as he studied Cael's face.

"I would like to know somewhat more about what power you hold."

Cael stifled a sigh of relief.

"Does it truly work as Devren seems to think it does?"

"Somewhat," Cael laughed. "I figured out, long ago, that I can manipulate my latent ability. I created a power that seemed to be altogether different. In truth it was merely a facet of my ability."

"I knew it was much too good to be true," Devren injected. "I was hoping to learn it."

"You're an intelligent lad." Islyr moved Devren's now forgotten belt pouch to take a seat next to the boy. "You have no need of a latent ability to attract women. Most respond to confidence and common respect. Although a well-kept appearance helps a great deal."

"Too much effort in that," Devren scowled. "I'd bet that Cael has had more women than you have, Islyr. Hundreds more, probably."

Cael raised a brow in the Devren's direction, the sign he had long used to let the boy know that, prince or no, punishment would be dealt if needed. Devren fell silent.

"So, what is the truth of it?" Islyr seemed unfazed by Devren's insolence. The Spirits knew that he had been around the boy long enough to become used to it.

"The slightest whisper of my latent ability draws a person's soul towards me for just a moment. The touch of their soul to mine causes an irrational feeling of attachment for them. It feels somewhat akin to love, or in some instances lust, as far as I am able to tell. It lasts only a few hours. Afterward nothing more than the thought that we are old friends remains, if that."

"What of your true ability?" Islyr asked. "You do not use it at all from what I have seen."

Cael pondered for a moment. "I have not used my ability, not in its true form, since my days as a Praecyr," he said, running a hand through his hair. "I have changed much since then, with time and experience. It grieves me to think of the innocent lives that were lost to my greed. I will tell you what I am, but only with your promise to consider me as I stand before you rather than judging my worth on what misdeeds I have committed in the distant past."

"The past cannot be changed," Islyr said evenly. "The wrongs of others pale when compared to those of a Rakaii."

"That may be true, but you were forced to do such things. I did them willingly. I derived pleasure from them."

"As did I," Islyr responded. "At times I still do."

There was a measure of hunger in Islyr's eyes. How many Marked Ones had the man slain in his short life? The list could not possibly be greater than Cael's own, one composed of Marked Ones and humans alike.

"Speak freely, for I will not judge you for the harm you have brought to others," Islyr promised. "I am in no position to do so, having brought numerous Bloodsoul into the world."

Cael lifted his head to study Islyr's expression. "I am able to take the life force of others into myself." He paused shortly to gage the man's reaction. Islyr's face showed no concern, only mild interest. "From it I receive strength, most usually. I have also gained abilities, though the life force I take must have mastered such things in order for them to be transferred. From some I receive feelings, thoughts, even memories. Those are the hardest to bear. There was a time when death haunted my thoughts without mercy."

Devren's face was agape with wonder. It was possible that his father had told him something of Cael's power, though surely he had not gone into such detail.

"I have very little control over my latent ability. A light touch will do no harm, but once our souls are fully connected it will see itself through. After that point I can take all of someone's life or none of it. There is no center ground."

Islyr leaned back into the shadow of the forest, which now stretched out into the Glade. It rendered his expression vexingly indecipherable.

Cael continued, for now he could do naught else. "I used my latent ability frequently in my younger days. It served to dispose of those who crossed me, and also brought me the strength I needed to rise from the rank of Rider to that of Praecyr. My temper was widely known at that time. Those who displeased me were soon found dead, and those who dared to lay the blame of it upon me joined them with haste."

"What happened?" Devren asked suddenly. "By using your latent ability like that you could have done anything you wanted. What stopped you?"

"The Aranth," Cael replied, his mind drifting away from the present. "Six came for me, each with an animal companion. I had not seen more than two Aranth in my short years, and that was at a safe distance. They waited until I was alone to approach. A young, ashen haired girl drew nearest. She demanded my peaceful surrender while a viper as long as a jousting pike coiled its way around her neck. She had heard the stories, I suppose. She assumed that I could not take her soul without touching her flesh, and that I would not dare to come so close to her for fear of her animal companion. She was wrong, at least on the second matter. I took her life, but was bitten by the snake."

"But you survived," Devren said, captivated.

"The Aranth overwhelmed me despite the strength I had gained from the girl. My training was nothing when compared to that which the Aranth receive, and the snake's venom coursed through my body, weakening me with every step."

"But who was she?" Devren asked.

"The girl's name was Novalin. She was the current leader of the Aranth and a companion to all. Her death enraged them, putting them at odds concerning what should be done with me though the king had ordered that I be brought before him." Cael pressed a hand to his temple. "It was taken to vote while I lay dying. An Aranth named Xaiden Basiir, who was Novalin's lover and the second eldest of the Aranth, would decide my fate."

Devren's eyes grew wide with disbelief at the mention of Xaiden's name.

"Most would demand your death for such a crime," Islyr said, breaking the awkward silence.

"I would have done so without a second thought, had our roles been reversed," Cael replied. "Xaiden did not. He offered me the antivenin in exchange for a vow of loyalty to the royal family."

"Why would he do that?" Devren cut in. "You killed Novalin. You slaughtered all of those people."

"I asked that as well," Cael replied. "Xaiden said that he would have known if I had spoken the vow without meaning it; that he allowed me this chance because of one that he had been given long ago. He also told me that he did not have any more than one chance in his soul to give. I followed the Aranth willingly to Evaria, trusting that Xaiden would hold to his word. He did. In fact, he used a boon owed to him by the king to spare me from execution."

"I must see your hand." Islyr reached for his staff.

Cael was prepared for Islyr's demand, though the fact remained that there were some things he simply could not permit.

"I cannot allow you to do so, for you know that I am marked. To honor my vow I would be forced to kill you."

Devren stiffened.

"I gave you back your life. The boy's as well."

"You have my thanks for doing so."

"I could have given you only that, and let you perish once again in the depths of the abyss. You would not have found your way to the surface without my help."

Cael ran his free hand through his hair.

"I do not enjoy being treated as a fool," Islyr continued. "I will not kill you, but know that my only reason for such mercy is the effort I made to bring your souls back to this place. Speak the truth now or I will leave you and the boy to face Damaeus alone."

Devren looked ready to flee, or perhaps to fight. He held his sword aloft with shaking hands. Islyr took no notice of him, though the boy's weapon was nearly at his throat.

"I will answer your questions," Cael said. "It will require a vow of secrecy, and a blood pact to seal it. The pact must be formed with the boy, for my own vow keeps me from doing so."

"Done," Islyr agreed, slicing his pact hand upon Devren's wavering blade. "I swear to the Spirits that not one word of what you speak will be told to another. May they bind me to truth."

The boy looked to Cael in fear.

"Pyre's Ash," Cael swore irritably. "If he was going to kill you he could have done so one hundred times over by now. Lower your sword and make the pact. We have no hope of defeating Damaeus without him."

Devren did as he was told, though not before exchanging his sword for an obscene gesture. The boy truly had the temper of his father. "May the Spirits bind you to truth," he muttered.

"You are one of them," Islyr said softly as he leaned into a patch of fading light.

"My vow does not permit me to tell you directly what I am because you know that I am marked," Cael replied, grasping the hilt of his sword. "But since you put it that way, yes, I am one of them."

"How long would you have kept it from me?" Islyr asked, standing. "And the boy? He is Aranth as well? One in training, I imagine?"

"No," Cael replied, keeping an eye on Islyr's movements in case he should think to harm Devren. "He is the heir to Evaria's throne."

Islyr pressed his palm to his forehead.

The air was cool and a slight breeze moved the branches overhead. Cael found it oppressive nonetheless. "You may leave us," he offered slowly. "I will not move to stop you."

"Tell me, before I make my decision," Islyr said, his blue-green eyes looking up between tendrils of dark Rakaii ink. "How does it feel?"

"I'm not sure I understand."

"Your latent ability. What feeling do you get when drawing the life from another?"

Cael did not speak. He knew the answer well though much time had passed since he had last used his latent ability.

"Answer me with honesty and I will stay."

Cael glanced uneasily at Devren. This was not something he wished for the boy to hear, but he would be a fool to send him out of earshot and thus out of sight.

"The feeling is greater than any pleasure imaginable," he said finally. "There is no other way to describe it. Anyone who has lain with another will know what I speak of. It is a similar feeling, multiplied one thousand fold."

"We are more alike than I imagined," Islyr said with a partial smile. "Since you were truthful with me I shall be so with you. I assume that you will not think poorly of me for keeping this from you," he added with a touch of sarcasm.

"The thought had not crossed my mind," Cael replied evenly.

"I did not accompany you solely out of concern for your welfare. I seek revenge. I believe that your Damaeus is the one who sold me to the Kerell, though I must see him to confirm it."

"If that is so," Cael mused, "then we may have more difficulty facing him than I at first thought."

"He has vast experience in killing and capturing Marked Ones," Islyr said. "We would have a much better chance with more allies."

"We may have some, one or two at best, if I can manage to enter the castle without being detected by Damaeus."

"And assuming that those you seek are not loyal to him," Islyr added. "How many of the Aranth are marked?"

"I cannot tell you that," Cael answered as he removed his sword-belt. It was well past time for him to go. He would make his way to the castle in the near-dark hours, by way of the windows on the Aranth wing. There was always one left open, most usually by Felan. He was not reliable in the least when it came to such matters.

"A great many of them are like us. It must be so."

"You could say that," Cael replied noncommittally as he pulled his shirt over his head. "I will bring king Graelen here as soon as time permits. You will guard the boy?"

Devren's frown was plainly visible. "You won't leave me here. I'll go with you to save my father."

"You will go nowhere, or else I will tell your father how you needlessly risked your life despite my warning. He will not be pleased, I can guarantee it."

"I would die to keep Damaeus from doing to another what he did to me," Islyr promised.

"Do not leave Islyr's side."

Devren opened his mouth to object. Cael placed his hand upon his mark. The boy's complaints were successfully drowned out by the cooling burn of Affinity. Cael welcomed the familiar pain. His body reshaped itself to falcon form as if he had been born to it. He took to the skies.

Darkened forest was replaced shortly by barely visible gardens and cobblestone. The castle loomed below him like an elder black dragon; its entrance barely visible by the light of low burning torches. He found the Aranth wing at once, and landed in the west courtyard upon the railing of Felan's balcony.

Memories of times past and of the Aranth that been lost visited him. He was certain that most had been taken by Damaeus, now that he knew the truth of Islyr's plight. It sickened him to think of his friends as Rakaii, or worse, slaughtered by that bigot of a Mage. It was Damaeus who spoke against recruiting once the disappearances began. The king's Elite Guard could well have numbered in the hundreds by this time. It was a sobering thought. Cael pushed it aside in order to concentrate on the matter at hand. Felan's room was unlit, which was typical at this hour. Dinner would begin shortly.

The balcony doors were closed, much to Cael's dismay, and he found all of Felan's windows to be shut tight. *The one time I'm in need of an opening.* He supposed that he could expect no more from Felan. The man had an uncanny way of doing exactly the opposite of what Cael anticipated. He liked him well enough despite it. There was nothing left to do but try the others. Xaiden's windows were locked, which did not surprise Cael in the least. Luca's were as well. Cael perched upon the roof a moment, his whispered curses coming out as a volley of low, hissing screeches. He headed for his own room. The servants may have come to air it out in his absence, or perchance to remove his belongings if they thought him dead. He tried the balcony doors and the study before coming to the bedroom window. It was, to his great relief, open just enough for him to squeeze through, though the fit was tight.

Cael glided to the floor and reformed himself, finding it rather more difficult than it had been before his time in the abyss. It would take several months yet for his body to become used to remaining in human form. He waited impatiently for his eyes to adjust before heading to the wardrobe and throwing it open. He would not like to make his plea to the king while naked as it would not bode well for his sanity. A quick study of the contents revealed it to be mostly full. They had not cleared it out yet, if they truly thought him to be dead. Cael lingered for a moment before admitting to himself that he could not tell what was what for the darkness. He settled for pulling out an item at random. It was of silk. Cael ran his fingers down the length of it. *Too much fabric to be a shirt.* His funeral robe, perhaps. He did own one, though thankfully it was not often used. Whatever it was it would not do for clothing. He found the bed by touch and threw the item upon it. His furniture had been moved. The bedside table held a lamp, beside which lay a metal box of striking sticks. He lit the lamp. His room looked out over the town, beyond which lay the ocean. No one who mattered would see its meager light.

Cael looked down at the item of clothing that he had thrown upon the bed. He would have laughed had he not been so bewildered by its presence. It was a silk dress of a silver hue. He turned back to his wardrobe only to find the whole of it filled with women's clothing. The second wardrobe was no better, and it looked as if someone had taken a portion of the contents.

Cael grabbed the lamp and headed out into the main room. Here he was confronted by three tapestries, all finely woven. The largest depicted a phoenix with wings spread. *So there is a new Aranth.* The fact that King Graelen had allowed it was unexpected, to say the least. The fact would have pleased Cael somewhat more had they not given her his room. It would make things complicated once he returned.

Cael listened at the door before entering the hall. He heard nothing and so sprinted to Felan's room, his bare feet making only the slightest sound against the cold stone of the floor. Felan's door was unlocked. Perhaps the man was not as unpredictable as he thought him to be.

Cael threw open the wardrobe and pulled on some of Felan's clothing. It was not a perfect fit, but it was far better than running about the castle nude. He would ask for his belongings back when the time came. Hopefully they had not disposed of all of them. His journal would be safe even if they thought him dead, for when an Aranth passed on to their next life their journal was added to the others in the king's private library. Cael headed for king Graelen's bedroom. The king would return there shortly after dinner. He would likely be alone, for Perfidia most often retired to her sitting room. It was then that Cael would make his plea.

It was in the Imperial Hall that Cael came across Sedna, her arms loaded with clean, folded bath towels. She had grown since Cael had last seen her, and now looked more woman than girl. Sedna's face paled upon noticing him. Her expression was one of pure terror, which made Cael's theory all the more likely. Damaeus must have told king Graelen that he was dead. The towels dropped to the floor as Sedna opened her mouth to scream. Cael wasted no time. He reached out with the slightest touch of his latent ability. Sedna's eyes grew distant for a fraction of a second. The girl's soul was soft and breathy, like a feather's edge. She was not yet truly a woman, as much as she looked it. Cael smiled at her, and was relieved when she returned the expression.

"Let me help you with those," he offered, reaching for one of the fallen towels.

Her cheeks shaded with embarrassment. "Oh," She stammered, scrambling to retrieve them before he had the opportunity. "You shouldn't suffer for my clumsiness. This was entirely my fault. I wasn't watching where I was going, but then I just didn't expect anyone to be in the hall at this hour. Mera is always saying that I should concentrate more on the task at hand. I suppose this just proves her to be in the right. I should really learn to keep my head out of the clouds. I am just so sorry, Lord Cael."

Rambling was a common side effect of his latent ability, at least in younger women. He felt a bit of pity for the girl, but he could not very well have let her scream out his presence.

"The fault was mine." He folded the last of the towels before handing it to her. "There's no need to worry on it. No harm done."

"Not true!" she objected. "Why, you could have fallen upon the towels and injured yourself, perhaps breaking a leg or your finely formed-" Sedna clapped her free hand to her mouth.

Cael wondered what part of him she had been about to name as finely formed.

"Please forgive me." She blushed all the more as she attempted to hide her mortification behind the stack of towels.

"It is of no consequence." It would take more than a few fallen towels to injure an Aranth, but he had neither the time nor the desire to argue with the girl. "I will consider all to be forgiven if you will do me one small favor."

Sedna peered around the towels with embarrassment so pure that it could only stem from love. Perhaps he had lingered a second too long with the girl's soul.

"Please do not mention to anyone that you have seen me." Cael placed a hand upon her cheek. The girl looked as if she might faint at his touch. "It is of the utmost importance that my presence is not known."

"Not a soul will hear of it." Sedna nearly dropped the towels once more as she bobbed a hurried curtsy. "Thank you, Lord Cael. You are so kind," she added before disappearing down the hall.

Cael waited until her footsteps faded to turn his attention to King Graelen's door. No light passed beneath it. He sighed. The encounter with Sedna had put a limit of time on his endeavor. He hoped that she would suffer no long lasting effects from his latent ability. Cael entered the room, closing the door silently behind him. Lamp light burst from the far corner, delivering the area from shadow.

"You are not the Aranth that I was expecting," Meiun said. The Khaloc stood in the center of the room, his massive wings bent against the ceiling though it stood well above Cael's head. "I had not thought to see you again, Logan Altayr."

"Meiun of Northlight," Cael answered formally, attempting to cover his shock. Meiun was the only one who ever called him by his true name. As a result he was unused to hearing it spoken. "It has been a long time, indeed."

"All Aranth have been exiled from the capital city," the Khaloc said, his clawed hand encompassing Cael's wrist with dizzying speed despite the closeness of the room. "The fact that Graelen Elyon considers you dead does not exclude you from his decree."

"I do not wish to battle with you, Meiun." Cael's thoughts reeled. The Aranth had been exiled, which meant that Xaiden was not here to back up the truth of his words. Things were worse than he had guessed. He wondered who would win if he and Meiun were to come to blows. With the luck of the Tides it would not go so far as that. "I wish to speak with King Graelen."

"You shall have your chance to do so, Logan Altayr, when your final plea is heard upon the executioner's block. I am certain that all will be curious to hear why you chose to return here after slaying the heir to Evaria's throne."

Bastard Mage. He should have known that Damaeus would cover his tracks in their entirety. "Meiun, listen to me, Devren is alive and quite well. He waits at the Aranth tracking ground. I will take you to him."

"What you claim is not possible," the Khaloc said firmly. "I have seen Devren's Stone. It is no longer linked to his soul."

"If you have seen his stone then you must have seen mine as well," Cael answered. "It would be the in the same state as the boy's."

"It is not so," Meiun replied. "Damaeus Severl was not able to find your Stone."

"The Spirits keep him," Cael cursed.

"I must take you below. I would be deeply dishonored if you were to escape before punishment is dealt to you."

"Wait," Cael said desperately. He was as good as dead if Damaeus came across him in the dungeon. "I have never lied to you. You know this to be true. Devren waits at the Glade, at the edge closest to the castle grounds, may the Spirits keep my soul if I lie. Take me there. If what I say is not true then I will go willingly to my death."

Meiun's ashen brow lowered as he considered Cael's offer. Khaloc were rational by nature, and thus took the time to consider any deal that was made to them. "I find your proposal to be fair," he said at last. "But I will go alone. You will wait in the dungeon; in the sorcerer's division."

Cael sighed. Magic had no effect in that section of the dungeon. His latent ability and affinity were included. Although, on the lighter side of things, Damaeus' magic would not work there either. "I agree to your terms," he replied. His options were few.

Cael allowed the Khaloc to lead him. The castle's familiar corridors were surprisingly barren, which served to unsettle Cael in the slightest. They reached the white walled rooms of the sorcerer's division in a short time.

"Bend forward, Logan Altayr."

Cael glanced at the smooth metal collar Meiun held.

"That will not work here," he said confidently. He hoped that it was true.

"Your words are not accurate," Meiun replied. "Damaeus Severl has made several changes to this place in your absence. He considered the dungeon's old form to be inappropriate for the continuation Graelen Elyon's safety. He is talented for a free-born of the Ethereal Realm."

"Indeed," Cael replied with more than a touch of sarcasm. "I don't suppose you would settle for a bracelet?"

"I do not believe that you are beyond severing a limb in order to escape," the Khaloc said as he snapped the collar around Cael's neck. "Is my assumption incorrect?"

Cael did not reply lest he say something untrue. He stepped into the nearest cell, taking a seat upon the straw filled mattress. Meiun closed the door without a word. The well-oiled lock turned smoothly between thick, metal bars. The Khaloc slipped the chain that held the key over his head before leaving the room.

Pyre's Ash, Cael thought as he took in his surroundings. *Couldn't have botched this more if I'd tried.* The area was clean for a dungeon. Cael had found himself in more than a few over the years. The white of the walls was nearly enough to blind a person with the way it reflected torchlight. Its spotlessness was most likely due to the fact that the sorcerer's division was not often used. Cael himself had seen this place only once in all of his years at the castle.

The only object in the cell besides the mattress upon which he sat was an empty bucket meant for use as a chamber pot. Cael kicked it in frustration. The thunderous sound it made as it hit the pristine wall was a fine match for his mood. "Not even a dent," he muttered as he examined the place where it had struck. The bucket, however, now looked as if it had been trampled by horses. It was a small comfort.

What seemed like ages trickled by as he waited. There were no windows in this place, which left him no way of telling the true hour. He passed the time singing ancient Riders' songs. Many of his nights were spent singing in taverns for coin before he discovered what great riches the use of his latent ability could bring. His talent for singing was a source of great pride, for he came by it naturally rather than having stolen it along with some poor fool's soul. Despite his best efforts, Cael was half asleep when the Khaloc finally returned. Devren was not with him. It was then that Cael began to worry.

"Logan Altayr, slayer of the heir and of Aranth Novalin Ralea," Meiun said with an expression of stone. "You will go willingly to your next life upon tomorrow's light, for you have promised it to me. You have been untruthful in your words. I do not know why this is so, for it has gained you nothing, but you may be certain that I will not forget this betrayal."

"That cannot be. I left the boy with one sworn to the Spirits to guard him with his life. Search the rest of the tracking ground. Their position may have changed."

"I have searched the forest entire. No trace of them was found."

Islyr had betrayed him, or Damaeus had found them. He could come up with no other explanation. "You must let me speak to King Graelen," Cael begged. "I may well be the only one left to carry the truth to the throne."

"You will speak with him at tomorrow's light, just before your soul merges for its time with the earth's spirit."

"Damaeus will kill him and you will do nothing to stop it."

"I will hear no more of your lies, Logan Altayr." Meiun flashed his teeth in the semblance of a smile. They were human in appearance save for two pointed, dragon-like canines. "May your next life be more honorable." The Khaloc strode from the room.

Cael rested his head against the bars of his cell. The field of magic created by his collar rippled at his touch. If only Meiun had placed him in the dungeon proper with the common criminals. Xaiden often said, partly in jest, that he would be hard pressed to keep either Cael or Felan in captivity should the occasion call for it. Cael had become quite adept at picking locks in his time as a Rider, with aid of the soul of a highly skilled rogue. He passed his knowledge to Felan at the man's urging, unbeknownst to Xaiden. It pained him to think that he may never again see any of his companions.

He returned to his mattress and sat with his head in his hands, trying desperately to think of something that would sway King Graelen towards the truth of his story. He worried for the boy. Both time and his sordid past were working against him. By tomorrow's light it would be too late. He hoped that his next life would be much less complicated.

Cael's Execution

Cael woke to the tapping of rigid heels against the floor of the sorcerer's division. Meiun entered, followed by twelve standard guardsmen garbed in heavy armor. They crowded behind the Khaloc, shrinking the space of the room by half.

"Graelen Elyon awaits you in the Hollow. I assume that you will come peaceably?"

Death and insult combined. Cael nearly laughed. His blood would darken the ground upon which all Aranth were trained. It was Damaeus' idea, he would wager.

"Of course," he replied. He had thanked the Spirits many times in the past that his vow said nothing of lying. He thanked them once again for good measure.

Cael waited with feigned patience while Meiun released his barricade collar. He bowed to the Khaloc before allowing himself to be led into the hall. Darkness more oppressive than that of the abyss met his eyes. Cael walked with the unwavering pride of an elder Aranth though he was certain that this morning would be his last. Guardsmen surrounded him. He gave the closest fellow a wink. The man paled considerably. As well he should. Pitting an Aranth against a Standard Guardsman was akin to setting a war-trained hound upon a suckling pup. After a sword was poached from the first guardsman the rest would have due cause to make their peace with the Spirits. Meiun was his only worry. Cael had no desire to slay the Khaloc, even if the feat could be managed.

A wooden platform had been constructed in the center of the sparring pit. Upon it sat the executioner's block.

King Graelen stood next to it with the knife of the Aranth bond in one hand.

The entire Second Quarter was present, by the look of things. Cael did not recognize most of them, for battle helmets covered their features. One face, however, made his prideful stance falter. Barrik sat to the far side of the platform upon one of the stone benches that had previously surrounded the training pit. The boy turned away as Cael passed him. It pained him to see it, for in his last years as Aranth he had come to think of the king's children as his own. *I am still Aranth*, he amended, *whether or not it is by Graelen's grace.*

"You have some honor left, it seems," King Graelen said, holding the bond knife aloft. "Some would say you were brought here by arrogance. Others would say by foolishness. I must say that I consider it a mix."

Unease settled upon Cael like morning frost.

"Do not fear, Logan. You will suffer greatly before dying, but you have always had the luck of the Tides. The Spirits may not keep you, and pain is nothing to one who is Aranth trained."

"Majesty," Cael said, climbing the few stairs to kneel before him. "I have failed to protect the heir to the throne. I gave my life for his, as was my vow, but my soul was not given the proper time to enter the cycle. It was returned to the earth by the latent ability of one I have come to consider a companion."

"You were the first Aranth to betray my trust," King Graelen said thoughtfully, oblivious of Cael's words. "It is fitting that you shall be the first to die." He touched the point of the knife between Cael's eyes.

Cael did not flinch though he knew that the magic of the knife would slice through the bone of his skull with ease.

"It was foolish of Xaiden to think that you could be redeemed. I should have rejected his boon, though it would have marred my honor beyond repair. There are some who may never be trusted. There are some who cannot be saved."

"It is not for Devren's murder that I accept this punishment," Cael said, "but for my failure to protect the life of one who has become precious to me. You may choose to send my spirit this day, but know this before it is done; Damaeus was never loyal to the kingdom of Evaria nor is he an ally of the Ethereal Realm. He is responsible for the downfall of the Aranth. He will see you dead when it suits his purpose."

King Graelen pressed the tip of the bond knife into Cael's forehead, igniting a spark of pain.

"When I last spoke with your son, less than a day from this moment, he still lived," Cael managed. "He may still retain his life, though I cannot be certain. Allow me to arrest Damaeus and put him to question."

"And still you persist?" King Graelen mused. "Such arrogance."

Cael held his ground. He took a firm grip of the King's knife arm. Weapons shifted across the Hollow as the Standard Guardsmen prepared for what would likely be a battle to half their ranks. King Graelen stilled them with a gesture.

Cael's eyes found Barrik. Damaeus was seated next to him, stroking the child's sandy blond hair. The boy buried his face in the Mage's robes. Damaeus flashed Cael a knowing half-grin.

"Have you anything else to say before your death?" King Graelen asked, his eyes distant.

"If thought or time brings to light the truth of my words," Cael whispered, "look to Damaeus for the answers you seek. I beseech the Spirits that it will not be too late."

"Have you some proof that what you say is true?"

Cael could see that King Graelen wished it to be so.

"I have nothing to offer you other than my word."
He knew it was not enough.

"Lay your head upon the block," King Graelen
ordered.

Cael followed what would be his last order as
Aranth. King Graelen came to stand to one side of him, and
Meiun to his other.

"May your death be honorable," Meiun said,
nodding his head accordingly.

Cael gazed across the courtyard, thinking of times
past. The Elite guard was no more. The Ethereal Realm would
fall to ruin under Damaeus' rule and he could do nothing to
prevent it.

King Graelen raised the bond knife above Cael's
neck. "It is for the continuing safety of the Ethereal Realm
that you die on this day."

The King's words receded beneath his hearing. Cael
looked to Barrik. The boy's expression was odd. It was no
wonder. A child of his age should not be made to witness any
execution; let alone that of one who was nearly a father to
him.

"May the Spirits allow his soul to pass on to its next
life though he has wronged in this one. May he grasp the
morals of higher power though those of men are lost to him."

Cael wondered what would happen at the moment
of his death. Would the souls he had taken with his latent
ability gain new, separate lives? Would they cling to his own
as they had for so many years, entering his new body as one?

"By the grace of the Spirits is this done."

Cael braced himself for the impact. The first strike
would be light. King Graelen would not allow him to die
quickly.

"Father, no!" Barrik twisted from Damaeus' grasp.

Cael held his breath, expecting that the blow would
still come. It did not.

"Barrik," King Graelen said sternly. "This must be done, as we discussed. Enemies of the Ethereal Realm cannot be given the chance to roam free. You must stay by uncle's Damaeus' side."

The boy looked to his uncle with uncertainty. Damaeus watched him through narrowed eyes. He crooked a single finger, muttering beneath his breath.

"No!" Barrik screeched, covering his ears.

"You would allow him to use the Mage's arts upon your son?" Cael slipped out of range of the knife in a single, agile motion. If Barrik was willing to fight Damaeus' treachery then he could not leave him to fight alone.

"Cease your magic, Damaeus," King Graelen commanded.

"It is merely a calming spell, Majesty," Damaeus answered smoothly. "Nothing that would harm the boy, I assure you."

"Do as I say, or you will find yourself in the sorcerer's wing."

"As you wish, Majesty," the Mage replied, folding his hands beneath his robes.

It seemed that the Tides had not completely abandoned Cael on this day.

"If he moves," King Graelen said, "you may kill him. Speak if you will, Barrik. My patience is short."

The boy pulled at the edge of his shirt.

"Speak against him if it is truth," Cael offered without shifting so much as an inch from where he stood. He could die from an arrow to the heart as easily as any man.

"I will tolerate nothing short of silence from you, Cael," King Graelen said. "Your next word will be your last. If you have nothing to say, Barrik, then you will return to your uncle and leave me to what I must do."

"Felan didn't take Cyanna and mother," the boy whispered, inching closer to Cael.

"It is common to become confused after something terrible occurs," Damaeus said. "Sometimes our minds alter events from what they truly were in order to make bad things easier to deal with."

"That's not what happened," Barrik insisted. His eyes were beginning to tear. "I saw it."

It was the first time that Cael had heard the boy contradict his father.

"What did you see?" Concern crept into King Graelen's voice.

"They knocked Felan out. They put a silver band on his head. He screamed." Barrik twisted the edge of his shirt. "Cyanna saw it too. She told me to run and hide in the wardrobe in her room because there wasn't time to find you. She said she'd come and get me if she could, when she knew it was safe." The boy began to shake.

"Who do you believe is responsible?" King Graelen asked as he placed a hand upon each of his arms to steady him. "Give me their names and I will see that they are put to question."

Cael beseeched the Spirits that there would be something of use in the boy's confession.

"Uncle Damaeus," Barrik said, "and…"

It was far better than Cael had expected.

"Majesty," Damaeus injected, "the boy is greatly distressed by the loss of his mother. His young mind has suffered some damage from recent events. Allow me to see to his welfare. Simply give me a few moments with him and all will be well."

King Graelen fell silent. Weapons shifted uneasily as he formed his decision. "Damaeus, you will accompany me to speak with Barrik when this is finished. You will retire to your quarters for the moment to prepare whatever you deem necessary."

Cael's last hope was smothered by the crooked smile Damaeus offered before turning to leave.

"It was wrong of me to allow Barrik to witness this," King Graelen muttered. "It is as Damaeus said; his mind is far too infantile to process such events."

Barrik's defiance visibly dissolved as two Standard Guardsmen ushered him towards the castle.

"Your son attempts to show you the truth and you are too stubborn to see it," Cael said. "You are not fit to be named his father."

King Graelen lunged for Cael. The King had been formidable in his day, but time and age had slowed his movements. Cael bounded from the platform, rolling beneath it. A flurry of arrows struck, raining upon the spot where he had been only seconds ago. Cael lay flat to the ground in the darkness at the center of the platform, knowing that neither weapon nor Meiun could reach him there. Silence settled around him.

"Come out and receive what is due to you," Meiun growled. His eyes shone red, like those of a dragon on the hunt, as he leaned into the darkness. "Your cowering brings you great dishonor."

"An Aranth does not cower," Cael replied before shifting to one side. The Khaloc wished him to speak so that he could determine his position.

"Promise me a half hour of life. Take me to the Glade so that I may show you the truth." He shifted aside once again.

"I will not do so," Meiun responded.

"Ten minutes, then," Cael bartered. He could think of a way out within ten minutes, surely. He had been willing to give up his life a short time ago. His thoughts had changed with Barrik's confession. The boy had spoken against Damaeus, and would lose his life for it.

"You will be granted five minutes," the Khaloc said after a moment.

"I have your word?" Cael asked. He noted the shadowed legs of three Guardsmen who had moved to his left.

"You have it, by the grace of the Great Cycle."

The Khaloc would take his own life before breaking his word. Cael crawled from beneath the platform.

"You," King Graelen pointed to the nearest Guardsman. "Garen?"

"At your command, Sire."

"Keep count of what time has passed. The rest of you; aim at the prisoner's heart and shoot when Garen gives the signal. You have my permission to shoot at will if Cael attempts anything other than speech."

"Pyre's Ash," Cael muttered. Graelen knew him as if there was a Stone bond between them.

"Foolishness," one of the Guardsmen muttered. It was difficult to see the man, as he was standing behind a line of his fellows. "That is no way to treat a trusted companion." The man stepped forward, and Cael smiled openly at the sight of him.

King Graelen angered at first, no doubt for the lack of sanity that Cael's expression betrayed, but his breath ceased as he took in what Cael had seen.

"Father," Devren said without a trace of pleasantry. "Where is Damaeus?" The heir to the throne wore an ill-fitting shirt of the Standard Guard and stolen breeches to match.

"You live," King Graelen uttered.

"Unexpected." Meiun turned to Cael. "I regret that I questioned your honor, Logan Altayr. I will find the Mage and deal with him." His wings flared as he prepared for flight. "Damaeus Severl's scent still lingers. He is not far."

"Do you wait for the Spirits to command you?" Devren asked, rolling his eyes at the men of the Second Quarter. "Find Damaeus. Recruit whomever you cross on your way to guard the doorways."

They scrambled to obey.

"How is it that you live?" King Graelen asked in wonder.

"Damaeus, too much the coward to slay us outright, left us to die in the Crimson Abyss," Cael explained. "We were killed after a time, though by the grace of the Spirits or the luck of the Tides we were found by one of our kind."

"He returned our souls to our bodies using his latent ability," Devren added.

"What of Islyr?" Cael asked the boy, expecting the worst.

"He was captured. Damaeus appeared suddenly while we waited in the Glen. The Mage was startled to see us, but not enough to give us any real advantage."

"It seems that the word of a Rakaii is worth something," Cael mused. "I would not have bet on it." He was relieved that Islyr had not betrayed him. He hoped that the man had not lost his life.

"You think you've seen Islyr fight," Devren said. "You haven't, not in truth. Damaeus had a good thirty Riders with him. Many were killed; the rest badly injured."

"You managed to escape by pure luck, I suppose?"

"I didn't want to leave Islyr, but he said that if I wouldn't go then he would kill me himself. I slipped away using my Affinity. In the cover of darkness even Damaeus could not find me."

King Graelen embraced the boy; something Devren would have protested at any other time. He fell gratefully into his father's arms.

"I thought you would be dead long before we reached you," Devren said. "Perfidia and Damaeus have been planning your death for some time. They have been doing away with the Aranth to gain access to you. You should keep Xaiden at your side. He is the only one whose loyalty we can be sure of."

"I had him exiled along with Selene," King Graelen murmured distantly. "I sent Damaeus to watch over them. He was to return to me to tell me of their actions. I gave him orders to kill them once they led him to Perfidia and Cyanna."

"Selene?" Devren asked.

"They came across her while hunting for Luca. Felan used a bit of deception upon her to force her to join the ranks of the Aranth."

"There is a chance that she and Xaiden are not innocent," Cael said. "We can trust no one who associates with Damaeus."

"There is a chance," King Graelen agreed, "though it is slight."

"Graelen Elyon." Meiun entered from the far side of the Hollow. "I was unable to find your Mage, though I assure you that Barrik Elyon is safe and well protected. I will broaden my search if you wish it, but Damaeus Severl's scent has dissipated. One of strong magic is left in its wake."

"There is no need," King Graelen replied. "Damaeus is not one to take risks. He will not return here until he has fully prepared."

"The boy is in shock and speaks strangely," Meiun added. "I am not certain what the Mage has done to him. *Acleiu imedimun reaulei.* Words of magic, I believe."

"He trusts you, Meiun," Graelen said. "I ask that you watch him for a time. I will join you momentarily when matters here have been settled."

The Khaloc bowed his head.

"We have to find Damaeus." Devren ran a hand across his brow. "But we're at a disadvantage. We have no idea where he and Perfidia are."

"That is true," Cael agreed. "But Selene's Stone will carry some memory of it if she sides with Damaeus. With the use of Devren's latent ability and the luck of the Tides it will show us enough. We can plan our next action from there."

"What about some object from her room?" Devren suggested. "She is bound to have something crafted of stone lying about. We wouldn't have to go anywhere for that, and it could tell us just as much."

"Half of the items in her room are gifts from Damaeus." King Graelen sighed. "He harbored a desire for her that bordered on obsession. Damaeus may have anticipated that we would use such means to search for information. To touch something he has given her with the magic of a latent ability could trigger a trap. I will not allow you to risk your life."

"It is decided, then," Cael said.

"I think it would be best to find their position first. Do not attempt to take anything from them. Damaeus has most likely rejoined the group. We cannot risk events turning out to his advantage."

"I will have no difficulty with them," Cael replied. He was not certain that it was true.

"Be wary of using your latent ability upon Selene," King Graelen warned. "She may tell Xaiden of the encounter after your power has dissipated. He has sworn to kill you for Devren's murder and the breaking of your vow. Find them first. From there we will decide on a course of action."

"I will proceed with the highest amount of caution, Majesty." Cael promised with a bow.

*　　　*　　　*　　　*　　　*

Islyr chewed on a stale end of bread and massaged his bruised neck as he paced the tiny cell. It was best not to sit in this sort of place if it could be avoided. The floor was damp, and the rats were bold enough to dine on human flesh when the thought occurred to them.

The boy had escaped. That was what mattered most. Islyr would not let another young Marked One suffer the torture of the Circlet. Its worm-like points of metal and sorcery had writhed their way into his skull once again, filling the holes that had remained empty so many years. He would have clawed his head to bloodied scraps if only to rid himself of the cursed band of steel. Its insertion alone shattered the will of most men. For Islyr it was much like an old companion come for an unexpected visit; familiar and irritating all at once.

Islyr pulled two tiny, brown insects from his bread before pushing the last of it into his mouth. He had escaped before. He would do so again when the chance presented itself. The trick was in timing, and in convincing your Holder that you cared for nothing but to please them. Mistress Nevane had believed every honeyed word of devotion he had offered her. A combination of skill and a feigned willingness to obey had prompted her to promote him to the rank of most cherished Rakaii. As an offering of thanks he had made her death as swift and painless as possible.

Unfortunately, such an opportunity was a rarity.

Islyr sipped at the battered earthenware cup of dirty water he had been given. The fight in the forest had been close. Not even the most skilled of Rakaii could hold his own against over thirty men, but he wagered that he had done well enough at it. Devren's mark was what had sealed the outcome of the battle. Who would have thought that the boy could turn shadeslight? Memory of Damaeus' vexed expression at finding that the boy had escaped brought Islyr pleasure no matter how often he pictured it. He shuddered as his master's attention turned to him. The feeling was wholly unique.

"Cease that idiotic grinning this moment or I will give you cause to do so," Damaeus hissed. He had grown progressively more irritable over the past few days, or perhaps that was simply his nature. "My methods of coercion are not pleasing, I assure you."

"As you wish, Master Damaeus," Islyr replied simply. He wiped the blood from his forehead before it could run into his eyes. It was common for a newly placed circlet to bleed for several days before settling.

"I have work for you." The cell's ancient hinges cried out like a rutting sidle goat.

"Ask what you will, Holder, and I shall obey." Islyr hoped that it was nothing involving a great effort on his part. He knew that Damaeus' sister wished for a Pleasure Rakaii to share her bed. He did not relish the idea of lying with her, for she was twice his age at least and time had not been kind to her in matters of the flesh. Then again, the muscles involved in such a feat were the only ones which had not been bruised by the beating he had received in the forest.

"I have another Marked One in my possession. He wears a Circlet, though his demeanor leaves much to be desired. The methods I have used thus far have not brought the desired effect. I wish you to train him in the ways of a true Rakaii."

"Yes, Master Damaeus." Islyr could feel the Mage's irritation through the Circlet, and thus knew that it must be severe. Just as a Holder could at times tell the thoughts of any Rakaii bonded to them, so could a Rakaii attune themselves to their Circlet Holder's sense and gain knowledge of their feelings. It was something few Rakaii thought to do, and something that fewer had perfected. It was absolutely necessary for one who had need of escape.

"Follow."

Islyr walked demurely behind him, keeping a proper distance of five paces. He kept his head down with none of the usual difficulty. The Keep seemed to be decaying from within. What may have once been splendor to humble the Spirits themselves had been reduced to nothing more than rot. The Mage's pungent odor seemed at home here. Islyr wondered if the fact had played a role in his choice of dwelling.

"He lacks etiquette, and is so unmanageable as to be dangerous. Perfidia wishes to work with him privately. You may tell Felan such if you think it will persuade him. She wishes him to be knowledgeable in the ways of the Pleasure Rakaii. I have denied my sister such access thus far so as to ensure her safety." Damaeus' speech wavered for a moment. The Mage brought a hand to his chest.

Worry, slick as lamp oil, slipped its way into Islyr's head. Would the bond of the Circlet take his life when the Mage's sickness was fully realized?

The dust of termites fell from the door, powdering the floor beneath, but it managed to hold together as Damaeus pushed it aside. "A Rider will come each morning bearing food and water. I have instructed him to fetch whatever you deem necessary for the Marked One's reform. Do not think to deceive me with foolish requests, however, for the consequences will be dire."

Islyr peered into the room. A small, framed bed stood in its center with a straw mattress and a woolen blanket whose color had been stolen by time or use. Nothing else was held there except for a threadbare, flowered rug. To many it would seem torture to live so. To Islyr it was Spirit-sent.

"You have my deepest gratitude, Master."

"The door upon the far wall leads to his room. Travel where you wish within this area, but do not leave the northern wing. Understood?"

"Yes, Master Damaeus."

"I trust you know better than to speak against me?"

"I do, Master."

Islyr had made the mistake of speaking against his first Holder; the one who had sold him to Mistress Nevane. *Spirits keep you.* Three simple words of hatred. It was not nearly worth the night of pain his Circlet had given him for it. Fortunately healers were plentiful amongst the Kerell.

"I do not care how you do this, but I expect it to be done with haste. You will have tasks enough to fill your every hour by the time the moon is new." With that he left.

Islyr lay back upon the straw. He enjoyed the dry feel of it somewhat, but most pleasurable was the lack of rats. He checked beneath the bed and found a cracked chamber pot.

"Hah!" And here he had thought he would have to use the window. As hard as he tried he could not remember ever having a real chamber pot. The barrel in his cell did not count, most obviously, for in all of the days he had been here not a soul had come by to empty it.

One of the doors near the bed creaked open, though he could see no one in the darkness behind it.

"Hello?" he called, repeating it in Kerell in case the man did not speak the common tongue.

A hand appeared around the edge of the door. The brand of the Aranth was marked upon it. This would be interesting, for certain.

"I am Islyr," he said in the language of the Ethereal Realm. He assumed that he could call himself such; Damaeus had not given him a name. "You may come out, friend. I swear I will not harm you."

The hand's owner stepped unsteadily from behind the door. His condition was deplorable. Deep blue eyes scanned Islyr warily from within a face composed of bruises and swelling. Unkempt hair, perhaps blond or light brown beneath the dirt, fell to his chin where a beard was attempting to grow. Streaks of dried blood stretched from his Circlet to his chest where it stiffened his shirt in patches of russet.

Damaeus had not been kind to the man, but Islyr could tell that his will was unbroken. A good beating brought most into submission, but for a rare few it had a very different, rather contrary, effect.

Islyr felt for Damaeus' presence within the Circlet's magic. His thoughts seemed distant for the moment, but that would change all too soon.

"Listen, friend," Islyr began, "there are many rules to this bout and you must trust me when I say that I have turned it to my favor once before. If you follow my lead there is a great chance of victory, yet if you continue upon the path you have begun you will gain nothing but hurt as your reward."

Something deep within the man's eyes flickered to life.

Thank the Spirits that he's an intelligent one. Islyr thought. He checked quickly to be sure that Damaeus remained distracted.

"Over the next week I will ask you to do some rather unpleasant things, but you must remember that every foul deed you commit brings you one step closer to our objective. You must listen as if your next breath would not come without my counsel. You must obey unconditionally. In time I will return your life to you. Do you agree to my terms?"

The man nodded.

"Someone is distracted at this moment. His feelings are weak to us whereas he feels ours quite strongly. Can you sense what I speak of?"

The man closed his eyes for a moment. Some semblance of a smile touched his lips as he opened them.

"You learn well for a-" Islyr cut his words short as Damaeus' attention slithered through his mind. "I am to train you as a pleasure Rakaii," he amended.

The man's brow furrowed. He did not seem to have any idea what the title entailed, or perhaps he was startled by Islyr's sudden change in demeanor.

"It would be helpful to have your name."

The man extended a scarred hand in greeting. "Felan," he replied as the warmth of his mark spread across Islyr's skin. "Can you truly do such a thing?"

"Most obviously," Islyr said, sensing that Damaeus' thoughts were now fully upon him. "With the training I provide you will become a passing decent pleasure Rakaii in under a fortnight."

"That's not what I meant," Felan protested. It was obvious that he did not grasp the extent of the Circlet's hold upon him, nor did he understand the knowledge Damaeus could gain from it.

"It is natural to be nervous when faced with bedding such an honorable woman as the sister of the one who holds your Circlet," Islyr said with just a touch of sarcasm. He hoped that it was enough to get his point across. "But do not fear; I was a pleasure Rakaii for many years, and was the favorite of my Mistress." He paused to be certain that Damaeus was listening. "It was in that way that I earned my freedom, for she stated as such in her will," he added, giving Felan a wink. "It pains me still to think of her untimely death."

"I have been a fool to act so hatefully towards Mas-" He choked on the word. "Master Damaeus." It seemed that he had at last caught on.

"True," Islyr replied, "but the Circlet Holder has been kind in sending me to you. You receive this second chance by his good grace."

"That is so," Felan agreed. "It was thoughtless of me to be so ungrateful." A smile lit his face, one filled with loathing such as Islyr had never seen. "And when the time comes you can be sure that I will thank him properly for his kindness."

comes you can be sure that I will thank him properly for his kindness."

Meeting Aurin

Snow covered leaves lay nestled above, clinging to their branches in a futile stand against winter and blocking the light of the barely risen sun before it could reach the forest floor. Xaiden still slept, his breath rising and falling evenly beneath the hollow tree that they had procured for use as a campsite. Damaeus' bedroll was empty, and no sound came from the forest beyond. Neither fact worried Selene. With the luck of the Tides he was far off, casting some spell or other. *Or in search of some ridiculous gift with which to court me,* she thought sourly. Either way, she could not truthfully say that she missed his presence.

Selene crept carefully over Xaiden, pulling her boots and cloak over the clothes she had slept in and grabbing her pack as she passed beneath the hollow of the tree. After a swift hello to Cyprus she dusted last night's snow from one of the tree's massive roots and sat to eat her breakfast. The strips of venison had lost their taste somewhat. It was probably due to the fact that she had eaten some sort of cured fare exclusively for the past few weeks rather than due to the actual taste of the meat itself. Seral was the last town they had passed through before braving the Magden Woods. It was where she had bought the pack and the food within it. The trip would be longer yet. Xaiden refused to travel the Crimson Abyss though Damaeus assured him that two Aranth and an accomplished Mage traveling together could not possibly come to any harm there.

Selene chewed thoughtfully upon a dried apricot, the last of her store of fruit. It was wonderfully sweet and it did not make her tongue numb as the meat did. The group would now be forced to travel around the abyss after leaving

Lystonne, which extended their journey by weeks and rendered it much less exciting in the process. She took a mouthful of water from her wineskin before attempting another strip of meat. The next town was not far. She would buy more fruit when they reached it.

Movement, too precise to be a clump of falling snow, caught her gaze. The falcon, pure white as the clouds of a summer's day, perched itself upon a nearby log. It cocked its head in her direction, watching with curious, ebony eyes. The bird's legs were free of any band. *Strange.* Surely a falcon of such unusual beauty could only be bred by the will of man.

She held a chunk of venison out to it. The bird ignored her, choosing instead to preen its already immaculate feathers. Selene lowered the meat to the ground and stepped back a few paces. The bird tilted its head this way and that, eyeing both Selene and the food in turn. After a moment of contemplation it coasted down from the stump, snatched the meat in its talons and disappeared into the forest with the prize.

Selene frowned. The bird had gone northwest. She would have liked to tame it, but could think of no way to do so. Besides that, the time could be better used for tracking Felan.

"Selene," Damaeus called. He emerged from behind a redwood tree as wide as Cyprus was long. The Mage was fond of materializing from nothing more than air. "You seem troubled. Is there anything in particular I could do to improve your disposition?"

"It is nothing, Damaeus," she began. It was still difficult not to become irritated with him. He had been kind over the past few days, but not overly so. "A falcon. I had thoughts of taming the creature, but we haven't the time." Selene pulled Cyprus' brush from his saddle bag.

"A falcon." Damaeus turned one corner of his mouth downward. "Beautiful creatures, but I would not worry over any particular one. They are common at market. At least one breeder can be found in even the smallest of towns, though the quality varies from one place to another. A young bird would be best, for it is then that they are most easily trained." He regarded her calmly. "I could purchase one for you if you wish."

"No," she said with a bit too much haste.

Damaeus offered her a pained look.

"No, thank you, I mean to say. This one was unusual. Its color was the purest white." She busied herself with brushing Cyprus.

The Mage's eyes narrowed. He pulled a corked glass vial, no larger than his thumb, from one of the myriad of pouches that hung at his waist. "Use this if the bird returns," he said, tossing it in her direction.

She caught it, barely. "What should I do with it?" The liquid within the vial shimmered even when held in shadow.

"Pour it on some bit of food. Once the falcon has consumed it he will bend to your every word."

"I didn't think such a thing was possible."

"Great things can be accomplished when the Mage's arts and Alchemy are combined. The results will be pleasing," the Mage promised as Xaiden emerged from the tree carrying his bundled bedroll. "I guarantee it."

"Thank you, truly." Selene slipped the vial into her belt pouch. Her words seemed to satisfy Damaeus immensely.

"It relieves me to see that you two are no longer arguing like children," Xaiden said sharply, "though your time would be better spent preparing to ride."

"Sorry, Xaiden," Selene replied automatically. She sprinted to fetch Cyprus' saddle.

Damaeus offered no apology.

Xaiden softened his tone. "No harm done."

He seemed to pity her at times. The last thing Selene wanted from anyone was pity. She prepared Cyprus quickly, being sure to face away from Damaeus as much as possible. She had not wanted to speak with him in the first place. Xaiden's chiding made the fact that she had done so, and the fact that she had not been irritated by his company, so much harder to bear.

The camp was emptied within minutes.

"Has his direction changed?" Xaiden asked.

Selene pressed her thumb to her Stone, thinking of Felan as she did so. He was closer, but the feeling was odd. She knew that it was not as it should be, but could not put into words just what was wrong. "Northeast." The feeling could be ignored for now. Once they found Felan all would be well. Xaiden was not convinced of his innocence, but given time he would be.

The first half of the day was spent journeying through forest, which turned to field as they neared Lystonne. Xaiden brought Requiem to a halt around mid-day.

"Use your Affinity to scout ahead. Take note of any pertinent conversations you may hear, and keep watch for signs of Perfidia and Cyanna."

He had given identical orders before every town they encountered. Thus far it had done them no good. Selene obeyed him without question nonetheless. She did not wish to anger Xaiden any further, and it felt wonderful to be in raven form besides. She dismounted and secured her sword to Cyprus' saddle. Xaiden, always the gentleman, turned his back to her as she prepared to disrobe. Damaeus, however, continued to hold her in a narrow, expectant gaze.

"Turn away, Damaeus," Selene said sternly.

He did so after a moment's hesitation. She would not let Damaeus' unseemly behavior ruin her mood. Selene's mark warmed in anticipation as she undressed. The cold nipped at her flesh for only an instant. She focused her thoughts, enjoying the familiar wave of pain that passed over her as she used her affinity. It was different now that she had her Stone. At least it seemed that way. Xaiden said otherwise. She had been tempted to take the Stone off in the beginning, for fear that some harm would come from using her affinity while wearing it. She was shocked to learn that the Stone, the setting that held it and even the leather cord were laced with magic and thus were absorbed in the process. She flew up to perch upon Xaiden's outstretched arm.

"Use caution," Xaiden warned.

"If you witness anything unusual you should return at once," Damaeus added with a scowl. "We cannot be left here indefinitely to worry on your safety."

Selene nodded her head to show that she understood. She lifted from Xaiden's arm, tilting her wings to catch the wind as she had learned from the ravens of Woods Edge.

Selene glided smoothly from the sky upon reaching what she gauged to be the center of Lystonne. There she settled upon a lamppost which stood to the side of the main road. It was now just beyond noon, and the main street stood empty.

She coasted down from her perch to get a better view, coming to rest upon an uncovered well backed by a line of evergreen shrubs. Light patches of snow, which covered the cobbles of the road in places, bore no tracks of any kind. Not so much as a bird's call reached out through the stillness. *The street should be filled with people at this hour.* She surveyed the area, searching for something to explain the oddity. Nothing looked out of place. She preened her feathers shortly, preparing to take flight. She should return to confer Xaiden and Damaeus.

A cold breeze of early winter drifted past her, carrying an oddly sulfuric scent. Selene stretched her wings and rotated her body in preparation for flight. She was met by her reflection, warped in a glass-like protrusion of silver and obsidian. She identified it, after a moment, as the largest eye she had ever encountered. The beast tilted its nostrils towards Selene, taking in her scent. The slight shimmer of its winter-white, pebbled skin blended perfectly with what snow surrounded it. The bitter aroma of its breath engulfed her. She would not have believed that the breath of any living thing could be so cold had she not encountered it firsthand.

When Selene was young she and Islyr had played at battling dragons of all types. They had imagined beasts that towered above the Elders' cottage. Their imaginings may have been an accurate representation of the creature's size, at least when it was of a weanling age.

Selene launched herself from the well, working her wings with enough vigor to make her muscles ache. The dragon reared up, snapping its massive jaws shut perilously close to her tail. The wind of it nearly pushed her from the sky. She tilted her body in attempt to regain her balance. Her wings brushed the edge of a rooftop. The dragon snapped at her once more, catching one of her flight feathers between its teeth. Selene held her breath as the beast tossed her into the air, opening its mouth wide in preparation to swallow her whole. She attempted to spread her wings, but found herself dizzied by the speed at which she was falling. The dragon shut its mouth without warning. Selene struck the creatures teeth and tumbled down the far side of the roof, her claws scrambling to gain purchase upon smooth ceramic tiles. There was nothing to hold. She fell hard upon a broken wheelbarrow that lay behind the building then rolled from its barren surface, striking the solidly packed dirt that lay beneath it.

Selene dragged herself beneath the wheelbarrow. There she lay still, allowing her senses to return to her. If the Tides were with her then the dragon would move off in search of some larger prey. After all, a raven would be no more than a bite for a creature of such magnitude. The air was silent now. She waited, breathing in time with the throbbing pain of her injuries.

Several more minutes passed. The dragon did not show itself. Silence had returned in complete disregard to the chaos which preceded it.

After a few moments more Selene clawed her way from beneath the safety of her shelter. An attempt to use her affinity resulted in agony. Never before had she attempted to change form while injured. Now she knew why Xaiden warned against it. Her next try was successful, though no less painful.

Tentative probing with her healing ability revealed that no bones were broken, though a muscle in her arm was torn. She healed the injuries with no difficulty. Winter laid its teeth into her skin as she peered around the side of the house behind which she had fallen. Freezing snow clawed at her bare feet. Other than a number of cobbles which had been pried from the road by the dragon's movements and claw marks the length of both of Ranur's hunting dogs combined, the street was bare.

A roar echoed past the empty houses, causing loose cobbles to shudder. Requiem galloped past her, followed by Cyprus and then Damaeus' mare. The horses were having a difficult time of it as the road was slick with ice. The sight did not bode well for Xaiden and Damaeus. If they had ever fought a dragon before this day she had not heard tell of it.

Selene whistled, which proved rather difficult to do while her body was quaking with cold. Cyprus skidded to a halt, his ears swiveling to find her. She breathed a sigh of relief. He could well have raced on. Fear turned a horse's mind irrational at best. She made her way carefully to his side so as not to startle him. Once there she dressed hurriedly. It was surely Xaiden and Damaeus that the dragon had found, for there did not seem to be another living soul within miles of this place. She untied her weapon and mounted, spurring Cyprus in the direction of the sound. It did not seem right somehow that a dragon could empty an entire town without disturbing any of the buildings, or that the beast would stay after the supply of food had run out. But then, what did she know of dragons and their habits?

She found no answers upon reaching the animal, but rather was greeted with a strange and disturbing sight. A barn lay ahead. Protruding from one splintered side of it was the back half of the beast. Its tail swished from one side of a fenced area to the other, leaving a pile of boards and wire that looked to have been a chicken coop moments ago. The Tides were with her, in a form. With its front end in the barn the dragon could not see her approach.

Selene dismounted. She could hear Xaiden's voice, but could not determine what was being said. She moved closer, advancing far to the side to avoid being struck by the creature's tail. The dragon's flank was tight against the broken section of wall. It left her no room to enter, though at least now she was near enough to understand what was happening within.

"You are not the most intelligent warrior I have encountered," noted a voice that made the ground quake. "You dare to enter my territory, and with no companions to back you. Perhaps you have no friends, yes?"

Selene had heard that dragons could speak, but had never believed the tale. She had also heard that they did not usually deign to speak with humans, or with any creature besides other dragons for that matter. She worried for Xaiden. He could not possibly face a dragon of such size on his own. Where in the name of the Spirits was Damaeus?

"I will tell you this once more, dragon," Xaiden replied. "This town is not within your territory. It is a human settlement and has been so for several hundred years. If you continue with your present course of action I will be forced to take your life from you."

Either Xaiden had completely lost his mind, or he was attempting to gain some time with the hope that someone would arrive to aid him. As Aranth they were bound to protect the lives of others, but she did not think that the vow included dying pointlessly in the face of impossible odds.

She considered rounding the barn to the front. It would be simple to enter from there, but would also bring her to the same position as Xaiden. That would be of no help at all.

"I find it is pitiable that you have no companions, and so I will end your misery. You should thank me, I think."

Selene could not wait for Damaeus to appear. He was already dead, for all she knew. Yet she had no idea how to fight a dragon. No regular sword could pierce its thick hide, though perhaps her Aranth blade might since it was Khaloc made. She crept as close as she dared.

The dragon's tail stopped swinging. She took the chance. The blade slid easily into the beast, at a spot where pebbled skin met a small cluster of scales. Wood splintered as the dragon's front end burst through the side of the barn. Selene realized suddenly that she had not planned her actions as carefully as she should have. The sword was wrenched from her hand as the dragon's colossal tail struck her in the chest. She landed flat upon her back, gasping for air. The dragon faced her then, holding her to the ground beneath a carriage-sized foot tipped with sharply pointed talons. Her ribs felt as if they might collapse.

"You do have companions after all, I see."

Selene noticed, through the silver points of light that threatened to claim her consciousness, that the dragon held Xaiden in a similar fashion. He looked to be unconscious. Blood marred the dragon's perfect hide. It brought Xaiden up for closer inspection.

"Decisions, yes?" the dragon tasted Xaiden's blood with its split-tipped tongue. "Which to eat first. A difficult decision, at that." Wings of pale skin flared out while it pondered. The beast's tongue slid across Selene's face like a length of cool silk. A soft warmth spread across her mark.

He was not a true dragon, but Marked.

"Release me." She struggled to break free. Her breath came with more difficulty as his grip tightened.

"This one for later, I think," the dragon rumbled.

Darkness closed in around her.

Selene woke to see Damaeus' face inches from her own.

"Did he injure you?" the Mage asked.

"Where were you?" she coughed. "Xaiden was almost killed."

"Back away," Xaiden said. "Give her room."

Selene fought a wave of dizziness as she sat up. Her chest ached horribly. "How long was I unconscious?"

"A minute or so," the Mage replied.

"You should be more considerate towards Damaeus," Xaiden chided. "We would not have survived without him."

"Thank you," Selene amended. She allowed the Mage to help her to her feet. His hands were as cold as the ground beneath her. "But I would still like to know where you were."

"I did not foresee battling a beast of such size," Damaeus explained. "Xaiden noticed the dragon's approach and offered to distract him while I prepared a practical spell."

"It was odd," Selene remarked. "He was about to swallow me whole while I was in Raven form. But he decided against it suddenly. He left, seemingly without reason."

"Peculiar," Xaiden agreed. He was wounded in several places, the worst of which lay across his temple and into his scalp. The area was bleeding badly.

"Let me heal you," she offered. Xaiden did not usually mind when she used her latent ability upon him, though she had learned that it was always safer to ask.

Xaiden nodded his head in consent. Selene probed his injuries shortly before beginning the healing. The dragon's talon had scored the bone of his skull, but thankfully had not gone deep enough to cause serious injury. When finished with Xaiden's injuries Selene moved on to her own. It was deeply satisfying to be able to breathe without pain. She did not offer to heal Damaeus, for she knew what his answer would be.

"The Marked One?" Selene asked.

"You are intelligent indeed," Damaeus said in a tone that reminded Selene of a proud parent speaking of their child. "You cannot feel the burn of another's mark through thick hide or bone. How did you know he was Marked?"

"He licked me."

Damaeus mumbled something beneath his breath. Selene was certain that she did not wish to know what had been said.

"The Marked One is in what is left of the barn." Xaiden used his sleeve to wipe the blood from his face.

"You're not afraid that he will wake and run off?" Selene asked. "He did attempt to eat us, after all. It is possible that everyone in Lystonne met the same fate. It would not be intelligent of us to let him roam free."

"I agree, but Damaeus has assured me that the spell he placed will leave him unconscious for at least one half-hour."

"I suppose you couldn't possibly have used *that* spell when you knocked me out in Lansfallow rather than the one that left me unconscious for weeks?" Selene asked the mage as she followed him to the barn.

"I use whatever enchantment is best suited for the situation," Damaeus replied evenly.

"We must decide what to do with him," Xaiden said as they reached the spot where the Marked One lay.

A good portion of the barn was now missing.

"You returned him to human form," she noted as she stepped around an upturned saddle. The thickly bearded man lay completely uncovered. She attempted to keep her eyes from straying to his lower region, as Xaiden would most likely find it to be improper.

"A Marked One's body will always return to its principal form when unconscious," Xaiden explained, "That form is human, for most."

"Do you wish for me to kill him?" Damaeus asked. "He knows of you, and perhaps of Selene."

"We have been exiled," Xaiden replied. "Our vows no longer hold us. We may need aid to restore the name of the Aranth. What do you say, Selene?"

Xaiden was the last person Selene would have expected to say that their vows no longer mattered. It shocked her more that he had asked her opinion on the matter. "He would make a valuable ally," she said finally.

"He is unstable, and thus is a danger to you both. I would strongly advise against it."

"We will allow him a chance to speak," Xaiden said firmly.

"It will do you no good," Damaeus growled. "The enchantment carries a few side effects, one of which is amnesia."

"Nonetheless we will hear what he has to say. His inability to remember will work in our favor. With the luck of the Tides he will not know the symbol of the Aranth on sight."

Damaeus stormed from the barn before Xaiden could continue.

"Selene," Xaiden ordered. "Go and find something to cover him with."

"Yes, Xaiden."

"Do not break into any residences if you can avoid it. You may enter shops, but be sure to leave coin in the value of anything you take."

"I will," she promised.

"See that you do. I am serious, Selene."

"I said that I would." Selene looked down at the man. "He is certainly in need of some breeches." She laughed despite her best effort.

"Go." Xaiden moved to stand between Selene and the unconscious Marked One. He did not look amused.

"Yes, Xaiden."

Felan would have found it amusing. Selene exited the barn, where she found Cyprus waiting. Requiem and Damaeus' mare grazed nearby. She was fairly certain that Damaeus had gathered them, yet as usual he was nowhere to be seen. She climbed into Cyprus' saddle and headed into town. Shops were plentiful in Lystonne, but none of the ones she passed looked to be clothiers.

"This is absurd," she muttered. "It is a waste of time to look for a clothier when there are so many houses about." Cyprus nickered as if in agreement.

Selene selected a row of houses at random and stopped at one end of it, leaving Cyprus to graze by the side of the road. The first and second doors were bolted tight, as was the third. She moved to the last with a sigh. The Tides seemed to be with her, however. Not only was the door unlocked, but it hung open in the slightest. She pushed the door aside, allowing light to sweep into the house. A putrid scent emanated from within.

"Anyone here?" she called, knowing well that she would receive no answer. A woven rug lay in the hall, its edges bent up against the walls that surrounded it. She took the stairs two at a time, anxious to be out of this place and back with the others.

Her search began at the far end of the hall. The room held two small beds and a shelf of toys, nothing of great interest. Even if there was clothing to be had it would not be of a decent size. She moved back to the bedroom nearest the stairs, within which was a larger bed and wardrobe. The scent of decay was stronger in this room.

An infant's cradle rested in the corner, covered by an indigo baby's blanket. The family was fairly well off, for dye of that color was difficult to come by. She certainly had not had anything so fine in her younger years. Selene hurried to the wardrobe, attempting not to become distracted by anything else as she did so. She was not here to ponder the financial standing of people who may no longer live.

Decently made women's dresses hung upon the wardrobe's bar, with men's shirts and breeches on the shelf above. A chest to the side contained corsets, petticoats, and other various undergarments. She moved back to the wardrobe, grabbing one each of shirt and breeches. The Marked One was larger than most men, but they should fit well enough for the time being. They may end up having to kill the man anyways, though she hoped that it would not come to that.

With the clothing in hand Selene sprinted out of the room and back downstairs. She paused at the door, turning her head towards the end of the hall. An irregular scratching noise came from that direction. *Sounds larger than a mouse.* Curiosity overwhelmed her and she headed towards it.

The noise stopped abruptly as Selene entered what appeared to be the kitchen. She ignored the partially set table and peered over the edge of an iron pot which sat upon the stove. A thick layer of brown mold had consumed its contents despite the cold. She wrinkled her nose in distaste.

The scratching noise greeted her once again. This time she was close enough to tell that it had come from the pantry. She opened the door slowly at first, then more quickly upon seeing no movement within. The space held all of the things a pantry should: flour, rice, bottled goods, and the like. Upon the floor was a strange assortment of items; all of which seemed mildly out of place. A silver hair pin with tiny crystals along its length lay next to a polished stone and a curled length of twine. Selene leaned forward, taking the pin from where it lay. It was similar to those Cyanna was fond of wearing. Something white caught Selene's eye as she straightened. She reached for the coin-like object, which sat upon a shelf beside a sack of flour.

A needle-like pain punched through her hand. Selene pulled back to find tiny points of ruby colored blood welling from it. She turned her palm up, where similar punctures resided.

A narrow-headed creature with a mask of dark fur popped its head from behind the sack. Selene had seen many ferrets in the past, mostly upon the arms of hunters in various taverns. Never before had she encountered one in such an odd place.

The ferret chided her with a volley of hisses and chatter before grabbing the object and leaping from the shelf. Selene could only watch as the speedy little creature bounded down the hall, sliding across the planked wooden flooring before bolting out the door.

Selene healed herself without thought. *Of all the things to find in a pantry...* She should get back. Xaiden would begin to worry soon. She dropped the pin into her belt pouch.

Selene placed a gold piece upon the table before leaving the house. It was more than enough to cover the clothes and the pin combined. She then returned to the barn where Xaiden and Damaeus waited. The Marked One was awake and standing, his body still as bare as a newborn. She noticed now that he was broad shouldered, with thick limbs and a chest that looked well-muscled enough to lift a horse. She offered the clothing to him with one hand while covering her eyes with the other. The clothes pulled from her hand.

"Milady. It is truly a pleasure to meet you. Marked ones of your type are rare." His thick accent was more noticeable now than it had been while he was in dragon form.

"It is nice to meet you as well," Selene replied, keeping her eyes averted, "though perhaps it would be better to hold this conversation when you are properly clothed. Or clothed at all."

"Ah, yes," he replied. "How thoughtless. Your exquisiteness caused me to forget myself."

"That is enough, Aurin," Xaiden ordered. "If you wish to travel with us you must act accordingly."

"I will keep my promise, Xaiden. I do not know what came over me, truly. I would not wish to eat one of my kind."

Xaiden offered Aurin an unsatisfied gaze.

"Nor one of human kind, most obviously," Aurin amended. "I much regret my attempt to consume you, beautiful one," he added for Selene.

"My name is Selene. You may call me by that."

"I will do so, if only to please you. No need to look away. I have clothed myself."

"He remembers little save for his name," Xaiden whispered as Aurin moved off to speak with Damaeus.

"Does he recall why he attempted to kill us, at least?"

"He does not. If not for my latent ability I would consider it a lie."

"What should we do, then?"

"I know of him. The Aranth have dealt with the chaos that he and his rogue partner have caused on many occasions. I think it is best not to tell him of his past. It will most likely return to him in time. He may become a companion to us, and a better person for it."

"Are you certain that it is right to do so?" Selene asked. She had never before had to pose such a question to Xaiden. His demeanor had changed greatly of late. "What right have we to deny him his past?"

"We did not willfully take it from him," Xaiden reasoned. "He will come to no harm from being without it for a time. He asked to travel in our company. I believe that we should allow him to do so. If whatever caused his latent ability to activate should occur again then no one within his vicinity would be safe."

"I do not believe that he is responsible for whatever happened to the people of Lystonne."

"Nor do I," Xaiden agreed after a moment of contemplation. "That does not make him any less dangerous."

Selene remembered the pin suddenly. "I came across something you may wish to see." She reached for her belt pouch.

"Your hand," Xaiden noticed. "A wound from the dragon?"

Selene checked her hand. The punctures were properly healed, but she had neglected to wipe the blood from them.

"No," she replied. "I came across a ferret. He was not pleased to see me."

"Trouble seems to follow you," Xaiden grinned. "I cannot leave you alone for any length of time."

Selene smiled as well. It was not often that Xaiden attempted humor. She hoped that it would continue.

"Here." She offered him the pin.

"It looks like one of Cyanna's. You are certain that Felan is not near?"

She checked her Stone once more for good measure. "Absolutely. His position has not changed."

"A ferret, you say?" Aurin interrupted. "Where did you find it?" It seemed that he had given up on befriending Damaeus.

"A house on the northern side of town," Selene replied.

Xaiden furrowed his brow in time with Damaeus, who joined the circle.

"I did not wish to waste time," she explained before Xaiden could speak. "There were no clothiers to be seen and the door to one of the residences stood open. I left coin for both the clothes and the pin, in case it is not Cyanna's."

"I appreciate your honesty," he replied as if she had any choice when he was involved.

"My weapon," Aurin exclaimed. "I must have my weapon if we are to travel, yes?"

"You remember where it is?" Selene asked.

"The Winsome Lady. I was lodging there, waiting for something." His voice trailed. "I cannot remember what."

"This is good," Xaiden said. "If his memory continues to return to him at this rate we will have the story in its entirety within only a few days."

"I will go with him." Damaeus offered.

"I believe we should stay together from this point forward," Xaiden replied, "for the safety of all."

"As do I," Selene agreed.

They followed Aurin to the Winsome Lady and waited in the common room while he fetched his things. The interior was more tavern than inn. An old wooden bar took up two thirds of one wall, behind which multiple rows of liquor occupied shelves from floor to ceiling.

The place had an eerie feel to it. Half empty cups of liquor and ale sat amongst mold covered bread and frosty cheese. It was if everyone in Lystonne had suddenly walked out without reason. Aurin returned wearing properly fitted travelers' clothing and carrying a heavy, spiked mace in one hand.

"Much better, indeed," he said. "Where are we headed, my fine new friends?"

Damaeus looked wholly disturbed by the idea that the man considered him a friend.

"Northeast," Xaiden replied. "But we will travel around the Crimson Abyss rather than through it."

"An excellent plan, I think. I remember somewhat of that place. It is horrible, yes?"

"Let us leave, then," Damaeus grumbled. "I have no desire to waste time. We will execute Felan and be done with it."

"We will not be killing him," Selene said vehemently.

"The decision has not yet been made," Xaiden injected. Selene could tell by his tone that he considered the conversation finished.

Selene's Obsession

"Barkeep," Aurin called across the din of the tavern, "A round of Pyrewood whiskey for my newest companions."

Selene watched curiously as Aurin finished his third plate of food. She could not imagine where he stored it all, for there was not a spare inch on the man.

"This drink will be my last, I believe," Xaiden announced. "I have received an offer to play Forces. I think I shall accept."

"You could find a Forces partner in the middle of the Barren Lands," Selene said, laughing.

"I shall take that as a compliment," Xaiden replied in kind.

"Pyrewood whiskey, gentlemen," the elderly Innmaster said as he approached the table. His clean white hair was tied neatly at his neck. "Will you have something, Milady?"

"The same," Selene replied.

"Begging your pardon, Milady, but Pyrewood isn't a drink for your breed. We've got some excellent Fenlaye wine, if you fancy that."

"Pyrewood will be fine," Selene replied, removing her riding gloves and tucking them into her belt so that her Aranth brand was visible. "Thank you."

"Yes, Milady." The Innmaster paled. "Right away." He shuffled off to fetch another glass.

"Selene," Xaiden chided, "You should not use your brand in such a manner. Especially considering recent events."

"No harm came from it," Selene reasoned. "Besides, who is he to tell me what I can and cannot drink? I never had such problems when I was a Rider. And of what other use is the brand now that the kingdom has abandoned us?"

Xaiden downed his shot of whiskey and rose from the table. "Perchance it is as you say," he agreed wearily.

Shame wrapped its tendrils around her, yet she found that her mouth refused to form any sort of apology.

"A game of Forces awaits me." Xaiden turned his back to her and headed off.

"Your whiskey, Milady." The Innmaster set it down upon the table with a bow.

"Thank you," she replied softly.

"You are the first woman I have seen to drink Pyrewood whiskey," Aurin said in an obvious attempt to distract her. "You are certain it is not too strong for you, yes?"

"A great many Riders have lost drinking bets to me," she informed him.

"Ah, it is so with all of our kind, I think. We have a greater tolerance for such things, yes?"

"I suppose."

"To our journey." Aurin raised his glass. "May it be swift and gainful."

"Here's to that."

Selene touched her glass to Aurin's before drinking. She scanned the room while the burn in her throat subsided, looking for anything of interest to take her mind off of Xaiden. The tavern of Miloren was filled from one wall to the other with people. It was of a better quality than most, and thus contained a stage towards which all of the tables faced. The ceiling high sheet of linen which had been hung upon the wall behind it was painted with a mural depicting the creatures of the Crimson Abyss. Dark wisps of shadeslight swirled amongst blye spiders and ruby eyed bats. Selene had never been to the Crimson Abyss, though stories of the fearsome creatures that lived there were abundant. She wondered if any of them were true, while at the same time hoping that she would never find out first hand.

A man cloaked in black climbed onto the stage carrying a battered guitar. The inn quieted somewhat as all eyes were drawn to him. He drew back his hood to reveal a face finer than any Selene had seen; so much so that she found it difficult to turn away.

"Time for a show," Aurin pushed away his empty glass. "A song to lift the spirits of this place. And in excellent company."

Selene followed Aurin's eyes, then noticed at once that many of the tavern's patrons were female. It was odd, to say the least, for this time of night.

The man removed his cloak and set his guitar atop it. He pulled a chair from a nearby table and placed it center stage. Serving girls around the room set down their trays to watch.

"Good evening, fine patrons. I present to you one of my most cherished songs. It has no name that I know of, but I am certain that you will enjoy it nonetheless." The man swept down into a graceful bow before sitting and taking up the guitar. He wore a tunic of ebony leather, beneath which lay a long sleeved, cotton shirt of a charcoal color. The shirt, Selene noted, revealed a healthy portion of the man's chest. She could not have honestly said that she was sorry for it.

A cloth bandage covered the man's left hand. Selene probed his flesh with her latent ability, but found no injury. The man raised his brow in her direction. She drew her ability back quickly, but felt immediately foolish for doing so. There was no way he could have known that she had used it upon him, or even that she had one.

The man sang with a voice like that of the Spirits. It carried well, weaving its story with perfect clarity and soothing her mind with its flawless tones. He was no less talented in the ways of the guitar. Selene smiled as she recognized a song from her childhood; one she and her father used to sing together. The melody was as beautiful as she remembered it to be. A thrilling tale of faraway seas unfolded before her, sweeping her thoughts to a land of impossibly deep caverns and the treasures that lay within.

The performance was finished all too soon. Wavy hair fell over the man's dark eyes as he bowed. Selene steeled herself. An Aranth did not fall lovesick at the first fine body she came across. And then there was the matter of Felan. She pulled her Stone from beneath her shirt, rolling it absently between her fingers for a moment before replacing it.

"Many thanks to you, fine audience," the man said. "With the luck of the Tides we shall meet each other once more before their next descent."

She could have sworn that he winked in her direction.

"Tips are greatly appreciated," he added with a smile that melted her resolve. The ladies of the audience rushed to comply. The men, to Selene's surprise, seemed just as pleased with the performance.

Selene had never seen the man with the guitar before, nor had she heard tell of his talents. The fact puzzled her greatly, for she had stayed in many taverns and inns during her time as a Rider. She would have remembered a man such as this one, of that she was certain. Perhaps he only performed at this particular tavern, though the chance was slight.

"The admirers of your splendor are many, indeed," Aurin said, scattering her thoughts.

Selene offered him a look of confusion.

"I will lend my company to some of the other beauties, I think." He plucked his drink from the table. "With luck I will not see you until tomorrow's light, yes?" Aurin whispered before making his way through the crowd towards a group of fair-faced young women who looked willing to share his time, to say the least.

The cloaked man appeared beside Selene as if brought by an enchantment. Aurin had noticed him, surely, but how he had done so in the disorder of the tavern she could not surmise.

"May I have the pleasure of your company?"

His manners are as fine as his look. Selene found herself wishing, for an unknown reason, that it was not so.

"Yes, of course," she replied. Her face heated like that of a girl at her first Festival of Low Tides. She felt horribly awkward around him, and slightly guilty about feeling so. The worst of it was that she had no idea how to make it cease. She folded her hands so that her Aranth brand was hidden.

"You may sit where you wish," she amended. "This is a public tavern." She regretted the choice of words even as they passed her lips.

The man was undeterred by her discourtesy. He sat next to her and raised a hand. Every serving girl who caught sight of the gesture rushed towards him. It was the eldest of them who reached him most quickly, causing the others to scowl at her with varying degrees of irritation. The woman held her tray beneath one arm, looking the man over with adoration that was unbecoming of her age.

"May I purchase you a drink, my Lady?" the man asked.

"You may," Selene replied, deciding at once to test him. "Pyrewood whiskey. A double, if you please." She might even drink it all, if it came to that.

The server looked hesitant, but made no comment on her choice of beverage. "For you, My Lord?"

"The same," the man said without hesitation.

It seemed that Selene would have to work much harder to be rid of him. He was pleasant enough, but she had matters of importance to attend to.

The woman sauntered off to fill the order, swinging her hips quite a bit more than was necessary.

"I would like to ask something of you," the man said suddenly, leaning in. "It is my hope that you will not think me too forward for it." There was something in his gaze that was familiar; an intelligence uncommon for someone of his years. His confidence reminded her somewhat of Xaiden.

"I was a Rider for many years," Selene replied. "There are very few things you could say that I have not heard before in some form or another."

"I understand that well. I was once a Rider myself; a Praecyr as well."

She was in no mood for idle talk. "You wished to pose a question? I must return to my companions soon so that they do not worry for me."

Xaiden would have been disappointed in her, for it was most certainly a falsehood. Aurin was surrounded by a sizeable group of ladies, young and old alike. He was weaving some tale or other, and all seemed thoroughly entertained by it. Xaiden was nowhere to be seen, though Selene guessed that he would remain engrossed in his game of Forces for the next few hours, if not longer. He said that he had once stretched a single game over a month's free time. The boast, if it could be called such, would have been completely unbelievable had it come from anyone else. And lastly Damaeus had retired early, as was usual for him. He rarely wanted any part of drinking or games.

"Well enough," the man said. "I have noticed that you journey solely with men, which leads me to wonder." He ran one hand through his hair as if nervous. Nervousness seemed unnatural on him.

"Xaiden and Aurin?" Selene laughed as his point became clear. "They are my traveling companions and friends, nothing more." She did not bother to mention Damaeus, for she did not know whether to name him friend or foe.

"Your words are deeply satisfying, I must admit." The man moved as if to place his hand upon hers, which were still folded.

Selene's Stone warmed against her chest. She pulled it from beneath her shirt. The clear center glowed shortly with a pure, white light. Felan was near.

"I must leave." Selene rose from her seat and levered her sword from its scabbard.

The man looked properly stunned, as if nothing of the sort had ever happened to him before. She guessed that it probably had not, if his appearance was any judge.

"My apologies," she added as she pulled her cloak around her shoulders. She did not linger long enough to witness his reaction.

The street was dark, and cold enough to send shivers through her. She rounded the building, using the feeling of the Stone as her guide. She was glad that Xaiden and Aurin were not with her. She would have a chance to speak with Felan alone.

Xaiden would be angry. It was his opinion that Felan was dangerous. It was one of the many points upon which they disagreed. She quickened her gait as she turned down a narrow road that ran between two buildings. Her Stone glowed once more, throwing light upon the snow that filled every crevice like builder's mortar. Felan was close. It would be simple to find him so long as he did not venture indoors.

She turned down the next alley she came to. Lamps did not hang between the buildings as they did upon the main street. The far end looked as if it may be blocked, though she could not be certain as it was blanketed by darkness. Selene continued down it anyway. A dead end meant that Felan would have nowhere to go, in the event that he was indeed running from her.

Her Stone became as cold as the surrounding air. For several seconds she could feel nothing of Felan's presence. She slid to a halt. Thoughts of Felan's whereabouts brought a feeling of emptiness deeper than the Crimson Abyss. When his presence finally returned it was much weaker. He was just as far from her as he had been at the beginning of the evening.

She sighed irritably. How in the name of the Spirits had Felan traveled such a distance in so little time? It made no sense. Nothing to do now but return to the tavern and tell Xaiden what had happened. She should have acted more quickly. It could be ages before another opportunity presented itself. She turned to leave, but shadows moved to block her path. Three men obstructed the alley less than a yard from where she stood.

"What's your price, harlot?" the middle one called.

"Why bother to ask of price," a second voice offered, "when we can simply take what is due to us? I consider a wench such as this one fair payment for a Rider serving the King and the Spirits."

Selene readied her sword. If the scoundrels were looking for someone to prey upon they had chosen poorly. All the more foolish were they for bringing King Graelen and the Spirits into their debauchery. Xaiden would not disapprove of slaying those who meant to harm her. What if it had been some innocent walking this alley? She could not leave the men to prey upon others.

"You may not defile her," said a voice that caused winter's chill to creep into her heart. "Our benefactor has ordered it so."

"Yes, Praecyr."

"And watch your tongue. The lowliest man is one who takes his satisfaction from a beast such as she. I will not have such Riders in my company."

"Yes, Praecyr," the man conceded.

"Ranur." Selene narrowed her eyes in an attempt to make out his face. A company of men stood behind him. Selene's confidence faded like the mist of her breath in the night air. "Face me alone," she attempted. "If you do not then all honor will be lost to you."

"A lone Praecyr against an Aranth?" he laughed. "I would not consider that to be an honorable fight."

"I am no Aranth," she lied, fighting the spread of fear.

"Then I am no Praecyr."

"Your Riders are undisciplined," she said as she pooled her concentration in preparation for the fight. "The battle will be lost when they see you fall at my hand."

"No need to worry, Selene. I will not fight you on this night. That honor has been reserved for another. You did attempt to kill me, but I am a patient man. There will be a time for us."

"Do you think that I'd be so foolish as to let you go?" Selene shouted as he walked away.

"No," he replied. "But I shall go nonetheless."

"You're responsible for what happened to Maye." What little was left of her composure was melting away. "The Spirits will keep you for slaying my family."

Several of the Riders shifted nervously as the walls surrounding them began to shake. Loose portions of brick clattered to the frozen cobbles. Selene struggled to keep control of her latent ability.

"The blood of all Marked Ones is tainted," Ranur replied. "Those who bore them are not worthy of life."

Selene readied herself to strike. Ranur's Riders may overpower her in the end, but first she would have him. Maye and Luca deserved as much.

"Your friend will know that you are well," Ranur said calmly. *"Acleiu imedimun reaulei."* He melted into the shadows.

The alley erupted into chaos as Riders closed in on her from every angle. Long ago she would have been frightened by such odds. With only the training of a Rider to call upon she would have been slain in an instant. But she was not a Rider any longer. She was Aranth, and Aranth did not show fear. Selene pooled her latent ability, releasing it through her Stone in a burst that swept out from all sides. Men were forced back against each other, with some striking the walls behind them. It gave her time, but did not provide her with an exit. A few Riders did not rise from where they lay. The others were up in an instant. They charged her almost as one.

Selene showed her former brethren no kindness. She used every opportunity she was given; slashing easily through a throat, a leg, an arm. She applied what she had learned, blending her swift, self-taught movements with Xaiden's bold form and Felan's feigning strikes. She killed any Rider that came within reach without thought as to who they were or if they had at one time been an ally. Anyone who stood with Ranur was now an enemy of the Ethereal Realm. Whether King Graelen accepted Selene's aid or not was irrelevant. She would do what was necessary.

The men did not seem frightened by the swiftness of their companions' deaths. Ranur must have offered them more than a kingdom's worth in gold for her head. No matter what the outcome of the battle, she was certain that they would never see it.

The man who had named her a harlot struck to her left, aiming for her heart with clumsy movements. He had not been a Rider for long, or else he simply had no talent for it. Selene thrust her sword through the man's stomach, twisting it as she withdrew. He fell to the ground. The second man she clipped in the skull before carving a deep wound into his thigh. Several more advanced to take his place.

Selene sliced her way through flesh and leather but there seemed no end to the flow of bodies. The Riders grew more daring as the fight wore on, though a great many of those who had been closest to her at the start were now dead. One man charged Selene head on in attempt to draw her attention while two others approached at her flank, one upon each side. She dispatched the decoy in a breath's time, moving to one side and sinking her sword between his ribs in a single, smooth movement. The man at her right was easily defeated. He was young and his lack of skill showed it. The one at her left, however, had more talent at weaponry than she had anticipated. A blow grazed her side.

Selene's concentration was split, and she could not spare any of it for healing. Worse yet, she was rapidly tiring. She parried a swing from a man armored in hardened leather only to be struck in the back of the leg by what felt much like a club. She collapsed with the force of the blow. It had surely broken the bone. Her sword clattered to the ground. She attempted to stand, but her leg refused to hold her. She brushed her hand against the cobbles. There was no sign of her weapon.

"Another-" someone shouted from near the alley entrance. He could say no more than that before his head flew from his body. It rolled crookedly, coming to a stop in a trampled drift of snow.

Xaiden had found her. It could only be him for he moved with the swiftness of an elder Aranth, cutting Riders down before they had time to identify him as Spirit or man. Selene took the opportunity to heal her leg enough so that she could put pressure upon it.

Most of the Riders turned to Xaiden. He did not draw the attention of all, however. Selene stumbled backwards through the snow until she could go no further. The Riders advanced. A stone wall pressed against her back.

"Leave us," one man ordered the others. "Kill the male." His voice was tight with fury.

The men did as he commanded.

"Fight me honorably, Selene, as you would have fought Ranur had he allowed it. Use none of your cursed spellcraft."

"Why should I afford you such an honor?" she asked, bargaining for time. "Who are you to me? You have not given me so much as your name."

The gash in Selene's side healed with ease.

"It wounds me greatly that you do not remember me." The man moved closer.

"You are a Rider," Selene replied. "You follow Ranur, which makes you my enemy. That is all I need to know of you." She healed her leg further, knowing that she would have to ask Xaiden to break it once again so that she could reset it properly. It would work well enough for the time being.

Selene's face was warm from the effort of the battle. The man's fingers were glacial against her cheek.

"I could have looked after you, Selene. Your mother as well. My family had wealth enough. *I* had wealth enough. I imagined that I was not worthy of your attention."

His free hand struck her cheek hard enough to turn her head. The strike would have pained her somewhat in her younger days. Compared to the use of her affinity or the fading pain of her leg it was nothing.

"You are a curse to everyone you come across. Ranur speaks truly when he says that all Marked Ones deserve to die. Your blood taints ours." The man pressed the tip of his sword to her chest. Panic swept her latent ability from her grasp.

"Other girls came to you, Terran," Selene said, recognizing him at last. Her voice did not shake though she felt that it should. "You bedded many, if my memory serves me. Why did you not offer to take your Caerim vows with one of them? Nearly any girl of age in Maresbane would have been happy to do so."

Terran's face crumpled as if he was in pain. "Tell me why you would not have me. I was kind to you. I was charming."

"You only wanted me because I would not have you." *I will not let panic control my actions. I open my mind to the winds of tranquility. My thoughts are pure serenity.*

"I wanted you because you were beautiful and strong." He backed her against the wall. "Because I did not know that beneath that alluring exterior lay the malevolent heart of a Marked One. Now tell me why."

"My spirit is as it has always been. You grow angry at something I cannot change. Being born with a mark does not make me a thing of evil." *I will not let panic control my actions. I open my mind to the winds of tranquility. My thoughts are pure serenity.*

"I have to know." His face contorted. "You were with others but never me. Why?"

"I do not wish to harm you, Terran. Leave Ranur and return to Maresbane. Your family is no doubt worried for you." *I will not let anger control my actions. I open my mind to the winds of tranquility. My thoughts are pure serenity.*

"My Lord has given me this opportunity with you and I will not waste it. He only asked that I not kill you. In case the fact escaped you, he is not here." Terran eased the tip of his sword into her chest. The scent of pipe tobacco wafted against her face as he closed the gap between them. "The Spirits keep you, monster."

My thoughts are pure serenity. The glow of her Stone illuminated his face as her ability returned to her. Selene hurled Terran back. The world spun as she forced the flesh of her chest back together.

Terran landed on his back near Xaiden's feet. Xaiden rested his sword on the man's throat. "You should kill him. He knows what you are. By the vows of the Aranth you cannot allow him to live."

Selene realized as she plucked her sword from the snow that it was not Xaiden who aided her, but the cloaked man from the tavern.

"What right have you to speak of Aranth vows?" Confusion churned within her head. "You cannot know of them."

"You would find that I know many things if you would take the time to speak with me rather than running off at the first opportunity."

Selene pressed the tip of her sword to Terran's chest. The cloaked man removed his weapon, though he did not sheath it. They stood an awkward moment in silence.

"Pyre's Ash," he swore, pressing his fingers to his temple. "You have earned this kill. End it now unless you would have me finish him for you."

"You do not deserve the honor of fighting me," Terran choked. "All will know of the treachery of the Graelen lineage. The future of the Ethereal Realm lies in the ways of the Kerell. Marked Ones will no longer be free to spread their filth amongst proper men." Terran's arm shifted. Selene doubled over as pain pierced her stomach. She moved her free hand towards the source, fearing what she would find. The knife's unadorned, metal hilt still held the warmth of Terran's hand. Selene pulled it out slowly, immediately healing what space it left behind so it would not bleed out. The blade had not severed anything of importance, with the luck of the Tides. She tucked it into her belt once it was free.

Terran's eyes grew wide. "The Spirits keep your damned soul," he spat.

Selene knelt down beside him. "You did not need to travel so far to ask why I chose others and not you." She leaned in close, no longer afraid. "It is as you first thought," she whispered. "You are not worthy of my attention."

The man from the tavern placed a gloved hand upon Selene's, forcing her sword through Terran's chest. Terran's mouth opened as if to scream but he was not given the chance, for the cloaked man ran the edge of his sword along his throat.

"Do not attempt to heal him," he warned. "The blade of my sword is coated with tincture of larien root. Use of your latent ability will only prolong his pain."

Selene had no intention of healing Terran, though the thought of saying it aloud made her nauseous.

"Who are you? Speak or I will kill you." It was a bluff and the man seemed to know it. She had seen his skill, just as he had seen hers. She was no more a match for him than she was for Xaiden.

"My name is Logan," he replied. "And you should not be visiting alleyways on your own in the dead of night. I suggest that you return to the tavern before more trouble finds you."

Selene glanced down at Terran. No breath came from him.

"Selene?" the true Xaiden called from the street beyond the alley.

"Please do not mention my presence to your friends," Logan said. "It will turn out poorly for all concerned." He vaulted up a pile of broken crates and onto the rooftop, where he disappeared from sight.

Xaiden quickly reached her side. "Would you care to explain what happened here?" the elder Aranth asked, surveying the bodies that lay strewn about like ocean-swept driftwood.

"Ranur attacked me." It was all that would come to her.

"That is why you should not be out on your own at this hour." Xaiden said, echoing Logan's warning. "No one should. You may be Aranth, but that does not make you immune to death itself. Why would you do such a thing?"

Selene found that she could not pull her eyes from Terran's lifeless body. The blood of her past seeped between paving stones powdered with snow.

"I am disappointed in you, Selene."

"Felan was here," she said, pulling herself to the present. "My Stone began to glow while I was in the tavern. He was close for a time, but he disappeared before I could reach him. I could not sense his presence at all for several seconds, and then he suddenly returned to where he was at the beginning of our journey."

"You should have come to me first."

"I did not think that there would be time."

Xaiden frowned.

"Alright," Selene admitted, "I wanted to speak to Felan alone. I thought that perhaps I could convince him to rejoin us."

"What do you think I will do when we reach Felan? Do you believe my character to be so shallow that I would slay a man without questioning him first?" Few others could make her feel like a wayward child the way Xaiden did. Selene had yet to figure out how he accomplished it.

"I am truly sorry."

Xaiden's expression softened somewhat. "What of Ranur?"

"Disappeared, just as Felan did."

"Selene," Xaiden began.

"I know," she interrupted. "It may be true that Felan is aiding them, but that does not mean that he cannot be saved."

"They could only have found you by use of Felan's Stone. They must be tracking us as we are tracking them."

"Felan will rejoin us," Selene said stubbornly. "I will reason with him."

"That may be so. Still, we must be cautious. Promise that you will not do anything so foolish again."

"I promise it."

"We are no longer Aranth. We cannot count on our titles to absolve us of blame. If we are caught within sight of this carnage we may be held accountable for murder."

"Is it safe to stay in town for the evening?"

"I believe so. No one in with any sanity would believe that you accomplished all of this on your own."

Selene hoped that he was not including himself in that statement, for she had absolutely no desire to speak with him about Logan.

"Also, if we were to leave Miloren at this time of night it would seem suspicious. Come, we need to clean you up before anyone sees you."

Selene followed Xaiden back to the tavern, leaving Terran's body to freeze in the cold of night.

* * * * *

"I was not successful." Cael plucked a roll of bread from the nearly empty basket. The meal had been fine, though small and rather lonely for one eaten in the main dining hall. "I shall have it next time, assuming that the circumstances are more favorable."

"More favorable?" Devren mocked. "Is there a woman that the great Logan Altayr cannot tame?"

"It has nothing to do with that," Cael replied, giving the boy an irate glance. "There were her companions to contend with, for one. She keeps odd company."

"I would hardly consider Xaiden and Damaeus odd," King Graelen said, "no matter what allegiance they hold."

"I was not speaking of Xaiden and Damaeus," Cael replied, "but of our dear friend Aurin Fetlask. Viverr was nearby as well, which does not surprise me. He and Aurin are never far from one another in my experience. My latent ability was immediately absorbed when I tried it upon Selene in the tavern. I would wager that Viverr's presence was the reason for it."

"The Sleeping Bandits?" Devren said, excited by the concept. "They're nearly as famous as father."

"I believe the word you are searching for is *infamous*," Cael corrected.

"Did you bring me something of his, at least?" Devren asked.

"Of course," Cael replied with a touch of sarcasm. "I had plenty of free time to search for souvenirs."

"If he had brought you anything belonging to those rogues you would not be allowed to keep it," King Graelen added.

Devren grumbled in his typical manner.

"We cannot assume that Selene is on our side simply because she was attacked by Ranur and his men," King Graelen said. "We do not know that Ranur and Damaeus are working towards the same cause."

Cael swallowed the bread he had been chewing. "It would not bode well for us if they were. A rogue Mage is enough of a difficulty without a Praecyr and a company of Riders to back him."

"We are still in need of Selene's Stone." King Graelen pressed his fingers to his temple. "We must know where they are headed."

"They are headed northeast," Cael offered, "though I do not know the exact location. They were in Miloren when I found them. One of the serving girls at the tavern said she heard that they were headed for Fyren's Glen, and then Fenlaye."

"So you did use your latent ability," Devren said with a grin.

"I used only my charm and fine features," Cael informed him between sips of wine. "I had no need of my latent ability."

"Fenlaye." King Graelen pulled his hand down his beard. "Selene's Stone is the only thing that will tell of her allegiance. We must have it. Perhaps your friend Kyrros could be of use."

"An excellent idea, Majesty, but it will be difficult to remain hidden from Xaiden. He guards the girl as if it is his one mission in life. If she was not so willful, and Xaiden was not so fond of Forces, I would never have gained the chance to speak with her. There is also Damaeus to contend with, though he will likely leave of his own accord if confronted with any social situation."

"Then what can we do?" Devren asked, resting his chin in his hand. "It will be over if either of them catches sight of you."

"The answer is simple," Cael replied easily. "I believe that Lord Kyrros Hane of Fenlaye will be throwing a masquerade."

The Masquerade

Fields of frozen plant life littered with groves of leafless trees passed Selene by at a frustratingly sluggish pace. The surrounding snow rose nearly to Cyprus' knees. Selene had lost count of the number of days that had passed since she left Evaria with Xaiden and Damaeus. The constant travel, though so familiar as to be comforting to her, seemed to be wearing on Damaeus' nerves. She hoped that they would reach Fenlaye before his' attitude eroded what was left of her patience.

"We could have found Felan and executed him by now if certain members of the party were not slowing us so," the Mage announced.

He was speaking of Aurin, at whom he had thrown hundreds of words of ill will since leaving Miloren. They had been unable to find a suitable horse for the man due to his size. Thus he had walked while Selene and the others rode. Aurin returned none of the Mage's discourtesy, for the most part. Yesterday he had finally told Damaeus that true enemies did not threaten, but rather met one in a straightforward battle to the death.

"There is no need for you to travel with us, Damaeus," Selene's responded, purposely allowing some bitterness to enter her tone. "You may return to Evaria any time you wish, unlike Xaiden and myself. We have no need of you to find Felan, nor do we need to hear your opinion on what we should do when we encounter him."

"Ah," Aurin injected. "You come from the capital city. I have been there many times. If only I could recall the purpose of my visits."

His memory had been steadily returning since Lystonne, though it seemed that all occurrences of importance were still buried deep within his mind.

"Silence." Xaiden's voice carried well over the snow-covered earth. "Someone approaches."

Selene saw the boy then. He was dressed in violet and black livery, upon the center of which lay silver embroidery: a thorned rose surrounded by twisting leaves. His slim, long-legged horse, whose blanket matched the boy's clothing, paced easily through the snow. He stopped several yards from the party.

"I bear a message for Lord Xaiden and his companions," the boy called out, brandishing a note sealed with violet wax. "You match the description I was given."

"I am Lord Xaiden. You may approach."

The boy dismounted and struggled through the snow to Xaiden's side. "Lord Kyrros Hane of Fenlaye sends his greetings," he said, handing the letter to Xaiden and receiving a silver coin in return. "He asked that I await your reply and relay it to him upon my return."

Xaiden split the waxen seal. His eyes passed over the words within the letter several times. At last he turned to Selene.

"What does it say?" Selene asked when she could bare the suspense no longer.

"Lord Kyrros sends us an invitation. It is for you, myself, and any companions that may travel with us."

"Of what sort is it?"

"It is for a masquerade."

"We have no time for festivities." Damaeus sat uneasily upon his mount. His hatred for riding did not seem to diminish no matter how much time he spent astride a horse.

"An excellent idea to go" Aurin said. "We are in need of some relaxation to ease our fears."

Selene had to admit that she would enjoy some leisure time, as well as a proper bath. She did not, however, think that Xaiden would approve of the delay.

"Tell your Lord that we accept his invitation," Xaiden said. "And that a single companion will be accompanying each of us."

"He will be pleased to hear it, Lord," the boy replied as he returned to his horse.

"You are wrong to assume that I will take any part in this," Damaeus said after the boy had disappeared from view. "I consider it to be an incredible waste of our time."

"I expected that you would say so," Xaiden replied as he spurred Requiem to a walk. "And I have no intention of attempting to convince you otherwise. We planned to stay the night in Fenlaye. We may as well make our trip pleasurable. It will be a good opportunity to gather information as well. Lord Kyrros is a friend of the Aranth. He rules his land well and is aware of most of the events that transpire within its borders. We will continue on tomorrow morning as planned."

"You do not think it odd that he knew of our approach?" Damaeus asked, looking more aggravated than worried.

"Not particularly, knowing Kyrros as I do. He was a friend to Cael, but I do not believe that he was involved in Devren's disappearance. He will not harm us."

"Tell me that you do not agree with this insanity," Damaeus said, turning to Selene. "Felan will not remain in one place waiting for us to find him. Hours of time that could be used for travel will be spent on revelry. My sister could be taking her last breath as we speak."

"If that is so then it is truly too late," Xaiden said. "We would not be able to save her even if we traveled without sleep from this point forward."

"Felan's position has remained the same for ages," Selene added as she pushed Cyprus to follow Requiem. "And

I will not go against Xaiden's orders." Xaiden was right. It was best that they gather information before continuing any farther. Besides that, they were beginning to run low on funds. She did not relish the thought of what would happen when their coin was gone completely. Selene's pay as a Rider had been sporadic at best, but the small piece of land she and Maye owned and the animals upon it had sustained them.

"You do not generally follow my orders, as I recall," Xaiden said with a touch of a smile.

"I have no idea what you are speaking of," Selene replied evenly. She did not think that she had ever seen Damaeus more discontent.

* * * * *

Cael's knife struck the door just where he had anticipated, completing a perfect circle of eight. It pleased him to find that he had not lost the skill, though much time had passed since he had last used it. Then again, he was not certain that it was possible to lose a skill that he had gained from taking another's soul. Some skills required that he maintain certain muscles in order to practice them, but that was a different matter altogether.

He threw the last knife, aiming for the center of the circle. The door opened just as the hilt left his hand. A young boy stood in the doorway, his eyes so wide as to show the whites surrounding them. He clutched a cloth-wrapped bundle to his chest. The knife had passed over him with no more than an inch to spare.

"Pyre's Ash." Cael leaned back upon the finely crafted, maroon settee that he had moved to the center of the room solely for the purpose of throwing knives. "You ought to knock before entering a person's room." Some of Kyrros' servants were not nearly as cautious nor as well-mannered as they should be. "Next time I will aim for your head. Be forewarned that I rarely miss." He hoped it would frighten the lad into being more watchful.

"Cael, my old friend," Kyrros said as he strode into the room. "I see that neither your personality nor your vocabulary has changed in the slightest from our last meeting." He gestured at the boy, who laid the bundle he held upon a nearby table. The lad left the room with no small amount of haste.

"You finally deign to call after leaving me to rot in one of your gaudy visiting rooms for such a length of time?" Cael said, rising to embrace him shortly.

Kyrros was dressed in clothing which followed the latest trend: a shirt of black silk and a long, open coat with the thorned rose of Fenlaye embroidered upon one corner. Hose, with a codpiece to match, lay beneath. His hair was worn shoulder length and bound by a dark, silk tie. It was typical of the man. Before Cael had time to realize that something had come into fashion it seemed that Kyrros had already obtained it in triplicate.

"My apologies for your painting," Cael added as he released him. His eyes strayed to the far side of the hall. His knife had gone through the portrait and into the wood paneling behind it. "And to the Spirit of your great aunt. May the old biddy find peace in her new life."

"I'll not hold you accountable for it," Kyrros replied. "I was not fond of the woman even while she lived. You know as much."

The barely perceptible, yet wholly distasteful scent of his cologne touched Cael's senses now and again. Women were drawn to it, or so Kyrros claimed. Cael could not imagine why.

"But on to matters of greater importance, such as where you have been hiding these past few years. I've vast lands of worthy women and no partner to conquer them with."

It pleased Cael that he was not the only one whose personality had remained constant despite the passage of time.

"I was beginning to think that you'd met an untimely end," Kyrros continued. "Especially so when I heard that you'd been accused by the throne. Men of our kind do have a tendency to die violent deaths."

"I was with the Spirits for a short while, but they weren't able to keep me."

"I would never believe that they could." Kyrros laughed as he moved to the bar.

He believed the words to be a jest, and Cael felt no desire to correct him on the matter.

"Something to begin the festivities." He opened a bottle of brandy and poured a glass, which he handed to Cael before procuring one for himself.

"I told Graelen that you could arrange this with no difficulty." Cael took a moment to enjoy the heavy scent of the liquor. "He claimed that the notice was too short."

"Because he is king I'll try my best not to think of that as an insult." Kyrros raised his glass. "To our Riding days and to the better days that followed them. May the numbers of the Elite Guard rise once more."

"Brethren, to the last," Cael added, completing the toast. "King Graelen, as always, wishes me to remind you that his offer is still valid."

"I wasn't made for the Aranth life," Kyrros replied between sips of brandy. "Tell him that I appreciate his persistence, but must respectfully decline."

"You cannot expect your people to accept a Lord who does not age," Cael reminded him. "There must be some position in Evaria that would hold your interest. If not then I'm certain that King Graelen would be willing to create one to your liking."

"My face matches my age perfectly."

Kyrros examined his reflection in the glass of brandy.

"In terms of our kind it does. In human terms you barely pass for what age you claim to be."

"Certain families have a young look to their faces."

"For a short while, yes," Cael agreed, "but time will continue on and suspicion will rise. It would be better to pass your legacy to someone trustworthy before it is too late. You should begin searching for another One to take your place. The Ethereal Realm must maintain a certain number of Lords whose loyalty is guaranteed."

"Your costume is in the bundle," Kyrros said, changing the subject suddenly.

Kyrros was not one who could be forced into speaking of something when he did not wish to. It was better to let the matter rest for a time.

"You've chosen something suitable for the task, I assume?"

"Obviously. I'm your host, am I not? Each costume is themed upon a poem of nature. I've given you 'Harvest Moon', which is crafted in midnight blue and gold. No woman will be able to resist you; that is unless I come across her first."

"And what of Selene?"

"Winter's First Snow. She is being fitted for it now." Kyrros continued to stare into his glass. "You've had fine taste in women since our first meeting, though those you choose to bed are somewhat spirited for my taste. I must admit that this one's beauty is somewhat of a rarity, even amongst those of upper breeding."

"I'd have thought you half Bloodsoul if you'd said otherwise," Cael replied. "But don't let any part other than your brain make your decisions for you. Remember what she is."

"She is one of us, and available."

"She is Aranth, and my target. Did you get what I asked of you?"

"Of course, though I can't say that I agree with you using it."

Cael extended his hand. Kyrros held back for a moment before dropping a miniscule vial of white powder into it.

"I've seen you use this on women more times than there are stars in a clear night sky. You would look down upon me for using it this once?"

"I'm not the person I was then, nor are you."

"True," Cael agreed, keeping hold of the vial. "Which is why you should know that I would not use it for its intended purpose."

"With use of your latent ability she would do whatever you asked of her," Kyrros said, looking quite blatantly as if he was gauging Cael's reaction. Then again, perhaps it was only the length of their friendship that rendered Kyrros' thoughts so easily interpreted.

"It's a crime against the Spirits either way," Cael replied. "I would not commit such an act against any woman, even in my darkest days."

"Of course. You should know before I go that the vial I gave you is the last of my store. It's ancient by human terms but it should still be potent. Are you certain you don't wish me to do something about the Mage?"

"No need." Powder clung to the sides of the vial as Cael rolled it between his fingers. "Damaeus has not attended a social gathering of this size since I've known him. The larger the celebration, the less likely he is to participate in it. I'm much more concerned about Xaiden."

"No need. I've set ten tables for Forces and given the best players in my guard the night off to join the festivities. Between that, the entertainment, and the copious amounts of food and liquor that I have so generously provided I do not think that he will cause you any difficulty."

"You think yourself clever enough to outwit Xaiden?"

"Most obviously," Kyrros replied with all of his typical conviction. "That is unless Selene told him of your presence."

"I don't think she would have."

Kyrros looked doubtful. "Your entrance will not be announced as the others are. My attire is based on 'Shadow's Descent'. Search me out just before the first dance. I will fight beside you if it comes to that, though I hope against both our lives that it will not."

"As do I," Cael agreed.

*   *   *   *   *

"I'm not sure that this is suitable," Selene said as she examined herself in an expertly silvered mirror that stretched from floor to ceiling.

The dress was exquisite; made of flowing white silk that was fitted above the waist and flared slightly at the hips. The fact that it fit at all was amazing considering that the seamstress had taken Selene's measurements while she was still fully clothed. Selene would not allow otherwise for fear of showing her mark.

"I see nothing wrong with it," Xaiden said.

His attire was based upon the poem 'A Summer's Storm' and so was comprised of blue-grey tones that matched his eyes. He looked quite dashing, though Selene would never have mentioned it aloud.

"Aurin?" he called. "Would you care to give your opinion?"

Aurin peered around the door that connected the room he, Damaeus and Xaiden shared to Selene's. "You are more beautiful than winter's snow. Those who say otherwise are idiots, yes?"

"Are you satisfied?" Xaiden asked.

"I mean the back." Selene scowled. It was open nearly far enough to be indecent, with a lacing of silk ribbon loosely connecting one side to the other.

"I have been to many of Lord Kyrros' masquerades," Xaiden stated. "There is enough fabric on this one dress to compose two or three of the type most usually worn."

"My mark is not covered," Selene said, at last simply stating the obvious.

"Of course. Forgive me Selene, for there is something I neglected to show you. I suppose it is due in part to our sudden departure from Evaria. That does not make it excusable, certainly. Felan became one of us at eighteen years; the youngest by all records. I have not trained any since that time. The official period of training for an Aranth is thirty years."

"Thirty years?" Selene echoed in disbelief.

"Thirty years is nothing to an Aranth. Your training was rushed due to circumstance." He pulled her left glove from her hand, exposing her Aranth brand.

"Angle your back to the mirror," he instructed. "Now turn your head towards it. It is not necessary to see your mark to do this, but I would like you to witness the transformation."

Selene did as she was told.

"Focus your Aranth brand, but be sure to leave your eyes open."

Selene pooled her concentration. She watched in awe as her mark faded into the flesh of her back, leaving no trace to show that she was anything other than human.

"It's a jest," she said as she brushed her fingertips over evenly toned skin. "You can't be serious."

"I am quite serious," he replied, sounding much like the Xaiden of old. "And I had better not hear so much as one combined word pass your lips while we are in polite company."

"Yes, Xaiden," she replied numbly.

She had yearned for a way to remove her mark since she was old enough to form such thoughts. The feeling of being without it, however, was much different than she had imagined. The sight of her bare back made her ill. She was no longer whole.

"Your mark is not gone," Xaiden said, perhaps sensing her unease. "It has simply melded with the flesh of your back, as it does when you use your affinity. It will return the moment you focus your energy upon it. Meanwhile, I suggest that you stay away from Aurin while it is not upon you. It is up to you to come up with an excuse for its absence if he notices it. It is only by luck that he has not yet remembered the meaning of the Aranth brand, and the Tides can only hold so much luck for any one soul."

"Yes, Xaiden."

He headed back towards the other room, but stopped short. "Many of those who join our ranks become thoughtless in their actions when confronted with such freedom. You may be inclined to try certain things that were far too dangerous in your former state."

"I'll try not to do anything you wouldn't approve of," she interrupted.

"What I am attempting to say is that you should enjoy yourself, but not excessively so."

"Of course," she replied in a second attempt to stop him from carrying on and embarrassing himself. She had nearly forgotten how strict Xaiden could be. Or perhaps he himself had forgotten it. If he continued speaking she might be forced to inform him of just how many times she had evaded Maye's guard to join the festival of Low Tides. She also considered relaying to him the fact that most people were not at all interested in what was upon your back when their thoughts were focused in a certain direction, but dismissed it almost at once as too crass.

"See that you do. I may come across you in the Great Hall later this evening. Remember that we are to meet at one hour past midnight."

"The East Gardens. Small door on the far side near the fountain."

"Correct." He headed back to his room, pulling the door closed behind him.

Selene's seamstress returned a short time later, bringing with her three other women who were to help prepare Selene for the festivities. Selene sat as patiently as she could manage while her eyelashes were darkened and a carmine and beeswax mix was applied to her lips. The woman then brought out a bit of waxed paper, folded within which was a powder that sparkled like fresh snow when the light of the lamp touched it. This she mixed with clear gel from a plant of aloe and applied to various places upon Selene's skin. The rest she sprinkled evenly throughout Selene's hair, which had been turned to a cascade of pinned, chestnut ringlets with aid of an iron rod heated over the fire. Selene looked into the mirror at the end and was well pleased with what she saw. She looked for all purposes like a proper lady of the Ethereal Realm. She thanked the women thoroughly and handed them each a few coins from what was left of her stock. They hastened from the room, whispering excitedly amongst themselves.

Xaiden and Aurin will not recognize me, Selene thought as she removed her Stone from her neck and tied it around her ankle. It could not be seen there, for her dress reached nearly to the floor, and there was no chance of it being lost if it was tethered to her.

Damaeus would not know her, certainly. She would gladly wager as much, as he had not seen her in the dress. The Mage's absence, she decided as she glanced into the mirror once more, was most likely for the best.

Selene clasped a necklace of cascading diamonds around her throat. She lifted the diamonds slightly, admiring each perfectly cut stone. The necklace was on loan from Lord Kyrros. She was not much for expensive things most usually, but somehow she could not help but wish to keep this particular item. Perhaps living as Aranth for so long had spoiled her. She vowed not to become terribly attached to the necklace as she knocked on the door that joined her room to Xaiden's.

"Enter," he called.

She did. The room was decorated in hues of green, as was the one she had been given. They were a bit gaudy for her taste, but what right had she to complain after sleeping with only a bedroll between herself and the frigid ground for months. And that was not to mention the itchy, straw mattresses of various inns that filled the rare days between.

Xaiden smiled openly upon seeing her. "You are truly a beautiful sight, Lady Selene." He bowed and extended his hand, offering her a mask of white leather. Feathers, like those of a peacock save for their lack of color, had been artfully placed upon one side.

"And you are truly a fitting escort, Lord Xaiden," she replied. Her first day in Evaria came to mind. To think that she had once believed all Aranth to be true Lords of the Realm.

"Are you prepared to meet your peers?"
Selene nodded reluctantly.

The musicians of the Great Hall ceased their song temporarily as Selene and Xaiden entered. The room was easily as large as the Seller's square and twice as crowded. The walls, which were composed of highly polished grey marble, were rendered dull beside vibrant costumes of cloth, feathers and fur. Embellishments of gold and precious stone caught the candlelight of a generously sized crystal chandelier. Selene noticed with awe that the ceiling above it was a maze-like pattern of gilded wood in varied shades of russet.

"Introducing Lord 'Summer's Storm' and Lady 'Winter's First Snow' of Aranth." a man dressed in Fenlaye livery called out.

Xaiden had explained to Selene as they made their way to the Great Hall that it was customary only to have one's costume and lordship announced at a masked gathering rather than their full name. She had not known that names were typically announced at formal gatherings, in truth, for she had never attended one. She did not see the need to inform Xaiden of such, however.

"Of Aranth?" Selene whispered while attempting to look as if she were not doing so.

"It appears that word of our exile has not spread," Xaiden whispered back.

Masks of every hue turned towards them, cocked in curious poses. Selene's face heated at the thought of so many eyes upon her.

"Smile courteously and keep your head properly level. Most will lose interest temporarily when the next attendee is announced."

It was true, to a degree.

Xaiden escorted Selene to one corner of the massive room, fending off lingering glances without pause. He pulled two crystal glasses from a nearby server and handed one to her. Selene sipped it carefully. She found the blush colored wine punch within it to be rather agreeable.

"You will find that nobles are unlike common folk," Xaiden cautioned after checking to be sure that no one was listening. "They are oftentimes deceitful. Many have nothing better to do with their time than turn gossip from one mouth to another. You should attempt to gain any information they may hold concerning Perfidia and Felan, but be sure not to offer anything of true importance in return."

"I will," Selene promised.

"They will approach you the moment I leave your side." He kissed her lightly upon each cheek, as was customary in polite company. It caused her mark to warm, serving as a pleasant reminder that it still existed.

Selene felt rather exposed. It took a great deal of control to keep from glancing at her mark just to be sure that it was not visible. She set her cup of punch on a nearby table upon finding that she suddenly did not have the stomach for any drink. A lady dressed in deep purple and white approached. Xaiden was right about the indecency of the costumes. The woman's dress had been shredded into long, thin, strips beginning at her thigh and moving downward, which served to reveal the greater portion of her legs as she walked.

"I consider it a great pleasure to meet with you." She kissed Selene upon each cheek as Xaiden had done. "It is not often that one finds oneself in the position to converse with an esteemed member of the King's Elite Guard."

Selene returned the gesture, noticing as she did so that miniature white roses had been woven into the woman's dusky blonde hair. Her poem was no doubt 'Blossom's Growth' or something very near to it.

"It is a pleasure to meet with you as well," Selene replied. She wished now that she had not abandoned her cup of wine punch. It would have given her something to do with her hands. The other women of Maresbane did not exactly welcome her into their social circles after her father's death, and female Riders were not common. As a result Selene was often unsure of how to conduct herself in the presence of other women. Men seemed much more forgiving in social matters, on the whole. She resolved to act properly. For once in her life she surely looked the part.

"Female Aranth are nearly unheard of," the woman continued from behind a mask covered in rose petals to match those in her hair. "You must be quite talented. Or perhaps you are merely so open in your affections as to gain Lord Xaiden's favor."

Selene was unsure whether the woman meant to insult her, or if bedding men of position was the usual manner for one of her kind to gain status. Either way, she did not appreciate what the woman implied. One did not title of Aranth by sleeping with one.

"I earned my title as any other would; with skill in weaponry and the ability to form an animal affinity."

"Is that so?" the woman pondered. "And where is your animal companion, if I may ask? Is he so small as to be hidden somewhere beneath your attire?"

"He is a hills wolf," Selene lied. "It is not considered proper to bring animals of great size to festive gatherings." The statement sounded true enough, surely. "I forced him to wait for me in my room. He was quite upset by it, you can be certain."

The woman tilted her head ever so slightly, causing the petals of her mask to shift like grass in the wind. "Wolves must be popular companions," she said. "I have seen Lord Xaiden with one on occasion."

"May I be so bold as to join you?" A willowy woman in pale yellow asked. Her bosom looked as if it would pop from her corset at any moment.

Three other women followed behind. One was plump enough to remind Selene of a sunberry, dressed in red as she was. Her skin was so pale that Selene wondered if she had ever seen the light of day. The others were of a darker complexion and were dressed in swatches of silver and forest green. Both were as well formed as their companion was plump. They looked to be twins, even with the leaves of various trees covering their faces. Selene could not imagine where they had found leaves this time of year. Roses could be grown indoors so long as you had the resources to do so. Trees required quite a bit more space, like that of the Sky Room at home.

"Certainly," the woman in violet said. We were just speaking of Lady Aranth's animal companion."

"You were speaking of hills wolves, were you not?" the willowy woman said. "Surely you do not claim to have bonded such a fearsome animal."

"Any animal can be tamed with time," Selene answered. She wished that the women would find someone else to pester. She could not possibly be the most interesting person here. Also it was doubtful that they knew anything about what had happened to Felan.

"A hills wolf is hardly a fitting companion," the woman who reminded Selene of a sunberry said. "I would tame a white heron, or perhaps one of those fine colorless peacocks Lord Kyrros keeps in his gardens. Something to match your costume for this evening."

The other Ladies made gestures of agreement.

"I do not think that I would feel at ease traveling the Ethereal Realm with a peacock at my side," Selene said uneasily. She would feel rather foolish, truth be told. What would King Graelen do with Marked Ones that could turn into frivolous creatures, if he even bothered to train them? *Have them stay in human form, most likely, and pair them with those who have powerful affinities.*

"Does your hills wolf have a name, Lady Aranth?" one of the twins asked. They looked to be the youngest members of the group by far.

"I call him Trinine," Selene said with hope that they would accept it. "The day, month, and year under which he was born all hold the number nine," she added upon sensing that they wished to hear more. It was what the one of the stable boys at the castle had told her of the horse she had been loaned. She would have used Cyprus' name had he not been standing in the guest stables at this very moment.

"I believe I caught sight of your Trinine earlier today," the other twin said.

Selene's breath caught. It was impossible, of course. Her Stone would have told her of Felan's presence.

"Large for a wolf, with a coat the color of storm clouds," the sunberry woman offered. "It was walking the Visitor's Hall. I thought I was the only one who had seen it."

Unless he was not wearing his Stone, Selene amended.

"Lords Kyrros and Cael," the twin to the left said.

The Ladies followed her gaze. They began primping almost as one, touching their hands to their hair and smoothing their dresses.

"How do you know it is them?" the other asked in disbelief.

"Lord Kyrros is 'Shadow's Descent'," the first replied, "Lord Cael is 'Harvest Moon'. You may ask until the next life takes you. I will not tell you my source."

"Any simpleton could tell them from the others," the woman in violet said. "Lord Kyrros has been our host on many occasions."

"And Lord Cael is as well-known as Lord Xaiden," the sunberry woman added, turning towards Selene. "Would you introduce him to me?"

"I am not certain where Lord Xaiden is at the moment," Selene replied. "But I will certainly do so when I find him." She did not think that any of the women were to Xaiden's taste, but she dared not say so.

"I believe she was speaking of Lord Cael," the willowy woman clarified, "though I would invite either into my bed. My husband has not been terribly attentive of late."

Selene was not certain why they assumed her to be a companion of Lord Cael. She did not know anyone by that name personally, and the only Cael she had heard tell of was long dead by all accounts.

"Your husband does not care that you take lovers?" Selene asked. The idea seemed absolutely absurd.

"He does not like me to bother him with such trivial requests," the willowy woman replied as she brushed imaginary wrinkles from the yellow fabric of her dress. "He is satisfied so long as I attend to his needs."

"We should speak no more," the left twin said. "They approach."

Selene realized with horrible certainty as the two men drew closer that she did indeed know Lord Cael. He was the same man who had aided her in the alley of Miloren. He had lied to her then, revealing his name to be Logan, but she supposed that was to be expected. With his knowledge of the Aranth he could be none other than the Cael who had slain King Graelen's first born son. His presence was unmistakable, though his fine face was hidden beneath a mask of midnight blue and gold.

"My Lady Selene," he said, extending his hand and bending at the waist.

Selene did not recall telling the man her name.

"Would you be so kind as to join me for the first dance of the evening?"

He was also more handsome than she remembered.

Selene hesitated. He knew enough about her to make her uncomfortable, and he was a murderer besides. Selene knew that Xaiden would not approve of her going anywhere alone with Cael, but she could not allow him to escape now that he was within her reach. It was likely that he had something to do with the disappearance of Perfidia and Cyanna, perchance Felan as well.

"I believe you owe me as much," Cael said. His dark eyes lit up when he smiled.

What harm can come from one dance? She placed her gloved hand in his.

Lord Kyrros led the willowy woman onto the dance floor. Silence fell as the other guests ceased their conversations and turned to watch. A menagerie of masked creatures turned in Selene's direction. She found that she did not care so long as Cael was nearby.

"I assume that Xaiden taught you to dance?" he whispered as they reached the center of the room. His breath was scented pleasantly of brandy.

"He did," she replied. "With Felan's aid."

"All is well, then."

The first song began without warning. The music of harps, flutes and violins surged through the room at such a frantic pace that Selene found it difficult to keep up. She finally counted herself decent at dancing after all of the work she had put into it, but Cael's ability was far beyond hers. The feeling of unease that had plagued her as she and Xaiden entered the room began to return. It was worse now, in fact, for several hundred people were watching her use a skill that she did not like to perform before even her closest companions.

Why in the name of the Spirits did I accept this offer? Her mind refused to form an answer. The thought lasted for only a moment before the feeling of comfort returned. Cael was near. It did not matter what the others thought of her dancing.

The music ended to a chorus of applause, during which Cael led Selene from the floor. Nobles moved in from every side to fill the empty space in preparation for the next song. Cael paused shortly to take several glasses of champagne from a nearby server. He handed Selene one, which she accepted at once. After all, it would be rude to refuse.

"Would you care to walk with me?" he asked. "Lord Kyrros is a close friend of mine. I know the grounds fairly well. His private garden is one of the finest on this side of the Ethereal Realm. It is indoors, so the famous roses of Fenlaye are not touched by the cold of winter."

Selene paused. She was certain that she should not accept his invitation. Her eyes flew over costumes of nature and beast, but she could catch sight of neither Xaiden nor Aurin.

"It also boasts a spectacular view of the vineyard," Cael added. "Though unfortunately it cannot be seen at this time of night."

Selene shuddered as the peculiar feeling of closeness encompassed her once again. She found suddenly that she did wish to join him. Where he would take her was of little consequence.

"It is rather crowded in here," she replied truthfully. "A short walk would be pleasant."

Selene followed Cael away from the rise of the music. He led her down sand-colored marble halls lit with gilded lamps of oil.

With use of a key that Cael pulled from his coat pocket they gained access to the gardens. The scent of roses greeted Selene as she entered the dimly lit room. Rose vines grew over an arched, wooden trellis, at the far side of which could be seen a small fountain composed of leaf shaped stone tiers. Water trickled from one to another, ending in the basin beneath. Surrounding the fountain were flowering rose bushes of every color imaginable. All were perfectly maintained.

Cael offered her a seat upon the wooden bench beside the fountain. Once there he removed his mask. He then reached for hers.

"How is it that you know so much of me?" Selene said, pulling away from him. Why had she followed him here so willingly? Had she lost her wits?

Cael's eyes narrowed in the slightest, as if in displeasure. The feeling of comfort returned to Selene in a rush. Cael's fine smile returned as well. She allowed him to take her mask and set it atop his.

"We met shortly at a tavern in Miloren," he said casually. "And again in an alley nearby."

Selene felt her face heat. *What a ridiculous question.* Why in the name of the Spirits had she been so foolish as to ask it? It was only natural that he would know her. She set aside her empty champagne glass and removed her gloves at his request.

"I also have access to your journal," he added playfully.

"I hardly think that to be possible," Selene replied with a laugh. It was pleasing that Cael had chosen to dance with her. The other women must be terribly jealous.

"Do you still believe that I am so horrible a companion?"

It occurred to her that he was by far the most handsome man she had ever come across. And he was marked.

"I would never say such a thing. I would not so much as think it."

"An excellent answer." Cael drew so close that the soft breath of his words brushed against her ear. "Now, I am in need of a small favor from you."

Selene was prepared to do anything he asked of her.

"I would like to borrow your Stone for a time."

The sound of trickling water covered the silence that followed.

"I don't think I should let you." Of course that made sense. Why should she give him her Stone?

"You can trust me. I will return it to you the moment I've finished with it. You have my word."

"I cannot," Selene insisted. She lifted her hand to her mouth to stifle a yawn. It must be later than she imagined.

Cael's eyes narrowed once again, seemingly more in confusion than displeasure this time. "Of course you can." He pressed his lips to her hand. A fierce burn rushed through her mark. "Simply hand it to me. You will be greatly compensated for your loss, trifling though it is."

Selene reached for the ankle upon which her Stone was tied, but thought better of it suddenly.

"Actually, I am due to meet someone." She had promised Xaiden that she would be prompt. And she did not feel as safe with Cael as she had moments ago.

Selene stood, intending to leave. It turned out to be rather more difficult than she anticipated. A wave of dizziness gripped her. Cael caught her as she fell. He lowered her to the ground. She sat back against the fountain, cupping her head in her hands. The room shifted and quivered as if she were viewing it through several feet of water.

"It seems that the Tides are with me today, my love," Cael said, offering her a wink. "I have learned, thanks to you, that my latent ability does not work as well upon marked females as it does on those of the human variety. Thankfully it lasted long enough for you to accept a glass of champagne without question."

"What did you give me?" Selene managed. She attempted to stand once more, but realized that she could not feel anything beneath her waist.

"It would do you no good to know its name. There is no antidote." Cael scooped her from the floor as if she had no more weight than a child and laid her across the bench. Selene did not have the strength to resist. "Do not worry," he added. "The drug is in no way permanent. It will wear off shortly before tomorrow's light."

"Why would you do this?" Selene's arms were becoming numb as well.

"I cannot say, for it is likely that you and I are not fighting towards the same cause. But you must believe that I will not harm you at this time. I cannot guarantee that my feelings will be unchanged by the next time we meet, however. Tell me where you have hidden your Stone. I will not remove any more of your clothing than is necessary."

"What do you want with my Stone?"

"You ask far too many questions," Cael replied. "And I am not known for my patience. Tell me where your Stone is or I will be forced to find it on my own."

"My left ankle." Selene struggled to fight off a particularly strong bout of vertigo. She found it difficult to form coherent thought and impossible to touch her latent ability.

"Thank you," Cael said.

He did not sound at all as if he meant it.

"If I see you again I'll kill you." She could not speak without slurring her words. Her hatred for Cael was growing steadily.

"I have heard that many times in my years," Cael replied, grinning. "Only once has anyone accomplished the feat."

"Wait, please. You wouldn't leave me unable to defend myself."

"You will be safe here," Cael promised as he headed back towards the hall. "Xaiden is an intelligent man. He will find you soon."

"Cael, please don't."

"I feel it only fair to tell you that the walls and doors of this place are enchanted so that no sound may pass through them. It seems the Lord Kyrros' first gardener thought that roses were best grown in silence. An odd fellow, he was. But I digress. Until next time, love."

Selene heard the distinct metallic sound of a lock being turned.

Her head was now tilted towards the ceiling. She found as she stared at the snow-covered glass that she did not have the strength to look anyplace else. The stubborn room refused to cease its spinning even when she closed her eyes. The constant movement was making her ill.

The clicking of the lock pulled her mind to consciousness. It was impossible to tell how much time had passed, though it had to be some decent amount, for she found that she was able to roll her head in the direction of the sound. Damaeus' winter blue eyes greeted her.

It was shocking that he had found her. Selene could not recall ever being pleased to see the man, and only grudgingly admitted to herself that she felt so at this moment. She wished to say something to him, to thank him, perhaps. The words remained jumbled within her head, refusing to become proper sentences.

"Selene." He looked concerned. "However did you come to be here?"

Selene would have asked him the same had she been able to speak. The putrid scent of him swept aside that of the roses.

Damaeus closed his eyes. His lips moved, yet no sound came from them.

"Limben powder," he said at last, drawing his brows together in distaste. "How unfortunate for you."

He lifted her head a few inches and then dropped it. Everything around her twisted.

"Such things happen when you lay your trust in the hands of nobles." He turned the palm of one hand upward, muttering what appeared to be another incantation. "You would think that Xaiden would keep a keener eye upon his one remaining charge."

Selene's stomach clenched as her body lifted from the bench. With luck Damaeus would take her back to her room and Xaiden would be none the wiser.

"Let us hope that Kyrros is the one who accomplished this," Damaeus said, sounding as if he were speaking to himself. "It is unlikely that you are with child from the encounter, but it is possible. It would be a waste for you to carry any child sired by human blood."

Selene opened her mouth in an attempt to say, first of all, that nothing of the sort had happened, and secondly, that it would be none of Damaeus' concern if it had. Unfortunately speech still refused to pass her lips.

"With a Circlet in place I will be able to tell."

Selene had just enough time to wonder how a circlet would help Damaeus determine if she was with child before another wave of vertigo struck. It was far worse now that she had nothing solid to lie against.

"Let us move you to a more secure place, shall we?"

Selene wished that he would quit talking and take her back to her room. She was beginning to think that she would have been better off left upon the bench.

The door to the gardens swung open once again. Selene's body floated softly towards it.

The Stowaway

Lieutenant Skye glared down at the Forces table, muttering to himself. He had done so for upwards of ten minutes, if Xaiden's estimate was correct.

"You've lost it, Skye," Captain Wenway called from within the crowd that had gathered around them. "You'll withdraw if you want to keep your balls and your honor."

His words drew a laugh from the crowd. Skye's furrowed brow was barely visible due to the mask of spotted rabbit's fur that covered his face.

Those who gathered around the Forces tables were of the less cultured sort; mostly Kyrros' Guard, though a few of the younger nobles were mixed in. Xaiden preferred it that way. Most upper class men counted themselves excellent Forces players. Few actually were.

Xaiden pressed a finger to his temple. The Lieutenant could ponder the rest of the night away. It would do him no good. No matter what his next action was it would be his last.

"The Spirits will have us before you've moved," a man offered from the back of the crowd.

"They'll have the Aranth as well with what time you're taking," someone else added.

Laughter burst from the crowd once again. It was best that Selene was not here to witness this. She would not be pleased to hear the men speaking in such a way when Xaiden had specifically warned her against using combined words in polite company. Indeed, most of them would not dare to speak that way were there women within hearing range. Xaiden frowned. He had neglected to warn Selene against cursing. Perchance he should have mentioned it, in retrospect. He could never be certain of her behavior, especially so since the incident with Felan.

"The game is yours, Xaiden," Lieutenant Skye conceded.

"You have improved since last we met."

"Next year I'll have you." Skye shook Xaiden's hand in a show of good sportsmanship. The amusing part was that he truly believed it.

"I look forward to it," Xaiden replied, rising from his seat. He hoped to have both himself and Selene back in King Graelen's favor by that time. By the grace of the Spirits it would not take Felan's head to accomplish the task.

Xaiden lingered by the balcony railing for a moment, scanning the crowd from above. The center of the room had long ago been sectioned off for dancing, which made the edges much more crowded. He could not spot Selene within the twisting mass of people. Kyrros, however, was plainly visible. The man was surrounded, as was typical, by a sizeable group of women. Aurin stood next to him. Xaiden had predicted as much. Both seemed to enjoy the thrill of the hunt. Their demeanors reminded him somewhat of Cael, in the man's younger days. Now *there* was someone he would give his sword arm to come across. He had sworn to slay him on sight and he would do so, regardless of how many lives passed him by.

Xaiden strode down the stairs that led from the balcony and into the Great Hall proper, fending off those who attempted to engage him in conversation with little more than a disgruntled expression. He levered his sword from its scabbard. The nobles nearest to him turned at the sound, but looked away upon realizing who he was. It was likely that most had been told of his costume by now, and so knew him to be Aranth. Gossip spread amongst the upper class as lice did amongst the lower.

The women surrounding Kyrros and Aurin parted as Xaiden approached. If Aurin thought to bed someone this night he was sorely mistaken. Xaiden would disabuse him of the notion one way or another, and he would feel no remorse for it. Taking such a risk was not acceptable. As Xaiden drew closer he noticed that a third man stood between them. He wore the maroon, orange and gold 'Mid-Autumn Grace' costume that Kyrros had sent for Damaeus. It was ill fitted to him, for his stature was more thickly set than that of the Mage.

Viverr Templain, Xaiden thought at once. Spirits, the man was bold.

"Leave us," Xaiden said, encompassing all of the women in a single glare.

They scattered at once.

"Where is Selene?" Xaiden asked.

"I have not seen her recently," Kyrros responded immediately.

The statement itself was true, though the swiftness of his reply was suspicious.

"She is enjoying herself, perhaps?" Aurin offered.

"Perchance," Xaiden replied thoughtfully.

"I noticed her at the first dance," Aurin added. "Not since then, and I am sorry for it."

"Viverr," Xaiden said, growing impatient. "Why are you here?"

Viverr jumped at the mention of his name, but he recovered quickly. "I've as much right to be at this fine gathering as you," he said.

"I would not go so far as to say that." Xaiden looked to Kyrros questioningly.

"He is a friend of Aurin so I allowed it," Kyrros replied.

"Damaeus has never expressed the need to show himself at any of my gatherings, though I continue to invite him. It would be foolish of me to let such a fine costume go to waste."

"Just like I said." Viverr grabbed a spring roll from a passing servant and pushed the full of it into his mouth.

Xaiden sighed. He always found dealing with Viverr to be greatly tiring.

"We are friends now, you and I," Aurin said. "I will keep watch of him and see that he does not steal, yes?"

Trusting one rogue to watch another did not seem at all like an intelligent idea to Xaiden. He had come to like Aurin, and did not want him to fall to his old ways. The history between the Sleeping Bandits and the Aranth was long standing. It was also fraught with unnecessary tolerance, as Xaiden had often mentioned to King Graelen and to his father before him. Viverr and Aurin's exploits gave people stories to tell, or so his Majesty claimed. It was true, in a way. Most people were elated to be robbed by the scoundrels. They spoke of each incident as if it were a symbol of honor. And, oddly enough, none of the victims Xaiden had spoken to had made any mention of the fact that the Bandits could have possibly been marked. Word of the Sleeping Bandits' comings and goings spread like fire on dry tinder, though no one was ever able to recall exactly what either of the two looked like. It did not matter to Xaiden what people thought of them. Stealing was immoral regardless of the circumstances.

"I haven't taken anything that wasn't offered to me," Viverr said. "You should be satisfied now that I've said it aloud."

Xaiden was not satisfied at all. He knew of Viverr's latent ability. The man could claim Sammeus Elyon as his blood-born kin and Xaiden's ability would not be able to tell it as false. He would have arrested Viverr immediately had he anywhere to keep him. Xaiden's intention had been to invite Aurin to join the Aranth once their name was restored. He was not sure that he wanted him if Viverr was part of the deal. The man was nigh uncontrollable.

"Xaiden, my friend," Aurin said slowly. He looked greatly disturbed.

"Do not be troubled," Xaiden said bitterly. "I have no right to harm Viverr considering that he is an invited guest."

Viverr nodded in triumph and grabbed at a passing tray of pastries.

"I would speak with you privately," Aurin said. "It is important."

"Fine," Xaiden replied, gesturing towards Viverr, "but he must come as well."

"It is best, I think," Aurin agreed.

Xaiden kept a close watch on Viverr and Aurin to be sure that they followed him as he exited the Great Hall. Kyrros stayed behind. He did not seem to want any part of whatever was about to take place.

"We should find Selene and leave this place," Aurin said once the doors had closed behind them. "It is not safe for us to stay here."

"There is no need to fear Kyrros," Xaiden replied. "He is one of us."

"I do not fear him. He is not as strong as you or I, yes?"

"What is it, then?"

Aurin's unease seemed to be contagious. Viverr began to shift nervously.

"You trust your companions, I can tell it, but you should not do so. A memory came to me a moment ago."

"I told you of it earlier," Viverr interrupted. "About the house in Lystonne, remember?"

"Yes," Aurin answered. "But I could not recall anything of what had happened at that time."

"What of the house in Lystonne?"

"Your so-called companion was there with more than a few lackeys," Viverr said boldly. "That blond Aranth you trained. I should be able to remember his name for all of the trouble he's caused Aurin and me, eh? There was a young girl too, and an older woman. I would've crept out to see more, but Ranur was there. Didn't want to be packed up for sale to the Kerell."

"Damaeus was the one who sent me to kill you," Aurin said. "I had a few meetings in the tavern with a strange man who said he would trade with me. He slipped something into my whiskey, I think. I do not know how many days passed, but when I woke the town was empty. Damaeus came to me speaking words I did not understand. After that it is still hard to remember. It is truth. I swear it."

Xaiden's sword rang out as he heaved it from its scabbard. "Open the door, Aurin," he ordered.

"I do not think that I should do so," Aurin protested. "Lord Kyrros would not like it. I cannot control it like others do, you know?"

"It will take far too much time to find Selene otherwise." Xaiden said impatiently. "I shall apologize to Kyrros later if it bothers you so. Now do as I say."

Aurin pressed his hand to the door and pushed it aside. Music rang out for no more than a second's time. It ceased suddenly, and was replaced by the sounds of thudding bodies and shattering crystal.

Xaiden pushed Aurin's hand out of the way and entered the room. Unconscious people lay sprawled across the floor of the Great Hall like autumn leaves of odd, rainbow hues. Some of them were snoring quite loudly. Others were muttering in their sleep.

"You two search down here," Xaiden said. "I will check the balcony." He sprinted towards the stairs, stopping briefly to remove a woman's face from a bowl of wine punch. He certainly did not wish for any innocents to be harmed as a result of an order he had given. That aside, drowning seemed a horrible way to die. He reached the top shortly and scanned over the people who lay upon the balcony before heading to the railing. There was no need to search it thoroughly. The only thing of interest up here was Forces, and Selene hated the game. Aurin and Viverr had each taken one side of the room and were searching diligently. They would not find her, for Xaiden could tell at once that she was not within the Great Hall. None of the people below were wearing white. He did not think that she would have any reason to change her clothing.

Xaiden was angry with Damaeus for betraying him, but even more so with himself for failing to discover that the Mage was the one responsible for the downfall of the Aranth. Why had his latent ability not warned him of it? The answer was simple and infinitely infuriating. As Xaiden thought back upon all of the information he had gained concerning the disappearance of the Aranth he realized that none of it had come directly from Damaeus. It had always been one of the others who had spoken to him, relaying some information Damaeus had found. The Mage had used those who did not think to question his word: Cyanna, King Graelen, and Felan. The one speaking the information thought it to be true, thus Xaiden's latent ability thought it to be true as well. The worst part of it was that without Selene he had no link to Felan. He now had no way of telling where Damaeus was located.

"How long were you in Lystonne?" Xaiden asked Viverr as he pushed past him into the hall.

"Long enough," the man replied cryptically.

"Long enough for what?" Xaiden asked, undeterred.

"I was supposed to meet Aurin there after completing-" he stopped for a moment, as if deciding whether it was safe to continue. "Well, I had important business in Vale, and Aurin had some in Lystonne, so we split for a time and I said I'd meet him there afterwards. Only thing is, I got held up for a while due to some unforeseen happenings."

Xaiden started back towards the room that he and the others had been given. He would check there for any signs of struggle, though he doubted that he would find anything of use.

"Aurin was still there when I got into town," Viverr continued, following him, "but the guy he was supposed to be dealing with was acting a little off. Aurin wanted a few more nights to check him out, you know, to make sure he was a legitimate seller. I decided I'd do a bit of exploring in the meantime. The second day was when I happened upon your friends. The last day was when things began to get strange. I was using my affinity during one of my explorations when events went a little awry."

Xaiden opened the door to Selene's room without bothering to knock. It was empty and undamaged. He pulled out a chair and sat, placing two fingers to his temple. It was difficult to decide what he should do next.

"It was the strongest magic I'd ever felt, I'd wager you that." Viverr plucked a silver candlestick from a nearby table and pulled it closer for examination. "Must have overloaded my latent ability too. I fainted like a nobleman's daughter. When I woke the next morning the whole town was empty. Well, except for Aurin. He wasn't himself at all though. Couldn't reason with him, so I stayed a while, living off what food the people had left and trying to figure out how to get close enough to use my latent ability on him without being eaten. That was when you three showed up."

"So you've been with us since Lystonne?" Xaiden asked incredulously.

"Yeah," Viverr replied. "Lucky for me Selene doesn't get into her saddlebags but once a day."

"You knew he was with us?" Xaiden turned an accusing eye to Aurin.

"Not until two days ago. I swear it. I did not think you would be happy, yes? That is why I did not tell you."

"And you remembered that we were Aranth?"

"I had thoughts of it. I was not certain until Viverr told me so. King Graelen is much more liberal than I had imagined, allowing Marked Ones to join his Aranth."

"Indeed," Xaiden replied. It did not matter if they figured out the whole truth. Not anymore.

"I had a greatly interesting encounter with one of your Aranth back in Vale as well," Viverr said as he set the candlestick back down on the table.

"You two have had more contact with the Aranth than all other criminals combined," Xaiden said wearily. If he had to count on Viverr and Aurin alone to help him rescue Selene then so be it. "The life you currently lead cannot possibly satisfy you forever. Choose to aid me and allow your time here to serve a greater purpose."

"I would like to see Selene safe," Aurin said.

"And what of you?" Xaiden asked Viverr.

"I could tell you, but I think you might be more interested in who I met while I was in Vale," Viverr said as he followed Xaiden into the next room.

"Is that so?" Xaiden replied calmly as he lit a lamp so he could see well enough to pack his belongings.

"A Marked One named Islyr."

"I have not heard of him," Xaiden injected. "And I am not interested in learning the names of your scoundrel friends."

"Let me finish. Cael was there and King Graelen's boy. The older one, I think. Called him Devren. That's the heir's name, isn't it?"

Xaiden stopped his packing to turn to the man. An expression of contentment spread quickly across Viverr's face.

"You lie," Xaiden accused. "Do so again and you shall regret your actions." He cursed the fact that his ability did not work upon the rogue.

"I've told many lies in my life but this isn't one of them. The boy and your Aranth were both in Vale. Their affinities weren't working due to some spell. I was kind enough to take care of that with my latent ability."

"I would be best if you do not speak more, I think," Aurin suggested.

The rogue did not fall silent despite the warning. "The white falcon I've seen you carry around from time to time," he said. "It was him. That's how I figured that most of you are marked." The rogue looked rather pleased with himself. "I saved their lives so you should thank me." He held out a cupped hand. "Monetary compensation would be best."

Xaiden pushed him aside and continued packing. Viverr was clever. More so than Xaiden would openly admit. That did not change reality, however. The rogue may have seen Cael, but it was impossible that he had seen Devren. The Stone that had been bonded to the boy clearly revealed that he was dead. Damaeus could not hold enough power to remove a Stone bond. Even with that fact aside, Viverr had never seen Devren and so had no way to tell him from any other boy. Most likely he had seen Cael with a marked boy he had picked up in preparation for his next meeting with the Aranth. It seemed like something Cael would attempt.

"We are leaving tonight," Xaiden announced. "Pack your things, Aurin, if you wish to come. Kyrros has kindly provided a horse that will suit you. I am certain that he will not mind if we take it a day early."

"You won't be leaving me here as a scapegoat," Viverr said. "I'm going with you."

"But you do not know where they are," Aurin protested. "You were tracking them by Selene's Stone."

"When she checked last they were northeast of here." Xaiden threw a plain shirt and breeches at Viverr before procuring a set for himself. "The only structure of any size in that direction is Greyridge Keep, so that is where we will go."

"Greyridge Keep was abandoned years ago." Viverr informed him as he removed his coat and mask. "There's a reason for that, eh? Plus it's at the far end of the Valley of the Eldai."

"I remember that place," Aurin said. "It is named after those who live there, yes?"

Xaiden had not expected him to have even that much knowledge on the subject. Few people did. "That is true," he replied as he pulled on his boots. "It is the place where creatures of magic go to die. It is surrounded by mountains save for a small opening on this side and one upon the opposite side, at the edge of the Barren Lands."

"What sort of people are these Eldai?" Viverr asked. "I can tell that you know."

"Pixies," Xaiden replied shortly.

"That doesn't sound bad at all." Viverr had finished dressing and was rummaging through a box filled with bottled colognes that Kyrros had provided for the masquerade. He splashed a bit of one under each arm before corking the bottle and shoving it into Aurin's belt pouch. "A bit like faeries, are they?"

Xaiden would have laughed if not for the horrible feeling in his gut. It was plainly obvious that Viverr had never encountered a Pixie. "You shall see for yourself once we arrive there," he replied.

Greyridge Keep

Selene pressed her forehead against the only window in the room, letting the pleasant chill of winter seep through to her skin. It eased the pain somewhat. Last night she had feared that she would never again be able to hold a clear thought. The twisting of the world had disappeared with time, however, and the paralysis had gone with it.

Time and the elements had robbed the courtyard below of its beauty. The lower half of a rearing horse stood at its center surrounded by piles of broken stone and plants that looked to have withered long before the onset of winter. All were blanketed in a thin layer of snow. Selene exhaled softly, fogging the window's glass and thus temporarily obscuring her view. She turned at the sound of footsteps approaching. Damaeus had promised her something to eat while they waited for Xaiden to arrive.

The Mage had said many things as he levitated her through the halls and out into the night. Few of his words had made any sense to her at the time. Upon waking this morning she could recall little more than that he had promised to take her somewhere safe. *Greyridge Keep. Safe from what?* He had not mentioned. She could only assume that he meant Cael. But why had Xaiden not traveled with them?

Damaeus entered the room looking rather more disheveled than was usual. He carried with him a chipped bowl of broth, which he set upon the decrepit table by the door.

"It would not be wise to eat anything of great substance today," he warned. "A small portion of the drug still resides within you."

"All right," Selene agreed absently. "Is Xaiden here yet?" The scent of the broth was wonderful, but she doubted that she would be able to keep much of it down.

"He is not. You ask of his whereabouts quite often. I am beginning to think that you harbor some feelings for him."

"He is my friend, so of course I am concerned for him, if that is what you mean."

Damaeus had rescued her, but that did not mean that she had to tolerate his prying.

"And what of Felan?"

Selene did not wish to give him the satisfaction of an answer. She was not sure that she *had* an answer, truth be told. She picked up the bowl of broth and the spoon which lay beside it. She could not be expected to speak with Damaeus while her mouth was full. The first sip singed her tongue.

"Shall I take your silence to mean that you do not wish to see him?"

Selene's hand hovered half-way between the bowl and her mouth. "Of course I would like to see him." She dropped the spoon and set the broth back upon the table. Damaeus was right about her stomach, though most likely it was the Mage's scent rather than the drug she had been given that was making her queasy. "But I have no way of tracking him without my Stone." she could not understand why Damaeus would see the need to bring up such a pointless subject other than to aggravate her.

The Mage offered her an empty smile. "That is so, but I have a gift which will certainly raise your spirits."

Selene's patience was rapidly waning, as it often did in matters concerning Damaeus. She did not wish to stay in this place any longer, and she certainly did not want any more of his so-called gifts.

"You may enter," Damaeus called out into the hall.

Selene was unable to do more than stare dumbly as Felan walked into the room. He was thinner than he had been when last she saw him and he wore an odd silver band across his forehead, but he seemed otherwise unharmed. He offered her a weak smile.

Selene embraced him with all of her might, but he stood stiffly within her arms. He shivered as she pressed her lips to his cheek. His eyes did not leave Damaeus. It seemed almost as if he were looking to him to be sure that his actions were acceptable. Selene dismissed the strange thought immediately. She was simply happy that Damaeus had found him. Damaeus seemed pleased as well, though the satisfied smile he wore as he watched them made her mildly uneasy.

"Are Perfidia and Cyanna here as well?" Selene asked hopefully.

"They are safe," Damaeus replied.

She could not have hoped for more than that. All three of those she had been searching for were alive. The Tides and the Spirits were certainly with her. She could now return to Evaria and restore the name of the Aranth. Would King Graelen be pleased to find that he had accused them wrongly? He owed her at least an apology after all that had happened, perhaps a raise in pay on account of how he had nearly strangled her. Still, an uneasy feeling lingered behind Selene's thoughts of joy. What had happened to Felan and King Graelen's family to begin with? And why had Damaeus not delivered the three of them to Evaria if he knew them to be safe?

"I will return shortly," Damaeus said to Felan. "You may do as you wish within the guidelines I have established. Remember our discussion."

"I will, Master Damaeus."

Damaeus pulled a silver band from one of the pouches that hung at his waist. It was similar to the one Felan wore, yet slightly more feminine in appearance, with lines of metal that swirled around one another gracefully like the lines of a mark. The inner curve of the band was lined with pointed, metal tines. Damaeus handed it to Felan before exiting the room and shutting the door behind him. Dust and bits of stone crumbled from the surrounding walls and clattered across the bare floor. Somehow the door remained whole.

"*Master* Damaeus? How in the name of the Spirits did he convince you to call him that?"

"Selene," Felan began softly.

"We'll head home as soon as Xaiden reaches us," Selene said with what she hoped was enough confidence for both of them. She wanted to ask what had happened to him; where he had been and why he had not returned, but his expression was one of such misery that she could not do so. "Whatever has happened can be fixed. Wrongdoings can be forgiven." She placed a hand upon his shoulder. "Things will be back to the way they were soon enough. Xaiden will know of your innocence the moment you speak it."

Felan did not seem at all calmed by Selene's words. His expression brought shadows of the past. Oddly, it brought her to the moment just before Maye had told Selene that Islyr and her father were dead.

"You're too late," he said simply.

"What do you mean by that?" Selene asked. His behavior was truly puzzling.

Felan seemed unwilling to reply.

"What is this, anyways?" she asked, thinking it best to change the subject. She pressed a finger to the silver band upon his forehead.

Felan recoiled as if she had struck him. His eyes narrowed as a trickle of blood flowed lazily from beneath the band. "Don't," he said through clenched teeth.

"I'm sorry," she replied, horrified at what had occurred. Her confusion had amplified tenfold. "But what is it?"

"It's a Circlet. A Kerell device. Only my Holder may touch it."

"Your Holder? Felan, you're speaking nonsense."

"I'd hoped that Graelen would not send you here. That he would order Xaiden to come, or that you would not be able to find me despite our Stone bond."

"Graelen didn't send me here. Xaiden and I were exiled for conspiracy against the throne. The Aranth were disbanded. King Graelen thinks that you kidnapped Cyanna and Perfidia, and that Xaiden ordered you to do it. We came for you to learn the truth. I came because you're my friend and I was worried for you."

"You don't have any idea what this place is, do you?" Felan said with an empty laugh. "You don't know what goes on here, or what plans he has for you. I'm right, aren't I?"

Selene thought she should say something, but she could not figure out just what that might be.

"Xaiden does not know where we are. He may well be dead. Either way, he will not come for you." Felan ran his thumb along the smooth front of the Circlet that Damaeus had left upon the table. It was the same motion he had used with Luca's knife once it had finally been returned to him. "Neither of us are going anywhere for a long while. The best way to get what you want here is to be sure that Master Damaeus is pleased with you."

"And exactly how do you propose that I accomplish that?" If this was some sort of jest it was in very poor taste. The familiar spinning sensation returned to her suddenly. She sat upon the corner of the bed before her legs could give way beneath her. She was still weak and hated that it was so.

"I've envisioned this moment so many times that it's difficult to accept it as reality." Felan sat next to her and pulled her close. "It's self-centered of me to want you here, and yet I do."

She returned his embrace and was comforted to find that he did not stiffen as he had before.

"I am truly sorry for doing this, but you must trust me that it is for the best."

Selene looked into his face. She was not pleased with what she saw there.

"Just do as Master Damaeus orders. He will treat you well."

Felan forced her down onto the bed. The room spun and twisted like wind swept waves as her head attempted to adjust to the sudden movement.

Selene struggled, but he was much stronger even in his present condition. "Felan," she managed, "let me up."

"Don't hate me for this. I beg of you." He pressed the Circlet to her forehead.

The hinges of the door squealed.

"Do not think to release her," Damaeus warned. "You know the consequence for disobedience."

"Yes, Master Damaeus."

Felan would not meet her gaze.

The Mage's hand replaced Felan's upon the Circlet. He edged its fang-like, metal points into her skin. What had once been a jumbled maze of events became horrifyingly clear. Damaeus was responsible for the crimes that she and Xaiden had been accused of. He was responsible for the decline of the Aranth.

"I trusted you!" Selene cried, struggling enough to loosen Felan's grasp. It was not near enough to gain her freedom.

Felan shifted his position, pinning her more firmly against the straw mattress and providing space for the Mage to reach her. Selene winced as the metal points touched her forehead.

Damaeus smiled, and for once there was true pleasure behind the expression. "I suppose you are wondering why I did not do this as you slept?" he asked.

Selene's stomach clenched and bile singed her throat.

"The answer is uncomplicated," he continued, heedless of the hatred that Selene felt must radiate from her. "It is quite painful for you, but to me, the feeling is absolutely breathtaking. It is your fear that makes it so." He centered his palm on the Circlet and pressed down firmly. Sharp pain cascaded through Selene's head with more strength than any her mark had ever brought. She was aware of each point as it impaled her, melting away bone to reach what was held beneath. It felt as dying must feel. For a moment she wished she would.

Selene gathered her resolve. She refused to turn away from Damaeus, whose eyes were half-closed in pleasure. She hated him, purely. It was within that hatred that she discovered what she sought. She no longer fought the pain of the Circlet or that of Felan's vacant acceptance, but instead allowed it to flow through her. She embraced it for what it was and found peace within it.

When it was over she looked to Felan. The strength of spirit that she had so loved in him was nowhere to be found.

Blood ran from Selene's forehead onto the white silk of the masquerade dress she still wore. Felan's betrayal burned within her. He released her only with Damaeus' permission. Selene slowed her breathing before standing to face Damaeus. She did not allow her expression to relay her heated thoughts.

Damaeus regarded her curiously. "The response you have given is unlike any of the others." He looked content. "It is as I expected."

"You won't control me with this," Selene said, touching her Circlet. She did not wince despite the jolt of pain that lanced through her.

"I did not think to," he replied. "At least, not fully. I would rather that you join me willingly."

Selene waited for him to continue. She could feel his presence within her, most likely by way of the Circlet. Instinct pushed her to recoil from his vile touch. Instead she stilled her thoughts. If she could sense him then he could certainly do so to her, perhaps more powerfully at that.

"I have something that may persuade you," Damaeus said. His eyes held some unidentifiable hunger. "The latent abilities you have discovered so far are trifling when compared to that which still lingers hidden beneath your beautiful flesh. I can draw it out, and when I do I promise that you will be pleased. You need only promise to join my cause."

"I cannot decide what I wish to do so quickly as that," Selene replied carefully. "I would like to spend some time here first. I must know that this is to be the winning side before I join it."

"A reasonable answer. I must admit that I did not expect such rationality from you, Selene."

"I do have several conditions." She beseeched the Spirits that he would not draw back his offer when she mentioned them. In truth, she was in no position to make requests of any sort.

"I will not remove the Circlet," Damaeus said quickly. "It is for your safety that you wear it."

"I would ask nothing so brash as that. I merely wish to have use of my latent abilities; at least as I know them to be. I am not comfortable without my powers, harmless as they are. You have my word that I will not use them against you. When you draw this mysterious third ability from me I will allow you to judge whether I should be able to use it at will."

"Done," Damaeus said.

The metal tines of Selene's Circlet warmed slightly.

"There was something else?"

Felan watched impassively. Only the pallor of his skin served to indicate his true opinion. Could it be disgust, or misery? Perhaps he was shocked by Selene's sudden change of manner. It was difficult to tell.

"I would also like to be able to roam wherever I wish within the walls of Greyridge. In return for these conditions I give you my word that I will stay with you for at least one month and will follow what rules you set for me. After that time has passed I shall make my decision."

"Very well," Damaeus said after a moment's pause. "The deal is done. I will not ban you from any specific action as of yet. What rules I make later will depend entirely on your conduct. There are, however, a few rules of the Circlet which cannot be broken due to the magic upon it. I feel it only fair to warn you of it beforehand, as the consequences can be excruciating." His eyes slithered over Selene. "You may not speak ill of myself, nor may you speak of escape. Also, you may not use your affinity without my specific permission."

"Yes, Master Damaeus," Selene replied smoothly. By the grace of the Spirits she managed to keep any sarcasm from her tone.

"You may simply call me Damaeus," he said with a cold smile. "I hope that you will come to think of me as a companion. We shall be partners, soon enough."

"Yes Damaeus," she amended.

"Felan, you will sleep in this room tonight. Be sure that no harm comes to her."

"Yes, Master Damaeus."

"Tomorrow, my dear," Damaeus said to Selene, "is the beginning of something that I believe will benefit us both immensely." His Mages' robes billowed as he strode into the hall. A flick of his finger and a few mumbled words caused the door to swing shut behind him.

Selene sat back down upon the bed and pressed her hands to her head, which was sticky with blood. The salty, bitter taste of it filled her mouth as she touched her tongue to her lips. She had used the last of her energy in confronting Damaeus. It was a miracle that he had left when he did, for she did not think that she could have remained on her feet for much longer. The attachment of the Circlet had cured her headache, at least, though perhaps that was Damaeus' doing. When his presence was gone from her head at last she breathed a sigh of relief.

"I have some clean water in my room," Felan offered, breaking the silence which had settled upon them in Damaeus' absence, "if you would like to wipe the blood from your face."

"Leave me alone," she replied, lying back to stare at what was left of the cracked plaster that had once covered the ceiling. A decently sized piece was missing from the center. Several wide cracks stemmed from it, causing the empty space to look much like a fat, white duck of the kind that were often used for roasting. Selene nearly laughed at the absurdity of the thought. *Fatigue must be tainting my mind.*

"I thought it to be more like a swan," Felan said, coming to lie next to her. It seemed that Damaeus allowed him some use of his latent ability.

Selene rolled over so that her back was to him. "Please go away, Felan." She had no desire to speak with him after what he had done. "I don't want to force you out but I will if I must."

"I can't leave for more than a few moments," he said quietly. "Master Damaeus has ordered me to stay in this room and watch over you. I must obey him."

"Fine," Selene replied. "I'll sleep in your room. He ordered you to stay in this room, not with me."

"He ordered me to see that no harm comes to you, and I'm going to do so. I'm not free to do whatever I wish as you appear to be."

"It seems that you have enough freedom to poach my thoughts."

"The price for so little a freedom was my honor. I've done things that won't be forgiven."

"You may have," she agreed, rolling to face him.

This time he did not turn from her.

"Stay then," she said at last, "just so long as you do not bother me." She was not at all certain that she *could* force him to leave, even if she wished to.

Selene slept with her back to him, and woke alone. Fresh clothes and a bowl of water had been set out for her. She washed and dressed quickly, for she feared that Damaeus may try to enter as she did so. He did not, much to her relief, but instead came shortly thereafter. He carried with him a leather-bound book.

"Read," he said, handing it to her excitedly. "I have marked the place of most importance."

A strip of red cloth protruded from between its pages. Selene opened to the marked section.

She shall arrive in the Aranth's decline, as the lands prepare for winter's sleep. And with the passing of the one she believes to be the last of her own shall she be promised to the ranks of the Aranth against her will. Selene recognized the words at once.

"It is a foretelling. The same that you read while in my room."

"You knew of that?" Selene said uneasily.

"Most obviously. I allowed you to enter. No void-stone could hold an enchantment such as the ones I would normally set upon my door. The magic you and Felan encountered would not have harmed the most base of creatures. It was a spell of light, no more."

"So you meant for me to read this?" Selene asked, holding up the journal.

"No," Damaeus replied. "I meant for you to read the knife. I hoped that it would aid you in unearthing your final latent ability, which I discovered upon reading Ander Daxun's journal. It would have done so if not for Felan's interference."

"But how did you know that I would find the knife?" She was intrigued despite her best intentions.

"I had no way of knowing such a thing. I merely left it in an obvious place and hoped that one of you would come across it. If you did not, then I had lost nothing, for I would have other occasions to prove that you were the one mentioned in the foretelling."

"So, just what is this ever-so-powerful latent ability that I supposedly have?"

"Now is not the proper time," Damaeus replied. "I would like it if you would read the foretelling in its entirety. I believe it will be beneficial."

"I may."

It did intrigue her slightly. Still, she was not certain that she believed in such things as foretelling. She liked to think that the future was rather more open than that.

"Come to breakfast," Damaeus offered. "Bring the journal. Once there we shall examine what little you overlooked."

As Selene followed Damaeus through the Keep she could not help but wonder at how the structure remained whole. From the look of it the place was ready to collapse at any moment. Scraps of what had been drapery, or perhaps tapestry, hung haphazardly from rusted pegs. Loose pieces of stone crunched beneath her feet, and any edges that she happened to touch while descending the stairs fell apart in a most distressing manner.

They rounded a corner and passed before a large, stone archway. Black cloth covered the opening, through which could be heard a loud mix of voices. Selene wished that the cloth was not in such good condition. As it was she could not catch so much of a glimpse of what lay beyond.

"I feel your curiosity," Damaeus said. "You may look within if you wish."

Selene peered around the edge of the cloth. It opened onto a balcony, which overlooked a lengthy common room set with many rows of tables. Within the room were what Selene gauged to be several hundred Riders. All seemed to be enjoying a leisurely breakfast.

"What is this?" Selene asked hesitantly.

"This," Damaeus replied, "is one half of the army that will aid me in gaining the Ethereal Realm."

"Where is the other half?"

"It is being created as we speak." Damaeus urged her away from the curtain.

"You mean to say that you are recruiting them?"

"No," Damaeus said firmly. "An army composed solely of humans would be of little use. What I have in mind will be much greater."

"How do you create an army?"

"I will show you when it has been completed. Not before."

"You sent those Riders in Miloren," Selene said after a moment's thought. Memories of Terran on the day of his death plagued her still. "When Ranur and his men confronted me in the alley, that was upon your orders."

"You are correct."

"I could have been killed. Why would you risk such a thing if you wished for me to join you?"

"Death is not as permanent as some would have you believe," Damaeus replied.

"Is he here?"

"Ranur? He is. He has been ordered to do you no harm. I ask that you return the courtesy."

"So long as he keeps his word I will keep mine," Selene replied. It was not at all truth, but she had no desire to lose Damaeus' trust so soon.

She followed him to the dining room, where Felan stood waiting. Damaeus seated himself and then offered her the chair next to him. It had no padding, though it seemed sturdy enough. Felan set out some jellied fruit and an end of bread for Selene before pouring her a mug of tea. For Damaeus he set out nothing. Each task was completed quickly and without complaint. Selene could not help but feel the slightest bit of pity for Felan, regardless of what he had done to her.

"Read aloud," Damaeus pressed. "From the beginning."

Selene opened the journal once more to the place that Damaeus had marked. *"She shall arrive in the Aranth's decline, as the lands prepare for winter's sleep. And with the passing of the one she believes to be the last of her own shall she be promised to the ranks of the Aranth against her will. Thus shall she battle for their cause, which she believes to be just.'*

"On the day of her bond shall the journey begin, as a raven's flight into darkness."

Felan raised a brow in Selene's direction. It was apparent that Damaeus had not allowed him to read the prophecy.

"By the given title of Aranth shall she discover the nature of trust in others, and thus shall that trust be forsaken. She shall unknowingly lay herself, in body or soul, before those four who she considers to be constant, their true motives mixed of love, power, greed and honor, thus allowing them to betray the faith she has offered. She is the one to

whom kingdoms may fall; in whose hands lies the unification of the Army of Shattered Souls."

The part which told of betrayal was true enough. Selene looked up to gauge Felan's reaction. He did not acknowledge her accusing stare.

"She, given a choice between honor and darkness, with the unwilling aid of her living flesh and blood, shall be inexorable in her rule; for she is the one who commands the flesh, the air, and the lost souls of the walking dead. She shall be the hope of the many or the ruin of all, for she is a creature in which evil may thrive."

"You may pass over the next few pages," Damaeus said. "They are of little importance. The final passage is also the most intriguing."

Selene did not wish to do so, but it was obvious that Damaeus would not allow anything else. She sipped at her tea before continuing. It was comfortingly bitter. She turned the yellowed pages to the last paragraph of the passage.

"And thus her love shall be shared by two whose power is strong; whose souls are marked by the Spirits. By her willing union with one shall be born a child whose power is beyond that of any yet seen upon the earth."

The foretelling ended there, leaving Selene to ponder its meaning. "Those whose souls are marked by the Spirits are Marked Ones?" she asked.

"Yes."

"It is impossible to know who one will love in advance, or what children they will bear," Selene said firmly.

"I thought so as well, at first. But in reading the beginning of the foretelling I noticed that it does indeed bear a striking resemblance to your life."

Selene found that she could not honestly dispute that fact.

"What say you, Felan?" Damaeus asked. "I have been told that you do not generally believe in such things as foretelling. You may speak honestly without fear of punishment."

For a moment Selene thought that Felan would not answer; thus it surprised her greatly when he spoke. "It seems to be accurate, Master Damaeus. I believe it to be written about Selene."

"There you have it," Damaeus said, sounding pleased. "The betrayer himself tells it to be true."

"You wish me to have a child for you?" Selene asked, becoming angry. Damaeus had firmly crossed the barrier of decency.

"Calm yourself. I would never force you to do so. The foretelling specifically states that the child may be conceived only by one for whom you hold feelings of love. More than that, they must be marked and must love you in return. Such is the way with prophecy." He stood. "But I shall move on to other matters. I do not wish to draw your ire. I would like you to begin practicing your weaponry each morning. It would be unfortunate if your skills were to decline from disuse. Felan will aid you. It will be as it was while you were under Graelen's employ, though I daresay that you will have much more freedom under my rule."

Selene could not imagine how that would be possible. Graelen had been free with her in most aspects. Damaeus thought he was being devious, when in truth his plan was as clear as a mid-summer's day. If he proposed to gain a marked child by forcing Felan back into her good graces he would have a time of it. Then again, she might be able to use that fact to her advantage somehow.

"You may practice in what was once the Throne Room. There is little left of it to be destroyed."

"Are you finished with him for today?" Perfidia asked, striding into the room and grabbing a loose chunk of bread from the center of the table with none of her usual grace. She looked well kept, though perhaps not so much as she had been while in Evaria. It seemed that her hair had been dyed a dark brown, no doubt in attempt to cover the ever multiplying pieces of gray.

"For today, yes," Damaeus replied. "Tomorrow he is promised to Selene."

"I see," Perfidia said, noticing Selene at once. The former queen looked as if she had just caught scent of something particularly foul. "But that is only for a short time. Surely he will be free to join me later in the day."

Selene cringed to think that she had accepted Perfidia's underhanded attempt to befriend her. The woman obviously deserved no pity, for she was as much a part of this debauchery as was Damaeus.

"I may need him for several full days after, as well," Selene said, giving Perfidia a pointed look. "He seems weak. It will take time to build him up to what he was. My need for him is of much more importance than yours." The woman probably had Felan fetching anything that came to her feeble mind, or perhaps performing a number of demeaning chores while she set her idle rear upon the plushest chair she could find.

"You know nothing of my need for him." Perfidia's face began to take on a reddish tint. "He enjoys the tasks I set for him. He will tell you so."

Felan did not answer, perhaps because he had not been directly told to do so. His face was flushed nearly as much as Perfidia's.

"And yet he does not speak," Selene replied.

"Close your mouth, repulsive harlot," Perfidia snapped, "before I string you up like your worthless mother!"

Selene's anger conquered her good judgment in an instant. She thrust Perfidia against the wall using the full force of her latent ability, holding the former queen so that her head hovered only inches from the ceiling. "You know nothing of my mother!" Selene screamed, pushing back from the table. "You are not to come near Felan for two full weeks. If I so much as sense your presence it will take more magic than Damaeus can hold to repair you."

"Damaeus," Perfidia gasped. It seemed that she had not expected Selene to be in control of her powers.

"Selene," Damaeus said calmly. "Please release my sister."

"As you wish." Selene withdrew her latent ability at once, causing Perfidia to plummet to the floor.

The former queen stood gingerly, backing away from Selene as she did so. She smoothed the dust from her dress in what seemed much like an attempt to regain her poise. It may have worked if not for the cobwebs that clung to her hair. "Why would you allow her the use of her powers? Can you not see that she is dangerous? You are commonly the first one to say that Marked Ones must not be allowed to do as they please."

Selene sat back, content with what had occurred. She wished that Cael had not taken her Stone. Then Perfidia would surely be sorry for her words. Whatever bruises the woman would suffer would not be punishment enough.

"Female Marked Ones are not nearly as dangerous as the males," Damaeus stated simply. "They are more easily reasoned with. She has shown interest in joining us of her free will, but wishes for some time to decide."

"And if she does not choose to join us?"

"Then she shall be treated as Felan. She is intelligent. I am confident that once she sees what I have planned she will choose the correct side."

Perfidia glared in Selene's direction. "You endanger our lives with an idiot's experiment. She will never join us willingly."

"In the meantime I would suggest that you keep from speaking about issues which are sensitive to her," Damaeus continued, seemingly oblivious to his sister's insult.

"Also, Felan does not belong to you. He has become soft because you have not forced him to keep up his training. I am his Holder and will remain so. Take him now, but he is to be back in Selene's room by sunrise tomorrow, at the latest. After that you may see him again in two weeks."

It seemed that Perfidia was unsure of how to respond. She fumed for a moment before grabbing Felan by the arm and pulling him into the hall.

"You are most gracious to grant my request, Damaeus," Selene said. Her anger faded with the noise of Perfidia's retreat. "My apologies for losing my temper."

"Not at all, my dear," he replied, patting her hand. His skin was as cold as stone in winter. "My sister can be willful at times. She often has need of someone to remind her that she is not in command. I am pleased that you were able to do so. It is the mark of a competent leader. You will do well commanding the latter half of my army."

"But I know nothing of commanding," Selene argued.

"You know more than you believe. You were made to lead them. It is in the foretelling, thus it is truth. In less than a week your forces will be complete."

Selene remained unconvinced.

"While I am speaking of such," Damaeus said. "Where have you hidden your Stone? It was not with your other possessions. I will not take it from you. I merely wish to be sure of its position so that I may bring it here for your use."

"You would know that better than I. It was one of your Marked Ones who lifted it from me, was it not?"

"One of mine?" Damaeus mused. "What would bring you to such a conclusion?"

"He did not have a Circlet, but I thought perhaps he had joined you willingly so that there was no need to place one. You mean to say that Cael is not working with you?"

Damaeus' eyes narrowed in a frightening way.

"He is also called Logan, I believe. But I do not know his family name."

"Cael is not one of mine. Nor is he one that can be controlled, even by a Mage such as myself."

"What would he want with my Stone?" Selene asked. "No other can use it while I live."

"It is of no consequence," Damaeus replied. "Cael cannot harm you while you remain within the Keep, and your power is great enough that you have no real need of a Stone."

"And if he comes for me?"

"He is the most dangerous Marked One I have seen, and I do not say such things lightly. He has taken many souls in his lifetime, both human and marked. You will stay away from him if he appears and inform me of it immediately."

"Yes, of course," she promised. She was so very tired. "May I retire to my room for a while? I am still feeling rather weak."

"You do look pale. You should not have used so much of your latent ability. Go to your room and rest. I will send someone for you in a few hours."

Upon reaching her room Selene collapsed onto the straw mattress. Broad flakes of snow fell gently past her window. She placed her head on the pillow for only a second, and was grateful when the world dissolved around her.

The Valley of the Eldai

Xaiden whispered to Requiem, guiding him towards the center of the path. The gelding's ear twitched. It was obvious by his posture that he was nervous. He was right to be so. This place was perilous despite its peaceful façade. Redwood trees, ancient beyond years that any Marked One could hope to achieve, reached to the sky with spiked, evergreen branches. The path beneath was carpeted with dry needles in shades of reddish-brown set amongst miniscule patches of snow. A soothing feeling surrounded Xaiden, as it had since he had entered the valley. This felt like home, though if he were to keep count of the number of times he had entered the valley upon one hand he would have several fingers to spare. The horses felt as much distress as Xaiden felt ease. It was to be expected, as they held no magic within them.

"Not so much danger here as you thought, is there Xaiden?" Viverr said as he pulled Cyprus up beside Requiem. Selene's horse had been less than willing to obey the rogue's whim in the beginning. It had taken a great deal of convincing before he would allow Viverr to mount him. The animal was still not completely under control.

"We could holiday in this place with as nice as it is. We'd be like men of the upper class; sipping our Fenlaye wine with no concern for the welfare of the lowly common folk."

Xaiden did not find the rogue's wit amusing, especially as Aranth were considered upper class by many. "Hazards are near though they may not be readily visible. Be silent Viverr."

"There aren't really fearsome beasts lurking in every shadow of this forest, are there?" Viverr continued after a disappointingly short bout of silence. "But I'm sure you're not above telling us so to be sure we obey you, eh?"

"This seems like a peaceful place," Aurin agreed. "It is comforting here. You are certain that we are traveling in the right direction, yes?"

"This is the Valley of the Eldai," Xaiden responded. "There is no other place that resembles it within the Ethereal Realm."

"I think I see one of those Pixies you mentioned," Viverr said, pointing. "Up by that dead branch."

Xaiden followed the rogue's gaze. There was indeed a Pixie less than a yard ahead. The creature had perched itself upon a fallen branch thicker than a man's torso. It noticed them as well, and hovered in the air for a second's time before heading straight for Viverr.

"A fearsome looking thing," Viverr added with a sarcastic laugh.

Xaiden shifted his jaw in frustration. He had hoped to traverse at least half of the valley before being noticed. Then again, he should have known better than to expect such a thing while traveling in Viverr's company.

The Pixie hovered before Cyprus' nose. It peered into the horse's nostril and was thrown back as Cyprus snorted in displeasure. Xaiden had always considered Pixies to be distasteful creatures. This particular one did nothing to change his view. It was a repulsive human in miniature; a half foot in length at the most and it wore no clothing save for a loincloth of furry black hide. Its short cropped hair was matted into clumps and tinted a reddish brown by dried blood. Four wings with the look and hue of withered autumn leaves sprouted from the Pixie's back. They moved with such speed as to be almost invisible save when they were at rest. The creature's body had been dyed in linear patterns of blue and dingy grey, marking it as one of lower status. The brightest plant dyes were reserved for those in command. As the color lessened, so did the rank.

"Whoa, now," Viverr exclaimed as the Pixie pried open his belt pouch and dove inside. "Stay out of my things, you."

The Pixie paid him no heed. It reappeared momentarily with an oddly colored platinum coin in hand. Viverr grabbed for it, but the Pixie evaded his clumsy motions with ease. It grinned, showing a mouthful of teeth like tiny points of rusted iron. It looked to be male, or perhaps female and young, for its bare chest had no breasts to speak of.

"Just let him have it." There was a good chance that the rogue had stolen the coin to begin with. It was fair, that being the case, that he be forced to give it up to ensure the welfare of the group.

"No," Viverr objected. "It's mine. Why should he have it?"

"Mine," the Pixie mocked, hovering just out of Viverr's reach. "I deserve it. I, the mightily Viverr."

"Give it back, you little bastard!" Viverr hollered.

"Dead magics have no need of wondrous, shiny coins," the Pixie said as it clutched the edge of the coin with its tiny, slender hands. "This goes to my hoard, where it will raise me to the two hundred and ninety-fourth position. Emm will cry with shame as he is crushed under the greatness of me."

"Aurin," Viverr pleaded between futile attempts to crush the Pixie between his palms. "Help me out? This thing is hostile. That's on top of thieving what's rightfully mine."

"It is best to do as Xaiden says," Aurin replied. His worried eyes followed the Pixie's every movement. "You should let him have the coin."

"Quick little son of a harlot," Viverr muttered, ignoring Aurin's words.

"Too quick for Viverr," the Pixie chanted, "Viverr, the most slothful of magics."

"How does that pint know my name?" Viverr demanded. "And what does he mean by calling me 'magics'? That some kind of curse in Pixie language? It's got to be."

"He is merely naming you for a creature of magic," Xaiden explained, "which you are. As for the other; Pixies are observant creatures. It is likely that he picked up your name by listening to our conversation long before we noticed his presence. It is the nature of Pixies to understand the language of any magical creature. They are able to speak those languages as well, though the accuracy of their words leaves much to be desired. Give him the coin and he will most likely leave."

"He said something about death," Viverr replied with a nervous expression that seemed natural upon him. "I'm not convinced that he'll leave without making good on that."

"Die faster, stubborn magics," the Pixie said as it hovered in Xaiden's face. "I would see what other things of position-raising greatness you hold in your delicious pouches."

Xaiden was now close enough to see that rows of sharpened, miniature rib-bones had been polished and pressed through the flesh upon each side of the creature's neck as a form of adornment. "We are not here to die," he said firmly.

The Pixie tilted its head as if pondering Xaiden's words. "Magics come to our valley only to die," it stated. "And I can see you in this place."

"That is true, but we merely wish to pass to Greyridge Keep."

"You'd send us to the Spirits, eh?" Viverr said as he tied his belt pouch as tightly as he could manage in attempt to keep his remaining possessions. "Bastard Pixie. You won't be gnawing on my bones if I've any say."

A sharp sound, like that of steel striking stone, sliced the air.

The Pixie brandished its teeth in something vaguely resembling a smile. "Lih will make it your time to be here," it said. "But I have the coin and I will keep it."

With that it flew up to the treetops and out of Xaiden's view.

"Can't understand that," Viverr said. "Most creatures of magic don't survive my latent ability."

"You used your latent ability on a Pixie?" Xaiden asked, knowing that he would not be pleased with the answer.

"Yeah. No harm done, though. Didn't seem to hurt him in the least, unfortunately."

"No," Xaiden replied. "It wouldn't. Pixie society, at least that of the Eldai, is based upon the consumption of magical creatures. Over time they have become immune to all but the most powerful effects of magic. That includes magic such as your latent ability, though it would not seem possible."

"Isn't that just grand," Viverr said, not seeming at all as if he meant it.

Xaiden urged Requiem forward. "We should keep moving. The Pixie will find us if he wishes to, no matter where we are in the Valley." There was little chance that they would get far before the Pixie returned, but they may as well make an attempt. It would do them no good to stand around waiting for death to catch up. Xaiden enjoyed only a fleeting moment of silence before Viverr spoke once again.

"Just when I thought I was rid of the cursed thing," the rouge mumbled.

The Pixie landed between Cyprus' ears, where it settled itself comfortably. The horse twisted his head in attempt to shake him off, but the creature had a firm grip upon his mane.

"Xaiden," the rogue began, but his words died as his eyes widened.

The forest was suddenly filled with Pixies. They hung off of every branch and fallen log; their painted bodies causing the forest to resemble a field of brightly colored flowers. Its beauty was breathtaking, at least from a distance. It was then that Xaiden began to worry over the fate of his tiny group.

A plump, male Pixie approached Xaiden. Its body was painted in splotches of white and yellow pollen, and its neatly clumped hair shone greasy and black. Fresh unicorn blood had been used, by the look of it. A black dragon's scale covered each side of its lower half, and the tip of what looked much like the talon of a young gryphon had been pressed through the skin at the center of its chest.

"I am Lih of the first position," it said. "I remember you, magic, and am glad that you have chosen to return here for proper death."

"We are not prepared for death at this time," Xaiden answered. "We wish to travel to Greyridge Keep. Please do not bar our way."

"Your insults are not allowable." Lih hovered so that he was level with Xaiden's eyes. His hideous little face contorted into a deep scowl.

"I had no intention of insulting you. Tell me how I have done so and I will make amends." Perhaps they could still be saved if he could turn the conversation.

"Magics' refusal to die is not agreeable to our peoples. We allowed it before, and not again. Kill yourself and we may forgive you."

"I cannot do so. There must be something else that you will accept as a form of apology."

Lih extended his belly, resting his hands upon it. "Then you will follow with us to the center," he said, turning away.

The flower-like mass of Pixies shifted, forming a clump of colorful movement behind Aurin, who was last in line. Xaiden urged Requiem on, motioning for Aurin and Viverr to follow him. It seemed the most reasonable course of action. He could not possibly defeat so many Pixies with such a small party of men.

Lih led them deep into the forest, between trees whose trunks spanned the length of a horse and carriage in full. It grew darker as they traveled, and the clean unnatural edges of bones poked out from beneath beds of dried needles. Scattered bones became piles, and soon twisted skeletal masses towered before them. They came at last to a mix of skull, claw, and bone which had been arranged in such a way as to create rows of miniature dwellings. Some of the parts had not been completely cleaned of their flesh. The stench brought Bloodsoul to mind.

"Leave your lesser creatures," Lim said, looking at Xaiden's horse. "They hold no magic and are not tasty enough for our liking."

"Uh, Xaiden?" Viverr whispered as they dismounted.

"They will not consume us while we still live," Xaiden said with conviction. "Do not fear."

"All you're saying is that they'll kill us first before eating us." Viverr's voice was quivering. "Why did I travel with you to this forsaken place?"

"Because we must help Selene," Aurin reminded him. He grabbed Viverr's collar before the rogue could slip away. "And you have agreed to do so." He released Viverr with more force than was necessary. The rogue stumbled, but quickly regained his balance.

"You are with those magics who keep our prey from us," Lim said. "The mountains hold hundreds of much tastiness, but we cannot enter. They are beyond barriers of strong magic that even we cannot pass. The Spirits know that the balance has been disturbed. We are keeping the balance, and so we will be blamed for its wrongness."

Aurin held his mace at the ready. Xaiden did not think that a weapon of that sort would be useful against such small enemies. Still, he did not dissuade him from brandishing it.

"I have no idea what you speak of," Xaiden replied.

"Lim is not as dense as you think me to be. Magics will not be fooling a Pixie of the first position."

Lim tilted his head to one side, waving a hand over the talon that protruded from his chest. The words that had been etched into it twisted under Xaiden's gaze. The air around him shifted unnaturally. Massive bones rose from beneath the needle strewn ground around the party, snapping together to form a ramshackle cage. Silence followed, disturbed only by Viverr's whimpering.

"We will be releasing you when your souls have entered the cycle," Lim said. He turned his back on them then, and the Pixies that had followed them scattered into the city of bones and the forest beyond.

Cael watched the three men silently from atop a nearby hill. Xaiden seemed completely undisturbed by the fact that he was now caged, which was not surprising in the least. It was odd that he was still keeping company with the two rogues, however. Xaiden was a patient man for the most part, but he was also an honest one. Viverr and Aurin were quite the opposite.

He dusted dry needles from his clothing as he stood. Viverr was now in a complete panic and was pulling at the bars of the cage like a rabid animal. Aurin looked as if he were preparing to strike out with his mace. Little good it would do him, for the bones that composed the cage were at least half as thick as the trunks of the trees that surrounded them. Xaiden knelt in a position of meditation.

It had taken Cael many days of hard riding to catch up with Xaiden, and he would not let those days go to waste. He had flown Selene's Stone to Evaria, where they had learned that the girl was innocent, amongst a few other interesting facts. Unfortunately, that meant that she knew nothing of Damaeus' plans. Cael had then returned to Fenlaye to discover that both Xaiden and Selene were gone.

Strangely, Kyrros knew nothing of what had happened to them due to the fact that he had slept through the entire incident. Stranger yet, the popularity of Kyrros' parties had risen a great deal because of it. Nobles from all corners of the Ethereal Realm were speaking with pride of their encounter with the Sleeping Bandits while at Lord Kyrros' estate. Most seemed disappointed that so few people had actually been robbed. One could never tell what nobles would find amusing.

Cael drew the sword he had borrowed from Kyrros and headed down the hill. It was by the luck of the Tides that none of the Pixies had noticed him thus far. He was certain that they would soon do so.

Viverr looked up at the sound of Cael's approach. He rushed to clutch at the bars upon recognizing him. "Cael, my old friend," he squealed with glee. "You're a great man, coming to my rescue once again. I can't thank you enough. We're even, you remember? I think I did you quite a large favor, so if you free me I won't owe you anything, right?"

Cael raised a brow in the rogue's direction. "I'm not here to speak with you, Viverr. And you'll owe me a large portion of your time if I do decide to free you."

"No problems," Viverr answered quickly. "Of course letting me out would require some sort of compensation, eh? I am absolutely prepared to give you whatever you ask."

Aurin nodded in agreement.

"And you?" Cael asked, meeting Xaiden's quiet scrutiny.

"I have sworn to kill you," Xaiden replied. "If you free me I will do so."

"I expected as much. Would you change your mind if I told you that I did not kill Devren?"

Xaiden's smooth expression did not falter. "Most likely not. Your statement does me no good when in the form of a question. You know as much."

"I did not kill Devren." Cael leaned close to the bars. "Is that more to your liking? I am not working with Damaeus. My loyalty is to King Graelen and the Ethereal Realm."

"The heir is dead," Xaiden said. "His Stone bond was broken."

"Devren lives. I returned him to his father."

"It is impossible," Xaiden said darkly.

"What I speak is the truth. Your latent ability must tell you so."

"Viverr is aiding you in your deception."

"You would know if he was."

Xaiden did not reply. He raised the blade of his sword to Cael's face. "Why are you here?"

"Your goals and mine are the same. I wish to destroy Damaeus for what he has done to Devren and myself. I also believe that a comrade of mine is being held within Greyridge Keep. Several comrades, if Selene can be counted as one."

"I do not trust you." Xaiden said firmly.

"You do not need to trust me so long as you agree to work with me. What if I were to convince the Eldai to release the three of you?"

"May the Spirits guide you in your quest. You will certainly need their aid." Xaiden returned to his position of meditation.

"I'll take that as an agreement."

He crossed to the city of bones and knocked upon the nearest dwelling, the entrance of which was composed of a sizeable pelvic bone. The spaces in the bone had been stuffed with dirt and dried needles save for a small, Pixie sized hole at the top. Imbedded within the debris were dragon's scales of all colors, several gems, and various other items considered precious by their kind. A female Pixie burst from within. Her body was painted in shades of maroon and copper, and a skirt of white hair much like that of a horse's mane fell half way to her knees.

"Why do you pound, magic?" she asked, hovering level with Cael's face. "Death does not seem close to you."

"Of what position are you?" Cael asked.

"Ara is of the fifty-sixth position," the Pixie replied proudly, raising a hand to her freshly blood-soaked hair.

"A very high position indeed. But it could easily be higher."

"You say so," the Pixie replied. "It would take many items of preciousness to make it truth. Do you carry such things?" The Pixie eyed Selene's Stone, which hung around his neck. "The magic from this is grand."

"Indeed it is," Cael agreed, pulling it from her fingers. "You may not have this, but there are many items like it within Greyridge Keep."

"I cannot enter Greyridge Keep," Ara scowled. "None can. What good to me are things I cannot reach?"

"Perhaps you cannot reach them, but I can. I will need the aid of my companions, however." He gestured towards the cage of bones.

"The other magics have been trapped by Lim. It is not the right of me to release them before they have accepted the cycle of death."

"There are enough items of magic within the keep to raise you to the first position," Cael informed her. "You will not have to worry over what Lim thinks."

The Pixie pressed its fingers together as it pondered. Its face puckered hesitantly.

"You will not return. You will take the objects of magic and flee without keeping our deal."

"I would never do so."

If only he could be sure that his latent ability would work upon Pixies. He doubted that a light touch of it would be sufficient. He did not wish to take the little creature's soul, only to push it to agree with him. He decided that it was not worth the risk.

"Here." He pulled the cord of Selene's Stone over his head. "If you like this you may keep hold of it, but only until my return. I will bring you an even stronger item of magic to replace it." Damaeus would keep many such items with him. At least Cael hoped that he would.

"So nice," the Pixie said, running a hand lovingly over the Stone. "Your terms are agreeable," she flew over and pressed a hand against the cage. It collapsed outward. The ground shook with the weight of the bones as they fell.

"You're going to get us into the keep, right?" Viverr muttered as they made their way back to the horses, which were pulling hungrily at the bark of a nearby tree.

"Of course not," Cael replied. "I wouldn't dare to touch a spell of such strength, especially one Damaeus has concocted."

"We're giving up, then?" Viverr asked. He seemed dissatisfied by the prospect, oddly enough.

"Don't be foolish. You will get us in."

"You think so, eh? Well, my magic isn't strong enough. And I'm not fond of being killed, I'll have you know."

"That is why I have brought you a Stone."

Xaiden's expression darkened as hastily as the sky of an early summer storm.

"Graelen's orders," Cael said.

"King Graelen," Xaiden reminded him.

"His Majesty's orders, then, if you prefer that I keep the title."

"I do," Xaiden replied. "I am not certain that giving Viverr a Stone is a wise action, no matter whose orders it is upon."

"Of course it is," the rogue said quickly. "I've never been surer of my King's wisdom than I am now." There was no way for the rogue to know what purpose a Stone served. He must have heard the Pixie name it for an item of strong magic, and so he wished to have it.

"Besides," Cael added. "We can just kill him if we have need of it again."

Xaiden's expression darkened all the more.

"Perhaps I don't want it," Viverr amended, looking ill.

They mounted their horses and followed Cael to where he had hidden the dun stallion that Kyrros had loaned him.

"That coin," Xaiden said suddenly. "What spell was upon it?"

"Coin?" Viverr echoed. "I don't know. What coin?"

"The one the Pixie seized. You know well what I speak of."

"Haven't got any idea," Viverr insisted.

"It was an item of magic, was it not? Why else would the creature have chosen it above everything else you have in your pouch? I know that you must have taken something while in Fenlaye. Gems, perhaps, or trinkets of some other sort? Be truthful unless you wish for me to find out by searching you. I am certain that Aurin and Cael would aid me."

"He did take a few items," Cael offered. "Kyrros said as much. It is of little consequence. I doubt that the nobles will miss them."

Aurin grabbed Viverr once again. He did not look pleased. It seemed that Xaiden's moral conscience had spread to the man. Such was often the way with those who chose to follow Xaiden.

"I didn't thieve it," Viverr said quickly. "I found it in Lystonne. It did have some magic to it. Strong stuff, and dark by the feel of it. I'm kind of glad to be rid of the nasty thing, to be honest. It had a way of sucking the warmth right from your chest. Pity though, I could've got a pile of coin if I'd found the right buyer."

"Items of dark magic are not to be trifled with." Xaiden gave Viverr a look that reminded Cael of the many times he had been caught doing something the man did not approve of. Xaiden had a way of making one feel guilty even when there was no real reason for it. It was an impressive talent.

"And they are certainly not to be sold to anyone who possesses enough coin. It is best that the Pixie has it. No human will be able to obtain the item while it is with one of the Eldai. If you encounter any other such items you will hand them over to me immediately. Do you have anything else of a sinister nature?"

"Of course not," Viverr said at once.

"And as for you," Xaiden added.

The woods grew silent, and Cael turned from untying his horse. It was abruptly apparent that Xaiden was speaking to him.

"I may still kill you if your words prove to be false. You agreed to my terms long ago, but oaths do not fade with time."

"I understand. I will accept whatever action you deem to be appropriate in the event that any of what I have told you proves to be false." If Xaiden wished to hold Cael's life in exchange for his loyalty then so be it. He could think of no other companion that had earned his trust so completely.

The group encountered no Pixies as they made their way to the far side of the valley. Cael was thankful of it, though he wondered why they had not come. It was doubtful that one small, female Pixie had successfully distracted the others. They most likely had more pressing matters to attend to. A fair number of magical creatures entered the Valley of the Eldai on an average day, if what Cael had read in Graelen's library was correct. The Pixies were most likely feasting upon them, or attempting to repair the unnamed balance had been so cruelly upset by whatever Damaeus was doing in Greyridge Keep.

"We stop here," Xaiden announced, breaking Cael from his thoughts.

Smooth, even cliffs rose to the sky across a treeless field of snow. Unevenly strewn boulders, which had likely fallen from the cliff at some point long past, were the only objects that dared disturb the expanse of white. Greyridge Keep lay far above them. Cael had not been inside, nor had anyone else he had spoken with in all of his years. The talk amongst Riders, at least during Cael's days as a Praecyr, was that it held fortune without measure, but men tended to think that of any place that they could not reach.

"Why here?" Viverr asked. "Greyridge is only yards away. We can't search for a way in from so far off."

"Pay attention to your surroundings," Xaiden ordered. "It astounds me that you have survived for such a length of time. I can only assume that it is Aurin who keeps you from being slaughtered by your own idiocy each day."

Cael focused his attention at once. It was reckless of him to drift into thought while traveling through hostile territory. Luckily Xaiden had the rogue to occupy his attention.

The sudden change from forest to field gave Cael an odd sensation now that he considered it fully, but he could not come up with any explainable difference between the space ahead of him and that which was behind.

Xaiden dismounted. He plucked a dead branch from the forest floor as he reached it. He advanced, holding the branch out before him as if attempting to impale some unseen creature. Nothing occurred. Cael resisted the urge to smile. Xaiden's was intimidating to most people whether or not he wished it to be so. At the moment he looked rather comical, brandishing the stick as he was. Cael's amusement vanished as Xaiden reached the edge of the forest. The air crackled like pine needles thrown upon a fire. Nearly half of the stick melted away. It acted much as candle's wax would when held to a flame, dripping down like liquid only to become solid once again upon landing in the snow beneath. Xaiden knelt, using what was left of the stick to place a mark before the barrier. Steam rose from the forest floor at its touch. He had traveled less than ten paces from where Cael stood.

"We could go around it, yes?" Aurin offered, breaking his silence. "The valley is wide here. Maybe it does not cross the whole. No one could enter at all if it was so."

"That's right," Viverr agreed as he climbed from Cyprus' back. "How would Damaeus and his lackeys get in if the entire thing was blocked? It would be too much work to undo a spell that powerful every time you wanted to get someone through."

"I have no doubt that this spell extends the entire length of the valley," Xaiden said thoughtfully. "A Mage of

Damaeus' talent has no need to walk through barriers. There must be a voyage ring, or something similar to one, nearby."

"Voyage ring," Viverr said as if testing the word. "That sounds useful. So once we find it-"

"Absolutely not," Xaiden said firmly, cutting him short. "It would be unwise to attempt to use it."

Cael expected no less. He pulled the unbonded Stone from where it was tied upon his belt. Its setting was a sheet of gold colored metal with scalloped edges surrounding the open portion. It was unusual in appearance, though not as artfully crafted as the others Cael had seen.

"Touch your thumb to the place where the Stone is visible," Cael ordered, handing it to Viverr.

The rogue looked terrified.

"Pyre's ash," Cael swore, pressing Viverr's unwilling hand to the bare portion of the pendant. Viverr was worse about following orders than Devren had been in his younger years. The boy had improved considerably since Cael's intervention. Cael did not believe that the rogue would do the same.

Xaiden did not look at all pleased.

Cael removed his hand. Viverr held the Stone out, pinching its leather cord between two fingers as if it might suddenly turn to a viper and sink its fangs into his flesh. A swirl of russet, closely followed by one of light blue, swirled through its center.

"Don't lose that," Cael warned, "or I'll be forced to kill you."

Viverr snapped from his stupor. "No problems," he replied nervously as he pulled the Stone's leather cord over his head.

"Now," Cael said, "concentrate your latent ability through the Stone and place your hand upon the barrier."

"You're mad. I won't get near that thing so long as I've wits left about me."

"There may be no other way for us to enter the keep," Xaiden explained. "Your power will be amplified by the Stone. The barrier should not harm you."

"You just want to see my fingers melted into a puddle. I know you don't favor me, but you could at least be civil about it."

"Don't' be a fool," Cael said as he ushered Viverr forward. "We just want to get to the other side of that barrier before the Pixies catch our scent."

"You may not need to physically touch the barrier," Xaiden offered. "Simply focus your magic towards it at first. If that does not work then we will try something more drastic."

"What if my magic can't be focused by one of your Stones?" Viverr asked. "It nullifies magic, and a Stone is a magical item."

"Try it." Xaiden seemed unconcerned. "I am certain that the men who created the Stones accounted for such an event. They were far more knowledgeable than any Mage of our time."

"Fine, fine," Viverr muttered, pulling from the group. "But if that thing scorches me you'll pay quite a high price."

He stopped several feet from where Xaiden had made his mark in the snow.

"I'm not going any closer than this."

"Just try it from where you are, then." Cael was growing impatient. "Take a moment to concentrate. You will need a large amount of power to breach the barrier." He could not fathom how Xaiden had put up with the man's attitude for such a length of time.

Cael's horse pawed at the ground, snorting in displeasure upon finding nothing to eat beneath the layer of snow and needles. His movements were the only sounds to be heard during the next few moments. The snap of Viverr's latent ability caught Cael unaware. His horse was just as startled as he. Cael took hold of his reins to keep him from running.

The barrier was now visible, at least in part. Viverr had created a small hole in it, the edges of which glowed with the yellow-blue color of a lighting strike. Viverr's face twisted and the hole stretched down to the ground. It was now large enough for a man to pass through, though Aurin would surely have to stoop. Frenzied strands of light leapt from the site of the disturbance, skimming along the unseen barrier for a moment before fading from view.

"Can you make it any wider?" Cael asked. It would be best if they could bring the horses through.

Viverr shook his head in dissent.

"We will go on foot," Xaiden said. "Take anything you may need from your saddlebags."

"What of the horses?" Aurin asked. "There is no food for them here."

"Creatures without magic find this place uncomfortable. They will leave the valley eventually. Cael's stallion is Fenlaye bred. It is almost certain that he will lead them there."

Cael knew that Fenlaye horses were distinctive in appearance; long legged and agile. Still, he had not expected Xaiden to be able to tell the horse's origin with a look.

Viverr grunted. The hole became smaller.

Cael rushed to remove his horse's saddle. He pulled out his food, bedroll, and other various items he thought he may need. He then set all of the extraneous things in a pile between the roots of a nearby tree and stepped through the hole. The air crackled once more and turned from frigid to searing. Cael pulled a cool breath upon reaching the opposite side.

Aurin bent low and turned to one side before passing through the opening. Even so, Cael worried for him.

Xaiden followed shortly behind, with no ill effects to be seen. The hole shrunk once again, this time by several inches on all sides save for the bottom. Viverr opened his eyes and passed through what was left of it, crawling on hands and knees. He emerged snow covered and more than a bit pale. The hole snapped shut with such force that it cleared the snow on both sides, leaving a disturbingly large patch of bare earth behind. Viverr flopped onto his back.

"Well done, Viverr," Xaiden said.

"Almost made it completely through," Cael added, slapping the rogue's shoulder as well as he could manage. "Don't worry. There's only a small portion missing."

"*What?*" Viverr rolled frantically around to examine his feet, looking as if he expected to find that a toe, or perhaps a whole foot, had been melted by the barrier.

"Your cloak," Cael explained, pulling a corner of the worn, brown wool from the snow.

"Oh," Viverr said, staring at severed end. "Of course. I expected that was what you meant."

"I have your things," Aurin informed him. "I took all of importance, I think, and unsaddled your horse."

"Thanks. But you guys could have been a bit quicker about getting through, eh? I'm holding that thing for all my life is worth and you're sitting around talking like a bunch of tavern girls."

"Quit whining," Cael ordered.

"I feel like I've been whacked in the head," Viverr said as he lowered himself back down into the snow.

"Overuse of your latent ability," Xaiden explained. "It will pass with time."

Cael peered up at the keep, ignoring Viverr's exaggerated moans of pain. Greyridge Keep seemed much closer now, though they had not traveled far. It also looked much higher than it had from the other side of the barrier.

"We cannot stay in the open." Xaiden started towards a rocky outcropping that jutted from the base of the cliff. It was barely visible from this distance, which was probably best. If they camped beneath it they would not be seen from above.

Aurin helped Viverr up from where he lay. The rogue stumbled along at the back of the group, pressing a hand to one side of his head.

"Don't worry," Cael said. "Islyr should be within the Keep. He may have some herbs to help your head if he still lives, and if Damaeus has not taken them from him. He may even have forgotten the incident in Vale, if the Tides are with you."

"The more I hear of this place the less I want to go in," Viverr muttered.

Cael scanned the base of the cliff as they approached it. Viverr may not have to worry about meeting Islyr, for there did not seem to be an entrance of any sort within sight.

"Do you know how to get inside?" Cael asked.

"I do not," Xaiden replied.

"But you do have a plan of some sort?"

"No."

"Some idea of where to start, at least?"

"None."

"How encouraging," Cael said sarcastically as he laid his bedroll beneath the rocky protrusion. The roof of the cave stood just above Cael's head. It was also narrower than Cael would have liked. The four of them would be able to sleep beneath it, but the fit would be tight.

"We should rest here for a few moments before beginning our search," Xaiden said, sitting back against the cave wall.

"Thank the Spirits." Viverr grabbed a handful of snow and pressed it to his forehead before heading to the back of the cave, presumably to lie down.

"He will be alright, yes?" Aurin asked. He could not stand within the cave, and so had decided to crawl in. He was now leaning against the wall opposite Cael.

"He'll be fine," Cael replied. "The headache should subside before it gets dark, perhaps sooner."

"That is good. We can enter this place then?"

"As soon as we figure out how to do so," Cael agreed.

The more he thought on the subject, the more he worried that the four of them would not be enough to stand up to Damaeus' magic. He wished there was some way to find out what the Mage had in store for them. Whatever it was, he was certain that they would not be fully prepared for it. Odds were that Damaeus already knew of their presence. He closed his eyes and leaned back against the wall. A few moments of meditation could do him no harm. He was not likely to have any time for it in the days to come.

Selene's Army

"Fatal Strike." Selene's voice carried with ease across a room of toppled columns and featureless statues. The throne room of Greyridge was twice as large as that of Evaria's castle. The stillness, when it fell, was one hundred times as suffocating.

Felan lowered his sword and settled himself upon a nearby block of stone. He pressed the tip of his weapon to the crumbled floor and leaned against its hilt, breathing hard. He had gained a good deal of his strength back over the past few weeks, but he had not yet been able to conquer Selene in a bout. And she had not yet used the whole of her sparring abilities upon him.

"Perfidia will come for me soon," he said as his breathing slowed.

Selene wished that Damaeus had provided her with more suitable clothing for sparring. Unfortunately he seemed to think that she looked far better in a dress than a shirt and breeches. The clothing was finely made, though a bit tight for her liking.

"She's frightened of you," Felan added when she did not respond.

"She's not as foolish as I thought if that's true."

Felan looked to her. "Your soul has hardened since arriving here. I'm not sure that I like what you've become." He had not spoken more than a few words to her outside of their training time, though he was constantly by her side and he slept upon a pallet in the far corner of her room. It was odd that he had chosen to start a conversation now, when their time together was nearly finished. Selene made only a mild attempt to suppress her irritation. "You're certainly one to speak of hardened souls. I'm the same as I've always been."

"You aren't. You would kill Mistress Perfidia without a second thought."

"Of course I would. Have you forgotten what she's done to you and Cyanna? And don't call her by that name. That woman doesn't deserve the honor of a title."

"You should watch your words. There is no safe place for Marked Ones out in the world. Without the Aranth we have nothing. It would be best if we remained here. We're well protected within the keep."

"If by well protected you mean beaten and starved then I thoroughly agree." Damaeus' hold upon Selene lessened with every day that passed. She still could not speak directly against him without a great amount of pain, but he did not enter her mind nearly as much as he had in the beginning. It gave her the freedom to say nearly anything that came to her. Checking for his presence before doing so had become automatic. He was thoroughly occupied at the moment. His enthusiasm and pleasure carried strongly through the bond of the Circlet.

"Perfidia has been nothing but kind," Felan insisted. "She cares for me greatly and she would not think of harming me."

And what of me? Selene thought. The words would not leave her tongue. "You cannot honestly believe that to be true," she said instead.

Felan brushed a chunk of rock with the tip of his sword, sending it clattering across the floor.

"Have some self-respect. You're Aranth, not a lowly slave to traitors of the Realm."

"The Aranth have been disbanded," Felan replied crossly. "You and I are Rakaii now, whether you choose to admit it or not. This is our new place in life."

"It doesn't have to be. There is a way to fix everything that's happened. Trust me on this, please."

"You don't know half of what's happened." Felan stood. "And you're wrong. Not even with the aid of the Spirits could you make King Graelen forgive me for what I've done."

"What of Luca?" Selene said, knowing well that it would rile him. "The man who killed your brother is within your reach. You're a fool if you think that Perfidia had nothing to do with Luca's death."

"Stop, Selene," Felan said, lifting the point of his sword towards her.

"You're angry because you know that I speak the truth," Selene replied, pushing his blade aside with hers. He would be forced to think about it now whether he wished to or not. "Damaeus may allow me access to Perfidia. I cannot guarantee that she will survive our next encounter."

"The Selene of old would never have acted this way."

"She would have slain an enemy," Selene replied evenly. "And perhaps someone she once considered to be close to a friend; who has turned to the wrong side. She is not one to break her vows, unlike some others."

Felan's eyes narrowed, and within them Selene could see somewhat of the living spark that had been absent since Evaria. It was a touch of true anger. "You can't change the past and the things you've been forced to do. Master Damaeus will make it so that you can't leave. Like me, you'll realize that you have nothing to return to."

"He won't control me," Selene said, ignoring the familiar tingle of pain that emanated from her Circlet. "My life belongs to no one."

"You're going to join him."

"Think what you will." She wished that she could tell Felan the truth, but she could not take such a large risk.

Damaeus would only loosen his hold upon her enough for it to be of use if he was certain that she was truly upon his side.

"I can't truthfully say that I would choose a different path," Felan admitted. "Then again, I was not given a choice as you were."

"There are options in everything," Selene said, "though they are not often exactly what you would like them to be. I simply chose the best of what was offered to me." She placed her hand upon his shoulder. Her mark warmed as she healed the bruises she had inflicted.

"I'll take my last breath in this place," Felan said. "We both will."

"You won't. I promise to take you with me."

"I'm not sure that I want to go where you're headed."

Damaeus' focus was upon Selene suddenly. "He's coming," she said in case Felan had not noticed.

"Seems content," Felan commented.

Damaeus strode beneath the entryway. The doors had long since rotted away, leaving the room open to the hall. The Mage did indeed seem pleased.

"Come, Selene," he said. "I have something I wish to show you. You may bring Felan if you so desire."

"What is it?" Selene asked as she exited the room. She motioned for Felan to follow. He did so, but stayed a few paces behind as they traveled the halls. More than likely his curiosity had gotten the better of him. It seemed that Perfidia would be forced to wait longer before she could have use of her Rakaii. It would make her furious.

"It pleases me to see you so content," Damaeus said, mistaking the reason for Selene's smile. "I doubted at first that you truly wished to stay here. I should not have done so. It is not surprising that a Marked One of your intelligence would immediately see the benefits of accepting my offer."

They came shortly to a portion of the castle that Selene had never before entered. It was no more dilapidated than any other, though something unnamed made her ill at ease. They climbed several sets of stairs before finally coming to a pair of closed doors. Shards of colored glass were set within the doors' edges, though whatever had been depicted within its center was no longer recognizable. Wooden boards, as fresh as the castle was ancient, had been nailed across them to cover the openings. Beyond them lay what could only be the outdoors, for drafts of air brushed past jagged edges of glass to find her. They carried the promise of spring.

Damaeus opened the doors with a wave of his hand. He stepped through and Selene followed.

"What you see below is my gift to you," he said, "and you are my gift to the Ethereal Realm."

The courtyard was somewhere within the center of the castle, for it was walled in on all sides. Nearly half of the balcony railing had been eaten away by the ages, and the remaining portion was encrusted with green moss as thick as the pelt of a mountain bear. Selene crept to the edge and peered below, being sure to keep to the side where the railing was mostly whole. Her breath stilled. Hundreds of Bloodsoul milled about the base of the courtyard, remaining firmly in place despite her best effort to wish them away. They wandered in a lifeless daze, colliding against walls and each other as they wandered. The creatures were of all sizes and states of decay. Some of the larger, adult sized ones looked to be decades old. Others looked fresh enough to still be living, at least from this height.

Damaeus came to stand to one side of her and Felan approached on the other. She wished that Felan would not stand so close to the balcony's edge, but she did not think that he would take kindly to her saying so.

"You pilfered these from the Holding?" Selene asked. There were far too many for all to be from Evaria, but she felt the need to ask nonetheless.

"Some," Damaeus replied. "Most were created here using those taken from the town of Lystonne."

Selene thought back to the city's eerily quiet streets. "But you did not take them all."

"No, some were much too young to be of any use. They were disposed of."

Selene pushed her thoughts quickly away from the children of Lystonne. She had not thought that even Damaeus could be so cruel. "I was speaking of Aurin," she said. "I assume that a dragon Bloodsoul would be greatly useful. Why was he left when the others were taken?"

"Marked Ones return to their human form upon death. He would be of no more use than any other. It was better for him to stay in Lystonne to meet Xaiden and dispose of him. He would have done so with ease had you not returned to Xaiden's side. I feared that your body would be far too mangled to be revived if your fight with Aurin were to continue, so I was forced to intervene."

"Aurin attacked me when I entered the town," Selene recalled. "He could well have eaten me then."

"You must accept my apology. One of my Riders slipped a concoction of Alchemy and magic into Aurin's drink several days before my casting of the spell that emptied the town of Lystonne. I designed the potion to be triggered by the spell. It was supposed to prevent him from harming you as well."

"Something was wrong with it," Selene said before he could finish.

Damaeus' mouth twisted in irritation. "That is none of your affair. The people of Lystonne traveled willingly to the voyage ring which would take them to Greyridge Keep. It was my perception that was faulty, not my magic. I did not think that Aurin would attack you while you were in raven form. The potion was set so that he would be aggressive towards any person who entered the town. He should not have bothered with small creatures."

Some of Damaeus' more recent spells had not seemed to work as they were meant to. She had not yet determined what it meant, if anything. She had often seen Damaeus wandering the castle at night, regardless of the hour.

"Perhaps Aurin was hungry," Selene offered bitterly.

"That may be so," Damaeus replied without pause. "Regardless, everything turned out as I wished. You need only look below you to realize it."

"You slaughtered all of those who were brought here?" Selene asked again in disbelief. She caught sight of a bloodsoul who, by his size, could not be more than six or seven years of age. She was beginning to feel as ill as Felan looked.

"Certainly not. I leave such menial chores to those beneath me. Ranur killed many of them, though I believe he allowed several of his favored Riders to claim the well-formed women for a time, so long as they disposed of them properly when finished and returned their bodies to the courtyard."

Selene choked down the bile that had risen to her throat. Felan did not do nearly so well with his.

"I would rather that they were all of pure bone," Damaeus continued, oblivious of Felan's retching. "They are far more deadly in that form. No insect will touch them, regrettably, and most any beast that would eat their flesh would likely be killed. Thus, we are forced to wait."

Selene thought back to all of the bloodsoul she had encountered. It was true that she had not seen so much as a single fly upon them, even the ones she had encountered in late summer when insects were upon most anything that held the slightest scent of decay.

"But how did they come to be what they are?" she managed. "Killing a person is simple enough, but there is no known way of creating a Bloodsoul."

"There is no commonly known way," Damaeus corrected. "A solution can be found for any problem, so long as a person takes the time to properly search. The item of magic that I used at first was misplaced, in part due to my ignorance. I was planning on making another, but I have no need to do so now. By happenstance I obtained the Marked One from whose bone the token was made. I cherish him above all of my Marked Ones save you, for he is both supremely obedient and valuable. I suppose such is the temperament of all Marked Ones who were trained by the Kerell."

"I wish to see him," Selene said at once. What sort of man would willingly create these creatures? She did not know anything of the Kerell, and the awe with which Damaeus spoke the name filled her with morbid curiosity.

"Perhaps when we are finished here. The day grows short and I have sent him to rest. We must see to your final latent ability."

Selene would have gladly taken charge of Ranur and his Riders rather than command the mass of death that milled below. She backed a few paces from the railing. Damaeus placed his arm around her shoulders. His stench overpowered that which wafted from the courtyard.

"Bloodsoul have no mind for anything save destruction," he said. "They cannot be forced to obey by magic or alchemy. Any killing would be purely upon the whim of their rotted minds."

"Which is why you have need of me," Selene said quietly. This place made any sound above a whisper seem improper, perhaps due to the large number of dead beings in residence. Damaeus' fingers were like cold blades against the flesh of her arm. She wished that she had remembered to unroll her sleeves after the bout with Felan.

"Indeed." The Mage's head rested at an unusual angle for several seconds before returning to a natural position. He offered Selene an unbound length of parchment. "You must read this and accept what it offers."

"What manner of magic is it?"

"It is a variation of Kerell written magic. It is meant to wake the latent abilities of Marked Ones; both those which are wild-caught and those raised in captivity. Most spells of this type are open, meaning that any Marked One may activate their magic. This version can be activated only by those with a mark of Raven."

"I have no Mages' talent," Selene said stubbornly. "I cannot read words of magic."

"It is true that Marked Ones cannot be born with Mages' ability. It is an honor afforded only to those of the pure human race. The Kerell are well aware of this and have accounted for it. Looking upon the first letter of the parchment will activate a lesser spell of understanding. Because you are of Raven affinity you will then be able to read the parchment with no difficulty. They are the same words that were etched into Luca's knife. You do remember reading those words, do you not?"

"I don't want to do this," Selene said. It was not a lie. "I cannot."

"We must each risk some small thing for the good of the Realm. You will read it."

Selene glanced at the scroll momentarily before looking to Felan. He turned from her gaze. She had seen enough of his expression to recognize it as disgust.

Selene made no move to take the scroll.

Damaeus crooked a pale finger and whispered something beneath her hearing. Felan slid across the balcony and through the opening in the railing.

Selene grasped frantically for her levitation ability in attempt to stop his fall. It would not come. Pain lanced through her head and warm blood leaked from beneath her Circlet. One corner of Damaeus' mouth twisted into a smile.

She reached the edge of the balcony in time to see Felan slam against the frozen ground. He did not move. Her breath held until she heard him moan in pain. It ceased once again as hundreds of Bloodsoul became still. The creatures turned in Felan's direction.

"Help him," she begged.

Damaeus gave no reply.

The Bloodsoul stood silently as if pondering the situation. The ones composed of only bones were the first to move, and they did so with speed. A low garden wall stood between Felan and the creatures. Fresh Bloodsoul were often clumsy. It would take them time to cross the obstacle. The ancient ones would climb over it in no more than a moment.

"You could help him yourself." Damaeus offered her the parchment once again.

The first Bloodsoul reached the wall and began to climb. She snatched the parchment from Damaeus' hand. The soothing feeling that she had experienced while reading the etchings of Luca's knife encompassed her once again. She embraced it as she had the pain of the Circlet and that of Felan's betrayal.

A vibrating roar filled the courtyard. Selene's consciousness lifted, as it had wished so desperately to do when she had encountered the words of magic before. She became aware of the energy that was drawn to every earthly thing. Waves of life's essence flowed in every direction; unseen and unnamed, yet forcefully present. Their types were more numerous than she could comprehend, yet somehow she knew which could be drawn for use and which were beyond her limited reach. She found her healing ability most easily amongst the intertwining rivers of essence. Next came that which she had named as levitation. They were hers, surely, yet one was missing. A vibrating cry emanated from the body below her. The final essence became known to her at once. She drew it in and allowed it to blend with her soul. The world became blissfully silent.

The feeling of frozen stone against her face was as unpleasant as it as unexpected. Selene opened her eyes and stood. Silken moss cooled the flesh of her hand as she pressed against the railing. Damaeus had disappeared, leaving her alone.

The frenzied wails of bloodsoul reached her ears. The only pleasure that touched their demented lives came upon taking something that they could never again have. They killed because they were meant to do so. The life essence of those they slaughtered blended with the magic that held their souls to the earth. It gave them strength.

The reason that she had accepted the scroll struck her like a rogue's blade. She rushed to the railing and forced herself to look below. Only snowdrifts, half melted and trampled, remained upon the far side of the courtyard. The bloodsoul converged upon the side where she had seen Felan last. She could not catch sight of him.

"*Stop*!" The words rumbled in her chest. They left her in the vibrating language of Bloodsoul.

The cries of the creatures ceased, as did the writhing of bone and rotted flesh. Several hundred heads turned upward. Their bodies swayed back and forth as they attempted to keep their balance, creating an effect much like that of a small ocean. Selene stepped carefully to the portion of the balcony over which Felan had been thrown. Eyeless voids followed her, captivated.

"*Do not harm him.*"

The Bloodsoul regarded her with curiosity. Several tilted their heads. They did not know of whom she spoke, or perhaps they did not consider what they were doing to be harm. Selene's mind raced to find a more straightforward command.

"*Move backward twenty paces,*" she said at last. "*Stay there until I command you to move.*"

The creatures shuffled to obey. They formed an unruly group at the far end of the courtyard. Selene scanned the area directly below her. In the shadows beneath the balcony lay Felan's mangled form. She reached for her levitation ability once more and found it easily. She drew the concentration that was needed to lift him to her, but then thought better of her actions. His injuries looked as if they may be serious. Moving him may kill him, even if she was careful when doing so. She had learned that from her lessons with Damaeus. *Damaeus.* She could not help but hate him after what he had done. She quickly stowed her feelings away. The Mage's thoughts were not upon her at the moment, but that could change with no warning.

Selene continued to look upon Felan, hoping that he would show some sign of life. He did not. She beseeched the Spirits that he was simply unconscious rather than dead. She was too far away to use her healing upon him, even to probe his condition. It was difficult to look away, but she would have to if she wished to save him. She was not certain that the creatures held any concept of time. They could attack again without warning, yet here was an equal chance that they would stand where they were for eternity awaiting her next command. She hoped that the latter was true.

Selene pushed through the balcony doors. She ran down the stairs and into the maze of hallways, opening each door she came across in the hope that it would lead to the courtyard. Most led to small rooms of decomposing furniture covered in layers of dust. Those rooms whose walls or ceilings had long ago collapsed were blanketed in snow. After what seemed like ages she came upon a crumbling hall that led in the direction of the courtyard. No lamps were lit along it and no windows graced its sides. It held the darkness of a clouded night. Selene pressed the fingers of one hand against the damp, crumbling stone. She held her other hand before her, advancing with uncertain steps. Darkness encompassed her, threatening at once to steal her courage and her breath. At last something cold and smooth touched her fingertips ahead.

The door creaked outward on rusted hinges. It opened just enough to allow Selene to slide through. A short stone passage opened into blinding light. Beyond that hundreds of Bloodsoul stood at attention, watching her. She had come out at the wrong end.

Selene's heartbeat quickened. She stepped towards the creatures with determination, stopping several feet from where they stood. They made no move to attack.

"*Move out of my way,*" she said.

The Bloodsoul did nothing. Their stench was nearly unbearable.

"*Create a pathway at the center of your group so that I may walk through it,*" she amended.

Her words looked to have some meaning to the creatures, for they parted as she had commanded. Selene stepped nervously forward. The path that they had created was narrow. She walked slowly amongst them, for she did not wish to do anything that may draw their ire. Many predators were momentarily confused by an unafraid animal of prey. Perhaps bloodsoul were the same.

Despite her careful movements she brushed against one as she walked. Flesh remained only upon the creature's chest, which made it an odd sight indeed. It most certainly noticed that she had touched it, but it did not seem to be angered by the fact. It simply regained what balance it had lost and continued to rock back and forth on bony feet. Selene turned her gaze to the freedom of the open space that lay beyond. The only sound was that of snow crunching beneath her feet.

She scrambled over the garden wall upon reaching it, and headed with haste through the shadows to where Felan lay. His body was curled as if in an attempt to protect his face and chest from the attack. What skin was visible beneath the shredded remains of his clothing was badly damaged. Both of his legs looked to be broken, probably from the fall, and the snow around him was tinted with blood. The sight brought Luca to mind.

Selene pressed her hand to the bare skin of Felan's back. Her mark did not burn, but instead warmed faintly. There was some life in him yet, slight though it was. She reached for her healing ability. It came to her at once.

She gathered her concentration and probed Felan's injuries. Many were external and would easily heal. The deepest of the lesions sliced through the muscle that lay between his ribs and into his right lung. She began there.

The courtyard was beginning to grow dark by the time Selene finished Felan's healing. The snow beneath her had melted and seeped through the cloth of her skirt while she knelt by his side. Winter's lingering cold attempted to claim it once again when she stood. Her head ached horribly from the extended use of her latent ability.

Felan was breathing easily now. It was only with the luck of the Tides that he had survived. It had taken what seemed like hours to fix the bones in his legs. One had broken almost cleanly, but the other certainly had not. She had used her sword to open the wound further in order to push the tiny fragments of bone back into place. She hoped that she had found all of them. It would not matter too greatly, for she had been taught that many of the smaller pieces would work themselves free with time.

Selene reached for her levitation ability. Felan's body lifted easily from the snow. It would be best to get him out of the cold without shifting him greatly. She was far stronger now than she had been when she encountered Luca's body so long ago, but lifting an unconscious person posed much the same difficulty as lifting a dead one. She had no desire to injure him further with careless movements.

The path to the doorway remained open, much to her relief. The Bloodsoul had not moved in the hours since she gave her last command. She placed Felan on the balcony near the doors so there would be no chance of him falling. She then returned to the stone passage and squeezed back inside the keep by way of the small opening through which she had come.

Selene found her way to the balcony with ease and pushed the doors aside. A feather's touch of pain crossed her hand as colored glass sliced her flesh. She did not bother with healing.

Felan slept as if the Spirits had claimed his soul. Selene gathered her concentration once again. Her head flooded with pain and the room twitched around her. She caught her balance against the nearest wall before lifting him carefully from the floor. He had lost a large amount of blood and was in need of a warm place to speed his recovery. There were only two rooms within the keep that would do. One of them belonged to Ranur.

Selene lost her way several times as she passed through the shadowed halls. By the time she found the correct hall her patience was waning. Her head felt as if it might tear in half. The thick wooden door that marked Perfidia's room was closed and no sound could be heard beyond it. It was new, like most everything in the hall. What had not been replaced had been expertly repaired. Selene set Felan upon the floor nearby. She released her latent ability with no small amount of relief. Her head did not hurt quite so horribly when it was not in use. She practiced a short breathing exercise in attempt to regain her calm, and then knocked upon the door. It opened smoothly on well-oiled hinges. Warm air rushed out to greet her.

A bitter expression hung upon Perfidia's face like salt at the edge of a tidal pool. The woman's hands found each other with haste, clasping beneath her plump stomach. It did not keep them from shaking. "Damaeus would not like it if you harmed me," she said, scrutinizing Selene with a nervous air.

Selene realized at once how she must look. She had not bothered to clean the blood that had leaked from beneath her circlet while upon the balcony, and then there was that which had splattered her clothing as she attempted to fix Felan's leg. She had spent hours kneeling in the snow and mud, and Felan's sword had clipped her once or twice during their bout, tearing her clothing.

"I am in need of your assistance."

Selene hated Damaeus all the more for what he had forced upon her.

"Is that so?" Perfidia replied suspiciously. "What sort of assistance are you in need of and what are you prepared to offer in return for my cooperation?"

Selene ground her teeth in frustration. "Can Felan stay here?" she asked. "I don't have anything to offer you. Damaeus has taken all that I had of value."

It was immediately obvious that she had gained Perfidia's interest. "You expect me to grant you a favor?" the woman replied. "Do you think that I've forgotten all that has passed between us?"

"I ask that you do this for Felan's sake," Selene said, "Not for mine." She would not forget what Perfidia said about Maye. It still angered her when brought to mind.

"The last time we spoke it seemed that you would send him to his next life rather than to me. It makes no sense that you would change your mind so suddenly."

"He is injured and unconscious." Selene gestured to Felan, who lay upon the floor just beyond Perfidia's view. "I've healed him as much as I can. He needs somewhere warm to stay and some proper food. I cannot provide him with either."

Perfidia scrutinized Felan from where she stood before turning back to Selene. "You did this to him?" A hint of concern crept into her expression.

"Do not accuse me of harming Felan," Selene said heatedly.

"Who is responsible, then?"

"Ask Damaeus. He may tell you what occurred if it pleases him." Selene would have gladly explained the situation to Perfidia if not for the fear that the magic of the Circlet would punish her for it. She was beyond exhaustion. It was unlikely that her body would tolerate much more abuse.

"Bring him in," Perfidia said as she retreated into the room.

Selene gathered her concentration for what she hoped would be the last time that day.

"Place him on the bed," Perfidia offered as she closed the door behind them.

Selene obeyed. She accepted the chair that was offered with as much grace as she could manage, but declined the cup of tea which Perfidia held out to her. She did not trust the woman nearly enough for that.

The room was lavishly decorated, though it was far smaller than that which Perfidia had enjoyed in Evaria. It looked as the rest of the Keep must have in its prime years, with thick patterned carpets and polished wood furniture. The doors to what Selene assumed to be the balcony were set with pieces of colored glass placed in such a way as to create a scene. Selene puzzled over the nude male figures depicted within it. They were human save for the feathered wings that sprouted from their backs. Such odd creatures could only be the work of a vivid imagination, for even if humans were to grow wings they would most certainly be of flesh rather than feathers. Selene had seen such creatures only once before; in a book of the Ancients that she had borrowed from King Graelen's library.

"I will care for Felan until he has healed." Perfidia seated herself in a chair across from Selene.

"Thank you." It pained her to say it, for the woman was partly responsible for what had happened to him.

"As payment," Perfidia began.

"I don't have anything to give you," Selene interrupted, pressing her fingers to her aching temples. "I told you as much." The flames within the limestone hearth, which lay directly behind Perfidia, gave off enough light to worsen the ache in her head. If she did not rest soon her body might force her to do so. She did not relish the idea of passing out while in Perfidia's presence.

"Tell me what this does," Perfidia said, holding up a tiny glass vial for Selene's inspection. "That will be payment enough. I do have some small interest in Felan's welfare despite what you think of me."

Selene recognized the vial as the one Damaeus had given her to use upon the white falcon early in their journey.

"You have all of my things," Selene said stubbornly. "I should think that that would be payment enough."

"We do not have to make this deal," Perfidia replied. "Felan can recover elsewhere if you would rather. It is obvious that Damaeus does not care what happens to him. He will not force me to take him in."

What she said was true. It was for that reason, amongst others, that Selene had decided to come to Perfidia on her own.

"It's a bit of alchemy which was given to me by your brother. He was trying to gain my favor, I assume. I saw a falcon in the forest and had thoughts of taming it. He gave me the potion shortly afterward, saying that if the falcon consumed some of its contents it would bend to my will."

"Why go to such trouble?" Perfidia asked. "It takes time to create a potion, as Damaeus is so fond of reminding me. Even falcons of the best breeding are not costly. You could have easily purchased one. Failing that, Damaeus could have purchased one for you."

Selene frowned. What was of little cost to Perfidia would easily take a common man a lifetime to earn. "This one was of an unusual color," she replied at last.

"It was white." Perfidia clutched the vial eagerly. "It must have been."

"Yes," Selene replied wearily. "It was white." She could not understand how the color of a bird that she had seen months ago could possibly be of any importance.

Felan mumbled in his sleep. His eyes began to open.

"It is time for you to go," Perfidia said as she tucked the potion away in a gilded chest that sat upon the mantel. "You have my word that Felan will be properly cared for."

Perfidia's word was worth no more than a glass of watered down ale in Selene's opinion, but circumstance had left her little choice in the matter. She reluctantly left the warmth of the room. Perfidia closed the door behind her, and Selene heard the hard metallic clicks of a lock being turned.

Selene lingered in the hallway for a moment. She would have slept where she was if she thought Damaeus would allow it, for it was far warmer here that it was on the floors beneath. The Mage had kept his word. He allowed Selene to go where she pleased within the keep. Nonetheless, she knew that sleeping in Damaeus' hallway would be overstepping her bounds. She left the hall and started down the stairs. The temperature dropped as she descended, sending chills through her still damp clothing. She walked in a daze. The fire in her room's tiny hearth would have gone cold by this time, but she had a feeling that by the time she arrived there it would not matter.

Something small and dark lay in a pile at the side of the hall near the entrance to Selene's room. The flame of a tarnished lamp burned weakly nearby. It was the only light within twenty feet of her door and it was not mirrored, which made it rather difficult to see. She approached carefully.

"Cyanna," she said upon realizing that the pile was a friend rather than an object.

The cat's head lifted at the sound of her name. Selene was not certain why Damaeus forced the girl to remain in animal form. She did not dare to ask him. She picked Cyanna up. The hinges that held her door in place screeched angrily as she forced it open. She was certain that Cyanna wore a Circlet, though it could not be seen. Damaeus would not let a Marked One wander the keep without one. According to the mage the metal of the Circlet temporarily combined with a Marked One's body when they transformed, and it returned to its regular form when they reversed their affinity. She did not believe it to be true until she caught sight of Cyanna.

Selene placed Cyanna upon her bed. She folded a blanket several times and placed it over the little cat, leaving her head free. She then moved to the windowsill where she had stored a hand-sized portion of boar's meat from her lunch. She often kept food for Cyanna. The girl survived off of what little she could find on the floor after the Riders had finished their meals. It was not enough to keep her weight up. Aside from that, it was dangerous for a Marked One to enter any place where Ranur could be found.

Selene set the meat before Cyanna, who ate it eagerly. She wished that she could speak with the girl, but perhaps it was best that she could not. She was not certain that she wished to hear what had been done to her.

Selene pulled several pieces of wood from the pitifully small pile that Damaeus had allowed her and placed them into the hearth. The ache in her head returned with full force each time she stood. The fire came to life with a bit of stirring and some tinder. After checking on Cyanna, whose breathing was deep and even, Selene crawled beneath her remaining blanket. She lay back against her pillow and allowed sleep to claim her.

Breaking

The door to Selene's room struck the wall behind it with a crash, sending a waterfall of stone pieces cascading to the floor to land amongst narrow stretches of mid-morning light.

"Transform," he said. His tone made her certain that it was not a request.

Cyanna's fur bristled and her ears flattened. She bolted from Selene's blanket to hide beneath the bed.

"Was my order not plain enough?" Damaeus asked, hovering over Selene in a manner that made her wish that she could join Cyanna in hiding. He was dressed in Mage's robes of deep red, which did nothing to improve the pallor of his skin.

Selene sat up, using the wall behind her mattress for leverage. She attempted to make sense of what he had said, but sleep muddled her thoughts.

Damaeus scowled. He raised a hand towards her. Selene moved back as best she could. He did not strike her, but instead muttered something under his breath. She could not understand his words, but her Circlet warmed as he spoke. Pain encompassed her with the speed of a storm at sea, but was not the familiar pain that Damaeus' anger was known to cause. It was the pain of using her affinity, and it was amplified by her Circlet.

Selene cried out in agony as her body transformed. The harsh metal combined with her flesh, spreading its bitter essence through her body and thus claiming it in the Mage's name. She gasped for air upon reaching her raven form.

Selene's clothing lay heavily upon her. She found the pressure, and the darkness that came with it, to be

---

comforting. She would have allowed it to embrace her forever, but cold hands grasped her feet. She was dragged into the light.

The mildly sweet scent of death surrounded her. Damaeus had been in the bloodsoul courtyard.

"I offered you a choice," he said, extending his arm as falconers did with their charges. "I consider this to be fair. If only you had joined me of your own will, and had simply read the scroll when it was offered to you." The corners of his mouth turned up into a humorless smile. There was little humanity within his expression. "This is for the better perhaps, for now I can do as I wish with you."

Standing did not come easily. Damaeus righted her and she climbed upon his arm.

"And now to breakfast," he said, ushering her up to his shoulder.

The journey was not smooth by any means. Selene found it difficult to keep her balance as Damaeus made his way through the halls and down several sets of stairs. He stopped at last before the doors that led to the Riders' dining area. The noise of many voices slipped through cracks in the wood, accompanied most noticeably by the scents of sweat and anticipation. Overshadowing both was the aroma of death, thick and pure. Selene drew a breath in attempt to clear her mind. With the stale air came a tangle of information. Some of the meat being served was nearing rancid, though heavy garlic and a mix of other spices had been used upon it to disguise the fact. A few of the men had already begun drinking as well. Heavy liquor rather than the watered down ale most Riders favored in the morning.

"You will use your ability to open doors as I near them," Damaeus ordered.

Selene had never used any of her latent abilities while in animal form. Xaiden said that it was beyond difficult to do so.

"The Circlet will aid you. There are few ways to anger me more easily than disobeying an order I have given."

Selene reached for her latent ability and found it, much to her chagrin. The doors to the dining hall swung open.

The room writhed with movement, and the noise was so loud as to be nearly unbearable. The scents that had reached her beyond the door blended with a hundred others of lesser strength.

Riders moved readily aside as Damaeus made his way through the center of the room. Quarters were close and so tempers ignited with the ease of a flame to late summer fields. A fight broke out between two Riders who were not yet old enough to grow full beards. Selene sidled towards Damaeus' head, watching the men nervously.

"Give it over," the first one said. His look was like that of most other untested Riders, though a rather detailed inking of a nude woman with legs spread graced his left forearm.

"Leave off," the other grumbled, turning his back to the first. "You've had enough fare for the king's left quarter. This bit's mine." He said something more, most of which was impossible to understand through the din. Selene was able to catch two words: Marked, and bastard.

It soon became apparent that the first Rider had heard the insult as well, for the sound of metal rang through the air as swords and axes were drawn. A few Riders shuffled to one side, but most readied themselves to enter the fray. Selene had worked with their type a few times on errand. The Praecyrs of the Realm generally attempted to stay within the law for fear of reprisal by the king, but many Riders would do whatever they pleased the moment they were out of their Praecyr's view. It seemed that Damaeus gathered only men of that sort to work under Ranur's command.

A gust of air ruffled the feathers of Selene's chest. The noise of the room lessened suddenly, leaving only low conversation. The man with the nude inking toppled into the aisle with a grunt. An arrow jutted from his right eye.

Selene twisted to see the source. There she found a small balcony. Ranur leaned upon the railing, surveying the scene below. It was then that cold and familiar fear began to slither its way into Selene's soul. Ormun, who stood by Ranur's side, lowered his bow to the floor. He ran a hand through his greasy hair and snatched a pewter mug from the table.

"Move him," Damaeus commanded.

Selene tossed the body aside. It collided with several Riders who were standing nearby, which caused Damaeus' lips to turn up into a smile. The sounds of the room escalated to a roar once again and the Riders continued on as if nothing out of the ordinary had occurred. Selene was not surprised by it. She imagined that this sort of thing was common amongst them.

A wooden table with room for no more than six lay ahead upon a low stone platform. Only one chair sat behind it. Selene struggled to remain upon Damaeus' shoulder as he sat.

A young serving girl set a plate of meat before them with quaking hands. She had a fine face, though it held the shallowness that starvation tended to bring. Her scent was one of fear. Damaeus paid the girl no notice. She bowed low as she backed away from the Mage and stumbled down the few steps that led to the platform. Her awkward movements brought the attention of several Riders who were eating nearby. The closest of them grabbed at her clothing, drawing her towards him. He brought his face to her hair, breathing in her scent for a moment before biting down upon her neck. The girl cried out in fear, which caused his companions to erupt into laughter. It also drew the attention of others. Selene grasped at her levitation ability. It would not come. She pushed her talons through the fabric of Damaeus' robe and into the flesh beneath. He glanced at her, but showed neither pain nor any inclination to aid the girl. The scents of panic and stimulation mingled strongly. The serving girl was torn from the grip of one Rider only to be taken by another. Her screams pierced Selene's hearing like a lance. The Rider who had first grabbed the girl pushed her to the floor and jumped upon her, loosening his belt as he did so. It was then that Damaeus raised a hand.

"Not here," he said. "*Igniria enchalist proprenius imapratalus corpus. Emana enleteni.*"

What seemed to be no more than mumbling while Selene was in human form was easily received by her improved hearing.

Flames, a color of blue as deep as the ocean's depths, engulfed the Rider. The girl's screaming ceased as the man atop her was rendered to no more than dust. The other Riders returned to their food without protest, though they continued to leer at the dust-covered girl as she lay paralyzed upon the floor.

Selene fluffed her feathers in an attempt to keep the cold of the room from touching her skin. A low whistle met her ears. It emanated from Ranur, who stood at the edge of the balcony. He eyed the serving girl. His expression made Selene shiver even at such a distance. He looked to Damaeus, who responded with an indifferent wave. Ranur touched Ormun's shoulder then and said something shortly. He received a nod in return. The Praecyr then pushed through the doors at the back of the balcony and disappeared.

"Take her upstairs," Damaeus commanded two Riders who stood near the girl.

Both bowed with more respect than Selene had thought them capable of. The girl became limp at their touch. They dragged her between tables and through the hall's double doors.

"Eat," Damaeus said, offering a small chunk of meat to Selene. It did not smell as much of decay as the meat that Damaeus' Riders were eating, but Selene was not inclined to consume anything while thoughts of the unfortunate serving girl shifted about in her head.

"Nothing I say from this point forth should be taken as a request," Damaeus reminded her.

Selene choked down the first piece and the few that followed it. They formed an uncomfortable lump in her stomach. Damaeus watched her. He ate nothing. It seemed that the food had been brought specifically for Selene. When she had finished most of what was upon the plate Damaeus rose from his seat.

The Mage found his way through the darkened halls without aid of a torch or lamp. The knot in Selene's stomach grew larger with each staircase they descended. Damaeus' gait became uneven as they slowed. The sound of scattering rodents rattled along the area beside an odd scraping noise that Selene could not identify.

"*Igniria quiatt-fornaxus faxeneus,*" Damaeus said in a whisper like sand falling upon stone.

Torches mounted in brackets of rusted metal caught flame, only to sputter and die before a minute had passed. A long hall flanked with prison chambers flashed briefly into view. The walls were thick stone and each chamber held a single door and small window of metal bars.

"*Igniria quiatt-fornaxus faxeneus,*" the Mage repeated irritably.

The torches lit once again. Their fires burned brightly this time, yet the brackets were so sparingly placed that the chambers' interiors remained in darkness. Foul smelling water dripped from the multitude of cracks that ravaged the ceiling, rusting metal bars where it touched them and leaving vein-like streaks of reddish brown upon the walls and floor beneath. Damaeus stopped so unexpectedly that Selene nearly tumbled from his shoulder. The Mage lifted his hand up to her, and she reluctantly stepped upon it. He placed her upon the floor.

The death-squeal of a rat was followed with a soft, squishing sound and what could only be the crunching of bones. Something thudded against a nearby wall. Fetid water sprayed Selene as the object hit the ground. She was thankful that it had landed in shadow, but appreciation turned quickly to shock as Damaeus spoke.

"*Infula raemes seirus.*"

Metal was torn from flesh to reform upon Selene's forehead. Her body snapped back to human form, leaving her naked and shivering upon the damp floor.

"Stand," Damaeus said, "and do not look upon me with such disgust. You rejected my offer and yet I still allow you the chance to be feared and respected by all. You did not choose to join me, but the masses will not know of it. They will think of us as one force working to purge the Ethereal Realm of Marked Ones and of one unfit to rule, all in the name of peace. But first, you must learn."

Selene lifted herself from the floor. "You will have nothing from me but hatred," she said, ignoring the rush of searing pain that accompanied the words.

"I shall have whatever I desire, for you are mine," Damaeus said, taking the whole of her in his gaze. "Beauty, power and anger combined."

He ran a frigid hand across her bare breasts.

Bile burned Selene's throat. Her Circlet warmed as she moved to strike him. Her knees struck the ground, jarring her bones to the hip. Damaeus' vibrating laughter cascaded over her as she knelt helpless upon the floor. The warmth of her tears mingled with that of the blood that flowed from beneath her Circlet.

Damaeus tilted her head up. "It is much too late for me," he said. "I could not have you in that way, even if the desire remained. But I shall have you in all others."

Selene stood once again. For the first time since the beginning of her journey she allowed fear to claim her.

Damaeus pushed her so that she faced the rusted bars of a cell door.

"Open it."

Something paced the back wall, blanketed by shadows. A low vibrating groan proved it to be a bloodsoul.

"Power is nothing without control. You must be precise when giving commands. Picture where the creature stands now and what you wish for it to do."

Selene could not keep her hands from shaking. "*Come*," she said in a vibrating groan that sounded foreign to her ears.

Damaeus closed the short distance between them with the speed of a striking snake. He grabbed Selene's neck and tilted her head back towards him. "Precise," he hissed. "Again, and think only of him."

Selene shifted her feet through the icy muck of the floor. They were nearly numb. She turned to face the chamber once more and thought of the bloodsoul within it.

"*Stand before me.*"

Gaping holes in the creature's chest and neck shifted as it ambled into the light. The flesh of its face was surprisingly whole and Selene could not help but stare. It could be no one but Terran.

"Continue."

Damaeus shoved her against the cell. Rusted metal scraped against the naked skin of her chest. Her nose was nearly touching the creature that had once been Terran, yet he made no move to grab her.

"*Move back five paces*," she choked, attempting not to breathe in the scent of him. She did not succeed. The room spun sickeningly around her.

Terran retreated as he had been ordered. He stared at her, rapt. She could hardly bear to look upon him.

Damaeus pushed Selene aside. The chamber door screamed in protest as he forced it open. Still, Terran did not move. The Mage approached him.

"Once more. And be certain to concentrate upon him."

"*Sit.*" It was the only command she could think of. Terran did so, though it was far from graceful.

"Well enough. Send him to the Bloodsoul courtyard."

Selene assumed that simply ordering the creature to go to the courtyard would not end well, thus she gave him directions as accurately as she could remember in the form of paces and turns.

Damaeus seemed pleased despite everything that had occurred. "You will follow," he said as he started for the stairs.

"But I have no clothes," Selene protested. A brief flicker of pain pierced her skull.

"I know very well what you do and do not have. I know that your consciousness drowns in a mix of hatred, agony, humiliation, and cold misery. Each feeling travels perfectly through the magic of the Circlet and each brings me pleasure. Beauty should be open for all to see. Now, follow."

Selene thought of the serving girl and of Ranur's expression as he watched her from the balcony.

"But where are we going?" she asked, fearing to know the answer.

"That is none of a Rakaii's concern," Damaeus replied.

Reunion at the Keep

Spring's first breath was tainted by the wafting scent of decay. It was at once familiar and discouraging. Islyr's first spring beyond the abyss would be spent in servitude. It was far more difficult to serve another now that he had experienced a few short years of freedom. He knew that with time the urge to leave would ease somewhat. He did not wish it to do so.

The dead man's eyes were as clouded as the sky above. He was like most of Damaeus' Riders; unkempt but well-built. Islyr turned aside to pull a breath. The scent of this one was terrible, like singed hair. A good portion of a long, black beard remained, and three metal rings pierced what had once been his left brow. The latter would loosen as his flesh rotted. The gold band that surrounded his neck would most likely stay, at least until he got into his first battle. The man's clothing was melted in places, and nothing but bone remained of the right side of his head. Killed by magic of some sort. True fire would not consume flesh so thoroughly and leave bone without a mark upon it.

Islyr lifted his head from his work as Damaeus stepped onto the balcony.

"How many have been completed?" the Mage asked.

Damaeus' dark robes fluttered as a gust of wind reached them. The fabric was clean and well kept, in stark contrast to what flesh was visible around it.

"This is the last of them, Master Damaeus."

Islyr pushed the dead Rider over the open edge of the balcony before he could rise and turn against him. It unnerved him to look upon his creations on any normal occasion. Seeing them as they were now frightened him more than he would ever admit. It was unnatural for Bloodsoul to stand in one place as these did; in swaying groups at the far end of the courtyard. Those that he had created most recently wandered freely, making the strange behavior of the others stand out all the more.

"Very well. You are dismissed for the moment. I shall call you when I have need of you."

"I understand, Master." Islyr had foolishly assumed that Damaeus would be content once the last of the people of Lystonne had been turned into unearthly creatures. He had been wrong. Dead Riders trickled into the castle carried by their brethren, who showed no more expression than the rock walls of the abyss. With each new death came more work for Islyr's latent ability. Damaeus did not care how many members of his human army were lost, for he considered them much more useful in Bloodsoul form.

"May I ask something of you, Master Damaeus?"

"You may, though I may not provide an answer if your question is inappropriate."

"The Marked One who is to command this army," Islyr said as he gestured to the courtyard below, "would you allow me to speak with him?"

One corner of Damaeus' mouth inched upward to form a sickly half-smile. "The particular Marked One you speak of is female, and was once Aranth. She is in what was once the Throne Room at this particular moment. You may converse with her if you so desire, providing that you do not disregard any of the rules that I have set for you."

It would seem that Damaeus was greatly amused by something Islyr had said. Islyr swallowed his irritation. "You are kind to allow this, Master Damaeus," he replied, bending at the waist.

Damaeus turned thoughtfully to the courtyard.

Islyr pushed open the balcony doors, intending to leave. The Mage often ignored him, drifting into what looked to be deep contemplation. Then again, it could also be that he was having difficulty concentrating, or even forming coherent thoughts. Islyr had found that it was best just to leave him in such situations, so long as he had previously gained permission to do so.

"Islyr," Damaeus called.

Islyr released the balcony door and turned to face him.

"I forbid you to tell her who you are."

Islyr puzzled over Damaeus' words for a moment. "I am not certain that I understand," he said at last. He had no desire to disobey his Holder, inadvertently or otherwise. He tolerated pain well, but he did not take pleasure in it.

"Mention neither your given name nor your family name in her presence. Tell her nothing of your background, your parents, siblings, nor of friends you may have had in your youth. Do not speak anything of the life you lived before becoming Rakaii. Above all, do not ask another to do the task in your stead. It will bring great pain to you both."

"As it pleases you Master," Islyr replied. Damaeus must have some reason for giving such an unusual and seemingly unfounded order, though he could not imagine what it might be.

"You may go," Damaeus said before returning to his trance.

"Thank you, Master."

Damaeus did not take notice of his words.

Islyr thought it strange that Damaeus had managed to find two marked females. The striped cat bound with an iron collar was one as well, if what Felan said was true. Female Marked Ones commanded such coin at auction that only the wealthiest of the Kerell could afford to bid upon them. Islyr had only come into contact with one whilst under Mistress Nevane's care, at a time when it had come into her head to breed him. He pitied the girl still, for she had been born and reared in captivity and would never know anything of freedom. Islyr pressed his hand against his Rakaii inking. Some memories were best left buried, he decided at once.

He descended the set of stairs that led to the main hall. Felan lingered near the door to the Throne Room with his back against the wall. He looked to be in better condition than he had since Islyr first met him. He was glad of it, for he would need strength on his side when opportunity to leave this place finally presented itself. Felan's hand rested upon the pommel of his sword so naturally that Islyr would have guessed him to be either Rider or Aranth even without knowing him. Islyr had recently decided that all Aranth must be Marked. One member could have passed through the training unnoticed, but the presence of three formed a much heavier load than coincidence could bear. It would explain Damaeus' hatred for the Aranth and the King, for he considered any Marked One without a Circlet to be a danger to the Ethereal Realm. The army that Islyr had created was Damaeus' answer to that threat.

Islyr nodded his head in greeting upon approaching the man. Felan returned the gesture. His clothing was finer than anything Islyr had been given, he noticed, but he supposed that was to be expected considering the man's position with Perfidia.

"Do you have time to spare?" Islyr asked.

"Some," Felan replied. "Mistress Perfidia requested that I be in her room by noon hour."

"My question will take no more than a moment. Do you know where I might find the female Marked One? Not the one who is trapped in her Affinity, but the other."

"Damaeus gave you permission?" Felan asked, raising a brow questioningly.

"Of course. I wouldn't attempt it otherwise."

Felan gazed at the floor for a moment.

"I'm not sure that you'll be pleased to see her, if you are who I think you to be." He glanced uneasily towards the throne room.

"I've never met her," Islyr replied. "Damaeus didn't give me so much as her name. He did say that she isn't to know who I am, though I don't know why."

"The moment she arrived here he ordered me not to speak of you in her presence. If you really wish to meet her I won't be the one to convince you otherwise," Felan said evasively. "But you know her much better than Damaeus would lead you to believe."

Islyr retained his doubts. "We shall see," he said simply.

"You've yet to keep your promise," Felan reminded him.

"You must be patient. I will honor our deal when the time comes."

"I have no choice in the matter, do I? I haven't had a choice in anything since the night of my capture."

"A path that is dark at first may turn to light in time," Islyr replied.

"Sounds like something Xaiden would say," Felan muttered.

"Is Xaiden of the Kerell? That wisdom comes from the Book of Life, upon which the religion of the Kerell is based."

"I very much doubt that he is," Felan replied. "Selene?" he called into the throne room.

Islyr thought at first that he had misheard what was said.

"You're still here?" Selene asked, entering the hall. She wore a dress of deep green, the cut of which did not look at all suited for sparring. "I thought you were to meet Perfidia. She'll be angry with you." She was far from the shy little girl that Islyr had played games of adventure with beneath the Elder's awning. This woman was fit enough to be a battle Rakaii, though she lacked the scars of one. She had their mother's eyes, and within them lay an air of determination that he had once associated only with Maye.

Islyr felt more than foolish. He had stayed in the abyss for years thinking that his absence would keep his sister and mother from harm. He should have returned to protect them; to take them where no Mage would find them. Then again, Selene did not look to be in need of his aid. She seemed to have done quite well for herself, at least before meeting Damaeus. And who would presume to protect an Aranth? They were beyond human. No man could best them. No man except the great Master Damaeus. The Mage knew that time and the Rakaii inking that crossed Islyr's face made him nigh unrecognizable to those from his distant past. The man's cruelty truly had no boundaries.

"You are the one who created the Bloodsoul," Selene said.

Islyr watched as her eyes turned from green to stormy grey. The sight brought a long forsaken sense of familiarity. He could not help but laugh.

"What is it that you find so amusing?"

"The irony of life," Islyr said calmly. "You wish to kill me."

"You cannot know my thoughts."

"True, but I have come across many Marked Ones whose only desire was to Send me. The expression is unmistakable."

"Don't fight me then," Selene said, drawing her sword. "I will make your death swift. It is for the good of the Realm."

She had their mother's eyes, but her fortitude echoed that of their father.

"Selene, no!" Felan's sword met hers. "You do not want to do this."

"He turned a town of innocents to abominations of nature. He created the army that will destroy the peace of the Ethereal Realm. Any marked one that doesn't have an affinity or latent ability of use will be slaughtered by his bloodsoul, and you'll let him walk free? The Spirits keep Damaeus and the both of you!" She touched her free hand to her forehead. The pain of the Circlet would grow stronger as she continued to speak ill of Damaeus. The thought of anything harming his sister angered Islyr.

"You are to control that army, Selene," Felan reminded her. "Perhaps you and he should both be slain for the good of the Realm."

Selene lowered her sword. She seemed more distressed than frightened.

"I will not be the one to do it, though," Felan continued, "for I don't believe that your actions were of your own will. Either of you."

"Enough," Damaeus commanded.

Only the Spirits knew where he had come from. There was no warning. The cloying scent that had followed the Mage for far longer than seemed possible had disappeared quite suddenly several days ago, making his presence infinitely more difficult to detect.

Although Damaeus' attention was clearly upon Islyr he could not sense it. He hoped that Damaeus was having the same difficulty in reading the thoughts of his Rakaii as they were in sensing his.

The Mage frowned. He raised a pale hand in Selene's direction. "You *will* learn to submit."

Selene's sword dropped to the floor. She winced in pain and cradled her head in her hands. Blood leaked from beneath her Circlet and dripped to the floor, highlighting the tiny cracks in the stone. It made Islyr's stomach tighten in an uncomfortable way. He recognized the feeling after a moment's time. It was fear. He thought that he had left it behind in the land of the Kerell.

Selene lifted her head after what seemed like half of Islyr's lifetime. It was not pain or fear that showed upon her face, but rather hatred and defiance.

"Do not lift your sword against this Marked One again," Damaeus ordered. "Your next act of disobedience will be Felan's last breath. Do you understand?"

"Yes, Master Damaeus," Selene said. "My apologies."

"For what reason did you attempt to attack him?"

"He said something that I did not care for," Selene lied. "An insult to myself and Felan."

"Save your violent thoughts. In one week's time the war will begin. It is then that you will need them."

"Yes, Damaeus," Selene reached up to wipe the streaks of blood that marked her face.

"Leave it."

Selene lowered her hand.

"I have sealed your latent abilities. Go with Felan to Perfidia's room. Do whatever she asks of you."

Felan started away. Selene followed him with a scowl, but not before retrieving her sword from where it lay.

"If only all Marked Ones were so obedient as those which are Kerell trained," Damaeus said, motioning for Islyr to follow him away from the entrance to the Throne Room and down the hall. "What did you say to draw her ire?"

Islyr was fully prepared for the question. "She is impatient for the war to begin so that she may show you what her army is capable of achieving. She said that you are foolish for waiting so long to begin your attack, and that the King will gain advantage if we wait any longer. I replied that a proper Rakaii would never question his Master's wisdom. She took offense to my words, perhaps because neither she nor Felan are Kerell trained."

"Selene is easily riled," Damaeus mused. "She is eager in most tasks since I managed to shatter her will a few weeks ago, yet it seems that pride has not yet abandoned her completely. Perhaps some time with Ranur could cure her of it."

Islyr knew well what Ranur would do to Selene. Those who did not survive Ranur's attention were sent to the Bloodsoul courtyard. The ones who retained their lives were those who should be pitied. Islyr had seen worse amongst the Kerell. At that time he had found peace in the fact that his mother and sister would never suffer such torture.

"Do you not think so?" Damaeus regarded Islyr closely.

"I am not in a position to know such things, Master Damaeus," Islyr replied as they turned from a mildly familiar hall to one that he did not recognize in the least. The words left a bitter taste.

"That is so." Damaeus stopped suddenly. He pulled an unlit torch from the rusted bracket in which it sat, lit it with a few mumbled words, and handed it to Islyr. "I leave you here."

The nearby walls turned gradually from block-like carvings to roughly hewn stone. The passage beyond looked to be more cave than castle. Damp, chilled air pressed against Islyr's skin.

"I have a very special task for you," Damaeus informed him. "Should you complete it to my satisfaction then you will truly be the most cherished of my Rakaii."

"I will do as you command," Islyr said without pause.

"I did not think that you would say otherwise. This natural passage descends to the base of the cliff. It opens into a small cave which lies directly beneath the Keep. It is there that my enemies wait." Damaeus reached beyond the torchlight. He pulled Islyr's staff from the darkness and handed it to him. "There are four and all are marked. They are far too dangerous to be kept as Rakaii, though they would almost certainly be of great use to our cause. I will be pleased if you are able to kill at least one of them before you are slain."

"With deepest respect, Master Damaeus," Islyr said, "If I do not return then how will Selene's army grow as you wish it to?"

Damaeus pulled a white object from one of the pouches that hung at his waist. "This," he said, admiring the coin, "is something that was made of you when we first met. Your latent ability resides within it."

The right side of Islyr's chest began to ache. It was one of the few scars that he had not gained while under control of the Kerell.

"It was lost to me for a time, but one of nearly fifty Riders that were sent into the heart of the valley managed to retrieve it. Sadly he blundered into my barrier while attempting to escape the Eldai. At least he managed to fall upon the Keep side of the barrier while dying. You may remember the man, as you added him to Selene's army only a short time ago."

"I do, Master." He remembered the singed-hair scent of him well enough.

"Cael may still think you to be an ally. You should use that to your advantage. He is the most dangerous, and he is also the most likely to defeat you. You must have killed many Marked Ones in your time as a battle Rakaii. There is no difference in this save that your foes are not Circleted. Separate the group if you are able, or wait until one is alone for the best advantage."

Islyr's jaw tightened. He had hoped that Cael and Devren would not be amongst those he was ordered to kill.

"Above all, do not think to betray me. Do not speak to them. I have set your Circlet so that if you should utter but a single word while outside the Keep it will kill you. Writing your betrayal, if you are capable of doing so, will have the same effect. We stand just before that border now. I have no doubt that you are as cunning as your sister. Do not think that you have gained my trust simply because you have not yet betrayed me. Only a fool gives complete trust to anyone other than himself."

"Those are wise words, Master Damaeus," Islyr said, leaning into a sweeping bow, "though you must know that I would never betray you."

"Do not dare to return to me unless they are dead."

"Yes, Master Damaeus."

The Mage left then. Islyr reveled in the comfort of gaining his staff once more. He would not be parted with it again in this lifetime, short though it may be. He stepped past the border of the Keep and into the cave beyond.

Beneath the Keep

    Cael pressed a knuckle to his temple. His companions should have returned long ago. Xaiden thought it likely that one of the passages would lead into the Keep. Long hours passed as they attempted to find it, and each trip seemed to stretch longer than the last. Was it possible that Xaiden was becoming desperate? The thought had crossed Cael's mind more than once over the past few days. Why would he insist that they continue to enter the cave when no real progress had been made? It was dangerous for the party to be separated. He could not help but think that their time would be better spent exploring the area surrounding the cave rather than what lay within it.

    "Should we go after them?" Viverr asked. He had taken a branch from a nearby bush and was breaking small pieces from it to throw upon the fireless pit between them. "You sure we can't light this thing?" he added.

    "It wouldn't be wise." The answer would do for both questions as far as Cael was concerned.

    "I really think we should go in. We can't defeat Damaeus with just the two of us. Or were you not aware of that little tidbit? They could be dying for all you know."

    "I highly doubt that they're dying as we speak," Cael said as calmly as he could manage. "And even if we did attempt to follow them we would have no way of knowing which passage they traveled through. We would all be lost then, which would do none of us any good. They'll return soon. Have some patience."

    "Well, think on it at least." Viverr threw the last of his branch upon the ashes. He brushed the dirt from his clothing and headed for the back of the cave. "I'm going to

---

get some food. I think I've still got a little bit of smoked rabbit in my bag." He disappeared into the shadows.

Cael pressed his back against the cave wall. How in the name of the Spirits had Xaiden convinced him to stay with the rogue? A muffled thud pulled him from his thoughts. Viverr could be clumsy at times and so Cael did not think anything of the noise at first. Only as seconds of silence turned to minutes did he become uneasy.

"Viverr?" he called, rising as much as he could within the confines of the cave. The ceiling was low near the mouth of the cave, leaving just enough space so that Cael could sit in comfort. Within the length of a carriage it became high enough so that a torch would not illuminate its entirety. It made no difference, Cael supposed, for he did not have a flame of any sort at the moment. They had only one torch amongst them and it was now with Xaiden and Aurin. Cael levered his sword from its scabbard and stepped forward. The only sound to be heard was that of his steady breathing.

The clatter of falling rock came from behind him. He turned to the mouth of the cave. Several large pebbles lay upon the ground near the dead fire. He pulled his focus back to the darkness immediately, but was unable to move quickly enough. He stumbled back as something collided with his chest. The invisible enemy struck again before he could gain his balance. It forced him to the floor and leapt from his chest. The slightest of sounds brushed his hearing as his foe landed. Cael rolled to one side. A hard, striking sound came from where his head had just been. A spray of dirt struck his face. His attacker was atop him in an instant. Cael gasped for breath. He pushed at the cold, hard object that pressed against his throat, inching it slowly away. His enemy pushed back. It could only be a Marked One, for no human would have such power or speed.

Cael summoned all of his strength; both that which he had earned and that which came from the countless souls he had taken. He launched his foe towards the mouth of the cave. The attacker moved with the grace of falling water, glancing off the wall and retrieving his weapon from the floor. He lingered by the opening, his form obscured by blinding light. It was a man, Cael noticed as his eyes began to adjust. Not that it made any difference. It had attempted to kill him, which forfeited any desire Cael may have had to spare its life regardless of gender.

Cael readied his sword. Damaeus was truly an idiot if he thought that this Marked One or any other would best Cael in a fight. The man sprinted from the cave. Cael gave chase. He stopped once fully outside. The man had disappeared.

The grass at the base of the Keep was just beginning to turn to green, and the few patches of snow that winter had left behind were quickly melting beneath the rays of the sun. It made a slick surface upon which to do battle. The Marked One may be expecting Cael to lose his footing. It was not likely to happen. The man had no idea how many times Xaiden had purposely over-watered the Hollow before one of his infamous training sessions. It had irritated Cael in his younger days. He had silently thanked Xaiden for the experience many times since.

The branches of a nearby evergreen bush moved slightly as if in a breeze. It was one plant within several broken rows that looked as if they had been part of a garden long ago. The smallest of them towered well over Cael's head. His enemy could be anywhere within the mass of greenery. Cael inched closer. The Marked One stepped from within them.

Cael considered himself difficult to catch off guard, but the sight of Islyr standing before him certainly caused him to falter. Islyr was an ally. Why was he now attempting to kill him? Before a single word could work its way free from Cael's mind Islyr was upon him. Cael's back hit the ground.

Cold water seeped through his shirt and breeches. Islyr's staff pressed against his throat, ceasing his breath. Cael stared at the silver band of twisted metal that crossed the man's forehead. What damage had Damaeus inflicted upon Islyr's already tortured mind?

"Islyr," Cael choked. "Release me." Shadows crept in, obscuring Cael's vision. "Don't make me kill you."

The pressure against Cael's throat increased. Islyr was beyond salvation. It was unfortunate. Cael released his latent ability. Islyr's soul was like an Aranth blade; finely honed and sharp to the touch. It was a thing formed of skill and suppressed emotion. He took it in. It was ecstasy. Islyr's grip upon his staff loosened, freeing Cael's breathing. Cael's power snatched greedily at his essence. But it must be pulled slowly, for souls were fragile and easily broken. The result for Cael's victims was the same whether he gained all of their soul or part, but it would be wrong of him to break the soul of someone who was once a companion. A broken soul could not have another life.

Islyr's muscles relaxed. His body rolled easily aside. Cael sat up, being sure to loosen neither his hold upon the soul nor his concentration. Islyr's eyes stared into nothing. Cael had promised Xaiden that he would never again use the full force of his latent ability. He hoped that Xaiden would understand, or if he did not that he would allow him to live until Damaeus had been defeated.

Islyr's soul began to flow into him more thickly. Cael closed his eyes. He did not wish to enjoy the sensation of taking Islyr's life. His latent ability gave him no choice in the matter. Threads of emotion lay within Islyr's essence. Cael only ever received those which were strongest, and Islyr's were more powerful than most. Fear at witnessing a loved one battle against many foes. Pain at the loss of someone very dear. The emotions were old and heavily buried. His thread of hatred for the Kerell was leather-thick and easily detected, as were the early memories that resided within it. A cold steel cage and the smell of the ocean. Points of steel penetrated the bone of his skull. Needles imbedded ink within his flesh. Later memories of that time were suppressed and thus blurred. Cael was relieved that he could not see them, for they smelled of violence and cloying blood.

Islyr's love for his sister and mother was tangled with memories of early childhood, some of which Cael recognized from the pages of Selene's journal. The threads shifted to reveal hatred which was rooted more deeply than that which Islyr felt for the Kerell. Damaeus. Islyr's loathing for the Mage was pure. It was with that thread that the flood of visions began. Dead bodies by the hundreds. An army of Bloodsoul created from them with use of Islyr's latent ability. Felan, bruised and swollen so much as to be nearly unrecognizable. A skinny striped cat bound with an iron collar.

Islyr's memories became his.

Blood dripped from the silver band that crossed Selene's head. He walked with staff in hand to meet his fate. The turns of the cave were firmly stored in his memory, and the way into the Keep was clear. Viverr lay unconscious as Cael dragged him around a corner. Then came something that was at once old and new. Damaeus was dying. Tears ran down Perfidia's cheeks as she screamed in Cael's face. Cael pressed his hands to Damaeus' head. The Mage rose. Fear cascaded through him. Damaeus' flesh fell from his bones as he ordered Cael to enter the cave and kill the enemies at the base of the Keep. It was part memory and part thought. If he spoke then his Circlet would kill him. He would sacrifice his life. It was the only way to ensure Damaeus' defeat and Selene's freedom.

Cael opened his eyes. A faint smile crossed Islyr's lips.

Cael panicked. Nearly half of the man's soul was within him. *Release.* He would give his own life twice over if just this once he could pull back his latent ability. He attempted to reverse the rush of essence, but his latent ability would not allow it. Its only purpose was to pull souls from their rightful place. It had been an eternity since the last soul, Novalin's soul, had been added to his own. His latent ability knew it, and it did not wish to let go of this new and unexpected find. The threads of essence slowed to a trickle, but refused to cease. Cael's vision blurred with the effort.

Light glanced unnaturally from the Circlet that rested upon Islyr's forehead. It was what Kerell masters used to control their Rakaii. But this one was different. Something more than Islyr's soul lay within. A second soul was connected, if only by a slender thread. Cael's Latent Ability pulled at it greedily. It was slick and as dark as the base of the Crimson Abyss. Such power lay within it that Islyr's soul was all but forgotten. The new thread fought against him as no other soul had, but his latent ability would not give in. Cael's eyes watered as agony filled his mind. The new soul would not be taken. It would poison them both to escape from his grasp. His latent ability recoiled, releasing its prize in an attempt to protect him. The soul slithered away leaving nothing behind.

Cael clutched his head as he waited for the pain to subside. The void within his chest was far from pleasant. Something struck the mud nearby. He looked up to see Islyr sitting. His forehead was bare. It was marked by gaping holes with even spaces between them.

"Thought you weren't able to reverse your latent ability," Islyr said as he pressed a finger to one of the holes experimentally. The man looked pale, as if some pain lingered. He looked at the fallen Circlet and smiled as if he could not help but do so.

"I can't," Cael replied. "It seems that the Circlet attaches the Mage's soul to his Rakaii in some way. My latent ability attempted to take his as well as yours. It seems that he did not wish for that to occur."

"Damaeus most likely thinks that I'm dead. I owe you my life and my freedom."

The words seemed odd to Cael, perhaps because they came from someone whose life he had been attempting to take only seconds ago. "I suppose that makes us even."

Islyr nodded. "I passed your friends on the way here, though they didn't sense my presence. One was reluctant to turn back while the other argued that they should continue on. It is unlikely that they'll find the entrance to the Keep without a guide. The passages of the cave must look very similar to the eyes of someone who is unused to living in a place of darkness and stone."

"The tall one is Aurin," Cael informed him. "The other is Xaiden. They, along with Viverr, are the only ones I could gather. The rest are with Damaeus, as you know."

"Devren isn't with you?"

"No, his father thought it best that he stay at the castle where he can be protected. The boy protested of course, but it did him no good."

"We can gather our supplies and meet them as soon as Viverr wakes." Islyr removed his shirt and wrapped it around his right hand, which he then used to retrieve his Circlet from the muddy ground. "I do not like to touch them," he explained. "There is a chance that Damaeus may still be able to sense me, as well."

Cael's clothing pressed wetly against him as he followed Islyr back to the cave. Once there they started a small fire to dry themselves. It was not likely that Damaeus would notice it given what he had recently learned of the mage. Islyr dragged Viverr out from where he lay.

"Didn't need to strike him," Cael said. "He most likely would have passed out at the sight of you."

"So he should after what he's put me through," Islyr replied as he pulled Viverr's satchel from where it lay and placed his Circlet into it.

"Is it true that Damaeus is Bloodsoul?" Cael asked after a moment.

"I'm the only one that knows of it save for Perfidia. She's the one who forced me to use my latent ability on him long ago. I can only assume that he has somehow slowed the decay of his body with mage's arts or alchemy, for you would not be able to tell that he is bloodsoul simply by looking at him."

"He has turned almost completely then? He'll lose his mind as they do?"

"Perhaps," Islyr replied. "The scent of decay that followed him is no longer present. I would say that he had found a cure for his state, but he looks altogether unwell and I've heard mention that some of his more recent spells have not worked as they should. This makes our task considerably more complicated. There is no known way to dispose of a bloodsoul, though if we can get to Selene then something may be done about it."

"Bloodsoul?" Viverr squeaked. "Are they near?" He caught sight of Islyr as he was attempting to stand. "What's he doing here? You're sitting around having a chat with him as if he hasn't just tried to beat me to death?"

"Calm down, Viverr. He only knocked you out. There isn't much that could leak out of your head, in any event."

"I don't find that amusing," Viverr replied.

"Islyr was saying that we may be able to dispose of Damaeus if Selene can be found," Cael informed him.

Islyr stared into the fire. "I ask for your trust."

"Then you shall have it," Cael answered for both of them before Viverr could open his mouth. "Stealth will be one of our few advantages. You know how many bloodsoul he keeps, but what of his human army?"

"They number more than the bloodsoul. Ranur is amongst them."

"That does make things difficult. What are the chances of receiving aid from Felan? Is he on Damaeus' side or our own?"

"He resisted in the beginning and thought of nothing but freedom. I taught him to be a pleasure Rakaii under Damaeus' orders. I believe that he has fallen, as many do who serve their masters or mistresses in such a personal manner. He may not side with us if we attempt to harm Perfidia."

"I see."

Cael did not like to think that one of his companions would act against him.

"We should leave before our few remaining allies become lost in the depths," Islyr said as he collected damp earth from outside the cave to throw upon the fire.

Cael placed a hand on Islyr's shoulder as he returned. "Selene spent a great portion of her life searching for you. It is the reason she became a Rider. She joined the Aranth rather than living a life of ease within Evaria's borders in part to avenge your mother's death, but also in the hope that her travels would lead her to you." He would certainly wish to be told such a thing, were their roles reversed. Either Xaiden had begun to influence him at last, or he had softened with the years.

"I had thoughts that Maye was dead," Islyr replied. "May the Spirits protect and guide her soul on this day and thereafter."

"It is by the grace of the Spirits that even one member of your family remains. Not many Marked Ones can say so." Cael's family was long dead. He did not think upon them often lest it distract him.

"I saw Selene once within the Keep. She attempted to kill me. Damaeus would not allow me to tell her who I was. She did not recognize me grown and with the Kerell inking across my face. Still, it was good to see her."

"You will see her again," Cael said. "And if she is not upon our side then may the Tides be with us."

Friendship's End

Selene's grumbling carried easily over the tray of fine china cups and the pot of tea that sat between them. Apparently it was not punishment enough that Damaeus had blocked her latent abilities once again. He had also ordered her to do as Perfidia commanded. She glared at the tiny yellow flowers that graced the edges of the pottery. The tea smelled wonderful, as did the warm bread that sat alongside it. She knew that she would not be allowed to have any. The fact pained her stomach as well as her pride. Selene balanced the tray with one hand and knocked with the other. Long ago she would have found difficulty coming up with anything that would be more degrading than acting as a ladies' maid to a traitor of the Realm. Recent events had changed her opinion somewhat.

"Enter," Perfidia called from within.

Selene sighed as she pushed her way into the room. The woman could have opened the door for her, at least.

"Set it upon the table," Perfidia said as she pulled a bath robe of maroon velvet over her shift. "And close the door behind you. You endanger my health with your carelessness."

It had recently become obvious that Perfidia was with child. Selene had since been attempting to guess who the father could be. It served to pass the time and to take her mind from the bloodsoul that awaited her in the courtyard. Ranur was the most likely candidate, for she had often seen him leaving Perfidia's room with a rather triumphant smile upon his face. It could just as easily be one of his Riders, however. Perfidia had taken several of them to her bed, and they were not shy when it came to speaking of the event amongst their peers. The answer might come with the child's birth, but

Selene hoped that she would not remain in this place long enough to see it.

"My apologies," Selene said. She bowed more deeply than was necessary in an attempt to hide the hatred in her eyes.

"Over there." Perfidia pointed to the corner nearest the stained glass door. "I may have need of you in a moment."

"As you wish," Selene bit her tongue and stood where Perfidia indicated. The scent of the bread was driving her mad. Damaeus had not allowed her anything to eat since yesterday afternoon. The feeling reminded her of the days after her father's death and before she was old enough to become a Rider; when she and her mother had survived on what could be grown in their garden and what little their neighbors were willing to give to the family of a suspected Marked One. All food had smelled wonderful to her then.

"Your tea," Perfidia said, offering Felan a cup.

"No, thank you." He sat upon a chair by the hearth and stared into the fire as if in a trance. "I am not feeling well."

"Come, you must have a sip, at least."

"I'd rather not unless you would force me to it, Mistress."

Perfidia frowned. "Is there something else you desire?" she asked in a silken voice. His argumentative demeanor did not seem to deter her in the least. "Selene will gladly fetch anything for you, my dear. Is that not right, Selene?" She stroked Felan's head as one would a favored hunting dog.

"Of course," Selene replied bitterly. "I will happily bring you whatever you would like." She glowered at Perfidia despite her best effort to keep a neutral expression.

"That blood looks well on you," Perfidia remarked, examining Selene's face. "It is an excellent reminder of your social standing. Do you not think so?"

Perfidia did not seem frightened of her now that Damaeus had locked her abilities.

"But I cannot say that I approve of Damaeus' choice of clothing," she added with a scowl. "A Marked one should not show so much flesh."

That was one way in which Selene agreed with the woman. The dresses that Damaeus made her wear were tight at the bodice and their cut reminded her of costumes at Lord Kyrros' masquerade. She found them far more comfortable than being bare, however, so she had not spoken to him concerning the subject.

"Why my brother would wish to look upon such repulsiveness is beyond my understanding. Marked females are the most disgusting of creatures. They were made to tempt pure humans with their harlotry. Tell me, are you now one of Ranur's playthings? He can be quite gentle in bed, though only if forced to do so. It is not what he favors."

Selene drew a deep breath. What would occur when she was finally given control of the bloodsoul army? A few nasty things involving Perfidia came to mind. Damaeus may not care what she did to the woman, depending what mood he was in at that particular moment. His temperament had been anything but stable lately. Selene silenced her thoughts. It was difficult to keep one's sanity when surrounded each day by death and violence.

I will not let anger *control my actions. I open my mind to the winds of tranquility. My thoughts are pure serenity.*

"You will respond when I speak to you," Perfidia said with a scowl. "I will not tolerate disrespect."

I will not let anger control my actions. I open my mind to the winds of tranquility. My thoughts-

Selene was forced from her meditation when Perfidia's hand struck her face. Her hand found its way to her hip, only to meet with an empty scabbard. Felan had taken her sword from her after their sparring match, on Damaeus' orders.

"You cannot harm me," Perfidia said confidently. "You have no weapon and you are without the use of your latent abilities. Your Circlet will keep you in your place."

"Say what you will, but do not touch me." Perfidia should not be allowed to treat Marked Ones as if they were less than human. Cyanna suffered for her mother's bigotry, as did every other Marked One that came within Perfidia's reach.

Perfidia smiled. She struck Selene again with more force.

Selene returned the blow. Perfidia squeaked like a cornered rabbit and fell against the chair in which Felan sat. Selene's Circlet warmed and the bitter, metallic taste of blood touched her throat.

"Stop," Felan said, gripping Selene's arm firmly. His eyes were alight with panic.

"And still you side with her," Selene said angrily. "We were friends once, you and I. We were nearly more."

"He may side with me if he chooses," Perfidia said as Felan helped her to the bed. "You do not own him." It was clear that she had not been injured by the strike.

"Nor do you."

"Not true," Perfidia countered as she straightened her robe. "He will defend me to his dying breath. Ask him if you do not believe it."

"Well?" Selene feared to know the answer.

"I must protect her," he replied. "My conscience demands it."

"It is as I said." Perfidia wore a pleased expression. "He knows his place in this world."

"No person should be considered of less worth than another."

"Marked Ones are not people," Perfidia retorted.

There was a knock at the door, and Perfidia turned at the sound. "Felan, get the door."

The door opened before Felan could stand and Damaeus entered the room. He wore a fine black cloak, the hood of which covered much of his face.

"Our enemies have gained access to the Keep," he said. "I have sent Ranur and some of his Riders to dispose of them, though I am not confident that they will succeed."

"What enemies?" Selene asked.

"That is none of a Rakaii's concern, no matter how lovely she may be," Damaeus replied. His gaze hovered over Felan momentarily, and one corner of his mouth turned up to form an empty smile. "Go now to your army, and may you have the intelligence not to question me in the future."

"Yes, Damaeus," Selene replied. She would do anything to be away from Perfidia for a time.

"Perfidia will accompany you to the courtyard."

Selene barely contained the frustrated scream that echoed through her head.

"Ready your Bloodsoul for battle, Selene. I have released your command latent ability, but do not think to try and use any of the others. I will meet you when I am finished." He handed a grey silken pouch to Perfidia. "Guard this well. We will need it in the coming days."

Selene's gaze followed Damaeus as he slid around the corner at the far end of the hall and disappeared from sight. She puzzled over his uneven gait and the way he tilted ever so slightly from one side to the other as he walked.

"Come on, Felan," she said as she stepped from the warmth of the room. "You wish to be a proper Rakaii, so we should do as our master has ordered."

Upon reaching the stairs she realized that neither Felan nor Perfidia were with her. "I'll leave you to defend yourselves," she warned, heading back towards Perfidia's room with steps hastened by irritation.

Her voice dissolved as she entered. Felan stood at the center of the room clutching at his chest. Perfidia's eyes were red. Her face was damp with tears.

"Look what your idiocy has caused!" Perfidia screamed. She grabbed Selene's dress at the collar. "You've poisoned him!"

"*I've* poisoned him?" Selene replied incredulously. "I have done nothing to harm Felan, nor would I ever. You were here with him." The anger that she had held back with such difficulty began to release.

"You said that it would tame him," Perfidia cried, tightening her hold. "Heal him, Spirits keep you."

Selene writhed from her grip and moved to Felan's side. His gaze was vacant and his breathing shallow. "What has she done to you?" she whispered. Fear slithered into her chest. She could not heal the effects of poison, if that was truly what he suffered from.

"Make him well. If you do not then I'll give you to Ranur whether or not Damaeus allows it."

"My Latent Abilities are sealed." Selene was unable to keep the panic from her voice. "I can do nothing for him unless it is Damaeus' will."

"You did this so that I could not have him, self-centered harlot!"

Selene was suddenly unable to stop herself from speaking. "You dare to call me a harlot, and yet I'm certain that the child you carry was not conceived by your husband." The pallor of Felan's complexion made her stomach clench, but it did not overpower the rage that was building within her. "What poison did you give him?"

"You know as well as I."

"I won't tolerate your games, Perfidia. Tell me what it was."

Felan clutched her arm. "Selene, please don't harm her."

The words severed her remaining patience like a fine blade. "Why do you care so much for Perfidia?" she demanded. "What has she done to deserve your loyalty? You're Aranth, not a slave to a fallen queen."

"I am no fallen queen!" Perfidia grabbed a silver candlestick from the mantle and lunged for Selene. Her movements were slow and clumsy. Selene avoided the blow with ease. She grabbed Perfidia's wrist with one hand and pulled the candlestick from her with the other. She was finished being kind to the woman. She tossed the makeshift weapon aside and pulled Perfidia's arms behind her back.

"Selene, stop!" Felan propped himself up against the wall between the Perfidia's bed and the table beside it.

"You betrayed me. You held me down so that Damaeus could claim me. Tell me why I should listen to anything you say."

"It's mine."

Her mind washed around the statement in a futile attempt to decipher its meaning.

"The child that she carries. It's mine."

He said that he had done something that could not be forgiven, but this? "Graelen will have you killed." The words faded quickly beneath the crackling of the fire.

"It seems that he won't have the opportunity. My hope is that you'll forgive me though the others may not. I meant to resist, but with time I found it was easier to bend. Islyr taught me the ways of a pleasure Rakaii. He promised me freedom when the time was right."

Felan twitched as if his flesh had been pierced. He pressed a hand to his Circlet. "You can have what I was promised, at least. Cael and Xaiden are here with several others. It seems by their thoughts that they have come for you."

"I will ask you only once more," Selene said, turning to Perfidia. "What have you given Felan?"

"It should not have harmed him," Perfidia said haltingly as she attempted to twist from Selene's grasp. "I have been lacing his tea ever so slowly with the potion that Damaeus gave you for use upon Cael."

The logs of the fire shifted and hissed over Felan's labored breaths. Damaeus did not know of Selene's encounter with Cael at the Masquerade. He assumed it to be Kyrros who drugged her. He certainly had not given her any potion to use upon Cael specifically, so far as she could recall.

"The one in your belt pouch, imbecile," Perfidia amended. "For the white falcon."

"You gave him that?" Selene tightened her grip. "I told you that I wasn't certain what it did. You risked Felan's life simply because he did not return the love you felt for him?"

"I have not ever claimed to love Felan. It is your folly that you do, for you will suffer far more than I at his death."

Selene wanted to squeeze the woman's last breath from her. She may have done so if not for the child.

"Damaeus will win this war with or without your aid," Perfidia said. "You will suffer doubly when he discovers your betrayal."

"I have had enough of you," Selene said as she pulled open the chest that lay at the end of Perfidia's bed. "King Graelen will decide your fate." She rummaged through it with her free hand until she found several pairs of stockings. "Sit." She pushed Perfidia down into the chair that sat by the fire, tied her hands and feet, and then turned her to face the stained glass doors. She could no longer bear the woman's knowing expression.

Felan's back had slipped from the wall to the floor. He moved so little.

"Please, Felan. You cannot go," she whispered as she knelt beside him.

The atmosphere was uncommonly peaceful, and it seemed odd to Selene that her emotions raced so within the lush and oppressive warmth of the room. She had thought, so long ago, that nothing could tear her soul as greatly as her father's death. That was before Kailia had been slaughtered by the bloodsoul, and long before Ranur had slain Maye. Now, as she placed her hand on Felan's cheek and his breathing grew shallow she found herself thinking not only of him, but of those others who had left for their next lives without her. But Felan was different, for it seemed that he had forsaken her long ago.

The flesh of Felan's hand was chill. "May our next lives bring us together," he said, struggling to embrace her.

"May my love follow you there, friend," she whispered.

His hold upon her loosened.

Selene placed Felan carefully upon Perfidia's bed. She folded his hands across his chest. He had held such anger for her at their first meeting within Evaria's castle. Thoughts of time spent with him and the love that she had thought he felt for her on the roof of the Aranth barn brought fresh tears.

"Your tears should be those of joy," Perfidia said from her chair. "The world can be more certain of its safety with each Marked One's passing."

"There are many things I can do to you that will not harm Felan's child," Selene replied as she gathered a silk scarf from the chest of clothing for use as a gag. "You would do well to remember that. And may your child be marked as well, for it would be just retribution."

"If it is marked then it will bow to me, as all of your kind should."

Selene forced the scarf into Perfidia's mouth before she could continue. She moved to where Felan lay. He deserved a proper sending. It distressed her that she was in no position to give him one.

"May the Spirits protect and guide your soul on this day and thereafter," Selene said as she placed her hand upon his chest. Her palm pressed against a small, solid object. She knew it to be a Stone even before freeing the leather cord from his neck.

She stared at it for a moment.

Damaeus' presence was barely perceptible within her Circlet and it was slowly waning. It was a strangely troubling feeling. She had not been truly alone since before becoming Aranth. She had found comfort in being able to feel Felan's presence through her Stone. With the Circlet came Damaeus' consciousness, which she had become somewhat accustomed to despite a strong effort to the contrary. She touched her latent abilities ever so slightly. It was as if they did not exist. Her Circlet warmed, yet it did not bring her any pain. Perhaps his hold upon her was loosening.

Selene touched Felan's Stone to the rivulet of blood that was quickly drying upon his forehead. The Stone glowed with a pure, clear light. She pulled the cord over her head, letting it rest above the fabric of her shirt. She did not know whether two Stones could be set to a single person, and she had no desire to discover the truth of it. Selene glanced back at Felan one last time before heading into the hall. He looked as if he was merely sleeping, and she found herself thinking that he may rise and move to join her. She closed the door gently behind her and wiped the tears from her face as she headed towards the stairs.

Invading the Keep

Cael kept his hand upon the hilt of his sword as he followed Islyr through the innards of the Keep. Somehow the walls of the place remained steady, defying both collapse and the rules of nature as one.

"This way," Islyr whispered as they rounded a corner that looked nearly identical to all of the others that they had passed.

The halls of the Keep twisted and turned like the center of a corn-field maze. The structure was built much like one, in Cael's opinion. Passageways changed direction often, seemingly without reason, and the crumbling walls of stone looked much the same throughout. All had been quiet thus far, but something told him that Damaeus knew of their presence within the castle. The Mage was most likely waiting for the best time to strike. Damaeus had always been one to lure his enemies into thinking that he knew nothing of their plans. In that way the attack, when it came, would be unexpected and thus much more likely to succeed.

"The Riders' quarters begin ahead, up the next set of stairs and to our right," Islyr whispered. "Ranur's army numbers in the hundreds, so it would be best to avoid detection completely."

"Agreed," Xaiden said.

Xaiden had disposed of the few Riders that they had encountered thus far with his usual deadly efficiency, giving neither Cael nor the others any chance to aid him. Cael did not consider himself to be sentimental. What was in the past should stay there as far as he was concerned, but he realized that had missed working with Xaiden, and also with other Marked Ones, though to a lesser degree. It reminded him of the days when he was new to the Aranth, and of a time when many more rooms of the Aranth wing had been occupied. He hoped that this task would not be their last together.

Islyr stopped with such abruptness that Cael nearly stumbled over him. "Damaeus," the man hissed. His stance was that of a snake coiled to strike.

"We must wait," Xaiden said softly. "We cannot hope to reach him while he is surrounded by Riders."

The Mage stood nearly twenty feet down the hall, wearing a black cloak that buried his face in darkness. A group of nearly twenty Riders in mismatched armor surrounded him.

Damaeus divided the group into two, waving half down the hall behind him. He ushered the remaining portion towards where Cael and the others stood.

Islyr inched forward.

Cael placed a hand on his shoulder. "You'll have your chance," he promised. "But the time is not now."

Islyr nodded reluctantly. His eyes narrowed as Damaeus disappeared down the hall.

"Islyr, take the first man that rounds the corner," Xaiden ordered in a whisper. "Cael and I will approach the rest from behind as they turn to you. Aurin, you will protect Viverr as we discussed previously. He is our only defense against magic."

Cael headed to the other side of the hall. He slid beneath the shadow of a stone-framed opening that looked as if it may have once held a door. At last Xaiden had decided to share the battle with the rest of them. Cael's chest ached with the familiar pull of his latent ability, but he dared not use it while Xaiden was so close.

The first man to round the corner fell to Islyr's staff almost immediately. None of the Riders' heads were protected, and Islyr's water-smooth movements found two others before Cael had a chance to pull his blade. The former Rakaii had an impressive ability to strike deadly blows.

Cael drew his sword across the unprotected spine of the man whose back was closest to him. A chest plate did its job well enough on most occasions, providing that you could see your opponent and move to keep your open areas from harm. This man paid attention to no one but Islyr. His armor was ill fitted as well. It ended more than an inch from the top of his breeches. The sword that Cael had borrowed from Kyrros did not cut nearly as cleanly as his beloved Aranth blade, but it did the job well enough when a bit of pilfered strength was applied. The man fell to the floor in several pieces. The next two that came into range did not fall as easily as the first. Even so, it took no more than a moment to defeat them. Cael searched for another victim, only to find the rest of the Riders sprawled upon the floor. He cleaned the blade of his sword upon the shirt of the nearest before sprinting after Islyr.

"The stairway is just ahead," Islyr called back as they turned a corner. The air warmed suddenly as they ascended the staircase, and the dust that had covered the floor where they entered the Keep was no longer present. Brightly burning lamps lined the walls. The area ahead was obviously frequented.

"This gives me an uneasy feeling," Viverr said. "I don't think it's safe for us in this hall."

"You have uneasy feelings about everything, friend," Aurin replied. "We have promised to go to this place, and so we will. You wish to find Selene, yes?"

"Yeah," Viverr replied, "But I also don't want to be killed."

"Be silent," Xaiden commanded.

The sound of footsteps and clattering metal reached Cael's ears. More Riders were on their way.

"At least thirty," Cael said in response to Islyr's questioning look. The sound amplified as he spoke. It now came from behind them as well.

"In here," Islyr said as he pulled open a thick wooden door. It was one of the few decent looking ones that Cael had seen thus far. They entered with haste and Cael pulled the door closed behind him, blanketing the room in darkness. He ran his hands along the length of it but could find no latch. It seemed that it could not be locked from the inside. The torches that he had glimpsed upon entering sprung to life, casting a bright glow upon the floor beneath. There was very little space between soot covered walls, Cael noticed. The space was more passageway than room. Jars of preserves and packaged dry goods lined the shelves upon each side above barrels of what Cael assumed to be either ale or drinking water. The only bare wall was that surrounding the torches.

"We can't linger," Islyr said, starting off once again. "They'll be on us the moment we stop moving."

"They won't find us so quickly," Viverr disagreed with what Cael sensed was more hopefulness than conviction.

"They will find us if Ranur is with them," Xaiden replied.

Cael was not given the time to ask why that would be so. The door creaked open and a burly Rider peered around the corner.

"Yah, Praecyr, they're here." The force with which he flung the door open caused several jars to crash to the floor.

"Move," Xaiden said. "The time for discussion has passed."

The fact that the passage was narrow was to their advantage, and it was well that Cael had entered last. He pulled a barrel from the floor and launched it at the Rider. It struck the man squarely in the chest. He stumbled back onto his companions, who were struggling to enter the room. The barrel split as it hit the floor. *Ale*, Cael decided as the liquid's odor reached him. *Northern brew, lucky bastards.*

Nearly twenty feet ahead the passage opened into an oversized kitchen. A large, wood fueled stove stood at its center. Pots and skillets of various sizes hung from the ceiling. Cael slammed the door shut after passing through it. He latched the iron bolt near the top. It was likely that Ranur had already sent a team of Riders around to cut them off. They would need to work quickly to find a way out.

They exited through one of several doors that led out of the kitchen, and Cael found himself in what looked to be a dining area. The room was similar in size to the Aranth Common Room. It held rows of roughly hewn wooden benches with tables between them. The air was silent save for the constant banging upon the pantry door and the clattering of small portions of stone as they fell from the walls surrounding it. The door was thick, and it did not sound as if Ranur's Riders were having any luck with breaking it down for the moment.

"Can we get from here to where you believe Selene may be?" Cael asked.

"Not easily without going through them," Islyr replied, gesturing back toward the kitchen. "There is only one other hall that leads here on this floor. They are most likely heading towards us from that direction as well."

"We'll be killed," Viverr moaned in fear, "butchered in this horrible place."

"Pyre's Ash," Cael swore. "Shut your mouth for a time, will you? I can't form a thought for all the whining."

"What was that?" Viverr said with panic in his voice. He pointed to the far side of the room, above which a small balcony hung. "Something moved." He cowered behind Aurin, who did not seem at all surprised that he had done so.

"It is only a cat," Aurin said, lifting Viverr by the back of his shirt and placing him where he had originally been standing. "You have more fear than even the smallest child."

"Search the room," Islyr ordered. "Damaeus mentioned that there are stairs leading to the upper balcony somewhere in here. We'll need to find them soon unless you wish to battle upwards of two hundred Riders."

"There are simply too many," Xaiden agreed, "even for Marked Ones of our skill."

Cael's eyes moved to the cat that had caused Viverr so much distress. It slipped behind the square cut base of a statue that stood upon the far left wall. "I'll take this side," he volunteered, heading after the animal. It seemed odd that any small creature could survive in this place with so many of Ranur's Riders around. Cael knew what crimes the man allowed them to commit, and most were far worse than anything he and Kyrros had ever come up with.

He approached the statue cautiously. The stone man was dressed in full plate armor. He was headless, and one arm was broken off at the shoulder. The remaining arm held a shield with stylized flames carved upon its center. As Cael drew closer the cat appeared once again, sticking its head timidly from behind the base of the statue. The animal was pathetically thin, and a collar of iron that would be better suited to a war dog surrounded its neck. He recognized it from Islyr's memories. The creature came to sit at Cael's feet. It looked up at him expectantly.

"What do you want?" Cael asked. He did not mind cats so long as they stayed out of his way. This one did not seem to have any intention of doing so.

"Mrrow," the cat said.

"I don't have any food, if that's what you're asking." He had not bothered to learn any cat speech or body language for he had never worked alongside an Aranth with a feline Affinity. He thought of calling Xaiden over. The man could understand most languages, human or otherwise. *Don't have the time to bother with cats*, he decided as he moved to examine the base of the statue. He pitied the animal, but the best he could do for it was to survive. If he succeeded in defeating Damaeus then he would find the cat and bring it to Evaria. King Graelen kept a few of them around the castle. Cael doubted that he would notice one more.

The wall behind the base of the statue looked to be solid, as did the stone above it. The back of the statue's base was as smooth as fine cloth and was unyielding, much to Cael's chagrin. The pounding at the pantry door ceased suddenly. Silence of that sort was never a good sign.

"We searched the entire wall." Viverr twisted his hands together nervously. "There is nothing. No stairs. No escape."

"I also found nothing," Xaiden said.

Islyr nodded in solemn agreement.

"What'll we do?" Viverr asked. "I can't die here!"

"Mrrow," the cat said once again.

"Be silent, cat," Cael muttered. "You and Viverr could be brethren."

"We may be able to climb up to the balcony if we pile the tables atop one another," Islyr suggested.

The cat rubbed its head against Cael's ankles. Cael attempted to shoo it away with his foot.

"Isn't that one of yours?" Islyr asked, pointing to the animal. "I know she's marked, at least."

"Cyanna," Xaiden exclaimed, pushing Cael aside to lift the cat from the floor. He furrowed his brow as he inspected her, and then frowned in Cael's direction.

"Damaeus does not treat his marked females with much care," Islyr added, "especially considering their rarity."

"I had no idea," Cael said helplessly. Guilt spread through him as quickly as well brewed ale. By all rights

Cyanna should have been too frightened of him to show herself. She had surely heard the tales blaming him for Devren's death. And how was he supposed to know of the girl's Affinity? It had never been mentioned in his presence. That aside, Graelen seemed completely against any male training her in the use of it. How did Xaiden know of it, for that matter?

"They're coming," Islyr said, looking not to the pantry but to the closed double doors that marked the room's main entrance. The clattering of armor echoed across the room.

"Aurin, you must use your latent ability." Tension shadowed Xaiden's words.

Only an idiot remained calm when Xaiden was tense. The man knew when death was approaching.

The doors crashed aside. Riders spilled into the room like floodwater.

"But, the doors," Aurin said. "I cannot use my ability without doors to open."

"The doors are a crutch," Xaiden shot back as he balanced his sword in one hand and Cyanna in the other. "You do not need them." The anxiousness in his voice was almost certainly for the girl. The man feared his time with the Spirits no more than Cael did.

"I cannot do it," Aurin insisted. "It will affect us too."

The first of the Riders caught sight of them. Their eyes were like those of dogs at the end of a long hunt.

"You can, and you will because our lives depend on it," Xaiden shouted over the noise of scraping metal and benches clattering to the floor. "Do it now or die here."

An odd warmth washed over Cael; like the waters of the southern ocean in full summer. The air around him wavered, distorting his view into a tangle of shapes. Riders on all sides slumped heavily to the floor. Many collided with tables or each other as they fell. The closest landed less than a yard from Cael's feet.

"There are so many," Aurin said. "I do not know how long it will last." His words were sharp with excitement, no doubt pleased that his ability had worked as Xaiden had said.

"Now what, oh wise and powerful leader?" Viverr asked Xaiden at once. The pallor of his face made it look as if he might suddenly join the unconscious Riders. "Aurin won't be able to use his ability for at least a half-hour, and there's more coming."

Cyanna writhed from Xaiden's arms to land upon the base of the statue once again.

"Mmrrh," she said.

Cael squinted in attempt to see through the shadows. She was not standing before the wall, but within it.

"The stairway," Cael said, pointing.

"Go," Xaiden said, grabbing Cyanna before Cael could get to her. It seemed that he still was not trusted completely. The man had not let him out of his sight except when it was unavoidable.

Viverr disappeared into the false wall without pause. Islyr and Aurin followed close behind. *Pyre's Ash, but that looks like true stone.* Cael forced himself to step through it. He flinched as his face touched its surface, for it was cold and had a feel much like thick fog. All was gray for a moment, and his eyes struggled to focus as he entered a poorly lit stairway. A tattered maroon carpet lined a flight of wooden stairs. The opening at the top was covered with a mirage in the same way as the base.

Cael passed through the second wall and found himself in a partially restored hall lined with paneled wood. The brass lamps which hung there were new, though they did not light automatically as the ones in the pantry had. Aurin stood at bright end of the passage, each side of which was lined with closed doors. Beyond him was a window composed of swirling shards of stained glass in shades of blue and green like the shallows of a warm ocean.

"I cannot find Viverr," Aurin said.

Cael sprinted to catch up with them. "You were only a few seconds behind him. What happened?"

Aurin shrugged. "I stepped through the wall and he was gone. He must be somewhere here, I think, within these rooms."

"And you?" Cael asked Islyr.

"He ran up the steps. I stopped to help Aurin. When I turned back he was gone. It would be foolish to raise my voice in this place so I did not call out to him."

"I have vowed to return Cyanna to King Graelen," Xaiden said, glancing at her.

"I thought you might say that," Cael replied. "I will not stop you. We certainly cannot battle Damaeus and protect Cyanna from him all at once. You and Aurin should try to escape with her. Islyr and I will search for Viverr and move on to find Damaeus."

"I accept." Impatience overshadowed Islyr's words.

"I will do what Xaiden thinks to be best," Aurin said with reluctance.

"So long as we all agree upon it," Xaiden said. "Fight well my friends, and if the Tides are with us I shall see you again."

"The Tides are with me always," Cael replied with a grin.

"And do not think that I have forgotten our agreement," Xaiden added. His face was marbled in stained glass shades of blue and green. "I will find you and kill you, if need be."

"I won't betray you," Cael promised.

Xaiden nodded in consent and headed off with Aurin close behind. Cael pressed his fingers against the pommel of his sword. Light spilled from one of the entrances at the opposite end of the hall; a pillar in the depth of shadow. It was the only door that was open. Cael entered the room to find Viverr standing within. A stained glass window much like the one in the hall hung above a decorated bed with dark fabric draped from its posts. The window stretched from floor to ceiling. It painted the room in tones of orange and yellow.

Viverr moved no more than the stone man in the dining area. Cael would have thought him under one of Damaeus' spells if not for the rogue's Latent Ability.

"Why did you not stay with Aurin as Xaiden instructed?"

Viverr gave no indication that he had heard what was said. Cael followed his gaze and found what had caught the man's attention. A chair had been set at the back of the closet. A skinny girl wearing nothing more than a cotton shirt sat upon it, tied at ankle and wrist. She did not stir. Cael approached and lifted her chin. She was most certainly dead.

The window darkened as if by passing clouds, and thunder rumbled from beyond it with enough strength to rattle its colored glass.

"I don't know," Viverr said as if responding to some unasked question. "What should we do?"

"Islyr," Cael called softly over the light tapping of rain against glass.

Islyr wandered closer, gripping his sword. He wore an uncertain expression. Cael nodded his head towards the dead girl.

Islyr pressed a hand to each side of her face. He stepped back after a moment, shaking his head.

"Let's go, Viverr," Cael said, touching the rogue's arm.

"I don't want to."

"It's been too long. She is beyond our aid." Cael untied the girl and placed her upon the bed, crossing her arms as one would when placing a body upon the funeral pyre. She was young, and thoughts of what she must have endured angered him despite his best effort to retain the serenity required by an elder Aranth. He pulled the quilted blanket up, half from each side, to cover her.

"Something is wrong," Islyr said suddenly.

"Yes, it is," Viverr agreed adamantly. He was most obviously ignoring Cael's attempts to lead him away. "We ought to be able to do something more."

The door to the room slammed shut without warning. Viverr's eyes grew wide. The window shattered, pelting the group a shower of red and yellow glass. Cael could do nothing to stop himself as he was pulled through the opening. He dropped freely for a moment. Cold air and rain rushed up to meet him. The impact was expected, but jarring nonetheless. Wet stone crushed his chest and legs. Islyr landed nearby with a grunt.

Cael picked himself up. Frigid rain pelted him from above. Nothing seemed broken, but the fall certainly had not done him any favors. He did not like to think what would have happened if they had not landed upon the balcony. He ran his sleeve across his face. It came away tinted with blood. "You alive?" he asked, fearing the worst.

"Barely," Islyr groaned. He pulled several coin sized shards of glass from his arm and tossed them aside. "This does not bode well for us."

Cael looked up to find Viverr's head hanging out the window. "Managed to save himself, at least," he grumbled.

"Typical rogue," Islyr agreed

"Find a way down here," Cael called just loud enough so that Viverr could hear him. The man nodded and moved away from the window.

Islyr began to laugh.

"Are you certain that you're ok?" Cael asked. He worried that the man had struck his head during the fall.

"Look," Islyr said, nodding towards the courtyard below.

The rain came so thickly that it obscured Cael's view, but after a moment he was able to make out what Islyr had spotted with such ease. "Bloodsoul," he breathed. There were hundreds. Enough for an army. "But why do they stand in rows? No Mage can control them. Damaeus himself has spoken it with Xaiden in attendance."

"Yes," Islyr agreed, pushing Cael down behind the railing that rounded the balcony. "But there is one who can, and she is controlled by Damaeus." He pointed to the far left of the courtyard, near a partially finished row of bloodsoul soldiers. A figure stood there with no cloak despite the pouring rain. It was certainly Selene.

"You said that she was likely on our side," Cael whispered.

"She may wish to be so, but that does not mean that she will be. If you had ever worn a Circlet you would know what I speak of."

"I do have some idea of it," Cael replied.

Selene ceased directing the bloodsoul long enough to turn in the direction of the balcony. She looked as if she wished to convey something, but Cael found that he was much too far to understand what was meant.

"He's here," Islyr said.

The balcony beneath Islyr crumbled like a body in pyreflame. Cael caught Islyr's wrist as he fell. The stone under Cael's feet dissolved. He grabbed what was left of the railing. Both arms felt as if they might pull from their sockets, but Cael did not let the pain impede him. He summoned the strength of his victims and attempted to pull himself up. His hands began to slip. He struggled to retain his grip but the railing was old and covered in moss made slick by the falling rain. He held for mere seconds before tumbling once again through the rain-spattered air to strike the ground beneath.

Storm clouds hung thickly, casting darkness over the courtyard. Islyr was nowhere to be seen, though Selene stood shivering less than a carriage length from him.

Standing came with great difficulty. Cael ignored the ache of his ribs and drew his sword. A figure cloaked in black appeared at Selene's side. His eyes, the color of ice just before spring thaw, glowed from within the shadow of his hood. Cael readied himself. He would have Damaeus, even if it was upon his last breath.

"You have come for me," Damaeus' voice slithered from him with a vibrating hiss. His words were easily understood despite the roar of falling rain. "Not a wise choice, by any means. But one cannot expect more from a Marked One. Even with Islyr's soul and strength within you it is the act of a desperate fool."

"This is no foolish act," Cael replied. "It is only fair that I take your life as you took mine. All of those whose lives you have turned to ruin shall rejoice at your death." His eyes caught movement far beyond the Mage, where Islyr struggled to his feet. His focus returned to Damaeus immediately. If the Tides were with him then the Mage had not seen his gaze stray.

"Ah," Damaeus said thoughtfully. "Perhaps Islyr's soul did not tell you of my secret. Death is my ally. It holds my spirit to this place with such force that even a Marked One of your strength cannot breach it."

"The most arrogant warrior is the first to fall," Cael replied.

"A Kerell saying, I believe. It seems that you gained at least some wisdom from your friend. Does it make you ill, thinking of Islyr? He brought you back from the realm of the Spirits and you repaid him with suffering and death. Perhaps I can ease the pain you must feel. The bloodsoul in this courtyard number in the hundreds. They will kill you at my command."

"At Selene's command," Cael corrected. "You do not control them."

"Not so."

Selene dropped to the ground, clutching her head in agony.

Damaeus' eyes fluttered closed momentarily. When he smiled there was true pleasure behind it. "Bring them forward," he commanded.

Selene opened her mouth, and a vibrating wail emanated from it, echoing from the stone of the courtyard. A wall of bloodsoul moved as one. Cael tensed, gripping his sword tightly though he knew that it would do nothing to save his life against so many. He resisted the urge to search for Islyr.

"My offer remains as it was when I approached you within Evaria's walls."

"So does my answer," Cael replied.

"You have always been obstinate. You lost your life once for defying me and yet you would willingly repeat your mistake. You embrace the stains of your soul rather than fearing them. It is admirable. Yet I cannot save you for that alone. Your tainted blood makes you a danger to the good people of the Ethereal Realm. You would be a risk, even while under the control of a Circlet. The joy of your second bout with death shall also lie with me, as will the pleasure of your torture. You deserve no less, old friend." The next words to pass Damaeus' lips were no more than a soft hiss to Cael's ears.

A glow of pale blue surrounded Cael, reflecting from the metal of Selene's Circlet with perfect clarity. Cael rushed forward. He leveled the blade of his sword with Damaeus' neck. Blue light blinded him. Burning pain engulfed his flesh and seared his bones. The air crackled with a noise much like that of the barrier beyond the keep as it melted whatever dared to touch it.

Cael's sword was pulled from his hand. Something unseen struck his side, sending him tumbling past Damaeus. He struggled against the magic's grip, but to no avail. Bloodsoul voices blanketed him, building with such ferocity that it caused his ears to ache. He landed amongst them, upon a bed of bone and rotting flesh. Eyeless faces tilted their heads towards him, hovering above as if their rotted brains were attempting to make sense of what had occurred. The scent of death burned Cael's lungs. They turned as one at the sound of a single, vibrating tone. The creatures' bony fingers pressed into his arms as they lifted him to his feet. Those who did not hold him followed closely behind. Cael did not bother to struggle as they dragged him back towards Damaeus. He was thrown to the sodden ground at the Mage's feet. Damaeus gestured towards Selene. She spoke something lengthy in Bloodsoul tongue. Skeletal hands moved from Cael's arms to his throat.

"How do you feel?" Damaeus asked. Pleasure oozed from his expression as freely as blood from a deep wound.

He felt as if he had been trampled by horses. "You cannot break me," he replied simply, ignoring the burning scent of his flesh and the sting that accompanied it. "Do as you will."

"Many Aranth have spoken those very words to me. I have proved all to be false. You will be no different except in that I do not care to break you." Light surrounded the Mage once again, yet this time it was the blue of deep ocean waters. Cael's thoughts turned frantically. Damaeus was much too far for him to reach. It was little wonder that he kept him at a distance, for the Mage knew the limits of Cael's latent ability well. And where was Islyr?

"Why waste his death, Master, when you could gain pleasure from it," Selene said suddenly. "Place a Circlet upon him." The blood that ran from beneath her Circlet in a constant stream was quickly washed away by pouring rain.

Damaeus ceased his mumbling and turned to Selene, tilting his head ever so slightly. His magic bathed him in colors that reminded Cael of the stained glass window at the end of the hidden hall. "True," he murmured at last. "So many bloodsoul are surely enough to hold him. Perhaps your breaking was more successful than I believed." He pulled a Circlet composed of twisted metal bands from the depths of his cloak and held it up, turning the pointed tines so that they were level with Cael's eyes before moving it up towards his forehead.

Cael surged forward. Bone snapped and flesh split. Fingers continued to press deeply into his neck despite the fact that they were no longer attached to hands. He took hold of the Mage's head. His latent ability screamed for release. It pleaded to add the Mage's power to its own. Cael set it free in full force, not caring if Damaeus' soul was shattered as it was taken. A shriek of fury, limitless and vibrating, came forth from the Mage. The light surrounding him disappeared, and he dropped to his knees.

"Your soul has lingered for far too long now, Damaeus. Release it to me and end your suffering."

Damaeus' threads of essence were sinister and mangled. They twisted together like the tendrils of a venomvine within the depths of the abyss. It was unlike any soul that Cael had taken. It was decomposing from within. The threads held little memory or thought, yet when brought together they held more power than Cael could fathom. Damaeus shrieked again. His soul twisted within Cael's grasp, attempting to tear and leave him with less than the whole of it. Cael's latent ability moved deeper in attempt to salvage what it could. The threads pounced suddenly, tainting

Cael's soul with their rot. He gasped as they polluted him. He struggled to force them away. Selene appeared by his side without warning. The weight upon his neck disappeared, and some small, frigid object pressed against his cheek. *A Stone.* Cael's latent ability melded with it. It drew strength enough from the union to regain what ground it had lost.

It was not enough. Damaeus slipped from Cael's grasp. The hood of his cloak fell to reveal a face overrun with decay. The glow of magic gathered around him once again as his mouth moved, speaking muted words.

An arc of swift movement collided with Damaeus' head. The strike was clean. The Mage's jaw shattered with the impact. *Islyr.* Cael jumped at the bare portion of Damaeus' leg, placing his hands around it with a grip of iron. The Mage's skin was slick and festering beneath Cael's palms.

"Viverr!" Islyr called between Damaeus' cries of fury.

The glow of magic vanished. The stench of death grew stronger as the Mage's flesh melted like wax put to a flame. It slithered over Cael's hands on its way to the ground beneath, sucking the warmth from his skin as it passed. Still, the last threads of his soul refused to release.

Damaeus' next cry was that of a pure elder Bloodsoul. Cael looked up. His gaze was met by eyeless voids within a casing of bone. Shards flew past him on their way to reattach themselves to Damaeus' jaw. The Mage reached down towards Cael once more.

"Damaeus," Selene said. Six perfect holes marked where her Circlet had once been.

Bone shifted as the Mage turned to face her.

"You will give your soul to Cael."

Cael shuddered as the last threads of Damaeus' essence entered him. His soul wrapped around them, purifying and claiming them at last. The power moved through him like a storm at sea. It was unlike any other soul that he had taken. This was not physical strength, nor was it the usual slight understanding of some mundane task that came with the claiming of a normal soul. This was enough knowledge of alchemy and the mage's arts to fill the library of Evaria's castle. Cael lay back against the muddy ground and drew a ragged breath of air. His head began to ache.

Battle's End

The chill of near-spring air crept across Selene's skin with unexpected ferocity. The rain no longer pelted her, though rumbles of thunder and the occasional flash of light still crossed the sky. Had Damaeus been in control of the storm? It made her stomach clench to think of it.

Swaying bloodsoul stood in motley groups scattered throughout the courtyard. They remained silent for the most part, which pleased Selene slightly. She wanted nothing more than to be left alone for a time. But the bloodsoul refused to be forgotten. They smelled far worse wet than they had when dry, and those few that she had given orders to followed her every movement as if begging to be commanded once more. The Marked Ones who had defeated Damaeus stood amongst them. She recognized Cael at once, and the Marked One who had created the bloodsoul, though their companion was unknown to her. Damaeus was right on one account. Cael was certainly one of the most dangerous Marked Ones she had ever come across. Though now, torn and doused in mud as he was, he did not look nearly as threatening as he had moments ago.

Selene ran her fingers carefully over the holes that the Circlet had left in her forehead. Even the light touch of rain upon the spots of open flesh made her ill. Any other wound would have been an item of curiosity, but these were far different. These were humiliating and sickening at once.

She reached for her healing and was shocked at how easily it came. The holes were sealed in seconds, though the nauseating feeling that came with thinking of them remained. Selene drew a deep, even breath in attempt to calm herself. She tried in vain to push thoughts of Damaeus from her mind. Beneath fear, pain, and the fading rush that came with battle lay thoughts of Felan.

"How about a bit of help?" Cael called from nearby. He had risen from the mix of mud and Damaeus' remains and was headed towards her. "I think I may have fractured something on that last fall." He slipped easily between groups of Bloodsoul, stopping momentarily to pluck Felan's Stone from the ground and pull the cord over his head.

Cael's Stone, Selene corrected, biting into the inside of her cheek in attempt to keep her feelings at bay. It worked, for the most part.

"I hope that with time you will forgive all that I have done to offend you," Cael said, bending slightly at the waist. "I would never have left you alone in the gardens if I had known for certain that you did not follow Damaeus' cause."

"You could have asked for my Stone, rather than drugging me," Selene snapped. Exhaustion settled heavily into her. "A bit of explanation would have gone far."

"You would not have believed my reasons," Cael replied, "and I needed to have the Stone before I could be sure of your allegiance. Laying our majesty's plans before the enemy like pelts set out to dry is not a mistake that would be easily forgiven."

Selene had no answer for that. She placed her hand upon Cael's neck, in part to cover the awkward silence that had settled between them. Warmth swept forcefully across her mark, adding to the pain in her head. She pulled from him.

"Something wrong?" Cael asked with a puzzled look.

"No," Selene lied, moving once again to touch him.

"The burn of my mark grows stronger with every soul I take," Cael explained. "I should have thought to warn you. But it isn't often that I come into contact with a Marked One that doesn't know of it. My apologies."

"Apology accepted," Selene replied absently. Her mind was elsewhere. How long ago could she have escaped this place? How long had she spent following Damaeus' orders when she could have simply commanded him to set her free?

"A man of intelligence learns from the past," Cael said. "A fool dwells within it."

"I'm sorry?"

"Xaiden is rather fond of that saying." Cael offered with a knowing smile. "He is rather fond of saying it to me, at least. Just something that you may wish to keep in mind."

"I expect no less from Xaiden." Selene attempted to push all thoughts but those of the present from her head. She placed her hand upon Cael's neck once more. His injuries were light when compared to what he could have suffered at Damaeus' hands; a few small fractures of bone and extensive bruising.

"Are either of you injured?" she asked as the other Marked Ones approached. She would heal them as much as she was able to with the ache in her head.

"You'd think that I would be, after all that you people have put me through," the shorter of the two men, the one she had never before seen, replied.

"You can't ever be silent, can you Viverr?" Cael said with the slightest touch of irritation in his voice. He was most definitely of fewer years than Xaiden, though she could not guess how many. His temperament confirmed it.

"Silence gets you ignored, most times," the man replied. "Won't get anything you want that way, eh?"

"Never take a rogue as a traveling companion," Cael warned, aiming a pointed look towards Selene.

Selene barely noticed it, for her gaze was upon the man who stood next to Viverr; the one with the inking that snaked across his face like tendrils of dark smoke. He was the one who had created her army.

"I assumed that you were on his side," she said as he drew close. "It was wrong of me to hate you for what he forced you to do. I acted foolishly and I am sorry for it."

"You are forgiven," the man replied, nodding his head. "I could use healing, if you would be so gracious."

"You'd all be dead now if it wasn't for my showing up at just the right moment to dispel Damaeus' magic." Viverr heaved his words in Cael's direction. "I won't ask for payment now, seeing as we still have some matters to deal with, but you can bet your mother's ashes that as soon as we're back in Evaria I'll be getting it."

Cael pressed his fingers to his temples.

"Don't think you could get rid of these Bloodsoul, do you?" the rogue added nervously, glancing at Selene. "They're making me a bit edgy. You've got control of them, right? I think that one's watching me."

"Absurd," Cael replied. "Why would it choose to watch you over any other? They follow no one but Selene."

"Islyr will protect me from them if you won't," Viverr said. "We're even, he and I. We're old companions."

"Islyr?" Selene said, distracted from her healing for a moment. The inked man had several broken fingers, and she was upon the last. "What do you know of Islyr?"

"Circumstances have made you a bit daft, eh?" Viverr laughed. "Can't have always been that way, with you being Aranth and all."

Cael cut the rogue's words short with a well-placed cuff to the back of his head.

"It's no wonder that you do not recognize me," the man with the inking said. "Few would. Many years have passed since we played beneath the Elders' awning."

Selene stepped back. There was nothing about the man that stirred her memory. But she had not kept any friends as a child. There was only one soul that she had shared time with beneath the Elders' awning.

"Your mark. I must see it."

"As you wish," the man said evenly. He removed his shirt and turned his back to her. Scars crossed his skin like branches scattered on the forest floor. He had been through much in his years. She pushed her eyes to the man's upper back, near his right shoulder. His mark remained as it had always been, though it seemed that nearly all else about him had changed. It could be no one else but her Islyr.

He turned to her once again, and Selene's eyes searched his face for any recognizable feature. There were few to be found.

"You look much like Maye now that you've grown. Your eyes most of all."

"She's…" Selene began as familiar ache that came with thinking of Maye gripped her chest.

"You can't blame yourself for her death. Thinking on what could have been serves only to corrode your soul. For years I blamed myself for our father's death. My thoughts often turned to how things could have worked out differently; of what else I could have done to save him. I realized at last that he would not have wanted me to waste the rest of my life doing nothing but pining for him. I'm certain that Maye would feel the same. I only wish that I had been there to aid you in singing her Sending Hymn."

"I would have killed you." How could he forgive her so easily after what she had attempted? "I tried for so long to find you." She gave up on speaking then, for she could not find any words that were fitting, and instead placed a hand upon him, sealing the damage that the Circlet inflicted. He smiled after she embraced him. She saw something of the Islyr of old within the expression.

"I didn't think that Aranth were permitted to cry," he said lightly. "You have not changed so much as Felan believed."

"Is Felan upon our side as well?" Cael asked. "He has moments of weakness and a penchant for fools' games, but I have always believed his morals to be strong."

"They are not as strong as I would like," Selene replied. "He would not be allowed within the castle walls even if he was able to return there." She choked on the words. "He did not survive."

"He sided with Damaeus." Cael's expression darkened.

"No. Not completely. Alchemy and spellcraft were involved near the end."

"Rakaii are forced to do many things against their will," Islyr said. "There is no choice while wearing a Circlet, only obedience. Damaeus commanded me to train Felan as a pleasure Rakaii."

"For use by Perfidia?" Cael asked.

Islyr nodded. "Perfidia carries Felan's child. It would be an uncertain future for the child were they of the Kerell."

"And where is she now?" Cael asked at last. He masked his astonishment well, if he felt any at all.

"The upper floor," Selene answered with a touch of satisfaction. "So long as neither Ranur nor Damaeus came across her."

"We have remained here too long," Islyr announced suddenly.

Selene followed his gaze to one of the few balconies that had not crumbled with the passage of time. Ranur stood there with Ormun at his side.

Selene grabbed at Ranur with her levitation ability, thinking to force him over the railing. Her power was sucked from the air as it touched him, leaving an empty feeling within.

Ranur looked down upon them with a condescending smirk. "Let us not linger in this place," he said to Ormun. His voice was calm and steady. By the time Selene had taken hold of her ability once more both men had disappeared through the balcony's doors.

"He has a void-charm," she said more to herself than to the others.

"It must be strong," Viverr said. "Couldn't have sucked up your latent ability like that otherwise."

Cael raised a brow in Viverr's direction.

"I can sense magic, though it's sometimes difficult to tell exactly where it's coming from," Viverr explained. "How else would I know when to use my latent ability?"

"Perhaps he obtained the charm from Damaeus," Islyr suggested, ignoring the rogue.

"We should split our forces," Cael said. "One group to retrieve Perfidia and another to go after Ranur. We can't chance losing either of them."

"I will go after Ranur," Selene offered. "You three can find Perfidia.

"You can't go alone." Cael's eyes were hard. His tone reminded her much of that which Xaiden used when a particular command was not up for discussion.

Islyr's face showed that he certainly agreed with Cael.

"As you wish." Selene scanned the bloodsoul that were nearest to her, searching out six of the eldest amongst them. Taking all of the creatures would most definitely slow her, and she was not certain that she could truly command an entire army of them at once. She called out to the few that she had chosen. Their language came differently than it had while she wore the Circlet. It was not the vibrating scream that she was accustomed to, but rather a whispered song, soft and flowing like fog upon early-morning air. The chosen bloodsoul parted from the others and came to stand obediently at her side. Viverr backed up several paces to cower behind Islyr.

"That's acceptable, I suppose," Cael said. "We'll meet with you outside the Keep once Perfidia has been secured."

"Fight well," Islyr added.

Selene nodded and headed off, calling to a few of the bloodsoul as she did so. She commanded them to surround her as she exited the courtyard. There was only one exit to the keep that she was aware of. By the grace of the Spirits it was the only one that Ranur knew of as well.

An unnatural silence had settled within the halls of the Keep in her absence. The bloodsoul lurched obediently behind her. A small group of Riders lingered near the throne room. Selene whispered a command to kill. She attempted not to let her thoughts linger upon the action lest guilt find and claim her. The Riders died quickly despite their clumsy efforts at defense. Their screams sliced the stillness of the hall like a fine Aranth blade. A swift death was likely more kindness than the men deserved. She pushed forward, not daring to look at their bodies as she passed. The aged stone was slick beneath her feet.

Selene reached the cave that led from the Keep after what seemed an eternity. She stopped just long enough to pull a torch from its rusted bracket before entering the darkness. Ranur would not wait for her to find him. The dust that covered the floor had been disturbed. The dirt beyond it, where the stone floor of the Keep ended, bore the footprints of many men.

Selene split her Bloodsoul upon entering the cave, sending three ahead and commanding the others to follow. She would not be caught unaware. Torchlight did nothing to keep the damp air at bay.

The passage was long and twisted. Time trickled past as she walked. Selene pressed her torch into the ground as she reached the end of the cave, extinguishing its flame. The outside light caused her eyes to ache. She lingered for a moment at the cave's mouth, remaining out of sight within a small cove. Distant shouted commands and the clattering of armor greeted her ears.

"*Protect me*," she whispered.

They seemed to understand.

The sound of weapons clashing was louder than storm waves striking the shore. More people filled the area before her than had ever graced the Seller's Square, even at full noon. It appeared that some of the Damaeus' Riders had begun to argue amongst themselves. Others fought armored men wearing Evaria's colors. Selene could not imagine how the men of the Standard Guard had come to be here, but she was thankful for their presence. She stepped carefully around what bodies lay strewn upon the muddied ground, searching desperately for some sign of Ranur's passing. She found none. The battling men were intent upon each other and none of them noticed Selene as she passed into the fray.

Armor rattled as a sound ten times the strength of thunder flooded the base of the Keep. Men were thrown to the ground. Selene struggled to gain her footing. A great, white dragon stood at the far side of battleground. The small groupings of scales that peppered its skin shone like shards of glass in torchlight. *Aurin.* His wings spread across the sky as he reared, throwing the far side of the battleground into shadow. Aurin struck at the men with more speed than Selene would have thought a creature of such size to be capable of. Scores of men cascaded though the air, landing upon friend and foe alike. The Riders and Guardsmen who had managed to remain upright headed with haste towards the dragon. Thus the battle shifted, leaving Selene much to herself amongst the dying and dead. At last she was able to spot Ranur and Ormun, who were running along the base of the Keep towards the woods. She followed.

Men surrounded Selene from all sides, halting her steps. "Stop in Evaria's name, fiend," one among them ordered. He was certainly the captain of the group, for two silver bars had been embroidered upon his left sleeve. Selene could not remember ever seeing that particular man before, but the Standard Guard was far greater than the Aranth in number.

"I am Aranth." Selene tilted the back of her hand towards him. "Move aside. I have no desire to harm you."

The guards stood their ground, swords at the ready and arrows nocked. "I have orders to detain all who exit the Keep," the man replied. "Aranth included."

Selene kept her eyes on Ranur. He and Ormun slowed their retreat to dispose of a few soldiers who attempted to bar their way. Most were dispatched by Ormun's arrows. She doubted that the guardsmen had come close enough to see his face.

"Surely they told you of me?" Selene attempted.

"King Graelen did mention a female Aranth. We will not harm you if you make no move towards us, but we cannot leave you roam free with those creatures at your side."

"The bloodsoul will kill at my command," Selene said in desperation. Ranur was slipping away and she could do nothing about it. "This chance is your last."

Several of the men shifted nervously. Beads of sweat trickled down the face of the one who stood closest to her. None made any move to leave. Selene began issuing commands to the Bloodsoul; one upon each archer, ordered to attack but not to kill. It left only one to defend her from Ranur. She would take the chance. The creatures seemed to understand her light, whispered words much better than they had the vibrating growl that she had been forced to use while wearing the Circlet. She hoped that no death would result from what she was about to do.

"Begin now."

The bloodsoul struck, throwing the archers to the ground. Arrows flew. She touched those she caught sight of with her latent ability, altering their course. One grazed her cheek. Her one remaining bloodsoul charged ahead, providing room for her escape. Selene ran, stopping only to retrieve a sword from a fallen Rider. She would surely need it.

Selene's eyes were drawn far ahead, to the edge of the forest where the air crackled as lightning would upon touching the earth. The barrier lit the clouded day like a mage-conjured flame. Damaeus had named it as one of his finest works, aside from the massive web of voyage rings that he had built over the years. Selene grumbled. If Ranur managed to reach any one of the rings then all would be lost. She picked up speed.

The sounds of battle faded beneath her hearing as she came to the edge of the woods. Ranur knelt upon the ground several yards off. His gloved hands swept leaves from the forest floor at a frantic pace. Tendrils of blue light arched across the sky in a brilliant display. Selene slid to a halt several feet from the line of singed plant life that marked the edge of the barrier. The burnt-flesh smell of those Riders who had collided with it lingered. She had no desire to have the flesh melted from her bones. It seemed as if the barrier had fallen, but she was no Mage. She would not risk her life on an assumption.

"It would be wise of you to remain where you are," Ranur said as he stood. "I have seen what Damaeus' barrier can do to a man and it is not at all pleasant."

"The barrier has fallen." Selene hoped desperately that it was true. "Damaeus may have given you the means to destroy it, but only a Mage would be able to erect it once again. Even the youngest child knows that much of magic. You are no Mage, unless I am mistaken."

"And if he merely allowed me a way to travel through it unharmed? Then you must realize that we are at an impasse. My void-charm has many charges left upon it. And do not think that I would travel with only one item of protection. You cannot cross the barrier, and so have no means of reaching me."

Selene started forward.

"Will you trust your life to your limited knowledge of the Mages' arts?" Ranur asked. His eyes flicked to her left.

"I have no need to do so," Selene replied, knowing well what he had seen. "*Kill him.*" The clattering of ancient bones rang out from behind her.

The bloodsoul charged Ranur, passing easily over the place where the barrier once stood. A low whistle reached through the woods. Ranur sprinted in the direction of the sound. It did not matter that he ran, for no human's speed could match that of an elder Bloodsoul. Selene struggled to keep up with them.

The bloodsoul reached forward as it ran, grabbing for the edge of Ranur's cloak. The fabric slipped from its bony fingers. Ormun came into view suddenly. The bloodsoul surged forward, eager for the chance to kill.

"*Aculeiu imedimun reaulei.*" Ranur's panicked voice echoed through the air as he reached Ormun's side. It was the first time that his words had held fear. Both he and Ormun melted from sight. The sound of bone striking metal rang out as the bloodsoul landed on the voyage ring. A vibrating scream of frustration echoed between the trees, mirroring Selene's thoughts. She could use the voyage ring, for she had heard the words of activation, but to which other ring had they traveled? There was no way to know. There could be hundreds of rings throughout the Realm, perhaps farther than the continent's end.

The bloodsoul rose from the forest floor and came to stand beside Selene. It looked at her for only a second before sensing something of interest beyond her view. Selene pulled its attention to her. She ordered the creature to follow behind her as she headed back towards the Keep. Next time she came across Ranur she would be much better prepared. He could not spend his life in hiding.

Men surrounded her once again as she exited the forest. Fingers of light stretched through what clouds remained to cover the sky. The captain was the same one that she had encountered earlier. He did not look at all pleased to see her.

"I demand that you take me to whoever commands you," Selene was in no mood for foolishness. Still, she wondered at the words as they passed her lips, for never in her earlier days would she have dared to speak to a captain of Evaria's guard in such a manner.

The captain grumbled a few words, all of which were impossible to make out. He then ordered his men to escort her towards a group who stood beneath the towering shadow of the Keep. It seemed that Selene still had some pull as Aranth.

The scene that came into view as she neared the Keep was near comical in nature. The bloodsoul continued to follow the orders that she had given them. They obeyed by lying atop the unfortunate archers as if tethered in place. Small groups of guardsmen hovered around each one. They seemed unsure as to what should be done to remedy the situation.

Riders were far more common amongst the dead than Guardsmen. The few members of Ranur's group that had escaped death were tied hand and foot and heavily guarded. A young boy with sandy colored hair wandered amongst them, wearing a thoughtful frown. He was dressed in finery of Evaria's colors, and could not be more than fifteen in years.

"There," the boy said upon noticing Selene. "I commend you captain for bringing her with such speed."

"You cannot bring an Aranth anywhere that they do not want to go, it seems." the captain muttered as he brought his free hand to his chest in a salute. "I will that you have better luck with her than I, my prince."

"Selene is an ally," the prince replied. "She is as much on the side of the Ethereal Realm as you. Gather the prisoners and escort them to Evaria. I have no further need of your aid at this time."

"As you wish, Sir Devren," the captain replied, saluting once more.

"Call off your Bloodsoul," Devren said, turning to Selene. "Free my men and I will take you to Islyr and Cael."

The boy gave it as an order, yet his eyes widened in the slightest as Selene whispered and the bloodsoul obeyed. They rose from the archers and moved to stand in a swaying group near the wall of the Keep.

The battle had cost Evaria dearly although they had won. A makeshift path had been cleared between piles of bodies, and men were walking methodically amongst those who were left in attempt to distinguish living from dead. Selene kept her eyes high. She could aid them with healing after she was certain that her companions were not in need of any. That was if Xaiden allowed her to stay here for any length of time. Exhaustion was returning to her once again.

Islyr, Cael, Aurin and Viverr stood in a small group. Xaiden was at its center. He held Cyanna, who was still trapped in her affinity. The iron collar that bound the girl seemed to be the topic of discussion. Perfidia sat upon the ground nearby. She was bound just as Selene had left her, minus the chair.

"We should not bring her to Evaria in this state," Xaiden said.

"What else can we do?" Cael replied. "There is no latch or clasp. The thing is most obviously held on by magic and we have no Mage amongst us."

"What of you, Cael?" Aurin offered. "You have some magic now, yes?"

"Pyre's Ash," Cael replied, "I'm not about to test that sort of thing on the king's daughter. May as well begin sharpening the headsman's axe. Besides that, I think Graelen should see what has been done to her."

"But you did gain some ability in the mages' arts?" Xaiden asked, forcing the subject of the conversation back to Cael's abilities.

"Quite more than a bit by the feel of it," Cael replied.

"It would indeed be unwise to experiment with your magical ability before you have been properly trained," Xaiden said. "There is nothing that can be done to remedy the situation for now. We will have to bring her as she is. Perhaps we will find something within Damaeus' room to release her."

Memories of entering the mage's room with Felan crept into Selene's mind. She could not help but stare at the blanketed form that lay by Xaiden's feet. She could swear that Felan's torso rose and fell with his sleeping breath. She had always found it difficult to distinguish the living from those who were freshly dead with only a glance. The mind tended to play fools' games in such situations.

"Did you kill him?" Viverr asked.

It was a long moment before Selene realized that the question was directed towards her, and another before she recognized that Viverr was speaking of Ranur and not Felan.

"No," she replied. "If not for the voyage ring I would have had him."

"Then there is no way to know where he has gone," Cael said. "We would have to know what place he was thinking of when he spoke the words of activation."

Selene's Bloodsoul turned from her once again, this time to look to the sky. Selene followed its gaze.

"What in the name of the Spirits is that?" Devren asked, squinting at the mass of movement as it swept over them like a flock of starlings in a farmer's field.

"The Eldai," Xaiden said. "They sense that the barrier has been removed."

One of the dark shapes parted from the others and descended towards them. The bloodsoul that followed Selene backed up several paces, as if preparing to run. "*Remain where you are,*" she ordered absently. She had never thought of them as creatures of feeling, but this one seemed almost nervous.

The pixie reminded her somewhat of a human, albeit an ugly one with tattered, leaf-like wings. It wore nothing more than a skirt of white hair to cover the patterns of maroon and copper that crossed its skin despite the fact that it was clearly female. The hair upon the Eldai's head had been twisted into points by use of what looked to be dried blood. It carried Selene's stone within its slender fingers.

"Our promise, magic," the Eldai said, hovering in Cael's face. "Your essence has changed, it has added, but I am not fooled by it."

"I did not think that one so clever as you could be fooled by something such as that," Cael replied, earning him a frown from Xaiden.

Selene recognized the grey, silken pouch that Cael pulled from his belt as the one that Damaeus had given to Perfidia less than a few hours before. It was quite a bit fatter than it had been at that time, however. Cael had obviously added a few items to it. He opened the bag and pulled an oddly colored coin from within. "This, in exchange for the Stone," he said. "It should be enough if what Islyr tells me is true."

"Magic's bone," the Eldai gasped, turning the coin over with slender, pointed fingers, "and attached with two powerful enchantments. More than good." She handed the Stone over to Cael. "But the rest? I am needing more than this to take Lim's rank."

"I have collected many things," Cael replied, offering her the bag. "You may have them all."

"Excellent, magic. I will be of first rank soon enough, and you will be eaten most quickly when you return here and your soul leaves you."

"It will be an honor," Cael replied, though his tone hinted otherwise.

"There are magics of unnaturalness in this place," the Eldai hissed. "The balance will be made well and the Spirits pleased by it." It looked to the Bloodsoul that stood behind Selene. "If this one is gone when we return then I will not tell." She flew off then, clutching the bag to her chest.

"That thing is coming with us, isn't it?" Viverr asked, eyeing the Bloodsoul nervously.

"It is," Xaiden replied. "Selene must learn the extent of her latent abilities if she is to use them to the greatest advantage of the kingdom." He handed Cyanna to Cael. "You have regained my trust. Take care that you do not lose it again."

"Not to worry," Cael said with a smile that reminded Selene of how handsome he truly was. She pressed a hand to her temple. Her mind was wandering so much that she must certainly be exhausted.

"Islyr, take Felan ahead please. We will return using the voyage ring."

"Tell my father of our victory," Devren said. "And if you would, thank him for giving me this opportunity to prove my worth."

"I will," Xaiden promised.

Selene looked away as Islyr lifted Felan from the ground, turning back just in time to see Xaiden pull Perfidia to her feet.

"You have been to the Glade, where the north wall meets the edge of the cliff?" Xaiden asked.

Selene gave a silent nod. Felan had shown her the castle grounds, the Glade included.

"Be sure and think of it as you step upon the ring, and keep it within your thoughts as you say the words of activation. You must be touching the bloodsoul in order to take him with you."

Selene grimaced at the thought of coming in contact with the creature, but she was far too tired to argue with Xaiden. Stones would fly before she talked him out of bringing the bloodsoul, in any event. "*Follow*," she ordered. The creature did as it was told. Viverr sprinted ahead of the others at the creature's first step.

Xaiden slowed his pace upon reaching the side of Keep where the cliff began to curve. Sparse patches of grass were crushed into muddy pulp, as if many men had passed through the voyage ring that lay beyond them. As the other Marked Ones disappeared bitter thoughts of Ranur's escape surfaced.

"It worries me," Xaiden said, almost as if speaking to himself.

"What worries you?" Selene asked.

"The prophecy of Ander Daxun."

It seemed that everyone had read the cursed thing, or at least heard tell of it. If Xaiden knew of it then surely King Graelen did as well. There would be no escaping its discussion now.

"This was a battle, surely," Xaiden said, "but it was no war."

"You believe that the war is still to come?"

"Yes," Xaiden replied. "But now is not the time to speak on it. Go."

Selene stepped forward obediently.

"I will converse with you at length when we return. But first you must rest, for you seem in great need of it. You will have two free days. If you are in need of more then I am certain that it can be arranged."

"Thank you, Xaiden," Selene replied. The bones of the Bloodsoul's arm were cold and slick from rain. "*Stand upon the ring.*" She uttered the words of activation just as Ranur had spoken them. Both Xaiden and the towering cliffs of the Keep faded from view.

Return to Aranth

Selene navigated the brightly lit halls of Evaria's castle with quickened steps. The last few days had done much to revive her body, though her mind turned all the while with memories of what had occurred within the Keep. She had thought that it would feel odd returning to this place after so many months away. Instead she found it to be much like returning to Maresbane had been in her days as a Rider. This place had become her home.

"They will summon us soon," Islyr warned. His fine clothing may well have been the only thing that tied his appearance to Evaria, for his Rakaii inking stood boldly against the pallor of his skin and his clean, dark hair was tied into a club near the nape of his neck.

"I only wish to visit for a moment," Selene replied. "King Graelen will send someone for us."

"That one," Islyr said, pointing to a nearby open doorway upon both sides of which stood a single Standard Guardsman, sword at the ready. Islyr was far better at remembering direction than she, and had memorized the layout of the castle and its grounds within a day of entering its walls.

"Is it true, honestly?" she asked, although she knew the answer well.

Islyr nodded slowly. "It didn't turn out as well as I hoped, you understand. I only wished to ease your sadness. We've both lost far too much in this life."

"I agree." Selene managed a grin. "But not all things that have been lost remain so. I've truly missed you, little brother."

The inking upon Islyr's cheeks shifted with his smile.

Selene paused before entering the room, to draw a breath. All that could be seen was a hearth of white marble. Above lay a ceiling of midnight blue inlaid with tiny, silver specs. It reminded her that she was once a prisoner of this place. She had come far since then and her regrets were many, though she was not certain what she would have changed were she able. *No gift comes without a price.* It had been one of Maye's less common sayings, but an important one nonetheless. Thoughts of Maye still brought sadness, though now there was some calm to be found within it.

"Please be wary, my Lady," the Guardsman to her right warned. "I would not wish for you to come to harm." She appreciated their wish to protect her, though she could hardly imagine a situation where two Standard Guardsmen could manage what an Aranth could not.

"Thank you, Warren," she replied. I will certainly do so."

The man blushed like a boy when she mentioned his name, though he was clearly at least twice her age. No doubt he had not expected her to remember it. Still, his hand did not move from the hilt of his sword, nor did his face shift in its somber expression.

Selene stepped through the door with Islyr following close behind. The room had changed little since her imprisonment. The tapestry of male unicorns in battle had been moved to her quarters long ago, of course, and one depicting the town of Evaria hung in its place. Beneath it slept Felan. His left wrist, which lay above the white down quilt, bore a metal Bracelet; perhaps the same that she had worn while held there.

"It was nearly too late to make use of my latent ability," Islyr said softly as if fearing to wake him. "His soul was on the edge. It hovered between its last moments with this body and the short time it would spend with the Spirits before journeying to his next life. I suppose that is why he will not wake."

"But he is not Bloodsoul?"

"No, he is not."

Selene sat on the side of the bed, watching the quilt rise and fall with Felan's shallow breathing.

"I wouldn't have attempted it but for you," Islyr said. "Though in truth it is my gift to the Aranth and Evaria as well for all that they have done. The loss of one Aranth is great when their numbers are so few. It is my hope that he can be redeemed."

"It's mine as well. But I fear that our friendship may not be so easily mended."

"The love of friendship has as much strength as any other. Hatred often fades with time, but love will remain if it is true."

"The Kerell Book of Life is right in many things, though the attitude of its people leaves much to be desired." Selene recognized Cael's voice at once and turned to see him lingering in the still open doorway. He wore the deep blue leather and white cotton of Aranth formal armor.

Islyr offered Cael a questioning glance.

"The hearing will begin shortly," Cael informed them. "Graelen asked that I find you both to let you know."

Selene wondered at the fact that Cael referred to the King without his title. It would certainly earn him harsh words from Xaiden, if not more. She would not dare to try it herself even in jest.

"I will see myself there," Islyr said. Whatever uncertainty he had held at Cael's first words had swiftly disappeared. "I shall see you again shortly," he added as he passed through the door.

Cael did not leave, but rather took a seat beside Selene upon the bed. He stared at Felan with an air of discontent. "He was a close companion. I can't seem to decide what I'll do when he wakes. Has he changed so much?"

"The weight of life burdened him much more in his last days than it did when I first met him," Selene replied. "It's my hope that something of what he once was still lives beneath the scars that Perfidia and Damaeus have left."

Felan slept without movement. It was said around the castle that he had been put under an enchantment while defending Evaria from Damaeus' army of Bloodsoul. Xaiden furrowed his brow each time the tale found his ears. He did not tell them the right of the matter, however, for King Graelen had forbidden him to do so.

Selene brushed a hand across Felan's forehead. Her mark warmed at the touch. It was also said that Felan did not dream. Such gossip flowed like the current of a flooded stream, especially amongst servants. Nonetheless, she could not help but wonder if it was true.

"You were lovers?" Cael asked.

"Simply friends," Selene replied after a moment's thought.

"I see. Then we are bound by the same worries, you and I." Cael placed his hand upon hers, and a heavy burn swept across her mark.

"Perhaps."

The knowledge that lay behind Cael's eyes put her in mind of Xaiden somewhat, though it was there that the similarity ended. Cael was more open in his words and his intentions. It also seemed that he was not bound quite so tightly to King Graelen's rules.

The king had announced that Cael needed to repeat the Aranth ceremony shortly after their arrival, stating that the first only bound him until his death. The oddly strong burn of Selene's mark as Cael placed his hand to hers for the blood pact had brought memories of the bloodsoul courtyard, but also of Kyrros' private gardens and what had occurred there. She felt close to Cael, though there was no reasonable explanation for it. It had been so ever since that night. That feeling did not, however, lessen the irritation at what he had done to her.

"Promise me that you won't use your latent ability upon me in the future," she said.

"You have my word." Cael seemed puzzled at the sudden change of subject. "I did apologize for all that occurred, if you remember, though if you wish me to do so again I will."

Selene shook her head. Asking Lord Kyrros to send Cyprus back to her and procuring her Aranth sword served as enough of an apology. It was kind of Cael to let her keep her room as well, for she discovered through Mera and Sedna that it had once belonged to him.

"I believe that this is yours." Cael held her Stone up by its leather cord.

"It is." She took it from him and pulled the cord over her head. Her levitation ability surged forth momentarily before settling. "Thank you."

"Graelen awaits us." Cael stood and offered his hand to help her from the bed. Selene accepted. She hoped that with time the heat of his mark would not draw such harsh memories. She placed her hand on the hilt of her sword, reveling in the familiar comfort it offered, and followed Cael from the room.

Islyr, Aurin, and Viverr stood on the white marble floors of Evaria's throne room, separated from Selene and Cael by the length of midnight Eyrisian carpet that flowed down its center. She would not have guessed the latter two to be rogues had she not known it, for they were dressed as finely as her brother though in light, natural colors rather than the tones of gray and black that Islyr preferred.

Devren stood near his father, a few steps to the rear. Cyanna lingered at his side. Her eyes lit up upon noticing Selene, and the smile she offered was quickly returned. The girl looked far too thin even through layers of finery, but her collar had been removed and she was back in human form.

Selene took her place at Xaiden's side.

"Bring the prisoner to kneel before me." King Graelen's voice was level.

Perfidia entered dressed in prisoners' gray and flanked on either side by three Standard Guardsmen, one of whom carried a smooth, metal collar. Her smile was that of a cat who had eaten her masters favored falcon. They stopped at the base of the platform steps, on the carpet which led to the throne. She did not kneel as she reached it.

"Aid her," Xaiden urged softly. "But be certain to use control."

Selene touched her latent ability, forcing Perfidia to her knees as gently as her conscience would allow. The woman attempted to rise, but Selene held her easily in place.

"Perfidia Severl," King Graelen began.

Perfidia's sly expression faltered for an instant upon hearing her family name rather than that of the throne, but it returned swiftly.

"Your crimes against the Kingdom of Evaria and the family of Elyon will now be named. You will answer in guilt or innocence to each charge as it is spoken. Do you understand?"

"Yes, my husband," Perfidia replied in a silken tone.

King Graelen's eyes narrowed.

Selene struggled to keep from tossing the woman across the room.

Xaiden stepped up to the platform. If he was angered by Perfidia's performance then he gave no indication of it. "You have been accused of aiding in the kidnapping and enslavement of Cyanna Elyon, daughter to King Graelen Elyon," he said. "How do you plead?"

"Innocent. Certainly I cannot be charged with kidnapping my own child."

Xaiden's frown was much deeper than that he usually held for lies. It was clear that Perfidia was attempting to draw his anger, or perhaps that of King Graelen.

"And for aiding in the kidnapping and enslavement of Selene Valenne, a member of the King's Elite Guard, how do you plead?"

"Innocent," Perfidia said once again. "I had nothing to do with Damaeus' plans for the girl. In fact, I cautioned him against keeping her."

"It is believed that you also aided in the kidnapping, enslavement and murder of Felan Hadrian, a member of the King's Elite guard. To this do you plead innocence or guilt?"

"Innocence."

Selene pressed her palm to the hilt her sword with such strength that the gilding bit into her flesh. Xaiden continued to speak, adding to the list of crimes, yet his words swept beneath her hearing. It was the burn of Cael's mark as he placed his hand upon her wrist that brought her to her senses at last.

"The child which you now carry," Selene would have thought the words to be hesitant had they been spoken by anyone other than Xaiden. "With whom was it conceived? You will not be punished no matter the answer, for this is not a crime against the kingdom, yet I urge you to speak the truth."

"You must forgive me," Perfidia begged, turning to King Graelen.

The queen attempted to stand, but her knees remained upon the floor as if they had been tethered. Though Selene's latent ability ensured that Perfidia did not move, it did nothing to cease the torrent of lies that flowed from between the woman's lips like soiled water.

"Do you think that I would betray you when you have brought such honor to my family and the Ethereal Realm? Do you think that this child is anything but your own?"

"For the Spirits' sake," Cael muttered.

The woman was more than a fool if she thought to save herself by acting so.

It seemed that Xaiden agreed. "Whose child do you carry?" he said once again, standing over Perfidia and lifting her chin with a single finger. "I require a straightforward answer."

"The child belongs to Felan," Perfidia said bitterly. "It was not of my doing. It was he who forced himself upon me."

Selene's mark began to burn. It enraged her all the more that she was unable to control it. How dare Perfidia speak of Felan so? For all the woman knew his ashes had already been scattered to the tides. She resisted the urge to place her hand upon her mark for comfort, though there was truly no need to control such an action in this place.

"Is this true?" King Graelen asked, turning not to Perfidia but to Xaiden.

"It is her belief that the child belongs to Felan," Xaiden replied. "Though Perfidia lies when she says that he forced himself upon her."

King Graelen's expression altered, gaining the darkness of a winter's storm. "Continue."

"Very well," Xaiden said, nodding his head in the slightest. "The prisoner's false words have proven her guilt on all accounts. Suitable punishment will be determined by his Majesty Graelen Elyon, guardian of the Ethereal Realm. May his wisdom forever guide us to righteousness."

Selene drew a breath in attempt to calm herself. No matter what King Graelen's decision, she would abide by it. *I will not let anger control my actions. I open my mind to the winds of tranquility. My thoughts are pure serenity.* A Spirit's whisper would have seemed thunderous within the silence of the room.

King Graelen's midnight blue robe swept around him like dark water as he strode to the edge of the platform. "Perfidia Severl, you have been found guilty of the aforementioned crimes in their entirety. You are given one last chance to speak truthfully before me. Have you anything to say?"

"You have always held my love," Perfidia said. "You continue to do so. I wish for you to know it."

King Graelen turned to Xaiden, who shook his head.

"You would believe this Marked One over your wife? You allow these monstrosities to roam the lands freely, doing as they will with the innocent people of the realm? They are a danger to any that come into contact with them. Believe me when I say that they will be the end of you."

"Enough. I firmly believe that punishment should not only be given in equal proportion to the crimes which have been committed, but also to the amount of true regret shown by the accused," King Graelen said. "Thus it is with a clear conscience, beneath the watchful eye of the Spirits, that I sentence you to death by beheading. Your punishment is to be carried out after the birth of the child you now carry."

Perfidia's smile faded at last. Her skin took on the pallor of the marble floor upon which she knelt.

"Remove the prisoner from my presence and return her to her cell," King Graelen said wearily.

Selene released her hold on Perfidia only after she was certain that the guardsmen had her firmly secured. The woman was silent as they led her from the room.

Cyanna began to sob as her mother passed out of sight. Her face paled more with each wheezing breath, and she wobbled as if caught in a breeze. She toppled suddenly. Selene reached out with her levitation, catching the girl before her head could strike the ground. She lowered her gently to the carpet. A light touch of her healing ability was all that was needed to know that she had not been harmed.

"She just needs rest," Selene said in response to King Graelen's worried look.

"Will you take her to her room?" Xaiden asked, turning to Devren.

The prince nodded, lifted his half-sister from the floor and carried her off.

"We will not speak of Perfidia again until the day of her death," the King said.

Selene nodded with the others.

King Graelen sat back upon his throne. "There are those of you here who have discovered the closely guarded secret of the Aranth. I owe you each a debt of gratitude for aiding in the return of my daughter and securing the safety of the Ethereal Realm. You will each be compensated for your efforts by way of coin."

Viverr had the look of a raccoon that had just captured a particularly plump fish.

"It is unfortunate, but I must also give you the choice that all Marked Ones are given upon learning the secret of the Aranth. Xaiden shall explain the situation to you after the proceedings here have finished. I believe that, given the situation at hand, the third option would not be suitable."

Islyr would not enjoy the options he was to be given any more than Selene had at first, even with the choice of hanging removed from them. He had never been one to take well to authority, even in his youth.

"And to the final matter of business, my Aranth. Your exile was revoked long before your return, but I have yet

to make my peace with you. My deepest apologies to Xaiden
and Selene firstly, for you remained faithful despite your
exile; and to Cael for accusing him of a crime which he gave
his life to prevent. I also grant you each a boon in return for
your service. Most anything that is within my power to grant,
you shall have. Selene, tradition dictates that as the youngest
of the Aranth you are granted the first request. Are you
prepared, or do you wish to take time to consider?"

Selene was not prepared at all, in truth. Never in her
years of dreaming had she imagined that she would be
granted a boon by the king.

"I know what my request will be," she said after a
moment.

Cael raised a brow in her direction as she ascended
the steps to the platform, but the expression was fleeting. He
turned suddenly to whisper something to Xaiden. Selene was
too far by then to understand his words, even within the
silence of the room.

Selene knelt upon the carpet that led to the throne,
for it seemed like the appropriate thing to do. She wished
above all that one of the others had gone first, for she was
completely at a loss as to the required formalities of such
things. She decided to speak before she lost her nerve. "I ask
for my brother's complete freedom, providing that he take a
vow of secrecy before the Spirits. May he not be bound to
Evaria or to the ways of the Aranth if he does not wish it."

King Graelen was silent for such a time that Selene
began to doubt he had heard her. "It is very bold of you to ask
such a thing," he said at last. "Cael told me that most of your
brother's short life has been molded by Damaeus and the
Kerell. I would like it if he would join the Elite Guard, but it
seems fair that he should be free to choose his path from this
point forth. He would not betray the Aranth were he to leave,
for it would mean betraying his blood. Your request is
granted." He lifted a small, silver box which sat by the base of

the throne and opened it. Within lay a branding iron in miniature, the end of which had been twisted into something that resembled a star with eight points. The pattern at its center was so intricate as to be nearly indistinguishable, even given Selene's close proximity to it. She could not imagine how anyone had managed to make the thing save through magic.

King Graelen pressed the iron against the skin of her neck, directly below her collar bone. Little pain accompanied the soft, cool burn of it. "To mark that your boon has been taken," he explained. "Islyr Valenne shall remain a guest of the castle for one week, during which time he shall make his decision. In one week and one day hence I will allow the vow to be given; that is in the event that he does not choose to stay."

"I thank you, Majesty." Selene managed to combine standing and bowing into one movement. She had gained her brother's freedom. A mere glance in his direction proved beyond words that she had chosen wisely.

"Cael, do you wish to make your request or to consider?" King Graelen asked, losing the formality that had encompassed his voice from the beginning of the hearing.

"I wish to forsake my boon." Cael unlaced the upper portion of his shirt as he placed himself before the throne. "I ask that Xaiden's request be given extra weight because of it."

"Time has not lessened your ability to complicate matters, I see," King Graelen said in a whisper so low that Selene was not certain that even Xaiden, who was standing no more than four feet farther from the throne than she, had been able to hear it. "Are you certain of this?" He pulled aside the cloth of Cael's shirt with one hand while holding the tiny brand at the ready with his other. "Xaiden needs no further aid in making any request of me. You know as much."

"I am most certain." A casual grin crossed Cael's face. "*You* know as much."

"I cannot say that I have missed your insolence, Cael."

"You need only deny my request if you believe it to be unreasonable," Cael offered.

"It is not unreasonable in the least, though you do understand that it will not soon be forgotten." King Graelen pressed the brand to Cael's skin, next to an identical mark.

"I am at my Majesty's command, as always," Cael replied, throwing a casual wink in Selene's direction as he headed back towards her.

"Make your request, Xaiden. It is obvious that you do not wish for time to consider it."

Xaiden's stance as he approached the throne conveyed all that an Aranth should be: power, grace, and wisdom combined. He knelt with the smooth movement of a lengthening shadow at dusk. "I request the rebirth of the Aranth," he said. "To allow recruiting to continue as it was in days before the traitors lived among us."

King Graelen shook his head slightly, though a smile crept onto his lips as he did so. "Your request is granted," he said warmly. He pressed the brand to Xaiden's neck, at the end of a row of six others.

Xaiden said nothing, though his satisfaction was plainly evident.

"Each Aranth is granted a week of leave," King Graelen said as he stood, "after which their training will continue as usual. An evening meal waits in the dining room for those who care to have it. May the Spirits guide you."

Low chatter sprung up between the rogues as King Graelen departed. Viverr's voice carried quite soundly across the length of the Throne room. It seemed that portions the King's decree concerned him. He contemplated what horrible limits would be placed upon him while Aurin attempted in vain to calm him. Selene wondered what Xaiden would think of being forced to train Viverr, were he to join the Aranth. He would not be altogether pleased. She would wager her next month's pay on that. Selene tuned both men out as Islyr reached her side. He embraced her at once. It was only then that she realized how much she would miss him when he finally left.

"You owe me nothing," she said, pulling back from him. "I want to be sure that you understand."

Islyr nodded. "Will you come to dinner?" he asked.

"Perhaps I could meet you for breakfast tomorrow," she replied. "At the edge of the Seller's Square?" the events of the day had stolen all hunger from her, in truth.

"Tomorrow, then," Islyr replied. "And I'll do you the favor of taking your portion of supper." He held a mischievous look that Selene had not seen since their youth.

"You're welcome to it," Selene replied. "May the Spirits protect and guide you, little brother," she added in whispered tones as he disappeared after the others.

Selene retreated to her room then. There she lingered on the balcony, breathing in the scent of spring while watching the colors above the town of Evaria fade from those of early evening to deep Aranth blue. The light knock at her door came suddenly, cutting through the silence of the night as well as thoughts of Aranth training and the bloodsoul which awaited her in the dungeon below. "You may enter," she called, not bothering to turn.

"Do you let everyone into your room so casually?" Cael asked, coming to stand beside her.

"Only those who I find most irritating."

"I suppose that you don't wish to hear what I've come to ask you, in that case." He made no motion to leave.

"Say it quickly and perhaps I'll listen," she replied, looking not at him but at the starlit sky. "That's providing that you don't speak to your fellow Aranth as you do your King."

Cael laughed. "Would you care to fly with me?"

"I'm sorry?" Selene looked him full in the face for the first time since he entered the room.

"Our Affinities are both avian, and tonight is as fine a night as any for flight. I was about to head out and I thought that you might wish to join me."

Selene raised a brow in the man's direction.

"A raven's flight is slightly different from that of a falcon," Cael added. "But perhaps I could teach you a few things."

"First tell me this," Selene said. "Did you truly read my journal as you mentioned in Kyrros' gardens?"

"Every word," Cael replied, making no attempt to hide his grin. "So, would you care to go with me?"

Selene paused as she considered his words. "Yes," she said at last. "I believe that I would."